# ONE *Wicked* NIGHT

COLETTE RIVERA

This book is a work of fiction. All characters, names, places and events in this publication are products of the author's imagination, or are used fictitiously. Any resemblance to actual events, locations or persons, living or dead, is entirely coincidental.

Edited by May Peterson

www.maypetersonbooks.com

Cover design by Ink & Laurel Design Studio

www.inkandlaurel.com

ISBN

Print: 978-1-99-118793-2

Kindle: 978-1-99-118792-5

# AUTHOR NOTE

Content guidance for One Wicked Night can be found on the author's website coletterivera.com/content-guidance/

# AUTHOR NOTE

Content guidance for One Wicked Night can be found on the author's website coletterivera.com/content-guidance/

## LOVE & MAGIC

GIVE A WITCH A CHANCE

KEEP YOUR WITCHES CLOSE

ONE WICKED NIGHT

# ONE *Wicked* NIGHT

COLETTE RIVERA

# 1

# TRISTAN

I had ninety seconds to resolve the war going on inside my head. It was a battle of lust versus logic, action versus inaction. Basically, I was screwed.

*Why did I leave this until now?* There was no excuse.

I was busy ringing up orders at my side-job as struggle raged inside me. I'd been working here at the Coffee Cat Cafe from the day my friend Owen Sanchez opened it four years ago, and this was my official last day. I'd finally landed a full-time salaried position copywriting, and while I was thrilled to no longer need a second job, I was going to miss this place like hell.

And a certain dashing customer in particular.

"He's either desperately in love with you, or hates the sight of you. Can't tell which." Tess leaned away from the espresso machine, enjoying her harassment of me.

"Shut up," I muttered.

Mr. Bickel, first name unknown, AKA my most baffling crush, stood at the back of the line. As always, he looked like he'd stepped out of a period drama or traveled through time just to wreck my little heart.

He was flawless in a 1920's-esque cream three-piece suit,

fedora, and baby-blue bow tie. The paleness of the suit didn't wash out his white skin; instead it brought him to life, highlighting his rosy undertones and well-placed freckles. Bickel held himself effortlessly, like he was posing for a cover shot, not standing in line to order coffee.

No one should look that good before eight in the morning. His bone structure was killer. Jawline and cheekbones you'd need to register as a safety hazard. They'd cut me deep, wrecked me for sure.

And he wasn't even looking at me. But whatever, I was busy at the register serving someone else and ignoring Tess's mutterings.

Bickel had glanced my way when he'd first come in, a flick of his piercing blue eyes and a flash of acknowledgment before turning his attention to the menu on the wall. No smile. I'd never seen so much as a hint of one on his flawless face, but the way he was glaring at today's list of fresh baked pan dulce was enough to make you fear for the chalkboard's virtue.

So fucking serious. So fucking hot.

And herein lay my dilemma. I was sure he had a thing for me. Well, mostly sure. We'd shared *a look*—fleeting but potent. Yes, it had been like a year ago, and yes we'd never had an in-depth conversation, but I'd felt the connection like an electric shock and never forgotten it.

Mr. Bickel was wound tight and extremely elusive according to my friend Aria, so I'd been playing a long game, employing a slow burn strategy trying to get him to open up to me. Every time he came in, I threw in some subtle flirting, we're talking ninja-level stealth, paired with genuine friendliness and a broad range of conversation starters. Anything to coax him to chat with me.

He was ever so subtly responsive, or I'd have given it a rest.

There were lingering looks, drawn out interactions, it was what he *wasn't* saying. You know?

But he never cracked. Never offered more than hints, except for his eyes. Those gorgeous blues packed an emotional punch, often giving away how much he was holding back.

I could practically see his thoughts churning when his gaze settled on me, his lack of smiles leaving room for some devastating frowns. It was like a complex code trying to read him, but I was positive he was trying to say—*something*.

Okay so, in reality Bickel maybe thought I was cute and that was about it. My cuteness was undeniable. The rest of it could *theoretically* be in my head.

My thoughts had grown more and more involved as this thing-not-a-thing between us stretched out. I had hopes and dreams of his hands all over me. This is where my lusty-self won out, told me this bonkers attraction was mutual even if my logical-self liked to draft dissertations on my ability to read into nothing.

Either way, this maybe-one-sided flirting was a bright part of my day and suddenly this was the last of those days.

I hadn't seen Bickel in weeks, since before all the changes in my life had begun. I'd be in New York City this time next week, and practical me had inexplicably gotten on board with my lusty agenda, agreeing that leaving him this way was unacceptable. The possibility Bickel liked me too meant I couldn't leave all the potent feelings and potential I'd imagined with him behind.

He could be the one to get me out of this dating rut, or even The One. The endgame relationship I'd been hoping for. However, it was now too late to do anything about it.

"I'll have a triple espresso, please." Mr. Bickel turned away from the menu as he reached the front of the line.

I couldn't help but notice how his bow tie brought out the complexity of his eyes, the lights and darks in his irises drawing me in. They'd softened, now they were focused on me. The man had kind eyes, that promised depth and—

I rang up the coffee. "How's your morning going?" I felt jittery knowing this was the last time I'd see him. Shit, I was on the verge of anxious.

"Better now. I really needed this coffee today." Bickel's voice was smooth, almost soothing.

And why the hell did I think he wasn't talking about coffee? He wasn't talking about me. Coffee wasn't a metaphor for Tristan.

"Hard day ahead?" I offered with what felt like a dopey grin.

He shrugged, pulled a money clip out of the inner pocket of his jacket and flicked through the bills.

Damn. That was all I was gonna get. My mind raced for a way to engage him, but all my charm was gone.

After he paid, Bickel shifted over to wait for his espresso by the window. The low morning light streamed in. Aww man, now he was literally glowing, all warm tones and soft comfortable promises of how it'd feel to be wrapped up in his arms. I should have said something—anything—more.

"Swap with me," I muttered to Tess.

She smirked. "Fine. You can make the half-soy-half-almond extra-hot decaf white mocha. And don't forget the vegan whipped cream."

I settled behind the espresso machine and tried to center myself. I hadn't been this fluttery nervous, on the verge of helplessness since my teens. What the fuck?

I was consumed with regret for not asking Bickel out and confirming if he was even interested. My slow burn had been a ridiculous game, just a tool to protect me from potential rejection.

Realistically, nothing had stopped him from making a move, and knowing that had made me hesitate. I'd gotten stuck wondering why he'd never suggested anything when I'd been clear enough to signal I was interested.

I had been clear. Right?

*Ugh*, I shouldn't have stopped at subtle hints. That way I could have moved on knowing: hey, this hottie's not for you, Tristan. Now I'd have to live with the what-ifs. Asking him out today was pointless. It'd be like, hi wanna date? Yes? Oh sorry, I'm moving. *God!*

Where the hell was that vegan whipped cream? I almost knocked over the trim milk as I bumbled through this simple task I'd done countless times.

*Maybe you don't need to date him.*

This was one hundred percent my libido talking. I was a relationship guy and I liked that about me, but right now it felt like a flaw.

Thankfully, I found the whipped cream right where it was supposed to be and finished off the coffee. I glanced over at Bickel. He was looking at his phone.

I needed a sign from him on what to do. Even asking to meet for a drink with the intention of a night together felt impossible. But why? I was sure he was attracted to me. Mostly.

What was my problem? I wasn't normally shy. I had no problem approaching people and handled disinterest as fine as anyone. But this time I'd left it too long, thought about him too much, let the effect he had on me take over.

I got to making his drink. Grabbed a to-go cup and had an epiphany.

I'd slyly give him my number.

Making a move this way fit right in with my ninja flirtations. I grabbed a sharpie and scrawled: *call me* ♥ *Tristan* and my number on the cup. Before I could think a second more, I shoved the cup under the portafilter and filled it up with a triple espresso.

Now that I'd committed to this minor action, I decided that my plan was ideal. Best case scenario, he called and we hooked up. Worst case, he ignored me and I never saw him again, my fresh start waiting in New York to cheer me up. There would be no embarrassment, no need to look into his eyes as he confirmed the reason this dance between us never went any further was because he'd never wanted it to. It was low risk, high potential reward.

"Your triple espresso." I set the drink on the counter.

Mr. Bickel slipped his phone into his pocket and retrieved the cup. He brought it to his lips and took a sip. I stared. He held my eye contact almost like he expected me to watch him rather than go back to work.

"Thank you." Bickel didn't look away or make any move to go. It was wonderfully awkward, standing and staring, stewing in the tension together.

This was so like him. See. *This* wasn't nothing. I swore to god there was longing in those eyes. That or I'd lost it.

"Hope you have a good day." I glanced out the window and back at him. "Maybe I'll see you later."

Bickel's brows crinkled, a quizzical expression blooming on his face. "Uh—yes. See you next time." He nodded, gesturing at me with the coffee in a kind of acknowledging way, and turned to go.

# 2

# EDWIN

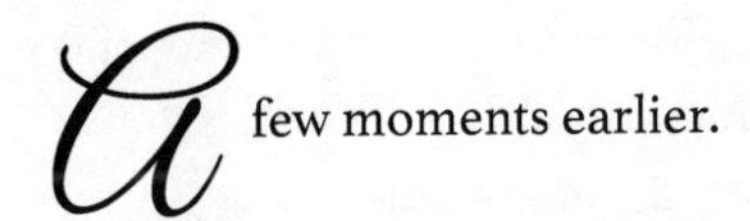

A few moments earlier.

SOMETHING WAS DIFFERENT TODAY.

As I scrolled mindlessly on my phone, Tristan moved from the cafe's register to the coffee machine. He'd seemed scattered when I'd ordered my espresso and now he was flitting back and forth from the milk fridge to the counter like he had no idea what he should be doing.

He was usually much more collected than this.

I couldn't help noticing how Tristan's beauty transformed in motion. He captured me with painted nails on busy fluttering hands, his slender frame lithe as he worked in the bustling cafe. But today an almost vibrational energy seemed to have overtaken him.

I tried not to wonder why, and managed to avoid staring, but only because there was no need. I knew what the man looked like.

Tristan was casually stunning. It struck me especially now, after I'd successfully stayed away from Coffee Cat for the past month. Even with my eyes averted I could picture the way his loose black curls framed his elegant sharp-featured face, constantly getting in his eyes as he worked, begging to be brushed back.

Somehow it was always my fingers I imagined doing the brushing.

I frowned at my phone, grumbling internally. Avoiding the cafe had done nothing to solve my current problem. My thoughts were as hopeless as ever, which was perhaps a given. More worryingly, my absence seemed to have had the opposite effect of what I'd intended. When our gazes had first met this morning, Tristan's light brown cheeks had bloomed in a blush like I hadn't seen since I'd first started coming around.

So I'd kept our interaction short.

I'd never intended to pursue Tristan and had tried not to encourage his interest in me. But I wasn't able to stay away and so the whole situation had become a ridiculous mess.

Tristan set my coffee on the counter. "Your triple espresso."

I met his eyes as I grabbed the drink. He looked bright and hopeful but still a bit off kilter. I took a sip of the hot coffee and wondered for the hundredth time what the hell I was doing.

"Thank you."

"Hope you have a good day." Tristan paused and I got lost in his crooked grin. "Maybe I'll see you later."

"Uh—yes. See you next time." I made an awkward parting gesture and turned to go, resisting the urge to ask him what he meant exactly. It was odd phrasing on his part.

Outside the cafe I turned right and walked briskly down the quiet street, letting myself have a brief moment of contentment.

Talking to Tristan brought out the simplest, most satisfying joy in me even though we never said anything of substance. He made normal magical, ironically giving me something I thought was no longer possible.

I picked up my pace, needing to get away as much as I'd needed to see Tristan in the first place. My espresso was too hot on the warm late-spring day, so I shifted my fingers to hold the lid with as little contact as possible in order to avoid scalding myself. As I did so, I noticed something on the side.

*Call me ♥ Tristan.*

I stopped, struck dumb by the perfect little heart he'd drawn for me. Heat flooded my face in a reaction completely out of my control.

*Hell.*

I made myself keep walking.

What was I supposed to do now? I couldn't call Tristan. I didn't date. Period. Not after Wyatt. It didn't matter how different Tristan was from the man who'd hurt me, he was no exception. I had no desire to experience anything like the twisted hold Wyatt had had over me, and avoiding relationships altogether was safer than trying to figure out which ones might turn down that road.

I wouldn't ever make the mistake of putting my trust in a partner again. Not when the risk they'd take advantage and abuse it outweighed any potential good a relationship could offer.

I thought I'd signaled to Tristan that I didn't want his romantic attention. But what else could the heart indicate? If he'd wanted something casual surely he wouldn't have waited until now to act.

A deep sigh passed my lips. Even casual was complicated. I had personal hang-ups there as well. Then there was magic. Its existence was unavoidably caught up in my less personal reasons for not pursuing Tristan. Magic was a secret all Witches had to keep, but I wasn't just any Witch. I wasn't Aria, free to be reckless. I'd already used up my second chances.

Any way I looked at it, I didn't need the drama of lying to a Mortal lover any more than I needed a partner. If only these complications had kept the man off my mind and my wandering feet out of his coffee shop. Why couldn't he have left me alone? We had a perfect, uncomplicated acquaintance going. We didn't know each other yet seemed to share something unique. It was ideal.

And what did he want exactly? Something substantial, the exact thing I was committed to avoiding? Or maybe his desires were more fleeting. Unwittingly my thoughts shifted to exactly what we might do together if I called.

There was no denying I wanted to spend the night with Tristan. But so what? This wasn't a new revelation on my part, just a longing I'd ignored. It was best not to go there. Leave the whole thing alone.

I passed a trash can, intending to throw the cup away, but somehow passed it by.

My idle morning was ruined, so I made my way to Juliet Herrera's office and teleported inside. She wasn't in yet. It was after eight and that was unlike her. With nothing else to do, I settled in the pristine waiting area to brood, staring at the cup.

His messy writing.

That heart.

When Juliet walked in, she stopped short at the sight of me. "Edwin, I wasn't expecting you. Was I?"

"Sorry. No." I stood, feeling off balance in front of Juliet for the first time in decades. "Shall I go?"

I didn't always have to call ahead before visiting my friend, but it'd been a number of weeks since I'd seen her—an isolating month all around—and it occurred to me I should have called this time. Juliet's habits had changed. She had more going on than her paranormal investigative work and my visits.

"No, no." Juliet waved away my concern with a hand adorned in exquisite crystal rings. "Come into my office. I'm not doing anything interesting today, just responding to emails Aria set aside for me while I was away. I'm not exactly itching to get started."

As I followed her into the next room, I slyly vanished the empty coffee cup, sending it home where I could throw it away later. Annoyingly, I already had Tristan's number memorized.

Juliet perched elegantly on the vintage-style chair behind her large wooden desk. "Are you working on anything interesting?"

I settled into the chair opposite, took off my hat and vanished it. "No. I'm between assignments. You're looking well."

Juliet looked fabulous. She was beautiful as ever in black pencil skirt and teal bouse, but it wasn't that. It was like a new happiness had settled over her.

A smile warmed her face. "Mea wants to get a miniature pony. Can you believe that?" Juliet laughed, like nothing could be better. "I've talked her down from a miniature donkey, but the pony might be unavoidable."

The news startled me, banishing my moodiness almost completely. "What? Why?"

"I have the space." She shrugged. "Mea's already moved ducks into the yard. They're cute, actually."

I laughed. "What, are you starting a petting zoo?" Juliet caring for animals was very out of character and hard to imagine.

"Oh, ha ha." She took an offended tone, but grinned appreciatively at my amusement. "They're pets. I don't know, Edwin. It makes Mea happy. Besides, they're rescues."

Another bout of laughter threatened to escape and I

wondered if something more serious than preoccupation with an overblown crush was wrong with me. "Rescued from what?"

"How should I know? The important thing is they're now spoiled rotten. Do you want to see pictures?" Juliet pulled out her phone.

"Um." I wasn't entirely sure what was happening. This was so unlike us.

Juliet scrolled through a dozen photos, telling me all the ducks' names. The silly pictures were surprisingly lovely.

She switched the phone off. "So what brings you over here this morning? You looked stressed when I walked in."

My amusement disappeared. "I'm fine."

Juliet's sharp eyes narrowed and I could tell she wasn't fooled. "Did you get coffee today?"

"That's irrelevant." I made a show of exasperation, frowning as severely as possible.

Juliet pursed her lips. "You know I think you're too strict with yourself, just talk to him."

She had been saying things like this for months, but today Juliet's encouragement felt like an unnecessary weight on my already strained mind.

Why was this situation with Tristan so hard for me to handle?

The problem wasn't me being strict, that was the solution. Wasn't it, or had that somehow changed? More and more it was starting to feel like everything was shifting out from under me, and I didn't know how to put it back.

Tristan shouldn't have given me his number. Something about his ability to alter our dynamic with nothing more than a permanent marker terrified me.

I ran a hand through my hair and watched Juliet track the nervous movement. At a loss, I gave in to honesty. "I don't know how my life got to this point. It feels ridiculous but I also can't image things being different."

Juliet's fingers twitched like she was thinking about reaching for me. "Edwin—"

"No. You know talking isn't the problem. It's become so much more than that." I averted my eyes, not sure how many of my issues I wanted to drag out into the open.

I'd avoided much more than relationships since Wyatt. It was as if one day I'd woken up and it had been, not just years, but decades since I'd been involved with anyone in any capacity.

It shouldn't have been possible to inadvertently give up sex, but before Wyatt I'd begun to prefer intimacy when it was with a partner I knew, someone I'd shared other aspects of my life with. So I'd forgone the company of other men when I wasn't in a relationship, finding casual encounters had left me with an uncomfortable sort of longing that I hadn't liked.

Maybe I should have seen my current lack of sex life coming but I'd never intended to be celibate after giving up relationships. It was just that the two principles didn't add up. And I couldn't deny that my feelings about intimacy had shifted after Wyatt. I wasn't as comfortable or confident as I'd been before. The aspect of trust in taking someone to bed had become much more apparent. It wasn't just that I liked being with someone I knew but was anxious about being close to anyone in that way.

When taken all together I didn't know where any of this left me.

I still experienced desire at the sight of someone attractive. Tristan wasn't the first man to catch my eye in recent years. Only now, it felt too significant to simply act on my attraction. Sex felt like a risk in a way it hadn't before. There were too many personal things I needed to address but instead had avoided for a very long time.

I didn't want any of this to be as big of a deal as it had become and I tried to convince myself it didn't have to be. When I looked at my life and how long I'd lived, was twenty-some years so long to go without sex? Witches lived for centuries and often got stuck in life stages as time passed us by. I'd seen almost the entire 1900's myself. Maybe the length of time between past partners and now didn't matter so much.

That only left me with all my other problems.

"Nothing is simple anymore." I twisted my hands in my lap, half voicing my fear that I couldn't readjust.

Juliet cocked her head in contemplation. "Is that what you want? Something simple?"

"I don't know." What I wanted was to go back in time and have sex now and again so it wouldn't feel so overwhelming that I wanted to do it with Tristan. So that I could be confident in this situation and not feel like I was giving in to emotions or a potential relationship just to indulge physical desires.

"Maybe what you want is changing." Juliet looked at me tenderly. She'd been doing this a lot lately too, and it made me fear she'd found some new perspective or understanding that I should also be embracing. "Change is okay, Edwin. It just means something new. Not that things will go back to how they used to be, or ever become what they were with Wyatt."

I shook my head. "You can't know that. If change isn't going to risk bringing me backward, how come you feel the need to reassure me all relationships aren't like the one I had with him?"

Just thinking about it made my chest tighten with anxiety.

I wasn't going to give up the only failsafe method I had to protect myself. Avoiding unnecessary vulnerability was sensible and knowing I was in control of what did or didn't happen with Tristan calmed me, my chest loosening almost as if it had never tensed.

I didn't want a relationship with Tristan. That would never

change and therefore we would never have one, but maybe I didn't have to ignore my attraction to him as completely I'd been trying to. There was nothing wrong with Tristan tempting me to sort out my messed-up sex life and get back out there. Find a middle ground where I could be comfortable in exploring my desires again.

Juliet was watching me closely, and much too thoughtfully. She tapped her polished nails on the desk. "Your world won't end if you spend a little time with a man you've liked silently for almost a year, Edwin. I'm not saying you should do something you're not ready for, but you can't keep this up."

I grumbled, hating it when she was reasonable. "No, I can't. I'm done going to Coffee Cat anyway. I stayed away while you were out of town, you know."

Juliet looked surprised, and maybe like she didn't believe me, but all she did was switch her computer on. "If that's what you want. So—how long has it been since your last job wrapped up?"

Work was the language of our friendship and these words brought me more comfort than all her prior assurances.

"It's been a few days, maybe a week." I regaled her with a somewhat typical case of magically influenced contracts signed by unsuspecting Mortals. "There's some tail end work to do, but it's mostly done."

Juliet was typing, probably already starting on her emails. "I have an idea of what you should do next."

"Oh? Do you need my help with something?" I leaned forward in my seat. A new job was what I needed. Preferably a complicated one I could get lost in while I found a new regular coffee shop. One located closer to my actual home, perhaps.

"I think you should take a vacation."

I scoffed. "Come on. What a waste of time."

I'd been trying not to think about what Juliet had said earlier this year, about the ways we'd helped each other hold back, even though I'd seen how the changes she'd made had helped her. We weren't the same; Juliet embracing new things didn't mean I was ready to do so. But I couldn't help wondering if I needed to anyway, ready or not.

Juliet stopped typing. "I'm serious. Mea and I went to Fiji. It was a damn delight. I really think you should try this whole taking a break thing."

I ran my fingers absently around the knot of my bow tie. "You two were practically on a honeymoon, it wouldn't be the same for me. I don't need a break. You know me. How can you think I'd do something so idle as take a vacation?"

"I'm talking about going and sitting on a beach somewhere for a few days. Not changing your whole outlook on life."

I broke eye contact and muttered, "Accepting I need a vacation would be life altering."

Juliet snorted a laugh. "Just relax, live a little. Drink something with a pineapple in it for fuck's sake. I can't believe *I'm* saying this to you, but if it's coming from me of all people, you know you need it."

She had me there. I'd never doubt Juliet's judgment on a case, but I was stubborn about my life outside of work. Mainly because it didn't exist, which was by design and not a loss. The work I was trying to do at the magical Authority was important to me and I liked assisting Juliet with her private paranormal investigator business. There was nothing lacking in my life that a vacation would solve.

Yes, the atmosphere at the Authority had been tense since the mess at the start of the year, but I needed to address the issue, not run from it. I hadn't told Juliet anything about the strain I was experiencing at work. I didn't want her worrying or feeling unnecessarily guilty. It wasn't her fault some of my colleagues had reacted predictably to my involvement in her mother's downfall.

At least the drama had helped me stay briefly away from Tristan.

"I can't take a break right now," I said firmly.

Juliet crossed her arms. "Can't? Edwin, you just said you weren't busy."

"I'm glad you and Mea are doing well. Truly. But I'm a completely different story. Nothing major is happening in my life. I don't see a reason I needed a break now over any other time."

"Then why are you so defensive?"

Sometimes it was inconvenient that Juliet actually knew me. She could tell something was up, but I didn't want her figuring it out more than she already had. I didn't even know why I'd come to see her. Juliet never helped keep my mind off Tristan.

Maybe I'd hoped she would convince me to do something I normally wouldn't. I didn't want to like that idea, but couldn't deny that I did. What if I managed one small change? Took a careful chance outside my comfort zone as Juliet was always urging me to do.

If Tristan was interested in a single night together, there was no reason we couldn't have it. Right?

The night would be the end of Tristan and me. Then afterward, I might be more confident in making a move the next time I found someone attractive.

"I can feel you overthinking," Juliet said into my silence.

"Yes, well. If you don't mind." I gestured for her to leave me to it.

"You're in *my* office." She seemed to barely suppress an eye roll, her lashes fluttering.

My grumpy defenses didn't want to stick today. Juliet's good-natured exasperation softened me. “Sorry. You’re right. Maybe I do deserve a little relaxation.”

Or at the very least a good conclusion to this crush. An acknowledgment that Tristan and I had a connection, even if it would never be more than a fleeting desire.

# 3

## TRISTAN

The brightly colored walls and familiar smells of Coffee Cat threatened to make me nostalgic all day. The owner, Owen, was family. Not literally in a blood related way, but we'd been each other's everything for more than a decade. This place was like home and part of me hated that I was leaving.

Tess leaned a hip up against the counter and turned to face me, the cafe in its usual late-morning-pre-lunch customer lull. "You sure you don't want a goodbye tattoo?"

I finished restocking the napkins on the counter and turned to her. "While I appreciate your generosity, yes, I'm sure."

Tess was a tattoo artist and had been working here to supplement her income almost as long as I had. Owen was a fan of her work. She'd done some really cool stuff for him as he continued his quest to amass body art, but I wasn't so into the ink. My one tattoo was all I needed.

She grabbed my wrist and turned my palm face up. "Get another matching one with Owen, like a metaphorical book end."

"Tess! How can you say that? Like he's leaving me forever?"

Owen popped out of the kitchen in time to express his offense. He quickly delivered a pair of tortas to a customer, eyeing us for further treachery.

Owen and I had gotten matching tattoos when we were eighteen, around the time we'd promised to always be there for each other. Maybe that sounded cheesy, but we'd both been alone back then and we knew a forever friendship when we found one.

I snatched my hand back from Tess. "This isn't the end."

She gave me an exasperated look. "Yeah, fine. I know how you two are. What about a tattoo for your time at Coffee Cat? A portrait of Piña, or one of Mr. Hottie's face?"

"Piss off." I glared and she let out an evil cackle.

Last summer Tess had been on a mission to convince me I needed a piercing. Any piercing, or all the piercings, depending on her mood. I mean, I'd already had my ears done, so it wasn't like I was totally uninterested, but you could never believe anything she said. Half the time she was just fucking with you. Or angling to practice her skills on your flesh. Still, I'd considered a nipple ring.

The tattoo, on the other hand, was a no and she was just going to have to accept it.

Owen joined us behind the counter, considering me with his brows furrowed. "I think it's crap you couldn't negotiate remote work for this company. These days, why need to be in person at all?"

I'd been freelance copywriting and working from home for years, so it was a fair point—one that Owen had been bringing up at least once a week since I'd applied for the job.

"One of the conditions of the salaried position was working on site," I reminded him. "The fact that they were even hiring so many new full-time writers was a miracle. I wasn't going to be difficult. They'd have given the spot to someone else."

Owen picked up a cloth and began wiping the clean counter. "I know. I'm just moping."

I bumped his shoulder with mine and he smiled. "I'm gonna miss you too."

Owen put the cloth down. "Yeah, but I shouldn't be whining when you've worked hard for this. I am happy for you. Promise."

He was right though, this whole thing was bittersweet.

My career was finally picking up. The last few years I'd had a significant uptick in clients, but this thing in New York was big. Thirty-one years old and this was my first permanent job in my chosen field. I'd be working for a major marketing firm with an office, a boss, no need to hustle for every project I picked up, and room for promotion and growth. It was what I'd been aiming for. If it hadn't meant leaving the West Coast it'd have been perfect.

Tess wrinkled her nose. "You might have worked hard for this, Tristan, but at what cost? You're going to start hating Mondays and celebrating humpday."

I looked down my nose at her in mock offense. "Call me a sell out and I'll never speak to you again."

"Yeah?" Tess had a devious gleam in here eye. "You'd cut me out like that? Fine. And just when I was going to offer to tattoo *property of Mr. Bickel* on your ass. Now who's missing out, huh?"

Owen made a startled sound as Tess snorted with laughter.

"Yeah, I wish," I muttered, giving in to checking my phone for the first time since I'd given the man my number.

There were no new texts or missed calls.

At least Owen hadn't been around to witness my little—whatever that episode with Bickel had been. Owen knew him better than I did, but not his first name. He and Aria both acted like it was normal to call him mister and not get familiar. It was strange.

Why had I never asked for his name directly? Probably

because Bickel's buttoned up nature didn't invite confidences, but he might have told me and that would have meant something.

Owen's partner Aria worked for Herrera Investigations, and so did Mr. Bickel. At least I thought so. Aria was never interested in telling me any more about him. For someone who claimed to be a psychic, she was particularly dense on this topic. Shouldn't Aria know I was desperate for tidbits of information about her gorgeously mysterious maybe-colleague? Not that I believed in any of her fortune telling abilities. But still.

She and Owen were quick to discourage my crush and I wondered what my friends disliked about Bickel. I'd always trusted Owen's opinion and gut feelings, except they usually weren't so contradictory to mine. You'd think he'd tell me what the deal was, but no. It was all a silly mystery.

Boxes crowded my loft. Movers were coming tomorrow, shifting everything to a room in Brooklyn. Now that the last of my life was packed, I didn't know what to do with myself.

It was nine at night, bordering on too late for anything other than sitting at home. The nice thing about being in my thirties was that I appreciated quiet nights in a way I hadn't five or ten years ago, but tonight I was restless.

I could call Owen, and what, just go over? I was anxious. He probably knew that, just as I knew I needed to start dealing with it on my own. Soon late nights with Owen and Aria would be a thing of the past.

My phone buzzed on the table, an unknown number lighting up the screen.

Hopeful excitement filled me, followed by nerves, making for a thoroughly uncomfortable cocktail given my already anxious state. I watched the phone ring, sure it was him and not sure if I should answer, then sure it wasn't him and filled with disappointment. Hesitation almost got the better of me.

"Hello?" I ran my polished fingers along the edge of the table as I waited for a reply. The silence stretched.

"Evening," came a clipped response. Then nothing.

I couldn't be sure it was him, not from that one word. My pulse quickened. "Yeah, who's there?"

"Uh. Sorry. Am I speaking with Tristan?" The voice was hesitant, tone apologetic and *yes*, beautifully familiar.

"You are." I smiled wide even though no one could see me.

"Oh, good. This is—um—Edwin."

Aww, my heart did something silly. Not the name I was expecting for him. It was kinda old-fashioned but I liked it. Edwin. Edwin Bickel. And he was so stiff and awkward, and *calling me*.

But I'd left him hanging too long, stuck in my own head instead of responding. Edwin sputtered on into the silence. "You—I thought—oh never mind." He huffed. "Sorry to have disturbed you."

The call disconnected.

*Well fuck*. The exchange was pretty much on par with our usual level of communication.

I called the number back.

"Hello, Tristan." Edwin's voice seemed almost relieved.

"Hi, Edwin." God I sounded eager, I tried to dial it back. "I didn't think you'd call." *Crap*, too far. Why say that? Confidence was sexy, not desperation.

"I didn't think I would either, but here we are."

*What did that mean?* "So—" I bounced on the balls of my feet. "How's your night going?"

There was a brief pause. "Better if you join me."

A hot flush of excitement enveloped me. "Yeah, that'd be awesome."

"Awesome." Edwin didn't sound enthused. It was like he found my choice of words unimpressive. I could basically hear him frowning. "That's one way to put it, I suppose."

Was this going to be the most awkward thing of my life? We could barely talk to each other.

But Edwin was already rattling off the name and room number of a hotel and saying, "Meet me in about an hour?"

"Perfect." My pulse thumped. It wasn't like he was inviting me over for a conversation, we'd be fine.

Edwin hung up without another word.

# 4

# TRISTAN

I arrived outside Edwin's hotel room squeezed into some tight skinny jeans that I'd paired with a loose fit V-neck, going for a hot-casual look. The jeans were probably out of style given I hadn't worn this pair in years, but I was meeting a man who ignored current trends and dressed exclusively in vintage clothes, so fuck it. I wanted to look different, a bit more enticing than I usually did.

I ran a hand through my hair so it wasn't in my eyes, leaving it to fall to the side in a not too tidy flop.

I knocked.

Fuck I was nervous. I never did hook-ups like this anymore. Worry that I'd trip over my own awkwardness and blow it bubbled up inside me.

The door opened.

Edwin was perfectly put together in his twenties-era cream suit. He'd removed his jacket, calling attention to his well-fitted waistcoat, and rolled his sleeves up to the elbow. The look gave him a casual vibe even though he was still dressed up.

Edwin's piercing blue eyes traveled down my body and back

up to my face. *Oh*. His blatant stare sizzled against my skin and I shivered like he'd touched me.

The man caught my reaction and his lips twitched, the flicker of pleasure lighting his face. It felt intimate and not just because I'd never seen him smile.

Edwin stepped back from the doorway. "Please come in, Tristan. It's lovely to see you."

I slipped past him into the swanky seating area of what appeared to be a suite. "Uh—woah." We were at one of the priciest hotels in town.

My nerves settled in my stomach, the urge to fidget almost overwhelming as I took in the modern, minimalist décor. It all made Edwin look even more like a time traveler than usual.

"Nice isn't it? I like space when I'm away from home." Edwin ran his fingers along the back of an expensive and uncomfortable looking couch.

I didn't know what to say.

*What does he mean, away from home?*

Edwin's eyes fixed on me as I floundered mutely. He still seemed reserved but his expression was unguarded in a way I'd never seen. Emotions looked good on Edwin and I didn't know why he'd waited until now to let them show. That subtle smile shouldn't be hidden from the world. And there was something else about him too. Was his hair always so perfect? The lightest brown gorgeously peppered with flecks of gray. How had I never noticed?

"You're not wearing your hat," I said as the realization clicked into place.

Edwin's smile widened, full of mischief. "I can go get it. Put it back on if you like."

"No, no. I like—um—your hair." *Shit*, I sounded as nervous as I felt.

What was my deal? Wasn't everything happening exactly as

I'd wanted? Edwin had gone from barely acknowledging a coffee order to overtly checking me out. I loved that, but the sudden shift in him was disorienting. It reminded me I didn't know Edwin despite how often we'd seen each other.

Maybe I'd get to know him.

Being here and realizing I was right about everything going on underneath our coffee shop conversations made me want to unravel all of Edwin's mysteries.

But to do that I'd need more than the one night I'd convinced myself was enough to move on. And it was getting awkward standing here looking at each other. There was no need to get ahead of myself. What if he changed his mind? What if I blew it standing here like a dope?

"Can I get you a drink?" Edwin asked as if prolonged silent gazing wasn't weird at all.

"Sure, yeah okay. Cool, thanks." *Oh my god*, why were so many words falling out of my mouth?

Edwin moved past me to where a bottle of actual champagne, not bubbly wine, and two flutes were arranged on a table. My heart skipped a beat. Um, all right. Like how romantic was this? He had a brand that cost—oh—way too much.

Edwin picked up the bottle, draped a crisp white cloth over top and popped the cork. I could watch those forearms do anything, but why had he gotten something so fancy?

My face must have been doing odd things because Edwin's smile faltered.

"I have whiskey, if you'd prefer?" He put the bottle down.

"Oh, no. This is great." I moved closer and picked up a flute. "I've never had this kind of champagne before. It's—thank you." I gave in to the urge to fidget and let some nervous energy out. Then I shoved my hand in my pocket to keep it still. Damn tight pants, it barely fit.

Edwin poured my drink. “Is this too much? Should I not have—” His voice petered out.

The man didn’t look at me before moving to fill his own glass and seemed to be focusing more intently than the simple task required. *Gah*, now he was acting shy and unsure. I swear a blush crept across Edwin’s freckled cheeks, but he was half turned away like he was trying to hide it.

“Not at all. This is nice.” I tried to make sure the sincerity showed in my tone.

It was more than nice; it was special. Well, to me anyway. You just didn’t say that when you were a hook-up. Maybe to Edwin this wasn’t anything special. It was looking like he might be rich, so who knows, this could be standard for him.

Edwin leaned his hip against the table, shifting closer to me. “Cheers.” He clinked his glass with mine, a tentative smile brightening his features and any hint of a blush gone.

We sipped our drinks.

I watched his lips on the glass. They were fuller, rosier than I’d noticed before. As soon as I looked up his eyes caught mine. No one had ever looked at me like Edwin did. It was like he could see through me, making my skin prickle in the most thrilling way.

Edwin reached out, hand hovering over my arm. He tilted his head as if he were asking a silent question. I nodded and he trailed his fingers delicately along my forearm. “You’re gorgeous, Tristan.”

I shuddered in pleasure at the small touch. There was no hiding my extreme reaction and my cheeks heated. “I—uh—thanks.” My fidgets were back so I took another, long sip of champagne.

Edwin withdrew his hand from my arm. “Are you nervous?”

“Not in a bad way.” I wished he was still touching me and shifted half a step closer.

"Is it anticipatory nerves?" Edwin gave me a searching look. "I hope I can put you at ease, darling. You can tell me what you want, or don't want."

Hold on—*darling?* No one had ever called me that, and the only thing more surprising than hearing it was finding out I liked it.

"Okay, Edwin." I nodded, feeling totally dumbstruck.

This was nothing like my other casual sex experiences. I hadn't expected to come in and like, get immediately on my knees or anything, well maybe something closer to that than this—romantic—formal—*whatever* was currently happening.

I took another sip of my drink and realized I'd already drained it.

"Oh. Do you want a few more drinks? Before we—" Edwin's eyes left mine and fixed on my empty glass. His expression closed off, leaving him looking hurt, almost embarrassed.

Wait, was I being totally rude? I didn't know what I was supposed to do here. This wasn't a date, but I kinda wanted it to be one now we were here and he was all attentive and giving me a window into who he was.

Edwin wasn't what I'd expected of the flawless, self-assured man who'd so often come to Coffee Cat. I was supposed to be the jittery one, but he seemed just as nervous as me, only in a shy, quiet way. It was the realization I needed to get my confidence in check. Edwin should know I was more than into this, and I definitely didn't need a booze haze to want him, if that's what he was thinking.

I reached out and put my hand on his arm. "If you'd put a glass of water in front of me I'd have downed that. You make me nervous because I've been eyeing you for like, ever. I can't get over the fact that we're finally doing this. You're so hot. Why do you always dress so—?"

Edwin's eyes found their way back to mine, mischievous smirk back in place. "You've had your eye on me, have you?"

Like he didn't already know.

I discarded my glass and tugged on Edwin's bow tie. He swallowed audibly. We were of equal height, perfect eye level as I leaned in close. I bypassed his lips and whispered in his ear. "I've wanted to take your clothes off since I first saw you all dressed up like this."

It was Edwin's turn to shiver. I pulled back just enough to see his blue eyes go wide, looking a little bit wild. Seeing signs he wanted me as desperately as I wanted him was all I'd ever wanted.

Edwin abandoned his champagne flute and shifted closer, bringing us chest to chest. He ran a hand through my hair, leaning in to kiss me but stopping before his lips touched mine.

A small involuntary moan escaped me.

Edwin's breath tickled my skin as he murmured, "Tristan, I've longed for this moment. I never thought I'd have it. May I kiss you?"

It was dramatic and romantic and so very hot.

My *yes* came out in a desperate whisper.

Edwin's lips brushed mine in a sweet fleeting touch. Tender and teasing. I was ready to pull him to me and devour him but before I could act, Edwin's lips brushed mine again and I felt him smile in an unexpected expression more seductive than the ravaging I wanted.

His lips twitched between smiling and soft kisses and I was putty in his hands.

# 5

# TRISTAN

Our kisses grew more urgent.

I wrapped my arms around Edwin. In response, his hand tightened in my hair. When his tongue found mine, he groaned, sending vibrations through me.

Edwin gripped my waist and pressed himself tight against me. My breath hitched. I couldn't get over the feeling of our bodies aligned and touching, together after so long. I was lost in sensation, his sweetness followed by raw desire completely unraveling me.

I wasn't wasting any more time. I needed all of him. My hands roamed, shamelessly feeling him up. Edwin's response was perfect, shivering as he clung to me.

He let out a strangled moan. It was the kind of exposing sound that made my heart pound.

Edwin pulled back from our kiss, his hand leaving my hair. He palmed my ass and let out a breathy laugh. "Your pants are so tight, Tristan. I thought I hated this trend but goddamnit, you should never wear anything else."

I giggled and gave him a wiggle. Edwin squeezed my rear, smiling at me in pure delight. I draped my arms around his neck. “That’s it then. From now on its skinny jeans or naked. You might have to write a letter to my boss explaining my lapse in professional dress.”

“Yes. Anything.” He kissed me. “But you make a good point. I need to see you naked.”

I extracted myself from our embrace, pulled my shirt over my head and tossed it across the room. Better to run with it before any nerves came back. Not that I thought they would now that I was high off his kiss and the look in his eyes.

Before I could give Edwin time to ogle me, I went for his bow tie. The silk felt like water between my fingers. “Why are these so hot?” I pulled the tie from around his neck.

He laughed more heartily this time. “Are they? I’d never have thought so.”

“Apparently it’s a huge turn on for me.” I ran my hands over Edwin’s chest. “I like a well-dressed man. What even is this fabric? It feels amazing.”

Edwin didn’t bother answering. He tangled a hand in my hair once more and brought our mouths together.

“I like the way you touch my hair,” I murmured into his kiss.

Edwin’s other hand found the curls at the back of my head. His touch was firm, but not rough or controlling. “Like this?”

I nodded, not pulling back from his lips. Edwin hummed in response.

We kissed and I got busy with his buttons. By the time we broke for air, his waistcoat and shirt were undone.

Edwin glanced over his shoulder. “Uh—bedroom?”

“Definitely.” I grabbed his hand and led us out of the room.

We both looked at the bed for a moment. I directed a sideways hell-yeah look at Edwin and he ran a hand through his hair, giving me a bashful smile.

I flopped back onto the mattress, half lying propped up on my elbows. Edwin stood up against the edge, between my dangling legs, and carefully pulled off his waistcoat, then his shirt.

"Why did you put your number on my coffee today? After so long?" Edwin gave me an inquisitive look, like my answer was a vital detail he needed to complete a puzzle.

"I'm moving. It was my last chance to see if you were interested." I sat up and trailed my hands over Edwin's chest. He had freckles here too, in amongst his chest hair and on his shoulders.

He made a small breathy sound, almost inaudible, before saying, "Tristan, I'm more than interested. I'd have been sorry to miss this."

One of my hands drifted lower and Edwin grabbed it. He looked at our clasped fingers like he wasn't sure what to do with them.

"I wouldn't want to miss this either." I squeezed his hand in mine.

Edwin returned the motion before dropping my hand in favor of stroking my cheek.

We fell into staring at each other again. It wasn't awkward, just more intense than I'd have expected now that we weren't grinding together or putting our hands anywhere suggestive.

I looked up at Edwin until I had to break the moment. This felt like too much. I had to stay focused on what this night actually was. The conclusion of a crush, not the start of something. Staring at his chest felt safer than wondering exactly what emotions lay behind those eyes.

Edwin leaned forward, gripping my thighs like he needed to steady himself and reestablished eye contact. He smiled. "Now—uh—how do we get you out of these jeans?"

I blinked.

"Oh, fuck. Okay. Hold on." I scrambled off the bed. I still had my shoes on but kicked them off in record time. Then I had to shimmy out of the pants. There was wiggling, and no graceful way to peel them off.

I straightened up, my face hot. Embarrassment at my silly little stripping display vanished when I saw the look of open desire on Edwin's face.

"You're the most beautiful man I've ever seen, Tristan."

A self-deprecating giggle escaped from me. "You think I'm beautiful?"

I wished I was sure enough in myself to take the compliment. I knew I was good-looking but I hadn't expected him to call me beautiful. Maybe he was just saying shit to get in my pants. But my pants were gone and a vulnerable part of me wanted to believe he was being genuine, not just saying things to fill the air or help him play a part.

Edwin reached out for my hair, running his finger gently through my curls. "I swear I've had dreams about your eyes. My sights have been set on you too. But I never thought—"

Oh, woah. *Dreams?* About my eyes? This was more than getting-in-your-pants compliments. Like he was almost old fashioned, or a character in a movie, saying things no one said in real life. But somehow it didn't feel like an act. Edwin really was nothing like any other man I'd been with.

I needed more. "You never thought what, Edwin?"

"You and I." He swallowed. "I never imagined—we might just click. Fit. What am I saying? Fuck, I want to do so many things with you, Tristan. But I never thought—never thought—you'd want to."

Edwin rambling was the best. He was so earnest.

"I want you," I told him in a rush. "Like, so, so much."

He looked almost surprised to hear me say it, like some realization had just hit him, but come on, look where we were. He'd known this was what we were about.

Edwin glanced down, his hand trailing away from my hair

and across my chest but stopping before getting too low, like he was suddenly hesitant about undressing me all the way. He hadn't made any move to take off his pants beyond slipping out of his shoes. Was he waiting for me to do something?

I ran my thumb along his waistband.

And there was that look of surprise again. I pulled my hand back but before I could wonder what was going through Edwin's mind, he unbuckled his belt and slid it off.

Edwin reached out and guided my hand back to his waist. "Undress me?" He sounded different than he had a moment ago, much more quiet but still very sincere.

"I'd love to." I gave him a playful look as I ran my hand from his hip to the button on his pants and dipped my fingers behind the fabric.

Edwin didn't return my smile. It seemed like he was concentrating solely on my hands as I undid his button and zipper, then gently tugged until his suit pants fell, pooling around his ankles. Edwin quickly stepped out of them, his breathing becoming more audible, almost a soft pant. He kept his gaze averted, standing extra still as a deep blush colored his cheeks, all the way to his ears.

"You all good?" I asked softly.

Edwin looked at me and cleared this throat. "Yes."

But the sense that something had changed didn't disappear. I reached out and placed a hand on his elbow. "You can tell me what you want too."

Edwin shifted closer until our bodies brushed. He settled his hands lightly on my hips, not responding to my words unless you counted his tentative touch.

He wasn't exactly hesitating, but something was going on. I didn't get the vibe Edwin was uncomfortable, he just wasn't as confident as his *darlings* and outlandish references to dreams had implied.

I traced the freckles on Edwin's cheeks, still pink from his persistent blush, and tried again. "You must have had some dreams about what you want tonight. Tell me, and I'll make it happen."

Edwin blinked. "I—everything."

*Everything* sounded perfect, even if he didn't mean it the way I hoped. But Edwin had avoided actually telling me what he wanted. Maybe he needed me to lead more than he liked to give direction, and that was perfectly fine as long as he wasn't going along with something he didn't want.

"Should we start with doing something about these?" I plucked the band of his underwear.

The blush spread down Edwin's neck. "Yes, I'd like that."

I knelt down and gently stripped his last bit of cover away, letting my fingers trail slowly down his legs as I did so.

Edwin was hard, and being down here temped me to lean forward and explore him with my mouth, but looking up at him, he seemed tense. And yes, sucking him off might have helped with that, but I needed a better idea of what Edwin wanted before I went for it. I could have asked but I had a feeling it would be moving faster than he wanted.

I ran my hands back up his legs and stood. "You're stunning," I whispered in his ear.

Edwin put his arms around me and let out a satisfied sound. I returned his embrace, letting my hands slip lower, going slowly to see if he like it. His eyes fluttered closed and when I got to his hips, he nudged them forward against me.

"More," Edwin whispered.

I gently cupped his ass. He leaned forward, opening his eyes and resting his forehead against mine.

Being in each other's arms, nose to nose, felt too good. I didn't mind this slow kind of intimacy but it threatened me with feelings that went beyond lust.

We didn't know each other. This shouldn't feel like more than any other casual thing. But we'd hovered around each other for so long, half flirting and wondering—at least in my case—that this tender touching felt full of meaning. Like there was potential here.

"Tristan?" Edwin pulled his face back a fraction.

My hands stilled where I'd been exploring the contours of his rear and lower back. "Do you want me to stop?"

"No—it's—for some reason I still can't believe we're doing this. That's all."

"Believe it—" I gestured to where we were pressed together. "We are happening."

A small chuckle bubbled out of Edwin. I felt his body relax, tension dissipating as he leaned more fully against me. Good. That's what I'd wanted. Maybe he just needed a bit longer to get into the mindset of what we were doing.

"Okay, my turn." I put Edwin's hands on my not-yet-naked hips and shimmied.

Edwin laughed again, a grin splitting his face with a mischievous twist. He wasted no time pulling my boxer briefs down to the floor. I kicked them away and Edwin pulled us back together.

We both made desperate sounds when our bare skin collided. Edwin's quiet hesitation seemed to disappear. He buried his face in my neck, kissing and groaning as he rubbed against me, our cocks trapped between us and sliding together.

I pulled Edwin onto the bed, guiding him on top of me and wrapped him up in my arms. I flung a leg over him to keep him pressed tightly to me as we kissed.

He rolled his hips, letting a deep sound escape his throat. "Yes, this is what I want."

"You like kissing? Or me underneath you?"

He shuddered. "Both. But please don't stop kissing me, Tristan."

My heart revved. "Not planning on it. I like this too."

And I liked figuring out what worked for him. I kissed him harder, holding him close.

Edwin's hands were everywhere, like he'd broken a dam and couldn't get enough. Our kisses became frantic, panting, lip-crushing movements. *I can't breathe and don't care* kisses. The longer our bodies ground together, the more we got lost in each other. It was consuming, like lack of coherent thought gave way to sparks and stars and things I never knew existed. It was more than worth waiting a year for.

We eventually came up for air, but only because the alterative was drowning in each other.

Edwin smoothed back the hair that had fallen in my eyes. "Look at you." His more confident, playful voice was back. "Flushed and rosy suits you, Tristan. And I didn't think you could look more gorgeous. I'm glad I was wrong."

I blinked furiously, a compulsive wiggle taking control of my body. "Are you for real?"

He lay a gentle kiss on my lips, exhaling slowly. "Yes, darling. And I suspect you'll look even more stunning when you come." He kissed me again before saying in a whisper so soft I could barely hear, "Nothing has ever been this real."

My heart thudded. Edwin's cheeks burned red.

*Who talks like this?* Edwin's earnest words combined with his earlier vulnerability made me want more than one night. For a second I was dizzy with it and filled with so much more than physical desire for this sweet, contradictory man. I was undone by his sincerity and seduced by every unexpected piece of himself he showed me.

But who was I kidding, this was still a hook-up, not a love story.

My feelings were unjustified. There was a lot of awkwardness between us. We could barely communicate. I'd learned Edwin's first name like two hours ago, and didn't even know how old he was.

I had to remember, Edwin had been attracted to me all this time, and yet never really talked to me. That meant he didn't want anything more from me. Sweet words didn't change facts, but hell if they didn't make this whole night better.

I tugged him back to my mouth. Kissing was better than thinking or hearing more of Edwin's outlandish declarations. Time didn't seem to exist when we were like this. There was nothing but touch. I lost track of everything until I was on the edge.

I pulled back just enough to say, "Edwin, please. Will you fuck me?"

"Yes." He groaned and pressed his lips to my neck, nibbling and sucking. "Say it again."

I begged for him and felt Edwin smiling against my skin.

He rolled off me and reached for a paper bag on the night-stand. A slight tremor took hold of Edwin's hands as he fumbled with a box of condoms, thwarting his attempt to open it. His shaking worsened as the box wouldn't cooperate and he let out a muttered curse.

I dunno, somehow it seemed like more than packaging-induced frustration and reminded me I had no idea what was going on with Edwin, no matter what I thought all these glimpses into his character meant.

Just as I was about to say something, Edwin ripped the box in two, sending all the condoms spilling onto the bed. He looked at me and we both laughed. Maybe I was trying too hard to read into things.

Edwin briefly covered my mouth with his before settling between my legs. His smile was sharp, eyes focused as he ran his hands up my inner thighs. Goosebumps followed his touch, lighting me up as his hand brushed between my legs.

He teased the sensitive skin at my hole with a leisurely lube-slick touch, responding to my pleasure like we had all the time in the world to do nothing but this. He pressed into me, slowly stretching me and finding that spot inside that drove me wild.

Edwin seemed to love every bit of it, all the needy moans and increasingly desperate words that passed my lips as I unraveled for him.

I moved against his hand. “Please, Edwin. I need you, now.”

“Yes, Tristan.” He sounded desperate too.

He pulled back, his skin flushed all over, the lines of his body taught as he rolled on a condom and slathered his dick with lube. I was captivated by the sight, sure I’d remember it forever as Edwin aligned our bodies and slowly pushed in.

When he was flush against me, I wrapped my legs around him and pulled him close. His mouth met mine, kissing messily as we found our rhythm. Everything was his body and mine. We felt so good together.

I let out a particularly exposing moan.

Edwin looked down at me with blazing eyes. “You like that, darling?”

My reply was an almost incoherent string of *yes*. I let the sensations swallow me as I wrapped a hand around myself. I swore nothing existed in the world but Edwin as my pleasure burst hot against my stomach.

The last of Edwin’s control frayed as he watched me. He came apart in a beautiful display of unrestricted emotion before collapsing against me, panting in my ear.

My heart raced. I ran my fingers through the sweat dampened hair at the back of Edwin’s head, making him sigh.

I was blissed out of my mind.

Moments crawled past. I wanted Edwin to hold me like this,

kissing my neck and jawline forever. I wasn't ready for our night to be over.

But we couldn't stay like this. Time hadn't stopped existing. Edwin slowly eased out of me and we cleaned up. He left the bed without a word.

I wanted to drift off to sleep, but instead my brain came back online. Would Edwin expect me to leave immediately, now we were done? I had no clue. It was too hard to figure out what he wanted. Was he tender or aloof? Or if he was both, which would he decide to be next? And what did he want from me?

Maybe next time I'd find out what made Edwin open up just that little bit more—and how great would that be? I wanted it so badly, even if I was leaving in a week. Maybe we could find a little bit more time.

As I noted my serious inability to be casual, Edwin returned. He crawled onto the bed and lay beside me, but not too close. He propped himself up on an elbow and examined me. For some reason it made my skin hot. I was consumed with the urge to hide.

"Come here, Tristan. Let me hold you?" Edwin's tone was soft but almost flat, like he'd used up all his unrestrained sounds.

I scooched closer and we wrapped our arms around each other. It was great. I loved cuddles. But I dunno, something kept me from enjoying this like I should have been. Everything felt conflicted. Were we starting something together? Or did Edwin just like this kind of physical contact? Liking my body pressed up against him didn't mean he liked *me* exactly.

Why hadn't he initiated something sooner? Edwin might just prefer to be approached. He'd waited for my suggestion on almost everything tonight. But how did that fit in with the rest of him? Especially the mysterious, flawlessly self-assured guy I'd thought I was meeting when he'd opened the hotel room door.

*Ugh.* What did the intricacies of Edwin matter? I was leaving regardless of figuring them out or not.

"I should get going," I pulled back so I could see his face.

Edwin's eyes were closed; he cracked them open. "If you want." He sounded as if he'd been on the verge of sleep, like my decision didn't matter in the slightest.

My stomach twisted. See. One and done. Edwin wasn't plagued by random feelings. His small vulnerable moments and hesitations didn't mean what we did was a big deal to him. I'd misread him. Over-analyzed everything. His sweet words must've been nothing but empty talk, he seemed one-hundred percent ready to doze off and move on with his life.

I sat up and scooted toward the end of the bed.

Edwin caught my hand. "Or you could stay."

# 6

## EDWIN

Tristan's grip was firm on my fingers. "Stay?"

"Only if you want. Maybe we could take a shower or—" I tried not to go red and failed. It was too bad you couldn't run out of the ability to blush.

Tristan was looking at me more closely than I wanted, making me regret reaching out for him. I felt like a ball of nerves, unable to stop thinking about all the reasons I'd shied away from physical intimacy and how long it had been since I'd let myself be in this position. I didn't want to sit by myself and stew, but even less appealing was the idea Tristan might clue into to my emotional state.

I should have let him go and hated that it wasn't what I genuinely wanted.

Unexpected things kept throwing me off. I'd underestimated the reality of tonight. Being with Tristan had been a sensory overload and I wasn't even talking physically.

"I'm down for a shower with you." Tristan scooted back toward me. "But if I'm not going now, you're risking me spending the night. It's pretty late."

Was I not supposed to want him to spend the night? I

supposed not. Once upon a time I might have been glad for him to leave.

"You can spend the night."

My words won me a dazzling smile even though I'd delivered them in a bored, almost unaffected tone.

Tristan tucked back into me, wiggling as he got settled. He rested a hand on my hip.

Laying together like this elicited a strange feeling in me that I didn't want to think about.

Yes, well. In that case I should have kept quiet and allowed him to walk away.

Why hadn't I?

For some reason I wanted to talk, not be left alone. Since when did I admit to being lonely? Why should Tristan tempt me to stay up all night and tell my life story? That wasn't a part of sex, or something I ever used to do in its aftermath.

I never wanted to talk to anyone.

Not that it mattered when real conversation was nothing but an idle fantasy. Tristan didn't know I was a one-hundred-and-twelve-year-old Witch only a third of the way through his life. How could I possibly tell him about my past, my day-to-day life or hopes for the future given that?

"You feel good," Tristan muttered as he snuggled closer.

My heart fluttered painfully at his easy intimacy in a feeling almost as overpowering as the rest of the night. This wasn't what I'd signed up for.

It was as if a wall of emotions and things I didn't care for were looming behind me. I hoped not acknowledging their existence would be enough to keep them away, but given how I'd been feeling lately, I feared everything would crash down upon me weather I liked it or not.

Would I have felt like this no matter who I'd slept with after so long?

I was unable to think of a satisfactory response to Tristan's comment and so lay there quietly and reminded myself tonight was nothing but the first step in getting my sex life sorted out. I wasn't having deeper feelings for Tristan than before we'd done this. I was just overwhelmed.

Slipping back into the habit of sex wasn't going to be as easy as slipping out had been, which was frankly bullshit. I just wanted to enjoy tonight as a simple pleasure. It was infuriating not to be able to.

Tristan ran his hand up and down my side as if he weren't bothered by my silence. He caught my eye and smiled before getting distracted and looking around the room. "I've never been to this hotel. I guess I thought you lived here in town, but you said you're away from home?"

"I'm only visiting for work," I lied. "As you've noticed, I'm here regularly, but this is only one of the many cities I travel to."

"Do you always stay here?" Tristan looked taken aback at the thought.

"Usually, yes."

I did stay at this hotel once in a while, when I couldn't be bothered teleporting back to my apartment three thousand miles away and didn't want to intrude upon Juliet's hospitality. The place was nice enough. I liked the change of scene, getting out of the city. Sometimes I'd sleep with the windows open and listen to the sea.

"Does your work take you near Coffee Cat? When you're here, I mean." Tristan propped himself up on an elbow. He wore small silver stud earrings and had a second piercing in one ear I'd never noticed before. It was adorned with a tiny silver heart.

The sight jolted something inside me and I didn't know why.

"No. Not really." I answered his question distractedly. What was happening? It was like that little heart was staring me down, confronting me. I didn't like it at all, but couldn't look away.

Tristan touched my chest absently. "You work with Aria and that one private investigator, right? Sorry. Am I asking too many questions?"

"Not at all."—except he was—"Yes, I work with Juliet. She likes the marranitos your friend makes, so it's worth the trip across town to buy a few when I'm here."

I suddenly felt like I needed to get away. I didn't want to leave the bed, the feel of Tristan against me, but also couldn't be here talking like this even if I was only telling lies and partial truths. And I'd thought I'd wanted to talk. It was ridiculous. I was all over the place and unable to collect myself as I normally did.

Tristan's hand stopped tracing circles on my skin, a puzzled look appearing on his face. "You didn't usually buy any pan dulce."

For a split second I wondered what he was talking about, then it clicked. I was more distracted than I'd realized, telling lies that didn't make sense. My whole body flashed hot with embarrassment at the truth I was clumsily trying to cover up. I couldn't break Tristan's stare. "I—"

Tristan didn't need to know I teleported across country to see him, and not just because I couldn't reveal magic to him. My behavior might be informed by decades alone, and I could almost convince myself there was little difference in getting coffee down the street, or from a different time zone when space and time were mine to mold and use at will. I popped over to Italy whenever I wanted good pasta or fresh mozzarella for fuck's sake. But it had been unreasonable of me to keep coming to the coffee shop to see him.

What would he think of me if he knew?

I'd used so much energy playing it casual tonight, trying to act confident, like I was as competent and unaffected in love and sex as I was in the other aspects of my life. Hiding the reality of me.

And I'd still almost blown it, hesitating and being unable to hide the fact that letting Tristan see me undressed was significant, but he'd met all my unexpected reactions with kindness and genuine care without making a big deal of it. Which was almost harder to accept than letting him see me so unraveled to begin with.

After all that, I didn't want Tristan to know how much trouble I had managing personal connections. That I'd put in so much effort just to see him and still hadn't been able to bring myself to talk to him properly. In Tristan's eyes I'd hoped to be the mysterious man who'd shared a good night with him, nothing more or less. I didn't want his opinion to change.

And most of all, I didn't want to face that after all this time a long dead abusive relationship still affected me in so many ways. I was never like this before Wyatt.

Tristan gave me a soft look, pulling me from my spiraling thoughts. "Doesn't matter why you like that coffee shop. I'm not complaining we met." He smiled wide, lopsided and so goofy.

I had no doubt he'd spared me on purpose, even if he didn't know the extent of what had come over me. He hadn't pressed me about the lie or called attention to my floundering, when either would have been reasonable. Gratitude burned through me, as uncomfortable as the rest of the emotions I was having.

"Me either," I mumbled.

Tristan ran a hand through my hair, down my neck and along my arm. I focused on his touch and took his hand in mine. I kissed his knuckles, trying get my bearings back.

"I like these." I shifted his nails so the blue-black polish caught the light, trying to focus fully on him rather than my messy self. "How'd you get the finish like that?"

"The matte look?" Tristan wiggled his fingers. "It's just, you know, the polish formula. Don't get me wrong, I love a good glitter polish, but dark colors look so good matte."

It came as no surprise that I found his fingers beautiful. Long and slender, well cared for short nails. *Hell*, I was infatuated with him. Not that it mattered. I wasn't changing my mind about never seeing Tristan again after tonight. No pretty nails or perplexing feelings would persuade me.

Tristan fidgeted. He was a wiggly man. "Um." He sat up and gestured to the bathroom. "I'm gonna go check out the facilities. Maybe come find me in the shower in a bit?"

Once Tristan was out of sight I forced myself to get up and slipped on the complimentary hotel robe. I did a quick cleaning spell, vanishing any mess from the bed, then turned down the covers and smoothed out all the wrinkles.

Some of my uneasiness disappeared. I could almost say I was relaxing. Maybe I'd be fine after all.

Now the bed was put right, I couldn't leave the rest of the room as it was. I tidied away the condoms and lube, then hung up my clothes before folding Tristan's things, fetching his shirt from the other room and putting everything neatly on a chair. I picked up his shoes—a lovely shade of mauve even if they were Converse sneakers and not something I'd ever wear—and put them with the rest.

I almost felt like my usual self, alone in the silent room, except for the fact that I couldn't stop looking fondly at Tristan's shoes for reasons that eluded me completely.

The water in the shower clicked on. I inched toward the bathroom door and knocked.

Tristan opened it and pulled me in. "There's a hot tub in here!"

"Technically, I think it's a bath. We can fill it if you like."

"Bathtubs aren't that big. Four people could fit in there and not even be touching." Hand on his hip, Tristan gestured pointedly with his other, still so perfectly naked. "It'd be a waste of water to fill and drain it."

I snorted, caught up in his carefree energy. "I'm sorry the bathroom setup bothers you."

"You should be."

"Get in the shower. You're wasting water," I teased.

"Join me?" Tristan's eager look brought a playfulness to his features, making everything feel all right.

"I will, just—I'll be right back." I ducked out of the bathroom and returned with the champagne and our flutes.

Serving it to Tristan had probably been over the top, but I'd needed to get myself in a celebratory mood and focus on what a good thing this night was for me.

I set everything on the counter next to the sink and poured two fresh glasses. I untied my robe, only hesitating a moment before shrugging it off my body. I *was* feeling good. See, I was already improving my confidence.

Tristan held the frosted door to the large tiled shower open for me as I carried the drinks over to him. I smiled.

"We can't drink that in here." Tristan was glistening with water droplets, his brown skin shimmering.

I handed him a glass and took a sip from mine. "Why the hell not?"

"Because." He made room for me under the water.

I brushed up against him as I tipped my head back, letting the water fall over my face. When I wiped my eyes clear, Tristan was looking at me, his thick lashes now glittering with moisture. His hair was plastered to his head, wet curls in his eyes and clinging to his ears and neck. I kissed him softly on the lips then pulled back to drink my champagne.

"This might be the only appropriate way to drink. I may never have champagne out of the shower again."

Tristan poked me in the side and laughed. Poked me! He rolled his eyes and everything was so light and joyous that I almost wanted more from us despite knowing it as a bad idea.

"We could break a glass in here," Tristan said in what I suspected was a mock-serious tone.

"We won't."

"Okay." He shrugged and took a sip. "It's your toes' funeral if we do."

"I'll risk it." I knocked back my drink and set the glass on the shelf, then grabbed the soap and lathered up my arms and chest.

Tristan drank his wine lazily, gaze tracking my movements as I washed. When he was done, I took the glass off him and turned the soap to him, rubbing my hands all over his body. The way he responded to my touch was so natural it made me light-headed. We moved together easily, like we'd done this a hundred times.

I leaned in to speak into his ear. "Can I wash your hair?" Maybe that was weird, but I didn't care. I suddenly felt great, like this wasn't as big a deal as I'd feared lying in bed.

Tristan gave me a surprisingly sweet look. "I think I'd like that."

Now my overwhelmed reaction had settled, I wanted to take everything the night had to offer. I was enjoying this simple pleasure just as I'd wanted.

Tristan let me work the shampoo into his scalp. He closed his eyes, leaning back into my touch.

I really should have cared that nothing about this shower said casual sex. I'd led us into a situation more dangerous than broken glass on slippery tile, where Tristan might expect more from me than I was going to give. I was a mess of mixed signals, but I couldn't treat him with detachment or keep playing it cool, even knowing too much of the wrong impression would disappoint him. Asking him to stay had been selfish in that regard.

Tristan let out a low moan. "Fuck, a scalp massage might be the best thing ever."

"Really? After everything we've done tonight, this is the best thing ever?"

He turned to face me. "Point made. But it's closer than you'd think." Tristan ducked under the water and rinsed, saying "Your turn," as he plucked the bottle from the shelf and spun me round.

"Okay, you might be right." But I didn't know why this felt so good.

The whole scene—wine, nonsexual touch—wasn't supposed to be what I wanted. It was too familiar, and I didn't need to grow attached.

I refused to believe I already was. This was just me making the most of the night. We didn't know each other. A rollercoaster of post-sex emotions wasn't going to trick me into thinking I wanted that to change. I'd barely handled tonight, even if I was feeling good now. Further intimacy and any kind of relationship would only be bad news.

I didn't want Tristan to hurt me, and within the confines of tonight I was confident he wouldn't. He practically couldn't, simply because he knew so little about me. Anything more between us and I'd lose the guarantee that vulnerability couldn't be turned on me, so I wouldn't give him any more than I already had, no matter how good a scalp massage felt.

This night had been exactly what I'd needed as first step to getting my sex life back. But that's all it was, and now it was over.

I rinsed my hair and we exited the shower to towel off. Tristan yawned.

There was a growing awkwardness as we returned to the room. I wasn't in the mood for more sexual activity and it didn't seem like Tristan was either, but getting off again would have helped bring back the façade that physical needs were all we were here for.

I liked façades, they were easier than anything else.

"You remade the bed." Tristan hopped in and pulled the covers up over himself. "How'd you get the lube off so well?"

I climbed in the other side, not so distracted that I couldn't come up with a reasonable lie. "There was another blanket in one of the closets."

"That was convenient." Tristan cuddled right up to me without hesitation, his head on my chest, yawning again. "What are you up to tomorrow? I'm not moving till the end of the week. If you're staying in town maybe we—"

"I have work early and then have a flight to catch. Another business trip. I travel often, all around the country. A day here, a few there. I don't get much time to sit still. You understand, I'm sure."

"Oh, yeah. Totally. I get it."

I waited to see if Tristan would say anything else, but he'd gone still as if all his euphoric energy had drained away. I wanted to take back my blunt dismissal, but it was better this way. Maybe not for him, but it was for me.

I often pretended to be a selfish jerk to keep people at a distance, but right now I didn't think I could claim it was an act.

After I left the hotel, I'd never see Tristan again and any feelings he might have about that weren't going to affect my decision.

## 7

# TRISTAN

A door closed and I blinked awake. It was morning.

The smell of coffee propelled me the rest of the way to consciousness. I rolled over and looked around the empty room.

I wanted to savor the memory of last night but couldn't. I hadn't expected to wake up alone. Had Edwin left already? I felt a horrible pang. If he had—

The bedroom door cracked open and Edwin poked in.

"Morning." He gave me a small smile, already dressed in a navy blue suit complete with white bow tie and hat.

"Did I sleep late?" I hated the insecure pitch in my voice. I needed time to wake up and get my head on straight before talking to him.

"No, I was up early." Edwin came to stand beside the bed. "I have to get going. You can stay in the room as long as you like. I've ordered breakfast. It's out in the sitting area."

"Oh, thanks." I pulled the covers around me, feeling too exposed next to him in his suit.

I'd been crushed when Edwin shut down my attempt to steer us toward a repeat. Part of me wanted to blurt it out now, ask him out on an actual date, tell him I wanted more, ask where he lived, or offer myself as a guaranteed no-strings-attached lay if his travels ever took him to New York. Anything so we didn't have to end it like this. The other part of me knew I couldn't take the rejection if he brushed me off again.

Edwin was hard to get a handle on. He'd been such a firm no to doing this again but up until then he'd acted almost like he was trying to woo me. His vulnerable moments made even less sense today, seeing him ready to walk out the door like nothing affected him.

No matter what I'd got myself thinking last night, this morning it was clear we were done.

Edwin looked down at me, his face gorgeous unreadable stone. "Thank you for putting your number on my coffee. I had a great time with you, Tristan."

"Oh. Yeah, me too. Last night was like, awesome." I cringed at my forced lightness and clumsy words.

Edwin smoothed his pristine suit jacket. "Goodbye." He doffed his hat at me and turned to go. He didn't look back.

"Bye." I couldn't help feeling shitty as Edwin disappeared.

The outer door to the hall opened and closed.

I got up and found my clothes folded on a chair. See, this right here. He was an odd one. Who folded their one-night-stand's clothes like this, socks and underwear included? All the champagne and *darlings* threw me off. Edwin must be weirdly formal. It didn't mean he liked me or cared, it was more like he subscribed to outdated manners or something.

I got dressed and wandered out into the sitting area. Maybe this was what hook-ups were like for rich people. Hotel suites, two-hundred-dollar bottles of wine, no second thoughts. This whole encounter was ridiculous, like something out of someone else's life.

I laughed when I saw the breakfast Edwin had ordered. The table was covered with enough food for four people.

With no reason not to, I sat down and helped myself, pouring syrup on everything. When I'd had enough, I refilled my coffee, grabbed one more waffle and went to snoop around the place.

There were several suits hanging in the closet, including yesterday's cream one. Edwin had laid out three different pairs of identical polished oxfords and an assortment of patterned socks, and had brought more bow ties than seemed necessary. I found ten, each in a different color.

With all this stuff I didn't see a suitcase anywhere. Shouldn't he be packed if he had to leave town today? What about check-out? The spent duvet was also nowhere to be found. Had it already gone for cleaning?

I stuffed the last of the waffle in my mouth and wiped my hands on my pants before running my fingers over the ties. I had a weird urge to steal one.

Right, time to go. I had to finish organizing my own shit and meet the movers. You know, get back to reality and stop wishing I could fuck rich hotties regularly. Okay, it was just the one inconsistently sweet hottie, but I needed to get my head out of the clouds.

I had my rideshare drop me off at Coffee Cat because who was I kidding, I needed an emotional support moment with Owen.

The place wasn't busy, so I stopped to chat with Tess and the other baristas, trying not to have too many feelings about no longer being their coworker.

There was an odd moment last night when I'd asked Edwin why he liked Coffee Cat and he'd panicked, making me wonder if he'd come here repeatedly to see me. Why else would he react like I'd caught him in something embarrassing? But it made no sense. Why come and not talk to me? Why seek me out at last, then have no interest in seeing me again when it went well—wait, did it not go as well as I thought?

Nope—I needed to stop. Looking for signs Edwin had feelings for me wasn't helping and wouldn't change the fact that our thing was so clearly over.

Suddenly I was glad my time at the cafe was done. The whole place was bathed in memories of Edwin. It would have been mortifying to go back to serving him coffee after the way he'd walked away from me.

I left the baristas and found Owen in the back office looking at orders and accounts.

He glanced up from his papers. "Haven't seen those jeans in a while. You look good."

I flopped into the only other chair in the tiny closet-turned-office. "Thanks. How's your month looking?"

Owen put down his pen and shrugged. "Good. Business is steady." He looked at me more closely. "Is that a hickey?"

I fidgeted, wishing I had a coffee or something to hold and hide my restless energy. "Yeah, had a bit of fun last night."

Owen knew my hook-up days were long behind me, but he could probably tell I didn't want to talk about it. "Are you ready for the move?" he asked instead.

I straightened a stack of post-its on the desk. "As far as chores and life admin tasks, yeah. But I don't know if I'm happy about it, now the moment has come."

"You can always come back if you want." Owen's answer came quick, like he'd been waiting to get the offer out. "You always have a spot at Coffee Cat. You're my business partner even if you never wanted to own a share of the place. This cafe will always be ours. And you can stay with me whenever you need, it's what the spare room is for. But you should give this new job a shot. Just don't worry if it doesn't work out."

"I know, I know. All the reasons I'm going are still valid. It's the stable job opportunity I've been searching for. I loved working here, creating this place, but it'll be nice not to need a second job, you know?"

Owen stroked his beard. "Totally. And you never know, it might be fun to live in a big city again."

We'd run wild in San Francisco during summers in college, but I'd loved the city less when I'd lived there as a mostly unsupervised teen. My high school days living with my uncle were hard to look back on, so I always focused on my time there with Owen instead. He was right, I'd liked the busy atmosphere then, but that hadn't been what made those summers memorable.

I made an unsure sound. "I won't know anyone in New York."

"You're the most loveable guy I know. I can guarantee you'll meet people." Owen gave me an I-believe-in-you look. Classic Sanchez. "And it's a whole new dating pool."

I groaned. "I'm sick of dating. I'm ready to be permanently off the market."

Owen cocked a brow. "What about last night's guy?"

I looked down at the tattoos on Owen's arms to avoid his gaze. "There was never a chance that was going anywhere. I keep picking people who are out of my league."

Owen crossed his arms and leaned back, balancing on the back legs of his chair. "No, you keep telling yourself lies like that. No one's out of your league. You're equal to anyone and worthy of someone who knows how great you are."

I squirmed under the assault of his sincerity. "I liked this guy way more than he liked me. I officially can't do casual anymore. Like at all."

"Well, he sounds like a fool. But so what? You'll probably run into your soulmate on the streets of New York City and call me up, telling me all about him." Owen's words were filled with the kind of confidence that only came from being in love himself. As if it were guaranteed for the rest of us.

If only Edwin were a fool and not—well, anyway—it might've made it easier to write him off. All our odd little moments added something, rather than took anything away, and made it feel like a real connection, or the beginnings of one.

But it wasn't like me to give up. I'd get over this and move on to something better. "I hope you're right, Owen."

"I'm only right because it's what you always say." Owen leaned in, giving me a conspiratorial smile. "So who did you see last night?"

"No one." I tried to sound relaxed and failed.

Owen narrowed his eyes like he was reading my mind. "You didn't—" There was a very pregnant pause. "You hooked up with Bickel? Really Tristan? *No way*." Owen looked mildly horrified.

I bristled. "Hey—his name is Edwin—and why shouldn't I have gone for it? I like him. And you've never explained why you don't. So why not reveal the big secret you've been holding back now it's done?"

Owen looked startled, and I'd almost say panicked, but I didn't get why. "What? There's no secret. He's just kind of a pretentious jerk—at least at work according to Aria. I don't know, Tristan. I guess I'm impressed you found another side to him. Um, you're definitely not seeing him again?" His expression turned worried, brows furrowed and mouth forming a subtle frown.

"He wasn't interested in seeing me again." I gave an account of his rejection and the awkward morning after. "I dunno. I tried to keep my head on straight, but I'm all feely and full of longing. Why do I do this to myself?"

"You're a romantic but that's not a bad thing. Look, maybe he's not right for you. That's probably best. You'll find someone who is, and it will be even better with them."

I slouched in my chair. "That's a high bar to clear."

Owen looked skeptical. "Was he really that different from anyone else? What did he do that was so special?"

"You know, magic sex stuff," I mumbled, a halfhearted joke, not knowing how to put the night into words. Maybe I shouldn't try to. I needed to accept it for what it was and nothing more.

Owen's eyes went wide at my poor attempt at humor. "Funny —uh—how are you not intimidated by him?"

It was my turn to give a strange look. "I don't get why you are. He's kinda sweet and weird, comforting and—*ugh*—I really want to see him again."

"Then it's the perfect time to move. Find a nice regular guy who'll treat you right. Forget about Bickel. Who, it sounds like, was a bit of a jerk to you, by the way."

I ignored that. "Why's Edwin not a regular guy?"

Owen looked startled. "I mean—not that he's not. Uh. But if he's not interested in you there must be something seriously wrong with him."

"Thanks for the pep-talk." I rolled my eyes. "I'm going to miss you." My voice broke unexpectedly on the last word. Shit. I looked down at the tattoo on my wrist.

"We haven't lived away from each other since we met." Owen got up and pulled me out of the chair into a hug. "I'm trying not to be selfish and sad you're going, but I don't know. I might have to get Aria on board with moving to the East Coast."

"We promised we'd never leave each other," I said into his shoulder.

Owen hugged me tighter. "You're not leaving me. This is just like when you moved out of the apartment, only with more geography. We'll still be in each other's lives. Plus, I can always expand my queer coffee shop empire. If you don't mind me following you."

I choked on a breath that sounded a whole lot like a sob. "I'll keep an eye out for coffee and pan dulce related business opportunities."

"Oh my god, what if you find someone who makes better conchas than me?" Owen pulled back and wiped his eyes, but he was smiling. "You'll replace me."

I shook my head. "Never. I'll leave anyone who dares tempt me a horrible review. I promise."

"No need to fuck with their business. Though I might secretly love it if you don't cheat on my baking."

We both laughed a little. "Deal, but you have to overnight a variety of sweets to me at least fortnightly—no weekly."

Owen pulled me into another bone crushing hug. "Come over for dinner tonight. Actually, want to stay with us for the rest of the week?"

"You have no idea how much I need that right now." I was smiling, my mood lifting at last.

Maybe I was disappointed about Edwin, but that was okay. I'd get through it, I always did.

# 8

## TRISTAN

Four months later.

I WALKED out of the conference room in a daze. How was I still underestimating the number of meetings I needed to attend each day?

I swear I could barely remember what that one had been about. It was like I'd been put into a trance as soon as our manager started talking. Was it something about a new workplace hazard reporting system? Or had it been about the company mission statement—oh—and how it informed processes like reporting?

Yeah, riveting stuff.

The rest of my team didn't look any livelier than me as we filed silently into the stairwell and returned to our desks on the floor above.

"Wanna go for a drink tonight?" Jonah asked as we sat down. His desk was next to mine and he'd become a work friend, though that was mostly due to proximity.

"Na. Sorry. Next time." I felt like crap and my neck itched intensely. Had something bitten me in that meeting? What the hell? Scratching it was only making it worse. I balled my hands in my lap.

Jonah swiveled his chair back and forth in quarter turns, an annoying habit of his. "Come on. It'll be fun. We've got a whole group going, even a few people from IT and the hot girls from admin—how can you resist?"

"Viv and Melanie aren't going to entice me."

"Yeah, I know. But I could really use a wingman." He gave me a weird eyebrow waggle.

I turned away and flicked my computer on. "I'm busy tonight. Maybe next time."

This whole office culture was new to me and so far I wasn't a fan. Most of the other writers in the team were all right, and the company wasn't terrible for diversity overall, but I didn't feel like I'd clicked with anyone.

For some reason I found Walsh Marketing Solutions dreary. Maybe it was sitting packed in a huge open-plan office miles from the nearest window, or maybe it was the obscene number of meetings we attended each week—I was salty about the meetings, okay? I swear I'd dozed off in one yesterday and had no idea how I'd gotten away with it.

The whole company had a weird vibe I didn't gel with. I couldn't put my finger on it, but something was off and I wondered if it went deeper than seating plans and boring lectures about policy. Then again, maybe I was the problem. When I actually got down to the writing, I enjoyed it. The work itself wasn't bad, I'd just been low-key miserable since my move. I missed my old routine and all the people in my life.

Owen said I was too used to his superior working environment at Coffee Cat. I dunno, I figured I'd adjust. Except it was taking way longer than I'd expected.

In an attempt to make an effort, I'd gone out for drinks with work people a few times. Last time hadn't been great on my part. I'd gotten too drunk too quickly. Cocktails were usually my downfall. I'd been a silly mess, which everyone else seemed to enjoy at my expense. Which was fine, whatever. I didn't do anything outrageous. It was when I got home that I had the problem.

I'd called Edwin, because of course I'd saved his number in my contacts. He hadn't answered, so I'd hung up. Then in a stroke of brilliance, I'd called *again*. Fuck. Even remembering it made my stomach cramp in humiliation. He hadn't answered my second call either, it had been about two in the morning, so shocker I know. But not to worry, I'd left a message.

Oh, the asinine horror.

The next morning I'd woken up with a hangover and a sinking feeling as I remembered my message had gone along the lines of: *I miss you and need to suck your cock*. Not want, need, a nuanced difference I'd explained at length. I had a fuzzy memory of calling Owen immediately after the tragic voicemail to babble incoherently at him. I may have also cried. He'd overnighted me some pan dulce the next day.

Edwin hadn't returned my call, but did that even need to be specified?

So yeah, I wasn't feeling the urge to go out drinking with Jonah, Graham, Rochelle, randoms from IT and the two hilarious girls from admin.

"My cousin is gay," Jonah said, abruptly pulling my attention away from my thirty-two unread emails and infinite self-pitying thoughts.

"Good for him." I didn't turn around.

"Yeah. So I could invite him out for drinks. He lives in Queens."

I swiveled to face my persistent desk mate. "Are you trying to set me up?"

Jonah shrugged. "Yeah?"

"Do you think he'd like me? Like, do we have anything in common other than both being into dudes?"

Jonah's dark eyes considered me with more focus than I'd expected. He stroked his chin. "You actually kinda remind me of his ex."

"Oh. Um. Yeah—I don't know if I'm in the right headspace for a set-up. But thanks." I tapped my fingers on my desk, the polish was chipped and looked terrible.

Jonah matched my rhythm, tapping his pen. "You sure? I could send him your picture and see if he's down?"

"Oh my god no. Please leave me to handle my own dating life." *Or lack thereof.*

Jonah finally turned his computer on and started working. I looked at the clock. I had enough time to finish off this piece for a financial software website before five if I wasn't distracted.

Dating post Edwin hadn't happened. I'd had to admit to myself that I'd spent so much time crushing on him that it felt like I was dealing with a break-up, even though we'd never gotten together, and I wasn't ready to get back out there yet.

My wistfulness seemed to be getting worse, not better. The actual move had been exciting and busy. I thought I'd moved on pretty quickly, but lately everything was getting me down and my mind kept wandering back to Edwin. Then that phone call had happened. Like fuck me. I'd ruined the memory of him. Now I couldn't even daydream without feeling like an idiot.

When five o'clock came I lingered at my desk, finishing the article rather than leaving it for Monday so Jonah wouldn't try and convince me to go out drinking again.

I found myself walking the empty halls, our floor a complete ghost town at 5:40pm. I passed someone pushing a cart laden with cardboard boxes, the sound of clinking glass unmistakable as it rattled by.

Weird. I wondered if they were product samples or something.

Walsh Marketing Solutions was a huge company; a recent buyout and a few mergers had berthed this beast. Everything was new, from the desks and computers to the coffee machines. It was like the place had gone from zero to a hundred overnight. There were so many teams and people it was hard to keep track. After four months there were still countless unfamiliar faces in the halls. Like random rattling cart guy.

Our CEO Emerson Walsh liked to be 'visible.' He was always popping onto the floor and catching people, chatting awkwardly as you tried to make your way to lunch or the bathroom. He liked saying how he was just like us, you know, except for his salary. He was here for us if ever we needed, and here ya go have a free company mug. His favorite thing was calling meetings about corporate culture, wellness, or anything buzz-wordy. The man was a walking office meme.

On a bright note, I'd remembered to text Tess every Wednesday since I'd moved to wish her a happy humpday. She'd already threatened to block me twice, then switched tactics saying if I didn't stop she'd sign my number up for daily inspirational quotes. I'd been forced to remind her that shit was a two-way street, and might have to give in to her tattoo-Tristan campaign on my next West Coast visit, just to appease her. But honestly, worth it.

I exited the high-rise where WMS occupied floors six through eleven and made my way to the subway to catch the train to Brooklyn. It was damn freezing. Not literally, but Southern California had murdered my tolerance for anything below seventy-five degrees. I'd had to buy a coat. And a scarf. Which was a lifestyle change I hadn't properly considered.

In mid-September most people weren't as bundled up as me, but this week had taken a turn for the colder and I was feeling each degree as they dropped. Turned out I liked scarfs as an accessory, so it wasn't all bad. Today I was wearing a purple one knitted by my apartment mate Avery.

The start of the fall weather left me wondering what kind of elegant coats Edwin would wear if he were here in the colder months. My mind seemed to want to wander his way when I walked the city streets and today was no exception.

I really should've started listening to podcasts. Something to get my mind under control and off that man.

I wished I could forget about Edwin and get back out there. Not with Jonah's cousin, but someone available. You know, geographically and emotionally. Someone who'd talk to me. No more mysterious hotties who dressed exclusively in vintage suits. I needed someone on my level, and deserved someone who'd see me as worth more than a good time.

I didn't like the idea of dating anyone at work, but I wanted someone in a similar space to me, like a peer. I was aiming for a solid professional writing career, but I wasn't overly ambitious. After dating guys whose level of aspiration mismatched mine, I was wary of it as a potential issue.

On top of that, people had often seen me as unsuccessful when I'd worked part time in a cafe. I'd never found that fair, and those people could fuck off. Even if it'd taken longer to get my chosen career going than I'd hoped, that wasn't something to judge and I tried not to wonder if that was what Edwin had thought of me.

He didn't seem like that kind of person, but then again, how could I possibly know?

This job was a big step. I'd come such a long way and, given where I'd started, it was a small miracle, but pressure to have gotten here sooner was ever present. I was on the older side of my team at work. They were mostly mid-twenties with a few just out of college, so not a huge gap, but sometimes the world made you feel like you needed to have everything *now*. Or yesterday. It was exhausting.

But I'd done all right. Life was more than a career, and I liked what I'd built of mine. I hadn't ever wanted to officially own Coffee Cat with Owen, it was his baby, but we created it together and sometimes it felt like the cafe was our relationship brought to physical form.

He was my only family, and I didn't say that to point out how little I had but the exact opposite. I couldn't have asked for more, and a big portion of my current melancholy was undoubtedly due to missing Owen. Of course I'd need time to adjust after twelve years of he and I navigating life together. So yeah, when I was getting down on myself for not being *whatever*, I just had to remember how much I had, and how lucky I was.

I reminded myself I wanted to be here, giving this job my best shot. Liking my new life was totally possible, I just had to find people to share it with.

I pushed through the crowd in the subway. The train ride was packed and stuffy, making me relieved to get back out into the cold air.

After another short walk I was home. I lived in a small old building in a third floor, two-bedroom apartment with a woman named Avery and her bonkers plant collection.

The common spaces, including the bathroom, housed hundreds of potted plants. We're talking all varieties, shapes and sizes. The balcony was completely inaccessible, and none of this had been advertised in the online listing I'd replied to.

I supposed it was better than finding out she had a shit load of cats when I'd showed up to move in, but oh my god.

As I entered the apartment, I swept a fan palm out of my

path. It was a bit like living in a forest, you had to watch your step and your head.

Avery was an herbalist. She grew all her own ingredients and made everything from teas to smudge sticks, from her own dried spices to pickled peppers. She sold things at a local night market and as far as I could tell that was her main source of income. It was kind of impressive Avery made enough money that way, I didn't see how it added up, but it must have.

Her work was super interesting, with the catch that Avery liked to test out her concoctions on me. This was possibly her main motivator for filling the second bedroom, other than you know, rent.

As the in-house taster, I felt somewhat coerced into drinking an energy tea each morning. But it was fine, we had homemade granola too.

As soon as I shut the front door Avery yelled out, "Tristan! I'm so glad you're home. Come try these vegan protein balls."

I navigated a new pot of chives—maybe new, maybe it'd been there longer than me, it was impossible to tell there were so many damn plants—and made my way to the kitchen.

Oh, the violas that resided in the doorway were in bloom and looking nice. The organic flower food must have been working.

*Meh,* I knew too much about these plants and their lives. They were members of the household, make no mistake. Some of them even had crystals nestled into the pots, keeping them company.

Avery was placing little turd-ish-looking balls in a glass container. "Try one, they're made with small batch peanut butter, supper seeds and dates. Unsweetened of course."

I took a ball. They weren't bad.

"How was your day?" I opened the fridge in search of something less raw-foodie.

Avery was also a health enthusiast. Honestly she was a little obsessed, and always trying to get me to eat unruly amounts of raw vegetables along with things that were trying to trick you into thinking they were sweets, but weren't.

"I had a great day. My harvest was the best of the month. We had twenty-two cherry tomatoes! And the herbs! Bananas! I mean not literally. I'm making cilantro water. It'll be great for you to take to work."

"I think I'm one of those people who finds that cilantro tastes like soap. Sorry." I pulled a leftover container of nachos out of the fridge and started eating them cold.

Avery eyed the container. She was way too parental for someone my age. "I'll make you a juice. You can't only eat *that*." She pulled the juicer out of a cabinet and grabbed a few carrots and a hunk of ginger.

This living situation was way more intense than I'd expected. The room had been advertised as queer friendly and close to local amenities and the train. Not false advertising but *how* had she not mentioned the plants? The listing photos must have been years old. Maybe the fact it was cheaper than anything else should have tipped me off, but as unexpectedly weird as living here was, I liked Avery. So far she was the best part of moving to the East Coast.

"Speaking of cilantro," I said between bites of cold chips. "Do walnuts, like you know, have a similar thing going on?"

Avery turned away from the juicer to stare. She had a smudge of something I suspected was peanut butter on her cheek. "I'm going to go with no. But how about you tell me what you could possibly mean."

I pointed at my own cheek and she wiped at hers with a grateful smile. "The taste thing. Walnuts always taste kind of like plastic. So I wondered." This was a genuine, if trivial, question mine and if anyone knew, it was Avery.

She huffed. “Says the man eating melted then resolidified cheese of unknown quality.”

I put another nacho in my mouth, chewing obnoxiously.

Avery shook her head, repressing a grin. “To answer your question, no walnuts are not like cilantro. All the nuts in this house are organic and taste delicious. I can’t account for anything you ate prior to living here, or explain what’s wrong with your taste buds.”

“Hm. They’re definitely not my favorite nut.” I unstuck a chip from the side of my container. “Got any apples for the juice?”

“Yes. Great idea—” Avery treated me to a tale of the apples’ origin as she lined a few up on the counter. “Want to watch a movie tonight?”

“Okay. But I’m painting my nails in the living room.” I tossed the empty nacho container in our compost bin. Avery took it to the community garden every night. Single use, non-compostable containers weren’t allowed in the apartment.

“Fine, I’ll burn incense. I don’t know how you can stand the toxic polish smell. Actually, maybe that explains your sense of taste.” She put several scoops of powder into our glasses before firing up the juicer.

“No supplements for me, thanks. Too chalky.”

Avery looked at me with serious consideration. “You need vitamins, Tristan.”

“You know I survived for decades without you. I think I’m fine.”

She raised her eyebrows. “Debatable. Pass that lemon.”

I tossed the lemon to her and went to change.

My room was a plant free zone. I slipped into joggers and a T-shirt then selected a few violently colorful glitter polishes. I needed to brighten my mood by any means necessary and green, blue and teal holographic glitter were a good start.

When I entered the living room Avery was settled on the

couch, our juices and some air-popped popcorn laid out on the coffee table. As promised, incense was burning on the mantle next to her basket of crystals.

I sat cross-legged on the floor and took a sip of the orange liquid in my glass.

Avery poked me with a sock clad toe. "Aren't you uncomfortable down there?"

"I always fall asleep on that couch. Tonight I need to make it to eight pm at the very least." I got to work removing my chipped polish with a cotton ball. "On Monday I fell asleep before seven. I swear that couch is too soft."

Avery repositioned a couple of lush pillows around her. "You're just tired because you don't get enough iron."

She'd tried to get me to start taking iron pills last week and I'd flat out refused.

"I don't need iron," I said firmly.

"Everyone needs iron."

I set aside my used cotton ball and grabbed another. "Then I'll eat some meat and call it done."

Avery pursed her lips but let it go.

You could mostly see the TV mounted on the wall. Of course, plants blocked a third of it, but the foliage of the tree fern was sparse enough you got the gist of the screen. Avery put on her favorite romantic comedy. Half watching, I mostly paid attention to painting my nails and eating popcorn while not messing them up before they dried.

I made it halfway through romcom number two before I curled up on the couch and fell asleep.

I WOKE WITH A START.

The living room was dark, TV turned off. A look at my

phone told me it was well into the middle of the night. Avery had put a blanket over me, but was gone.

I sat up and my head pounded. *Ugh.* It was like I'd gotten drunk or something.

Standing made me lightheaded but I managed to stumble to my room and flop on my bed. How long had I been asleep, and why did I feel like absolute shit?

There was a glass of water on my side table. I guzzled it down. I needed to be in a blanket cocoon, stat. As I pulled the covers over me, I noticed something on my wrist.

Damn it. There were four tiny red dots in and around my tattoo.

Occasionally, when I fell asleep on the too-cozy couch, some bug-or-other would take the opportunity to bite me. They looked like mosquito bites, but that made no sense at this time of year and I refused to accept they were spider bites. It was weird, I'd never seen so much as a single bug around the apartment and the bites were always on my wrists, maybe once on my ankles, as if whatever was getting me was targeting specific parts of my body.

A compulsive shiver went through me. I hated creepy crawly things.

Exhaustion engulfed me even though I'd just slept for hours. Maybe I did need iron. Or a trip to the doctor. I hated the thought that I might be lovesick or broken hearted. No way a one-night stand had screwed me up this bad. Even missing Owen and my old routines didn't feel like the whole story. Something was up with me. I never got caught in these low moods anymore. My resilience was usually robust.

Right. Next week I was seeing a medical professional, not Avery, for a real health check. Then I was going on a date. Or let's be honest, I'd make a dating profile and proceed to ignore the app, but it was still a step in the right direction.

# 9

# EDWIN

I stepped out of the elevator onto one of the Authority building's upper floors and made my way to Judge Geer's office.

I hadn't been busy when I'd received his summons and was glad to have something with which to fill my afternoon. I knocked on his door and waited, wondering what he needed from me.

The judge greeted me with a smile and I doffed my hat.

Charles Geer sat on the Judicial Committee at the branch of the Authority where I was based. I followed him into his wood paneled office and was greeted by a familiar, stuffy atmosphere.

He led me past his massive mahogany desk to a pair of leather armchairs arranged in front of the fireplace. "Edwin, it's good to see you." Charles poured two whiskeys from a drink cart set up in the corner of the room and handed me one. He looked a bit ghostly, his white hair wild, sticking out every which way like he'd been pulling it out in frustration. I'd never seen him look otherwise.

I set my glass on the side table without taking a sip and crossed my legs. "What can I do for you?"

As an investigator for the Authority, anyone sitting on a Judicial Committee was my superior, but the ones here in New York were the Witches I reported to directly. This wasn't the usual set up. Most investigators had partners and line managers, but I was a unique case with my own reporting rules. For quite a long time that had been perfectly fine with me, but more recently my position had begun to feel complicated.

Charles was old, about two-hundred and eighty years, and a powerful Witch. I liked him to an extent. He was always in my corner, which I appreciated even if I didn't like needing his support.

It'd have been nice not to need anyone, but I had chosen to work here and tried to accept all the things that entailed.

My position in Witch society was a strange one. I was still relatively young, yet my raw magical power was greater than anyone else's and would only continue to grow as I aged, as it did for all Witches. I also had a few unique magical gifts that made me an anomaly no one knew what to do with, including the judges I reported to.

Geer was the only one who didn't make a big deal out of it.

"I wanted to check in, Edwin." Charles sipped his drink as if he'd had a long day. He refocused on me with a satisfied smile. "How are you? Tell me how things are going."

On second thought, I did need a drink for this conversation. I picked up my glass. The whiskey tased smooth and perfectly aged. "Fine. Why wouldn't they be?"

Charles gave me a kind look. "I know it's taken a little while for things to settle down after the tension at the start of the year."

"You mean when one of your colleagues tried to frame me and Juliet for kidnapping?"

"Yes." Charles' expression turned pinched, like he'd wished I'd stuck to vagaries. "Everything has been disrupted since then.

We've had to fill Judge Herrera's spot in a horrible rush. I feel like you and I haven't caught up properly. I wanted to make sure there's no lingering problems. It can be hard to see what things are like in the wider organization when I'm stuck in court and all that."

I took another sip of whiskey. If I'd know this what Charles wanted to see me about, I'd have found an excuse to avoid him. "The wider Authority stays away from me, but that's nothing new." It was how I liked it. I'd worked hard to foster my particular work persona.

Geer tapped his fingers on the side of his glass. "Yes. You like your solitude. But I'd wondered—collaborating with Ms. Dubois didn't change your mind about having a partner to work cases with?"

"I considered taking on an apprentice." This was true. My restless boredom had gotten the better of me, but it wasn't the right time of year for new recruits.

Charles bobbed his head enthusiastically. "Working with young Witches is always rewarding, but I was hoping you'd given some thought to having a permanent partner."

He caught me off guard. "No, I haven't. Why would you think that?"

The judge waved a gold-and-crystal-ring clad hand. "Working more regularly with people can be nice. And if there's tension around the Authority, not setting yourself so far apart might be helpful."

I glared and Charles took a sheepish gulp of whiskey. "I said things are fine. Unless you know something I don't. What are people saying?"

The judge put his glass down and flapped his hands in a shewing gesture. "Nothing. Nothing. No one is saying anything. The Committee has moved past it. I can assure you that."

I frowned. "Well that's a relief, since there was nothing to move past."

"Indeed."

There was an awkward silence.

Despite Charles' assurance, I wasn't so sure the Committee had overlooked the incident involving Juliet's mother earlier in the year. Judge Herrera's framing plot could have been a lot worse for me, but it had still done damage even though I'd been cleared almost from the outset.

I didn't need more suspicion and rumors circulating around me. It made my position at the Authority feel precarious like it hadn't in decades.

Catching a judge involved in criminal activity should be seen as nothing more than my job. Investigating magical crime was what I did. But many of Charles' colleagues on the Committee had never trusted me, and being part of taking down one of their peers had complicated fallout.

I had a long and legally fraught history of my own and too many of my troubles were known around the Authority. It was as if the whole mess with Wyatt was doomed to haunt me forever. He'd been convicted of organized crimes in the eighties and while I hadn't been part of that, it had taken a long invasive trial of my own to untangle.

Some of the judges who'd overseen my trial still worked here and thought I'd escaped the law unjustly. My particular blend of strong magical powers made it hard for them to believe I'd been the victim of a manipulative man, trapped in an abusive relationship. I suspected one or two of the judges still believed I was responsible for the whole criminal debacle, but I wasn't. Nor was I responsible for how Wyatt had mistreated or used me. And while this old situation wasn't actually related to what had happened recently, all these old suspicions had been dragged back up.

My magic, which came from a particularly potent earth affinity that allowed me to command time and space, made other Witches uneasy. The most obvious daily use for this power was teleportation, but I could also freeze time and move independently from it. The more complex the interaction my magic had with time or space, the more problems and ripples emerged as a result. There was a lot I could do in theory that I didn't ever mess with.

Most of the Witches on the Committee with Charles didn't like that I possessed these unique abilities, but at the same time coveted them. I suspected that was part of the reason they'd hired me, even in the face of my dubious history.

After my complicated time with Wyatt, and a period of time spent floundering as I tried to recover, I'd settled on a path I thought would help me do some good.

Charles had been keen to bring me into the Authority when I'd applied after gaining my investigator's license. He'd probably seen it as some sort of second chance, which I suppose it was. The rest of his colleagues had begrudgingly accepted me after they realized working here meant I was easier for them to monitor.

The Authority liked to collect employees with magical gifts and having me on their 'side' looked better than having me against them. Not that I'd ever seen it that way.

All this was old news but having a judge try to frame me for crimes I didn't commit at the start of the year brought my past back to the forefront. It made people wonder. Why was I always on the outskirts of trouble? What was I actually trying to achieve by working here? Had I been after her position on the Committee? And so on.

So yes, I had been experiencing tension at work. It felt like I was being watched more closely again, even though the framing plot had been exposed before any accusations could be made against me. The Committee trusted me less than ever before and the lower-level employees always liked to talk. But I didn't need Geer's help dealing with office politics. I didn't need to be coddled.

I eyed Charles over my whiskey glass. "My assignments have been uncommonly light this year. You wouldn't happen to know what that's about?"

The wild-haired judge gave me a stern look. "It's nothing to do with trust in you, Edwin."

"Who said anything about trust?" I sounded cold to the point of unkindness, but that's just how I was at work.

Charles seemed to suppress a sigh, his shoulders sagging. "I know where your mind goes. Maybe we just thought you deserved a break. I don't want you overworked."

"Hm." I liked that idea less than my lack of assignments being due to suspicion I was up to no good.

"Besides," Charles added with a serious nod. "There's that massive black market problem. The huge uptick in the illegal blood trade. Everyone is working on that. It's a priority."

I swallowed the last of my drink. "I'm not assigned to the core team, but yes. Everyone is working on it in theory."

We moved on to social topics after that, culminating in Charles trying to get me to attend a party and me deflecting by asking about his wife. In other words, our usual dance.

After our meeting concluded I left the Authority building feeling exhausted. It wasn't five but I didn't care. If no one had anything for me to do, I'd twiddle my thumbs elsewhere.

The past few months had passed slowly, the lack of work grating on me more and more. A few weeks ago, I'd attempted Juliet's recommendation of a vacation out of sheer desperation. Turns out brooding on a beach and brooding in New York were no different. And I didn't like pineapple.

Hopefully the black market investigation would pick up the

pace. It would keep everyone occupied and all my drama might actually blow over.

My thoughts swam as I walked the streets of Manhattan, work failing to hold my attention. Sometimes it was nice to travel mundanely rather than teleport from my apartment to the Authority building. I liked walking the familiar streets and remembering what they used to look like. I'd lived in New York since I was born in 1908, and loved the business of cities where I was only one more person flowing through time unnoticed.

But I had a lot of bad memories of this city too. It had taken a long time to push them back, not have Wyatt consume all my thoughts. There were a few neighborhoods I still avoided, fearing familiar sights would trigger unwelcome recollections, but they weren't places I wanted to go. Everywhere in the city I loved I'd worked to reclaim. Time had helped. Things looked very different than they had in seventies and eighties, and I had more good memories than bad, proportionally speaking.

I'd always loved the park, ever since I was a boy, and headed that way now. I enjoyed watching things change over the years. Buildings going up, getting torn town and replaced, trees growing into towering things that looked like they'd always been there.

Sometimes it didn't feel like a century had passed since I'd run these streets as a child, but there was no doubt when you looked at the world. I dressed in the styles of my youth, but I wasn't stuck in the past. I hadn't always dressed like this. It was something I'd started after deciding to be an investigator. I'd committed to building a new life, one separate from everything that had come before. I'd wanted a physical reminder that things with Wyatt were in the past, something that showed me I could create myself anew and be something that had nothing to do with him.

I'd chosen the vintage suits because they reminded me of my

father. My parents both passed away in the 1950's but my memories of them in the twenties were particularly strong and filled with nothing but fondness. The suits made me feel good, gave me joy, and had the added bonus of playing to the austere Witch-society persona I'd adopted as part of my new life.

Despite reminding myself of the good times I'd had a hundred years ago each time I dressed, I never felt old. For a Witch, I wasn't. Would a Mortal ever understand that?

Was there any point denying I was thinking of age because of Tristan? I only looked about forty. What would he think if he found out I was older? Would we have had our night together if magic weren't secret and he knew everything about me?

The answer didn't matter, but somehow I doubted he'd have been interested if he knew everything there was to know.

I'd tried not to think about Tristan over the past months, to varying degrees of success. The thought of seeing him again and our feelings growing made me deeply uncomfortable, but I couldn't seem to keep him off my mind. I didn't want a relationship so why had this empty feeling crept up on me?

On particularly confusing days I wondered if my feelings had somehow grown in his absence, despite my efforts to prevent this exact thing from happening.

Maybe not moving on to the next step of my half-thought-out plan to restore my sex life was the problem, but I felt a Witchy timeframe on sleeping with someone new was reasonable. Within a year I'd do it. Surely by then I'd find someone who intrigued me at least half as much as Tristan had, and the void he'd created would go away.

He'd called me recently, setting back all my attempts to forget him. I'd woken up one morning to a voicemail. From the message it was clear Tristan had too much to drink but he'd been sweet and rather charmingly explicit in his inebriated attempt to seduce me.

I hadn't returned his call. I was sticking to my decision, one night only, no further contact. I hadn't even asked Aria where he'd moved to. It would have been too easy for me to 'take a business trip' to wherever he was. Then I'd only end up getting hurt.

But nothing stopped me wasting time daydreaming about Tristan's offer. It would have been better if he'd never called. That way I wouldn't know he was still thinking about me.

Worst of all, he'd said he missed me, which made it impossible to deny I missed him too.

## 10

# TRISTAN

It was the kind of Thursday that made you think you'd never reach the weekend.

My workday ended with a meeting on productivity, in which Jonah and I had fallen asleep.

I jerked awake to find his chair rolled right up to mine, his head resting on my shoulder. No one reacted to the fact we were blatantly passed out. The team manager just continued to talk tonelessly while everyone else stared off into space.

I rubbed my brow and suppressed a yawn as I tried to focus on what the manager was saying. My head was pounding despite the nap and having given in to Avery's rigorous supplement, raw food, and no-sugar routine for the last week.

My trip to the doctor had revealed I was indeed low in iron, a fact I'd kept to myself. Imagine what Avery would make me do if she knew she'd been right. Anyway, the doctor prescribed an IV drip infusion but I wasn't sure how much it had helped. I was still so tired and generally *blegh* all the time.

As soon as the meeting ended, I was overcome with the need for fresh air. I barely said goodbye to Jonah before getting the hell out of the office.

I skipped my usual subway station in favor of walking. The meeting and the headache weren't my real problem. My mom had emailed me last night. I hadn't slept—other than at work—and had hardly been functioning since.

Mom and I hadn't seen each other in fifteen years. I'd spoken to her in that time, and this wasn't the first out-of-the-blue email I'd received, but it had been a while.

The message was still sitting unread in my inbox.

I walked head down, pounding the pavement with angry steps. The last time I'd heard from her was a few years ago and I'd ignore the email at first. Eventually I'd given in and replied out of guilt, only to have our correspondence fall back into the familiar, hurtful pattern I'd been trying to avoid.

I felt sick, full of a jittery hopelessness not knowing what I wanted to do this time around.

My mom had moved to Florida when I was sixteen. She hadn't taken me with her. Not that she'd run off unexpectedly or anything like that. She'd deemed me old enough to not need her around, but I'd disagreed pretty adamantly.

My mom hadn't been blessed with an easy life and had to deal with a lot of things I hadn't understood as a kid, but I'd thought things had been getting better by the time I was in high school; even looking back it seemed like we'd turned a corner.

When mom had first said she was moving I'd tried to get on board. I'd told her it sounded great even though I didn't want to go somewhere new. Then she'd made it clear she'd meant just her, and I hadn't known what to do.

After a lot of questions and alternate suggestions on my part, mom's moving plans had changed to a break, not a vacation but time away she was supposed to come back from. So I'd gone to stay with her brother, keeping one eye on the calendar. He was even younger than my mom and not the parental type, but he'd been fine with having me at his apartment as long as I had a weekend job and went to school, or left the house and pretended.

Other than that, I'd been on my own, but it was supposed to be temporary so I'd been determined to deal with it.

Then my mom's plans had changed. She extended her stay and stopped calling me as often. She changed the date she'd be back in San Francisco again and again. Things kept coming up. And maybe that was true, or maybe I'd been a kid who'd believe what he was told. I still didn't know exactly what had happened, what bits had been true and what bits hadn't.

She never came back and by the end of high school she'd started ignoring my calls. This was followed by a period of years in college when I'd hadn't heard from her at all.

Then suddenly she began calling and emailing me regularly again, as if she'd never stopped. She'd said was going to come and see me for college graduation, but it had never happened.

For the next ten years it was periods of silence, then a flurry of messages and a promise to see me, then nothing. So the last few times I'd heard from her I'd tried to stop the cycle, telling her not to say she was planning to visit but to wait and call me when she'd actually showed up. When she had the ticket booked, or had arrived in town. Then, after I'd laid out my boundaries, I'd stopped responding to her messages about visits. At least until a fit of guilt got the better of me.

This time I didn't even want to start the conversation. I didn't want the how-are-you emails, knowing they would be followed by empty promises that I always got sucked into no matter how much I knew better. Why did she have to do this again? Why now? I just didn't want to deal with it.

I hated feeling guilty for ignoring her. Like, fuck that. I had no obligation to her, yet all day I'd felt like an asshole who couldn't be fucked to open and respond to an email.

So I walked and tried to lose myself in the sea of people. It almost worked. I ended up near Central Park barely remembering how I'd gotten here from the part of Manhattan where WMS was located. The sight of greenery was a relief, probably from too much time with all the plants at home.

The cold felt good tonight, like a slap in the face I needed. It was getting dark, the setting sun reflecting off the tall buildings. I looked up and caught some of the last rays of light on my face. This wasn't an area I knew well and right now that felt good. Like there were still possibilities and positive things out there to discover despite everything dragging me down.

As I glanced around someone caught my eye up ahead. Actually, it was a hat. There was Edwin, standing still in the middle of the sidewalk as people flowed around him. He looked devastatingly handsome, like he'd walked right out of my fondest memory.

He was staring right at me.

My heart skipped. Excitement flared in me, warm and inviting. It felt like fucking fate. I craved Edwin. I was desperate and broken, and right now remembering the feeling of holding each other gave me a wild surge of hope.

I smiled, realizing I'd stopped walking and we were doing that thing where we stared at each other unmoving. But his expression wasn't like any of those times at Coffee Cat. He looked shocked, and not particularly happy.

My little flood of relief vanished. I remembered my embarrassing voicemail. How he'd left me in the hotel room like nothing between us mattered. Right. Seeing him wasn't the thing to brighten this horrible day, it was more shit on top of the crappiest cake.

I turned to walk back the way I'd come.

My cheeks burned with embarrassment. How could I have thought seeing him meant anything good? Like it was a second chance? At least Edwin wasn't aware of my reaction. Hopefully my smile hadn't given me away. If only I could be as cold and calm as he was and not consumed by this burning rejection.

Someone caught my hand and pulled me, turning me around. I stumbled with a yelp and Edwin caught me. I blinked furiously in confusion. What was he doing coming after me?

Edwin held me delicately as I regained my balance. When he let go, he didn't step back.

My mouth fell half open.

"You moved to New York?" Edwin sounded like he didn't believe it.

I looked around absurdly, as if I was checking where I was. "Yeah."

Edwin still wasn't smiling but his eyes were bright, maybe with excitement. "I live here too. In New York. Actually, my apartment is only a block away."

Was he implying we go there? Together? Now that I was in front of him, did he wanted to screw me again or something? I stared unbelieving at his neutral expression.

Nothing had changed. Edwin was barely making an effort, not saying anything directly, only dropping subtle hints while hiding all his thoughts and emotions. Leaving me to make a move and take all the risk.

I gave in anyway. I felt so alone and didn't want to be. I wanted even temporary comfort. I'd rather have Edwin for a moment than not at all. It was reckless and that only made me want him more.

I swept my hair back from my face. "Let's go then."

For a moment Edwin didn't react and my stomach churned.

He blinked almost like he was surprised, but the shift in his expression was so infinitesimal it could have been nothing. Then he grabbed my hand and led me down the street, pulling me along quickly like we'd miss our chance if we took too long.

Edwin's fingers interlaced with mine. Was it sweet that he was holding my hand, or did I only want it to be?

The walk didn't take long. Of course Edwin lived in an Upper West Side apartment adjacent to Central Park. The building was old and beautiful. So classy. *So Edwin.*

Inside the pristine tiled lobby he pushed the elevator button, then pushed it twice more in quick succession.

A little thrill wound through me. I relished seeing him act as jittery as I felt. Any crack in his composure, any hint I affected him at all fed the flames that burned inside my wayward heart.

"I can't believe this," Edwin muttered, more to himself than me.

The elevator arrived and we slipped inside. The doors slowly slid shut. As soon as they clicked closed Edwin pulled me into a kiss. The ferocity of it caught me off guard. I gasped. It was like something between us snapped.

His tongue was hot on mine, his hands in my hair. Edwin pushed me back against the wall, pressing his body against me.

"Oh Tristan, darling. This is even better than I remembered," he muttered into my mouth.

He wasn't wrong.

My thoughts spun. I wanted to believe Edwin's enthusiasm came from more than your average lust. He was acting exactly how I felt: like I was getting what I desperately needed, kissing the man I liked more than anyone else in a moment that had meaning beyond lips and touch. This didn't feel like nothing, surely there was no way he thought it was.

The elevator stopped with a ding. Edwin pulled me out into the hall, but we didn't get far before he was kissing me again, his hands running all over me, pulling me into him, crushing us together.

"Oh my god, we need to get out of the hallway," I gasped with a frantic laugh.

"If you say so." Edwin walked me backward until I bumped into a door frame, still kissing me like he didn't want our lips parted for more than a moment. He reluctantly pulled back to rest his forehead on mine, taking keys out of his pocket. "I never thought I'd be this lucky."

He inserted the key in the lock.

"Uh, you're definitely getting lucky." *Lucky?* Why did he feel lucky? He'd walked away from me. He could have been this lucky every week if he hadn't shut me down.

We entered the apartment and the door slammed behind us. Edwin was already tossing his black coat—as gorgeously styled as I'd imagined—suit jacket and hat to the ground.

"You look good all buttoned up." Edwin reached for my own coat and helped relieve me of it. "But I still prefer those jeans to professional attire."

"Thanks, but no need for compliments." I pulled his mouth back to mine, not wanting any sweet words to leave me with more things to read into.

We stumbled our way past the discarded coats before colliding with a wall. I laughed, my breath almost knocked out of me.

"Sorry, I'm too carried away." Edwin ran his hands over me in a gentle caress.

"It's okay. I like it."

This wild physical thing we had going on was good. It was more straightforward than last time. If I played into it maybe we'd steer clear of all the stuff I found confusing.

I put my hands over my head and shook the hair out of my face. "Pin me to the wall and take advantage of me." *That way I don't have to think.*

Edwin clasped my wrists. "If that's what you want?" His eyes traveled up my body and fixed on mine, waiting.

I nodded and his look turned desperate. Edwin ran one

hand slowly down my cheek, my neck, my chest, making me quiver before he undid my belt.

Good. Yes. Straight to it. This was one-hundred percent different than last time. So why were my emotions in tatters? Everything felt charged. I was wildly happy but couldn't shake that thrown off feeling. How could we have we gone from nothing to *this* if there wasn't more under the surface? It was hard to believe the intensity of this moment was all about sex, but I tried.

"Edwin," I whimpered, a helpless, confused plea.

He held me with his stare, his grip, the position of his body against mine. Focusing on these things anchored me. I was here. With him. Edwin looked at me like I was the only thing in the world. Nothing existed but us and I loved that. It was what I needed, and I didn't need to think about why.

My pants fell to my ankles. Edwin's breathing was ragged as he looked down and freed me from my underwear. He held my dick and kind of caressed it with his thumb. Like it was almost too tender, a touch that elicited small, desperate panting breaths from me before he closed me in a tight fist. We both watched his hand move until I couldn't take it and begged him to kiss me.

He didn't deny me.

When Edwin let go of my wrists, I put my arms around his neck. He smiled against my mouth as I embraced him.

I wanted so many things. I wanted to tell him how much I liked him, how my thoughts ran wild for him. Instead I let sensations rule me and tried to tell myself our physical connection was all I wanted.

As we kissed, Edwin undid the buttons on my shirt. He fumbled and pulled, impatient until his hands found my skin. "I missed this, Tristan—I missed—" he murmured into my mouth, cutting himself off with a kiss.

"I missed you too," I confessed. He knew that, but even the thought of that phone call couldn't dampen the moment.

Edwin pulled my shirt off. He kissed my chest, teasing my nipples with his tongue and fingers before moving up to my neck. Words spilled from his lips, the vibrations of his voice sending shivers through my bloodstream. "*God*, I missed you, Tristan. I need you."

"I need you too." Admitting it made it too real, but his voice was raw and I couldn't hold back, even if none of this helped stave off my wild hopes.

Edwin's lips remained on my neck, his words buzzing on my skin. "What do you need from me? What do you want?"

"Everything. You. Us—" I reached for his belt. I needed to be quiet. Now really wasn't the time for us to start talking.

I undid Edwin's pants and let them fall. He didn't have the same reaction as last time, so I kept going, encouraged by the moan he made when I pushed his underwear down just enough to free his dick.

Edwin pressed up against me as I aligned our erections and stroked us together. He groaned and trailed kisses along my neck, not seeming to feel the same urge I did for silence. "I need all of you too, Tristan."

I wrapped my other arm around him. The soft fabric of his waistcoat teased my bare skin. Something about being mostly naked while he wasn't, pressed against a wall in a space I'd barely registered, was intoxicating. I dropped my head back, giving Edwin better access to my neck, and let go of all my reservations.

His hands moved frantically over me, like he was memorizing me through touch. I continued to jerk us both, Edwin panting like he could hardly breath, yet couldn't bear to take his lips too far from my skin.

"I couldn't stop thinking about you, Tristan," he moaned against me between ragged breaths.

Edwin's words were a hit of the most potent drug. I begged for him as I held us tight, keeping my head thrown back, face angled toward the ceiling, not wanting to look down. It was as if we could be anything while we were this close but hidden by our averted eyes. The idea that eye contact would remind Edwin of whatever had held him back before took hold of me. I had no desire to risk finding out if it was true.

Like this, everything was perfect.

I couldn't seem to stop saying Edwin's name. Hearing it drove him wild, leaving him thrusting into my fist and panting beautifully in my ear.

Edwin's hands guided my hips to meet his movements until we were thudding frantically against the wall. Suddenly the lights on the celling flared bright. The power surge gave the impression that this moment wasn't real, like it was part of some sort of fevered dream.

Edwin pressed harder into me, his mouth near my jaw under my ear. "Tristan, I never want this to end."

His words came out like a command, and I could have sworn the ground shuddered momentarily in a vibration that somehow made my ears pop. I must have imagined it. There were so many sensations going on at once. I became hyper aware of us. Edwin's breath, everywhere we touched, where I held us together, the way his cock slid against mine. It was as if the rest of reality fell away.

Maybe this would never end.

Edwin came hot over my hand and onto my stomach, moaning my name. I followed a few strokes later with a breathless cry. We stood there panting, Edwin's face buried in the crook of my shoulder and neck while I sagged against the wall.

I was spinning. The feeling that nothing else existed lingered in the air. I didn't want to break the moment.

Could I believe Edwin meant the things he'd said? His sentiments had come out of nowhere. If he'd missed me that fiercely, it had to mean he cared. I wasn't just another hook-up. Right? But then why hadn't we been doing this for the past four months?

I could ask him how he felt now we could both think straight, but that left me terrified. I wanted to live in a reality where he liked me as much as I liked him, even if it was just within this moment, extended forever.

Edwin lingered against me, his lips brushing the arch of my neck. After a few more soft kisses he pulled back and withdrew a handkerchief from his waistcoat's pocket.

The silence was consuming, like we were the only two people moving in the entire world.

# 11

# EDWIN

Tristan averted his eyes as he pulled up his pants.

This whole encounter was a lapse in judgment I should regret, but seeing Tristan turn away from me in the street, clearly hurt by my non-reaction, had been a punch in the gut I hadn't been prepared for. It snapped something that had held me back for years.

Whispering my longings in Tristan's ear had had been a release even more potent than an orgasm. Only, I didn't know what to do now we were spent and standing awkwardly in my entryway.

I cleared my throat. "Well, that was—" I reached out and trailed my fingers along Tristan's bare shoulder.

He buckled his belt and his eyes flicked up, gaze hitting me like an emotional train. He looked uncommonly shy. A blush bloomed on his cheeks and something in his look turned hopeful. I felt so close to him just then, like we were connected though shared feelings.

My heartrate spiked in the beginnings of panic. I didn't want to hope for things with him.

"You like me." Tristan's voice was soft and vulnerable.

My flare of anxiety eased even though there was no reason for it to. "We wouldn't have had sex if I didn't like you." I was trying to keep this light and fun, make a joke, but realized too late how dismissive I sounded.

Tristan rolled his eyes and his expression turned guarded. He looked away, scanning the space around us like he didn't know what to do either.

No, I didn't like this at all. He was closing off and probably thought I didn't care. My rules and limitations were fine for keeping me from getting hurt, but if they hurt him in the process, what was the point? I'd been wrong before, trying to tell myself his feelings didn't matter.

Of course they mattered. Of course I cared.

"Yes, Tristan. I like you." I ran a hand jerkily through my hair, tugging until it stung.

I didn't want to push him away again. There had to be a middle ground between nothing and giving my messy self over to him, a space where I could stay guarded while not torturing myself with denial.

Why did I have to sort out my sex life with a string of new partners when I didn't want to? I didn't have to commit or give in to anything romantic to see Tristan a few more times.

I let my had fall from my hair. "I like you, Tristan. So. We should do this again. Tonight even, and on other, future nights. Sex I mean. Uh—if you want?"

He probably didn't after that awkward proposition. Fuck.

Tristan looked back at me, his face transformed in an unrestrained smile that was more than worth my babbling. His eyes flashed with amusement, or maybe something playful. "Are you saying you want to do it in your hallway again?"

He trailed a painted fingernail down my chest, teasing me.

Relief rushed out of me in the form of a laugh. I matched his tone. "Maybe not in the hall. There are so many other places in the house better suited to promiscuous activity."

Tristan picked up his shirt and shrugged it on, slowly doing up the buttons. "Then we'll have to make our way through them. I'd like to see where this goes. You and me. But you already knew I wanted to keep seeing you. I like you too, Edwin."

My pulse jumped into my throat.

Tristan was looking at me like I was something special. He needed to stop it. I didn't want to walk away and never see him again, but *this* was exactly what I didn't want to deal with.

When you're treated badly for too long you begin to fear you aren't worth being treated any other way, that no one will see you as something to cherish. It wasn't true or right, but I'd still found it a hard notion to shake.

I didn't want to expect Tristan to treat me right when I couldn't escape the fear he'd disappoint me. More than that, I refused to give Tristan the opportunity to treat me badly—that was why I'd abandoned relationships altogether and would always say no to commitments and promises.

I didn't want to have expectations of Tristan, and that tender look was full of expectations for both of us. He might be the sweetest man I knew, but I didn't know him well, and I was too much a creature of my past to trust in hope that things could ever be different.

I ran my hands over my clothes, making sure I'd tucked everything back into place. "Yes, I thought you might. But—my lifestyle isn't conducive to anything serious, if that's what you're thinking. Even though I'm based here, you saw how much I travel. Dating never works when you live like I do. I don't want to make promises I can't keep, Tristan."

"Hey—" He reached out and straightened my bow tie. "I get it. I'm happy to see you when you're here." He hooked his finger under my shirt collar. "Let's see where the fun takes us. Okay? That's all I meant. Nothing more."

I doubted it was all he meant, but we were both committed to pretending, and Tristan seemed happy enough to accept what I was offering. I gave him a smile. "You make it impossible to disagree."

Tristan tugged me into a quick kiss. "Wanna give me an apartment tour? We can make plans for all the places we want to get each other off."

My cheeks burned hot.

He was much better at this than me. I had no idea how to maintain a casual sexual relationship anymore, which was why I'd told myself to keep my encounters to single nights. But people did this all the time. How hard could it be? Guarding myself with Tristan should come as naturally as it did in other areas of my life. I'd had more than enough practice keeping people away.

"A tour is a great idea." I hung up our coats and led Tristan down the hall.

"So you're like totally rich, huh?" Tristan asked as we entered the living area.

We paused behind the couches. "I do all right. This building has been in my family since it was built."

Tristan mustn't have noticed much on our trip up the elevator. I lived in the penthouse, mine was the only residence on this floor. It was spacious and well decorated with modern pieces, both furniture and art. My home was one of my biggest comforts and the living room was my favorite place in the whole apartment, with a wall of spectacular floor to ceiling windows overlooking the park and city.

"'Wow' is all I can say." Tristan walked right up to the glass and looked down on the nightscape.

"Stunning view, isn't it?" I may have been looking at him, but I might as well indulge fully now we were here.

"Hey, look at those cars." Tristan pointed down to the street. "Nothing's moving."

I didn't take my eyes off him, the faint light from the city outside the window gave Tristan a soft glow. "Must be a long stoplight, sometimes traffic seems to stand still for ages."

"No, look. That person has been standing in the crosswalk not moving either. I swear." He tapped the glass with his finger.

What was he talking about? I scanned the street. Tristan was right, nothing was moving.

There wasn't even a hint of a breeze in the trees. Under a streetlight a flurry of fall leaves was caught, frozen in an updraft. The twinkling city wasn't twinkling. I went stiff as a cold stone settled in my gut.

*I never want this to end.*

No. I didn't. There was no way I'd stopped time without realizing.

But now that I was paying attention, I could tell I was out of time. There was that subtle sensation of unreality and the silent stillness that separated you from everything like a hair-thin film.

I quickly called on my magic to unfreeze the world. Remembering to distract Tristan just in time, I turned him away from the window, pressed his back up against the glass and kissed him. My heart thudded in my ears as I surrounded us with magic and forced us back into time, breaking our never-ending moment and releasing everything around us with a faint pop and ripple of the air.

It hadn't been long. We'd been out of time a handful of minutes, not more than twenty. *Fuck!* How had I not realized? I'd wanted to stay in that moment with Tristan so badly I'd refused to let it end.

My frantic reaction to the mistake gave my kiss a wild edge. I couldn't collect myself and stopped trying, just for a minute. Everything was a mess, from my emotions to the way Tristan's lips clashed with mine. He had inspired this loss of control, but somehow I was desperate for him to anchor me.

Almost as if he knew, he held me tight until I settled down.

When I eased up, Tristan looked ravaged. His lips were rosy and swollen, dark eyes half hidden by his lashes and hazy with desire.

I willed my features into a mask of calm. There was no harm done. Tristan's skeptical mind would have naturally framed everything he'd seen as explainable oddities. Most Mortals had to be pushed quite far before they'd believe magic was real.

But this was way too close a call and wouldn't go unnoticed. My alterations to time were detectable to the Authority. Monitoring my power was a condition of my employment put in place due to my rocky past. I'd need to come up with an excuse to explain myself.

"Would you like a drink? I think I need a drink." I pulled away from Tristan before he could see how jittery I'd become and made my way over to the full bar built into a corner of the room. I poured two whiskeys, downed mine, and poured another.

Tristan remained hovering by the window. "You all right?"

"Perfect." What else could I possibly say?

I turned and gave him a smile but he looked ever so slightly wary. I sipped my drink in a manner I hoped looked relaxed, then tucked the bottle back into its place, fiddling with things on the bar to keep my hands busy.

If Tristan had looked a bit longer out the window, or seen the floating leaves, this could have turned into an unplanned magical revelation.

Witches needed approval before Telling Mortals about magic. Bringing them into our world had consequences and it wasn't a decision to be made lightly. We had laws protecting Mortals from being influenced or exploited by magic and the inequality its existence created, but once a Mortal was no longer ignorant they could be manipulated with the threat of magic. *Do this or I'll curse you* was hard to counter when you had no power of your own.

Any spells placed on a Mortal still needed consent—otherwise they were illegal—but the secret was meant as an extra layer of protection, aiming to level out an impossible imbalance and keep society from becoming a dystopian us-verse-them class divide. There was enough of that in the world already.

The rules guarding magic's secret, especially on a large scale, were among Witch-law's strictest regulations. If I went to court for revealing magic recklessly it could further complicate my strained work situation, never mind any legal trouble that might come from a negative ruling. There were still judges who'd love to catch me breaking the rules and punish me for it. They'd use any slip up as proof I'd had criminal tendencies all along and was some sort of fox in the henhouse.

It was a serious relief that Tristan hadn't noticed properly.

Was it a mistake to proceed with this casual arrangement in the face of such a close call?

I didn't think so. Now that I wasn't worried one more tryst was all we had, there was no reason to *literally stop time*. I would keep myself very carefully controlled and never unleash like I had today.

That meant no more whispered secrets in Tristan's ear. I'd never planned to do that. Nothing about tonight had been my intention. I hadn't even really meant to ask him to come back to the apartment with me, but Tristan had said we should go as soon as I'd mentioned I lived nearby. And I hadn't been able to resist.

Next time would be different, it would be planned. I wouldn't be caught off guard and do anything foolish. In fact, magic might help me keep us casual. It was a natural barrier, preventing me from getting close and sharing my life.

That thought calmed me like nothing else could have.

I retreated from the bar, handed Tristan his drink, and led him to the couch.

The view before us was so full of motion.

"What brought you to the city?" I asked to keep Tristan's mind from straying back to what he'd seen and how different things looked now, but unmoving pedestrians didn't seem to be on his mind as he put an arm over my shoulders and pulled me close.

I melted into him.

Tristan told me about his job as a writer. He talked about his office and the people, how this new position was what he needed for his next step in his planned career. Having someone hold me and talk to me, letting me soak up their life like this, was beyond relaxing.

That was another reason to never Tell Tristan about magic. It would break this companionable dynamic. I liked to be an average man with him, free from my past and unburdened by judgments.

Sitting on a couch in rumpled clothes, I could try to be me.

## 12

## TRISTAN

I woke up held gently in Edwin's arms. The only light in the room was a gas fire flickering in the hearth, casting warm tones over our bare skin. Edwin's features were softened by sleep in a way I'd never seen before. It was enough to make me never want to get up; too bad the floor was so hard. Damn reality.

Our couch cuddles had turned into kissing, which led to quite a bit more and I guess, being so blissed out, we fell asleep on the floor. It was honestly cozier than any fancy rug on hardwood had the right to be.

I got up, stretched, and found my phone and a throw blanket to wrap around myself now I was away from the fire. Edwin didn't stir, so I crept off in search of a bathroom.

I still didn't know what to make of Edwin. Even if you put some of his affection down to brainless sex talk, repeatedly saying he missed me didn't mesh with his aversion to any small level of commitment. He'd been conflicted all evening, kissing passionately, then looking panicked, and to top it all off, being intimate in front of the fire had seemed ridiculously romantic. I just wondered if I was the only one feeling that way.

A date would have been good for us. We'd be forced to talk with no opportunity to distract ourselves physically. It'd be an opportunity to get a better handle on Edwin. But dating wasn't happening and I was glad I'd stopped short of asking directly.

I was out of my depth creeping through the apartment. Everything was meticulously coordinated like Edwin lived inside a fancy magazine. He was next-level rich, not just successful but entrenched in money. The building had been *in his family*. Like what? And *I* wanted to date him? What was I doing?

I tried not to poke into too many doors and quickly found what looked like the master bedroom. I could see an open door to the ensuite, so I crossed the room and entered a bathroom fancier than the one at the hotel, though without the spa-sized tub.

Everything was tidy to the point I worried about knocking stuff out of place or leaving finger smudges. All Edwin's bath and body products were of the same high-end brand, neatly displayed and color coordinated with the room's décor. Maybe that wasn't a big deal, but I'd never met anyone able to afford to be that brand loyal.

As I lingered with the cold tiles under my toes, I texted Owen. I needed to share this day with someone. I'd had such a low low and then been higher than a damn kite.

I could still feel all the ways Edwin had held me, like he was imprinted on my skin. When I remembered how he'd touched me and let me touch him in return, how things had seemed to build on our first time together, I wasn't so worried about lack of dates or what was up between us. As much as I wanted a relationship, I couldn't see it working. All I had to do was look around to know that.

I sent Owen a quick message: *Guess who lives in NYC.*

My phone started buzzing. I swiped to accept the call.

"Wow. That was quick. Couldn't live with the suspense?" I whispered.

"Not exactly." There was an awkward pause as Owen cleared his throat. "So you ran into Mr. Bic—Edwin?"

It was a creepily good guess, though maybe I was just that obvious. Who else would I be talking about? Still, it was almost like Owen had expected this.

I gave a run down, but Owen didn't sound as excited for me as I'd hoped.

"I don't want you getting hurt," was all he said.

I clung to the throw blanket as it slipped off one of my shoulders. "Why would I get hurt?"

"I don't know—" I could hear Owen rustling around on his end of the line like he was pacing back and forth. "Your one night together left you feeling so—and the way he abruptly pushed you away after—I don't get what you see in him."

"I still don't get what you have against him. It wasn't like that. There was no pushing anyone away. He's not the most straightforward, but he's kind. And the man is basically magic when his lips are on mine."

"*What? Magic—*"

"I'm joking, Owen. Chill out. We just have good chemistry. I don't see why you keep trying to convince me not to enjoy it. You know I need something good right now."

"Um—sorry. I'm didn't mean to. There's nothing against him. Look, you know Edwin better than I do. I just hope he deserves you."

I made a dismissive sound. Owen was dampening my Edwin buzz so I changed the subject and told him about my mom's email.

Not even this night could banish her intrusion from my brain permanently. I should have called Owen about it earlier in the day, but sometimes you had to wallow in it.

His outrage was the satisfying balm I needed. Owen ranted and we rehashed familiar thoughts on this infuriating situation. Even with nothing changed, I felt better.

Then Owen asked, "Did you mention it to Edwin?"

"What? No. That kind of thing is *not* within our dynamic. Come on, you should know that." My stomach fluttered at the thought of telling Edwin my problems. What would he think? My mom's situation and my childhood only highlighted how different the two of us were. "We're keeping it low key. I'm not telling Edwin anything. I want him to like me, not feel sorry for me."

"If he'd judge you for that he's not a great—"

"That's not what I—"

There was a knock on the door. "Tristan?"

"Gotta go, bye!" I hung up on Owen and checked myself in the massive mirror.

Seeing my reflection, it suddenly felt like I was being too familiar. Was it presumptuous to wander the house in nothing but a blanket like I had a right to be here?

I opened the door to find Edwin standing there wide-eyed in a black silk robe with lace trim. "I thought you'd gone."

His expression threw me. Edwin looked all sweet and vulnerable, worry lines on his brow, those blue eyes fixed on me like he almost didn't believe it.

Here was the man who'd admitted he needed me between panting breaths.

Seeing him like this, I wanted to help Edwin feel comfortable enough to be like this more often. Show him he could talk to me instead of closing off.

I reached out and placed my hands on the front of Edwin's robe. "Sorry. Went looking for the bathroom and my phone rang. I'd never sneak out and leave you in the middle of the night. I know you'd miss me."

Edwin's freckled cheeks bloomed with color. "I should've known better."

"Plus, my clothes are all over your living room. Where would I have gone dressed in a blanket?"

"Oh. Right." Edwin kissed my cheek. He was being affectionate, but the gesture could also be a way to hide his embarrassment and not look at me. He lingered, lips caressing my skin.

When he pulled back, his calm, confident expression was back in place and no matter how much I hoped he'd open up, I had to remember we were keeping this light. Simple. Even if half the time it didn't feel like that at all.

## 13

# EDWIN

I checked my correspondence as soon as I arrived at my office in the Authority building the next morning. A quick glance showed there was nothing about my time stop from the night before even though I'd failed to follow up as promptly as I usually did.

That was good. I sometimes waited a day to check in, especially when things happened in the evening. I'd write up my report and bring it by Geer's office before lunch.

I just had to figure out what to say. There was no way my private life was going to be detailed in an official document.

In need of inspiration, I looked more closely at my emails. Finding some truth to base my report around was probably the best course of action, so I scanned the rest of the messages keeping an eye out for any leads that had come in regarding the black-market blood.

There were several. I'd even been tagged to follow up on one as a regular informant of mine had given the tip. This was excellent, a cover and actual work to occupy me, but I really should check in with the informing Witch before shoehorning his tip into my report. If I teleported over now, I'd have more than enough time to get it all done before midday.

Blood was tricky as far as magical substances went. My magic was strong enough that I didn't need conduits to focus or enhance it, but most Witches needed crystals to cast spells. Herbs and other natural elements could be used in conjunction, as could blood.

Mortal blood brought a potency to magic that couldn't be achieved any other way, but sourcing it ethically was not usually viable. Most blood magic was outlawed, both to prevent leaching blood from unsuspecting Mortals and because the spells that specifically required blood tended toward the sinister.

Witches couldn't legally cast spells on Mortals without their consent, and with it all being secret, only those who Knew about magic could donate blood for use in spells. There was no way the volume of blood being sold at the moment had come from consenting parties, just based on the number of Mortals in the region who Knew.

There was a knock at my door.

One of the other investigators poked his head in. "Bickel, the compliance team has asked me to fetch you."

I went still in surprise, reflexively glaring at the man in my doorway. Fetch me? Now? That had never happened before. I was required to detail what I'd done while stopping time but it wasn't a standard compliance issue. Why were they even involved?

"They'd like to see you now." The Witch wrung his hands and took half a step into my office.

"Yes, fine. Thank you, Mr. Morby." I got up, grabbed my hat and followed the waspy man down the hall. He left me to enter the stairwell alone, probably heading back to his desk.

There was no way for anyone to know the magic I'd done

last night was anything less than planned, so why was the reaction different? Maybe this deviation from the norm had something to do with the growing tension I'd been experiencing. I knew certain judges were watching me more closely since the mess with Judge Herrera, but that distrust bleeding into how my position was handled didn't bode well. Things should be getting better as more time passed, settling down, not getting worse.

My nervousness mounted as I descended the stairs.

In a meeting room on the compliance floor, I found Judge Geer and Ms. Soto—head of the local team who oversaw the various enchantments used to detect lawbreaking and monitor offenders who'd been given restrictions. This didn't put me at ease. Why was Soto here? Why hadn't Charles waited for me to find him later like I always did?

I took a subtle calming breath as I crossed the room to join them. If Judge Raven were here, I'd need to be worried. Charles implied everything was fine.

When I'd been hired in the late nineties, I'd agreed to have monitoring spells cast on me so that my superiors would always know when I used magic to alter time. Some of the judges had wanted to cast surveillance spells on me the decade before, after my trial, but I hadn't been convicted of anything, so they'd had no grounds.

I didn't really care about the spells. I could break them if I wished; I had the power. But I'd agreed to their casting in hopes it would show the judges I could be trusted. I wasn't trying to hide anything or do anything wrong, and my desire to work here had been stronger than any reservations I'd had about being watched.

The Authority and the court system had handled my trial, and surrounding situation, poorly. Victim blaming had only been the start. I didn't like or trust most of the Witches here anymore than they did me, and that hadn't changed in the last thirty-three years. I'd taken this job to try and improve things, push for progress and help future cases be handled better, and if I had to be monitored to do that, so be it.

I took a seat across from the others. "I know I sometimes come into the office at night to do my reports, but I wouldn't have started doing it if I'd known you'd come to expect it."

Charles laughed. "No, no. We don't expect you to write reports after hours. Though you're right, you've spoiled us with your work ethic, Edwin."

"I wanted to check in with you." Soto leaned forward, placing a hand on the papers in front of her. "You seem to have affected a Mortal when you altered time."

"What?" I snapped.

She flinched, but I only glared.

This was my Mr. Bickel persona at its best. Though I'd wanted to gain some trust from the judges, for the most part I leaned in to intimidating people in order to keep them away. It was my response to having personal things leaked all over the Authority during my trial. I didn't want anyone to know anything else real about me, and if they were intimidated they were less likely to pry and gossip.

Soto gave in to my stare and looked down at the papers. "A Mortal, Mr. Bickel. It seems you directly affected one when you stopped time."

"No, I didn't. Why would you think that?" My composure held despite my anxiety, one of the upsides of being an uptight control freak. I'd had plenty of practice and, in this familiar environment, being anyone other than the arrogant jerk everyone knew was near impossible.

"Really, Ms. Soto." Charles leaned in as if he were trying to interrupt the animosity. "There's no way a *Mortal* could have been detached from time without noticing."

"Not to mention there's absolutely no reason to take a Mortal with me when leaving the timeline," I added coldly.

*I never want this to end, Tristan.* The memory flooded me and I almost blushed. They didn't have a right to know about my personal life. It was ridiculous I even had to lie about this. I'd done nothing wrong.

"Yes, we know the Mortal didn't notice magic." Soto tapped her fingers on the table. "The Telling sensors didn't go off. But the spells monitoring your time magic were linked to our detectors when they were cast on you. Last night we had an alert."

I hadn't known they'd been watching my use of time alterations to check if I ever took a Mortal with me, had I? I couldn't remember that stipulation. Could I really have forgotten it? I supposed I might have dismissed it, since I almost never took anyone out of time with me, other than Juliet.

Teleporting was different. The Authority didn't care about that, only my ability to alter our timeline. They feared what I could potentially do and disliked that no one could stop me. Monitoring upheld their illusion of control.

"Are we sure that link was set up properly?" Charles asked. "If Edwin says no one was with him, something must have gone wrong." He turned to me. "What were you doing, by the way?"

Okay, so maybe I should stop begrudging having Charles in my corner.

I kept up my haughty attitude because it was what I did, and grabbed a form from Soto's stack. "I was following a lead on the blood problem. There's a tip in the inbox this morning, but I saw the informant last night. I paused time for a few minutes, as I often do when I think it will help me catch something in the moment. I wanted to keep my actions from the informant, so a small stop was ideal to discreetly check his story. Nothing came of it, but at the time I thought it worth trying. There weren't even any Mortals there."

I reached into my pocket, extracted a pen, clicked it and began writing as if all was business as usual.

Soto's frown caught in my peripheral vision. "I suppose there could be something wrong with the enchantments. It really is hard to imagine a Mortal disconnecting from time without noticing what was going on around them."

"I can't image how distracted you'd have to be for that," Charles said with a laugh.

I RETURNED to my office and slumped into my chair. After a quick glance to double check the door was closed, I put my head in my hands.

One breath in, one breath out. Everything was fine, ridiculous, but fine.

I pulled out my phone and sent a text to Mason, saying to meet me in his store room. Once I received his reply—a thumbs up emoji—I teleported to Mystic Pawn & Treasure, an awfully named paranormal pawn shop in Brooklyn.

Teleporting took some getting used to; I'd thrown up on more than a few occasions when I was learning how to do it, but now it felt like nothing more than stepping through a tight space as I materialized in the crowded storeroom.

Mason poked his ginger head through the doorway. "Hey—get out the front where you belong." He added a toothy grin.

I followed him out of the back room into the familiar pawn shop. The shelves seemed even more disorganized than I remembered, but it had been a while since I'd popped in.

Mason Foxhall was a tall lanky man who looked about twenty-five but was actually somewhere around sixty. He'd been an employee of Mystic Pawn & Treasure for forty years and was a quality source who let me know if any seriously dangerous objects showed up at the shop, or if anything untoward happened at one of his band's shows.

I leaned up against the front counter and surveyed a stack of cauldrons beside me. "How's business?"

"Same as always." Mason picked up a gold watch that had been sitting out on the counter. "This has been enchanted to make the wearer dopey. The owner said it slowed down time. Ha. It just makes you think that. A bit like weed."

"How interesting."

Mason put the watch down. "Yeah, a silly gimmick. So you're not surprised about the blood?"

I made a show of examining my fingers before glancing back at Mason. "We're aware of a problem."

"I was surprised." Mason laid both elbows on the counter, leaning across it to get closer to me and whispering even though we were the only ones here. "I came in on my day off because I forgot my good centering candle. Anyway, I was looking for it out back when I saw this box. It wasn't there the day before. The shop was closed and Al wasn't around, so I snooped inside and found vials of blood."

I matched his low tone. "Are you and Al the only ones who can get past the locking enchantments when the shop is closed?"

"Yeah. But if Al gave someone else access he might not have told me. I'm only his hired help. He's getting too big and important these days. Wouldn't be surprised if he let all kinds of people in here without me knowing."

"Oh?" I gave Mason a sympathetic look.

"He's the leader of his coven now and getting all into the Witchy hierarchy shit. The shop would be in disarray if it weren't for me. Al isn't keeping up with the books. Really, I need to buy the place off him. Dunno if he'd sell—" Mason stared off into space, probably lost in his ever-growing thoughts of owning the pawn shop himself.

"Do you think Al is dealing in blood?"

"Must be. Dodgy jerk. Maybe the money he's earning from that is why he doesn't care about the shop anymore. Even if he was just holding it for someone, I bet he's getting paid. The box wasn't here when I came in for work the next day, so it wasn't around long."

"Holding it for someone? You don't think he's collecting it himself?"

Mason straightened up and shoved his hands in the pockets of his worn jeans. "Oh—well, I don't know. He could be. But it was a lot of blood."

That gave me pause. I'd assumed the box was relatively small. The crowded shop was a good place to hide things, but leaving something large lying around seemed risky, even if Al hadn't expected Mason to come in out of hours. "When you say a box of vials, how much would you estimate it held?"

"Big box." Mason made an approximation of the shape with his hands. "Few hundred vials at least."

That was more significant than I'd expected. Where would Al get that much blood from? I could see why Mason might have thought the pawn shop owner was holding it for someone. "You'll let me know if you spot anything else?"

"Definitely. I wish I could let you put surveillance spells on the shop, but Al would know." Mason gave me a what-can-you-do look. "Though I have another idea."

The man brought an old, tarnished mirror out from under the counter. "It was on that shelf over there"—he pointed to the front of the shop—"on the night the blood was here, so it didn't record anything useful."

Mason offered the mirror to me and I took it. The glass had been enchanted to record everything that happened in front of it, and scanning back through the images by swiping the glass with my fingers revealed no one in the main part of the shop on the night in question.

I handed the mirror back. "Do you think you could leave this out back? In case that wasn't the only crate of blood due to pass through here?"

Mason nodded. "That's exactly what I was thinking."

I clapped him on the shoulder. "Thanks. I'll be in touch."

## 14

## TRISTAN

My apartment was empty—okay, it was never empty—it was just me and three hundred thousand plants this evening and I was taking advantage of the relative privacy to examine Avery's crystal collection while she was out at the night market.

The crystals were in a little basket next to some candles and incense in the living room. As I picked one up, I felt something odd. Like they were magnetic, maybe? But that didn't make sense.

My nosiness had peaked yesterday after poking my head into Avery's room and finding her sitting on the floor with a wooden salad bowl of water, some candles and a circle of herbs. In my defense, I'd knocked and I'd thought she'd said come in, but I must have misheard. Avery had shrieked as I entered, knocking everything over. Luckily the water had put out the candle flames.

After I'd helped her clean up, Avery had explained that she hadn't wanted to share all of her spiritual beliefs until we knew each other better. I mean, I didn't care in a judgy way. She should be free to do her thing in her own apartment. But the vibe between us this morning had been awkward, like she was embarrassed I'd found out about her rituals.

It got me thinking. The more I looked around the apartment, the more I noticed how the candles were arranged in particular configurations, or how carefully constructed all the bundles of herbs were. The painted symbols all over the potted plants and windowsills no longer looked random, there was a pattern to them, almost like they could be part of a language I'd never known existed.

Avery wasn't a casual believer in—what, exactly, she hadn't said.

Now that I was pondering all this, Avery seemed to subscribe to the same kind of alternative spirituality as Aria. Not that I'd ever talked to Aria in depth about the specifics of her beliefs.

I certainly didn't believe these crystals held any power. If Avery's stuff really worked, I'd be rid of my headaches and inexplicably low energy after drinking all her tea. Instead, I was still exhausted and consistently falling asleep on the couch even though I'd never been a nap person. And I was less interested in the herbs and crystal's supposed properties than Avery helping me figure out what had been biting me during all these naps.

This morning I'd had an unplanned second sleep on the couch and had woken up to little itchy red dots on my ankles. It was happening regularly enough that I was constantly on the lookout for any sort of bug or spider in the foliage of the many plants, but I hadn't spotted any and Avery seemed unconcerned, like I was worrying over nothing.

I abandoned the crystals in their basket. They weren't going to help me with the possibly trivial but incredibly aggravating bug bite mystery and besides, I had other things to be concerned about tonight.

Edwin was coming over. He'd arranged a time for our next —not a date—*encounter*—before I'd left his place the morning after our reunion. It was oddly formal, scheduling a time for sex in advance rather than saying *message me when you're horny*.

I'd been at a loss. He'd wanted to come to my place. No idea why, when his was so perfect. All day I'd been overthinking my host duties. There was a bottle of red wine in the kitchen I'd considered opening, but now that Edwin was due to arrive, I was falling victim to self-consciousness, remembering the expensive stuff we'd had that first night.

Honestly Edwin had the right idea: stick to what we were good at together. This wasn't a date so none of that other stuff should matter. I'd rather stick to sex than find out firsthand how poorly we matched in all of the other ways I wanted.

The buzzer sounded, pulling me out of my self-doubt-induced floundering.

I let Edwin up and opened the door. Did I even need to detail how handsome he was anymore? Tonight his suit was charcoal gray paired with a black and blue paisley bow tie and black fedora.

Edwin's expression was serious as his eyes roved over me. His lips twitched in an almost smile, like he couldn't help himself. "Hello, Tristan."

"Hi." I didn't hold back my smile.

He stepped inside and I shut the door.

"Oh my—" Alarm flickered across Edwin's features as he maneuvered through the hall.

Right, the ridiculous amount of plants. Maybe I should have forewarned him. "Yeah—my roommate. She likes greenery."

I held some foliage out of our way as we made our way to the living room.

Edwin looked around, eyes wide as he took in the clutter of the small apartment. His posture was rigid, expression bordering on shocked. Next to his place my house must seem—

no—there was no need to compare. He'd wanted to see where I lived and it wasn't a mess, just packed in.

We stood awkwardly for a few moments too long. It seemed like Edwin was unable to get over the semi-forested state of the apartment.

"Is this all your roommate's stuff?" He ran his perfect fingers over a hanging pot of sage covered in intricately painted symbols.

"Yeah. She's cool. Um. Can I get you a drink?" I fidgeted, but his eyes weren't on me so it didn't matter.

"A drink would be lovely, Tristan." Edwin turned and gave me his usual reserved look, no smile, all trace of thoughts and emotions hidden.

I retreated to the kitchen to open the wine. I decided to leave the bottle in here so it wouldn't be obvious I hadn't bought anything too nice. But then, he couldn't expect that. Surely he didn't care. I shouldn't either. It wasn't like I'd pretended living in a penthouse was *my* style.

Fuck, I needed to turn my brain off.

Returning to the living room, I found Edwin examining Avery's crystals just as I had been earlier. "That focuses healing energy. Supposedly."

"Yes." Edwin put the crystal down. "Did you know her before moving in?"

I hovered by the couch, holding our wines. "No. But it's not as weird as you might be thinking. It's kind of fun living here."

Edwin looked around the room again and picked a half-used smudge stick off the coffee table. From his expression I'd say he wasn't into the idea of alty-spiritualism.

Man, was this going badly already? I mean, I wasn't lighting candles and contemplating the divinity of the universe, but I wasn't uncomfortable with it either. Was all this too weird for a man who meticulously refined everything from his personal style to his home décor? Maybe it was just unexpected since it wasn't actually my stuff he was looking at.

As long as Edwin didn't react like this to my excessive nail polish collection, we were fine.

I handed Edwin his wine and he put down the bundle of dried herbs with a tiny shake of his head. He raised the glass, eyes focusing intently on me.

"Cheers, darling. You have a very cozy home—if a very eccentric roommate."

We clinked glasses and I felt myself blush, not knowing if he was being genuine or not.

"She isn't home, I gather?" Edwin paused, glancing around again before sipping his wine.

I hoped he liked it, though he didn't react, so maybe not. "She's out for the evening."

"Good. I prefer privacy." He took another sip.

I tasted my own drink. It was familiar, which I liked in a wine. "We could've gone to your place. Then you wouldn't have to worry."

Edwin looked surprised. "Oh, I'm not worried. I'm sure we'll enjoy ourselves just the same here."

This awkwardness should have been expected. We didn't have the best conversational track record, so why did this odd exchange feel different? I needed to stop reading into everything, but it was impossible not to when Edwin seemed to constantly hold himself back.

I looked grudgingly at the plants. "Just be careful you don't knock over a Ficus while we do."

Edwin sniggered and I looked up in time to catch the quick, brilliant flash of a smile break through his composed features.

I relaxed.

He took off his hat and set it neatly next to the smudge stick.

We settled onto the couch and talked about nothing really, but the conversation began to flow more easily.

When our glasses were empty Edwin put his hand on my thigh and I turned my attention to his suit, another vintage piece that looked wildly out of place in my apartment. I refused to see it as a metaphor for our compatibility.

Edwin pulled me onto his lap.

I straddled him and began undoing his fancy clothes. "You like dressing up all the time?"

He smirked. "I know you like it."

I pulled off his tie. "Yep, you got me. But why do you like it?"

Edwin leaned in and kissed my neck just below my ear. "I've dressed this way since it was in style. That, *or* I just like to indulge in eccentricities."

I let out a breathy giggle as he plied me with kisses. "What—you're not a hundred years old. You're just making things up to avoid answering me."

"Perhaps." Edwin's hand slid up the back of my sweater sending shivers down my spine.

I leaned back so I could see him better and ran my fingers through the peppering of gray in his light hair. "Can I ask, Edwin—um—how old are you?"

His face was free of wrinkles, except when he let his emotions show. Edwin's smiles cut gorgeous lines around his eyes and mouth while his frowns furrowed his brow, but guessing his age was somehow impossible. He looked younger than the average person who'd be going gray—maybe his freckles gave him a certain youthfulness—but at the same time he seemed older.

Edwin's movements stilled in response to my question, but he didn't try to look away. "I'm forty-five. I hope that isn't too middle aged for you?" He sounded more serious than I'd expected in response to a simple question, but then he was back to kissing my neck.

"Not at all."

His hands found their way to my ass. "Glad to hear it, darling."

My breath hitched and I swallowed my next question. Everything about Edwin felt like a mystery. I couldn't help wanting to try and unravel every bit of him. But getting to know each other wasn't part of our arrangement and I shouldn't push it when he didn't seem interested in sharing.

I WOKE from a doze as Edwin ran his fingers through my tangled hair.

We were in bed, my head resting on his chest. Edwin had been quieter during sex this time. The only whispers he'd breathed in my ear were to tell me how good everything felt. There'd been no more raw emotional confessions from either of us.

"Sorry, didn't mean to fall asleep," I muttered. It was early. We could still go out for a drink or even dinner if we'd wanted.

Edwin massaged my head. "That's all right. I like lying together like this."

A sweet, tender feeling unfurled inside me. I smiled goofily knowing he couldn't see it the way I was tucked into him, but a yawn overtook me. "I've been so tired lately. Ever since moving here."

Edwin paused his rubbing. "Moving's been hard?"

My hand trailed down his chest, touching his freckles. "It's not what I expected. Maybe I didn't realize the extent of everything that would change, or everything I was leaving behind. I'm taking longer to settle in than—anyway, it's fine."

I didn't want to unload worries on Edwin or admit how happy I was we'd crossed paths again. I'd been increasingly lonely, Avery feeling like the only one close to a real friend. Edwin's affection was strong, no matter what he wanted—or said he didn't want—from us. Lying together like this, he seemed to care, and that was enough for now.

"It must be hard being away from everyone you know," Edwin offered, resuming his absent stroking of my head.

I looked at the tattoo on my wrist. "Yeah."

Edwin picked my hand off his chest. "Can I ask about your tattoo?"

I squirmed. "It's Owen and me. You know, Owen from Coffee Cat." Edwin touched the inked lines as I spoke. "The date is when we met, and the stars are our signs."

"You're the Pisces." He traced the small constellation.

"Mm, good guess."

"Not a guess, darling." Edwin placed my hand back on his chest. "Were you and Owen together?" The last word sounded tentative, like maybe he wasn't sure if he should ask.

"No. Owen and I are like family. I met him at a really low point in his life. He needed someone, and so did I. It's weird not seeing each other all the time. Sometimes I don't know what I was thinking coming here."

"I could take you to visit him," Edwin whispered.

"I can buy my own flights," I responded automatically.

He went still and took his hand out of my hair. "Of course. Sorry."

Wasn't that a weird thing to offer a man you weren't dating, or did Edwin just have that much money? I'd never let him buy me expensive stuff like that even if we were together. Still, I wished I hadn't shut him down so abruptly.

The conversation didn't pick back up, though I tried a few times. Edwin didn't want to answer any questions about himself, deflecting all my curiosities no matter how small, and he didn't ask anything else of me before we both drifted off to sleep.

THE NEXT MORNING we both woke up in the mood to get off.

I could almost convince myself more sex was the reason Edwin stayed over, and if I'd asked him I had no doubt that's what he'd say, but I knew what that dynamic felt like and it was worlds away from this. Edwin liked cuddles and comforts as much as I did.

Avery was brewing tea in the kitchen when we emerged.

"Good morning." She gave me a wicked grin, letting me know Edwin and I hadn't been that quiet.

Just as I returned Avery's smile, she caught sight of Edwin and her expression wavered. A flash of something—recognition?—crossed her face. She didn't say anything about it as I made introductions.

The dynamic was weird. Edwin and Avery were both stiff and almost formal with one another. That was typical Edwin when he wasn't undressed and pressed against me, but I was surprised in Avery's changed personality.

Edwin wasn't one for small talk and disappeared off to the bathroom as soon as politeness seemed to allow.

"Where did you find him?" Avery raised her eyebrows so high they disappeared in her bangs.

I cradled my hot mug of tea, blowing on it gently. "Long story. We actually met over a year ago, in California."

Avery narrowed her eyes in the direction of the bathroom. "He's not who I'd expected you to be into."

I put my mug down on the counter. "Rude."

She flinched. "Sorry. I don't mean like, judgmentally. He's got a vibe—his aura. I know you don't believe in that stuff, but just be careful."

"What do you mean?" I crossed my arms and stared at my roommate. Why were people constantly warning me about Edwin?

"It's just a vibe, Tristan. But vibes aren't insignificant." She looked at me sternly and for an absurd moment it felt like she could be my mother—not my real mom but a parental figure who did typical parental things like tell you not to date bad boys.

Edwin took that moment to re-emerge from the bathroom looking disappointed to see Avery still in the kitchen. "I need to get going, Tristan." He seemed expectant.

I wasn't sure why but took a guess. "Here, I'll walk you out." I looped my arm through his and pulled him along.

"Pleasure to meet you, Miss Heyde," he said over his shoulder.

Avery retreated behind her mug. "Likewise, Mr. Bickel."

I stopped in the kitchen doorway, almost tripping over the violas. "Do you know each other?"

They both looked at me quizzically. Right. Stupid question. How the hell would Avery know Edwin? And he'd just said *pleasure to meet you.*

As soon as Edwin left, Avery disappeared into her room. I was hoping to get more detail on her comment about his vibe. I didn't believe in her crystals or Aria's ability to read people, but I still wanted Avery's take. Why had she felt compelled to warn me when she didn't even know Edwin?

I settled on the couch—making a mental note to buy a bug spray to deploy in the living room just to see if it would help, regardless of having seen no bugs—and wasted time on my phone waiting for Avery to reemerge. I had a bunch of emails, so decided to clear them out. This was a huge mistake. The most recent one was from my mom.

My stomach dropped, deciding to hang out near my toes with no plans to return to its rightful place in my anatomy. She hadn't even waited for me to reply this time. What did that mean?

I read the email subject line: *Tristan please read this*. Shit. Her last one had just said: *hi*. My face felt hot and my throat was doing that achy thing it did when I was about to cry. This was bullshit. But what if something was wrong? What if my mom was sick? What if this time she actually needed me? I was so angry at her and sick of her predictable let downs, but that didn't stop me from worrying.

However, I'd been here before. Gotten all concerned about her only for her to blow me off.

I had the urge to call Edwin. I closed my email app and opened my contacts. Then I remembered that was absurd. No one *called* anymore. I scrolled to my messenger. What would I even say?

Then it dawned on me, Edwin and I didn't even have a text history.

He wasn't someone I could turn to.

I felt so consumingly awful. Alone. I didn't actually want to tell Edwin about my mom. Not at all. It was comfort I wanted, a thing I couldn't request from him except physically.

Since demanding Edwin come back and hold me for no reason wasn't socially acceptable or casual, I called Owen. He talked me down and by the end of the long conversation I felt better, but I fucking missed him. Maybe I did need to organize a visit soon. I was going back for Thanksgiving but that was months away.

I archived the email unread and tried not to feel guilty about it. I had a Sunday to see to. Maybe Avery would emerge from her room at the offer of a vegan brunch.

## 15

# EDWIN

ne month later.

I WOKE up on my hundred-and-thirteenth birthday feeling strange.

For the most part I ignored my birthdays. They'd lost their luster after so many years. I hadn't done anything to mark the sixteenth of October since Juliet had insisted on celebrating my hundredth.

Even though we hadn't made plans for today I hoped she'd be free to see me. I didn't really want to celebrate, but lying here I was filled with a longing to have not woken up alone. Which was a thought that had nothing to do with Juliet in itself. However, she was my only friend and I supposed I might want to talk to her about it.

Grimacing at myself, I got up and showered, then dressed in a brand-new bespoke suit. After a lengthy consideration, I paired it with one of my more ostentatious bow ties. I'd bought it some years ago and not yet worn it, which was a pity since the gold thread embroidery was artfully done.

I stopped in my new—local—cafe and bought three coffees before finding a discrete place to teleport away from.

Ever since Juliet had started seeing Mea, I'd taken to appearing in Juliet's front entryway and calling out to announce my presence, whether I'd texted ahead or not. I might have chosen the front stoop as a more logical destination but Juliet insisted that making me knock on the front door was unacceptable.

"Hello?" I listened carefully but didn't hear anyone in Juliet's living room, so I poked around the wall blocking the entryway from view. The house looked the same as ever, crowded with books and homey.

"I'm in the kitchen," came Juliet's response.

I found her arranging what looked like home-baked scones and fruit on a plate. She was dressed casually in leggings and a sweater. I looked around the tidy kitchen, scanning the small breakfast table and glancing out the French doors to the back yard. "Where's Mea?"

"At her studio." Juliet took the coffee tray from me. "That's sweet you got her a coffee though. We can reheat it for her later."

I set Mea's coffee aside. "I assumed she'd be here and wasn't sure you'd be free. But I figured I'd stop in quickly anyway."

"Edwin, of course I'm free today." Juliet gave me a scolding look.

"Right." I sipped my espresso. "How are the animals?"

"Let's go see." She picked up the plate and her coffee while I grabbed a few napkins and the two of us traipsed outside.

We sat at the small garden table tucked off to the side of the lawn. The yard was lovely and private, dominated by large trees and given character by a small creek. A few ducks came waddling up to us, quacking and looking for food. A pony walked out of the trees and began grazing.

I blinked. "Is his mane—*purple?*" My question was more a shock response than a request for information.

"Mea enchanted him." Juliet popped a strawberry in her mouth gazing adoringly at the pony.

"She's not content with setting the place aglow with magical lights at night then?" I meant to sound cynical but something about the—now I looked closer—*sparkly* purple mane made me smile.

Juliet reached down to pat one of the ducks. "The yard's nightscape is ever evolving. It's been fun. And I think George likes it."

The pony did look quite pleased with himself.

My stomach felt suddenly hollow.

Sitting here with Juliet like this was strange and wonderful, so different than anything we'd have done a year ago, but it still felt completely like us. I liked this better than she and I sitting around, talking about work, even though I still enjoyed our more serious chats.

"We should meet Mea and go to the beach later," I said before I could think about the whim and change my mind.

"Yeah?" Juliet looked pleasantly surprised. "That sounds great. I'm sure she'd love to join us."

I picked up a scone and put it on my napkin. "She'll make fun of me for wearing a suit in the sand."

"I doubt Mea would hassle you on your birthday."

I grunted in response. Mea was hard not to like and I was only complaining half-heartedly. I enjoyed getting to know Juliet's girlfriend and felt like Mea was actually warming up to me now that she knew me as more than the closed off, arrogant Witch I tricked everyone into thinking I was.

I picked up a blueberry and examined it. "I've been seeing

Tristan." I popped the fruit in my mouth before looking sidewise at my friend.

Juliet didn't look surprised, she just beamed at me. "That's great, Edwin."

"Great? Is that all? I thought you'd be surprised. Oh—Aria told you, didn't she?" For some reason that disappointed me. I had to resist asking what the young Witch had said exactly.

Juliet only nodded. "I was wondering when you were going to tell me."

"Sorry." I felt guilty for keeping it a secret even though Juliet looked nothing but happy to be discussing this new development in my life. "I didn't know what to say about it. We're just sleeping together."

But that statement felt vaguely wrong. It somehow didn't fit, even though it was true. Tristan and I had only spent a handful of nights together over the last month.

Juliet put down her coffee as if I suddenly required her full attention. "And you're happy with that—just sleeping together?"

"Yes, I don't want more." As I said the words they still felt like an absolute truth, but didn't comfort me as they had before. "I haven't changed my mind about that, but—"

Juliet waited patiently.

I took a sip of my coffee and shifted uncomfortably in my seat. "But I woke up wishing I'd told him it was my birthday today. Isn't that absurd?"

"No. That sounds like a very reasonable desire, Edwin."

"For most people. But it doesn't fit. How can I not be comfortable with more than seeing each other occasionally for the night, and also be disappointed that I couldn't spend today with him? If Tristan knew it was my birthday he'd have wanted to celebrate, or have done something thoughtful and painfully sweet. I don't want him to do things like that for me."

Juliet was giving me that tender expression again. She placed a hand gently on mine, which had been tapping out a nervous rhythm almost without me noticing. "To me, it sounds like you might actually want those things, but aren't ready for what opening up to more means for you."

I snorted and almost pulled my hand away. Juliet couldn't be right. But her statement rang true despite what I wanted to believe. "In that case I should probably stop seeing him."

Juliet retreated and picked up her coffee. "If you're uncomfortable then maybe you're right. There's nothing wrong with change taking time."

I bit into my scone and chewed. It was buttery and delicious, flavored with an expert balance of cinnamon and dates.

Change hadn't taken this much time for Juliet, but we didn't have the same problems, and she was younger. Besides, I wasn't fully admitting I wanted change beyond reengaging in an active sex life, but one thing was certain: I didn't want to go back to nothing.

Meaning, there was no way I'd actually stop seeing Tristan. Nothing had actually changed between us in the last month. We weren't getting any more involved. Part of me wanted to see him today and I'd needed to voice it, but in the end I'd done what I needed to. I'd kept Tristan at a distance even if my feelings about that were becoming complicated.

And if I were—hypothetically—ready to face a more committed arrangement with Tristan, what would that look like? I couldn't have taken him teleporting across the country with me to sit in Juliet's yard with her enchanted pony. He might be living with a Witch, but had no idea what world Avery and I existed in. I couldn't tell Tristan about the spectacular hundredth Juliet had arranged for me, or confide in him about the birthdays I'd had with Wyatt in seventies and eighties that I'd rather forget.

Reality was disappointing, but then it always had been. It was only another reason not to want these things.

Juliet and I finished our breakfast in companiable silence. She was used to me getting lost in my thoughts. Sometimes it was comforting just to be around her, knowing she understood I didn't always want to detail everything on my mind.

George came over to sniff the crumbs on the table.

I reached out to pat his soft nose and his breath tickled my palm. "We should go somewhere outrageous for dinner, like Paris or Tokyo."

Juliet gave me a sly look. "That sounds a whole lot like celebrating."

"Maybe I've decided I want to." I gave her a haughty look, making her laugh. "Here, I'll look up the time zones and restaurants and you can tell Mea the plan for the day."

# 16

## TRISTAN

Jonah lifted his head off his desk. "I feel like crap."

"Me too. Have you been like, *really* tired lately?" I fiddled with a wellness crystal Avery insisted I carry around in my pocket. Most of the time I forgot it at home.

Jonah groaned. "Only in meetings. I feel more achy than anything. I swear I twisted my ankle running last week and it's still not right."

He continued to detail his various aches and pains and so I returned the favor and whined about my sore head and persistent fatigue. This prompted Rochelle to pop her head over the partition between our desks to add her grievances to the list.

Looking around the floor, all of my colleagues seemed glum. Like, I wondered if I was imagining the almost comical levels of dreariness, but deep down I knew something was off about WMS.

For starters there was my continued inability to pay attention in meetings, which was maybe a me thing, except no matter how awake I thought I was, half the time I'd come away drained and unable to remember what we'd been up to. I'd fallen dead asleep in a meeting today, yet no one commented. It wasn't the first time, and nothing about that was normal.

The problem with WMS had to be more than my potentially poor work ethic. The oddness here couldn't just me being unaccustomed to the corporate grind, not after this many months. I was starting to think Avery's ideas about energy and moods affecting the world around us might not be so far-fetched.

Maybe I'd ask her to light a candle, or do one of her rituals for me.

WEEKS SLIPPED BY UNNOTICED.

I'd had no new messages from my mom but opening my email app still inspired a mess of anxiety. The stress wasn't good for my wellbeing, not that mom had ever been stellar for that, but I was really trying to look out for myself, supplements, healing 'spells' and all.

I saw Edwin occasionally and couldn't deny that always helped. I could forget about the other parts of my life when we were together, like he and I existed inside a bubble.

Edwin remained mysterious. He didn't like to talk about his work, and never mentioned friends. Not that he was cold, Edwin's evasiveness never came off as unkind, more like he didn't enjoy talking or thinking about himself. His interest in my life always felt genuine, and unlike other casual arrangements in my past, he never canceled or blew me off.

Jonah had noticed I was seeing someone, picking up on the small change in my life quicker than I'd have thought. His new campaign was to get me to bring my boyfriend out to drinks with the work crowd. I'd told him I didn't have a boyfriend. He'd only insisted he wanted to meet my guy.

Like that was ever gonna happen.

Edwin's mannerisms around the apartment with Avery were still as weird as they'd been that first morning. Combined with the other thing I'd observed about him, it got me thinking Edwin's aloofness was a cover for shyness, rather than arrogance as Owen and Aria claimed. Still, the reason Edwin and I didn't go out wasn't to do with that. We only met at each other's apartments. Any sort of meeting where the purpose wasn't solely sex was a boundary we weren't crossing for reasons that were murky at best.

One Friday night in early November I left work and a crowd of colleagues who were disappointed I wasn't coming for drinks to go to Edwin's place instead.

He'd hung a new painting in his entryway. Some modern abstract thing. It was stunning and weirdly cold. It looked kinda sad for a bunch of colors.

Edwin stood beside me staring at the painting. "Do you like it?"

I cocked my head, feeling my phone vibrate in my pocket with text after text, undoubtedly singing the praises of two-for-one cocktails. "It's pretty, in an unsettling way."

"Pretty?" Edwin chuckled, causing me to bristle.

"Like *so pretty*." I didn't know shit about art, but why would I? Sarcasm on the other hand—

"No, no. I agree, Tristan." Edwin draped his arm over my shoulders. "Its beauty somehow reminds me of us."

"How?" I looked closer at the painting. I wasn't getting that at all.

"I'm obviously projecting. The artist isn't even alive, it's not commissioned. Nothing to do with—it's a feeling, I guess."

I turned to face him, my hair catching under his arm now I was growing it out. "Is that why you bought it?"

"Mm. I like it." Edwin freed my curls and let his arm drop, his cheeks displaying a faint blush.

Okay—who bought art because it reminded them of their not-boyfriend? Well Edwin obviously, but what did that mean? His contradictory actions were baffling. I was alternately struck by his sweetness and disappointed by his detachment, and always overwhelmed by his intensity. Edwin didn't want to share his life with me but often seemed over-invested in the time we spent together, and then he went and did something like this. None of it added up.

I couldn't help noticing Edwin had hung the painting in the entryway where we'd, uh, had our reunion. I mean it was a natural spot for a big piece of art, on the wall across from the front door, but heat crept across my cheeks as the memory of us sparked in my mind.

Edwin looked at me like he knew exactly what I was thinking, his features shifting to something seductive. He had such control over his expressions, allowing the most subtle movements to transform him. I found it endlessly captivating.

Maybe this odd gesture was a shift, showing me there was depth to his feelings and thoughts of us. It wasn't subtle, but it was *something.*

"Want to go out tonight?" I asked as we turned away from the painting to walk down the hall. "Some friends are meeting up—"

Edwin stopped and peered at me, his expression completely unreadable. "Tristan, meeting friends isn't my scene. Sorry. I told you I don't date, and don't want your expectations of us to—" He made a vague gesture with his hand.

*But you hung a painting to commemorate us reuniting passionately like a pair of long-lost lovers,* my brain screamed. It was the most extra thing anyone had ever done in my direction and was in no way casual.

"I'm not talking dating, Edwin. Just a low-key drink to start the night off." I walked past him and continued on to the living room.

Damn it. Now I felt ridiculous for thinking the painting was a gesture even though he practically said it was. Really, it was nothing but a fancy signpost for why we weren't together saying: *you aren't part of this art-buying rich-guy world.* No amount of sexual compatibility made up for our differences. Why couldn't I accept that? Edwin didn't want to date me because I didn't fit his life, and I never would.

Edwin walked up to his fancy, fully stocked bar. "I can make you any drink you like right here." He looked over his shoulder and hit me with this shy little smile. It was the epitome of sincere affection.

The look threw me.

I was nothing but a helpless pinball pinging around with no idea what we were doing. Did he really not know that a fancy cocktail wasn't the point?

Edwin's smile slipped when I didn't respond. "Tristan, I don't mean to disappoint you. We can go out for a drink next time, if you really want. The two of us. I only want to be clear, I'm not after a relationship."

I wanted to ask why. Demand some actual clarity. But in the end, I'd rather enjoy the night for what it was than risk having to hear truths I didn't want to accept spoken out loud.

"I know. Never said I was either, Edwin."

# 17

# EDWIN

An awkward air settled over us as I stood at the bar, Tristan still on the other side of the room.

His expectations of our arrangement were shifting as I'd expected they would eventually, but the uncomfortable truth was I found it increasingly hard to deny that I wanted more too.

Trust had naturally crept into our dynamic and while it felt good in the moment, I wasn't entirely comfortable with it. Trusting Tristan only meant I was giving him the opportunity to break my trust. I still didn't want to let him in, but ever since my birthday I'd been wanting to spend more and more time with him.

I was constantly conflicted. Details about my life were messy, even disregarding Witchery. What if I showed Tristan something he didn't like? What if parts of me really were fundamentally unlikable and he soured on me? Tristan might never hurt me deliberately but that wasn't enough to make me give up the protections I'd clung to for decades.

So what did I really want here? What more could the two of us have if I couldn't accept the risks that came along with opening up in any context other than sex?

If only I could focus on what we had. Our sexual relationship was better than I'd hoped. I'd stopped holding back in that area at least, and had grown more comfortable communicating my desires. I liked to let Tristan lead, but no longer shied away from his direct questions about what I wanted or failed to make suggestions of my own.

It was the only way I'd found I could be emotionally open with him. Equating physical things and abstract yearnings helped me be comfortable with all the uncomfortable feelings that had been roiling around inside me. It helped me hide how much I was slowly sharing pieces of myself with him.

"Let's skip the drinks tonight." Tristan came over to me and pulled me away from the bar. He kissed me roughly, almost like he was claiming me. Or maybe he just felt pent up after a few extra days of not seeing each other.

My body responded quickly to his enthusiasm, and we abandoned the living room for the bedroom. Tristan teased me through my clothes so long the anticipation almost became unbearable. I begged him to undress me and soon we were in bed tangled together, slowly touching each other and kissing.

My insides fluttered as I focused on the weight of Tristan on top of me. I put my lips to his ear, feeling the smooth brush of his silver earrings as I whispered, "Would you fuck me?"

He pulled back, looking down with sharp—and I'd say—excited attention. "You want me to?"

I felt like sinking into the mattress. "I wouldn't have asked otherwise."

Tristan smiled and wiggled against me. "I just didn't realize you were interested."

I let myself blush for him without trying to hold back. "Well, I'm setting the record straight. It's—ah—been a long time since I've gone there with a partner. Is all."

Now wasn't the time to think about when I'd last been with

someone in this specific way, but I needed Tristan to know I hadn't done this in a while. And not for logistical reasons. I hadn't spent my solitary years, or recent lonely nights, without self-pleasures. But unlike our first night, I wanted Tristan to get a sense of what was actually going on with me.

He kissed my cheeks, following my freckles over the bridge of my nose with featherlight lips. "I'd love to do this with you, Edwin. If you're sure?"

"Yes. I want you, Tristan. Please." I let myself beg and released my desperation into the air between us.

His eyes dazzled me in a bright, fiery brown. "I want you too, Edwin."

I pulled his mouth down to meet mine before he said anything more, scared of all the possibilities Tristan offered me.

Even if I couldn't have it all, I could have this.

My concentration didn't stray from Tristan as he slowly undid me. I gave in to my emotional nerves enough that he seemed to sense it in my movements and hear it in my noises. He soothed me with whispered words, sure fingers and wet lips.

Tristan fucked me like I'd always wanted, tenderly but not at all tentative. I wouldn't call it making love when it couldn't be. We weren't in love. I didn't even know why I thought about it like that. Maybe I didn't know any other way to describe something this good.

Regardless of what I called it, I was able to hand over everything I wanted to give.

LATER WE LAY ABOUT KISSING, tangled together as we'd been before. Neither of us talked for the longest time.

The mood might have turned heavy—for me at least, as the weight I'd put on this spun around in my head—but Tristan was all smiles. He was relaxed and his grin took on that genuine, lopsided quality I adored.

As Tristan's energy slowly came back to him, he playfully ran his fingers through my hair and down my neck, teasing me and almost tickling me until I smiled.

"There it is," he whispered, trailing a fingertip along my lips.

I was determined to get out of my own head. I didn't necessarily want Tristan to know how much tonight meant to me. It was key that he only saw pieces of me, so we should talk to lighten the mood.

This was perhaps my favorite time to talk. I just didn't know where my voice had gone tonight.

Maybe I should apologize for letting Tristan down earlier, and not going out when he wanted—but no, I wasn't doing that anymore. I didn't need to apologize or do something I didn't want to do. His desires didn't come before my comfort. I didn't want to share my social anxieties with Tristan and didn't need to feel guilty about them, or act like managing them came second to everyone else.

When I couldn't be the 'legendary Authority Witch,' I no longer knew who to be, or how to act. I didn't know how Tristan would want me to be around his friends. He'd expect I'd be nice at least, not rude and standoffish. He'd assume I'd be the way I was with him.

I didn't know how to do that. And didn't want to try. Not around nameless people I'd never met before. The fear of their rejection would leave me scattered if I was trying to get them to actually like me.

Somehow Tristan fell outside my uncertainty and it was easy to relax with him. Especially in moments like this. Was this who I really was? This man loosened by sexual satisfaction and left open, reaching out for connection?

If so, I didn't know how to be this man in any other context, for anyone but Tristan, and I certainly didn't know how to be likable around his friends. Which was for the best. I may have given certain things away tonight—in my own veiled way—but that was more than enough. Too much, probably.

Tristan stretched, reached for my hand and interlaced our fingers. He had purple nails tonight. I ran the fingers of my other hand over his, across his knuckles and down to the soft underside of his wrist.

He wiggled and squeezed my hand.

I noticed two small red marks on Tristan's wrist partially hidden by his tattoo. I ran my thumb over them. They were raised, the skin inflamed and felt almost as if— No, surely not.

I was only paranoid because of all the blood siphoning talk at work. The black market investigation was progressing at a glacial pace, my lead at the pawn shop going stale. Even so, I pulled Tristan's wrist closer to examine the marks.

There was the faintest trace of magic lingering on his skin.

"There's bugs in the couch." Tristan pulled his arm away and itched the spots.

"What?" I almost choked on the word, my mouth suddenly dry.

"In the apartment. Something's been biting me when I sit on the couch."

"Biting you?" I sat up abruptly, shifting Tristan off me so only his head rested on my thigh, his dark hair fanned out on my pale skin. I leaned back against the cool headboard and tried to think.

How the hell could Tristan have blood-siphon marks on his wrist?

He turned to look up at me. "It's no big deal. It's not like there's a bug problem infesting the whole apartment. I haven't even seen any around. I just get a few random bites when I fall asleep in the living room. I'm sure I'll be able to sort it out, only Avery is particular about non-organic spray."

"Does she get bitten too?"

"Nah, don't think so. I'm too sweet or something fucking dumb like that." Tristan rolled his eyes.

Damn her. If these were siphon marks, and there was no doubt about it, she was stealing his blood. A surge of adrenalin shot through me. Tristan had been complaining he was unwell and over tired.

"What did Avery say about the bites?" I surprised myself with an even tone that hid my anxiety well.

This wasn't supposed to happen. This wasn't what tonight was about.

Tristan rubbed his wrist again. "Avery thinks I'm overreacting. I think she's in denial that something is hiding in one of her plants."

"You can't go back there." This time my words didn't come out even. They were sharp and commanding, surprising me as much as the man lying against me.

Tristan sat up and looked at me with narrowed eyes. "Why?"

My hint of anxiety was becoming full-blown panic, making me feel close to sick. I didn't like the sharp attention Tristan was giving me. All trace of his blissed out, post-sex haze was gone.

I tried to think of a justification for my outrageous demand. "Y-you can't live like this. You can't have something biting you."

Tristan laughed. "It's not a big deal. I've lived way worse places. Avery's apartment is so not a problem—it's great except this one small thing."

I should agree. It was what he expected. But I couldn't let Tristan wander back into harm's way unaware. I had the urge to protect him. He was everything to me, even if I was too cowardly to say it. The least I could do was not let him be assaulted in his own home.

I had to get across the gravity of the situation. I pointed at his wrist. "What if this is what's making you sick?"

"That's ridiculous. Bug bites don't cause fatigue. It's not like a vampire is sucking my blood. Draining my life force." Tristan made fangs with his fingers, mouth open and hissed absurdly at me.

"Obviously vampires aren't real, but something is—" I couldn't think fast enough. How did I solve this? I could have Avery brought in, but how the hell would I explain coming across her crime without involving Tristan? Whatever I did, I needed to keep him away from her until she was dealt with.

"Nothing is sucking my blood. These aren't *fang* marks." Tristan laughed again. "Oh my god, you look so serious, Edwin. Why are you worried?"

I felt weak. Why was I acting like this? "You've been complaining about being tired."

"The doctor said I have low iron. It's fine." Tristan was dismissive but sterner than before, like he was telling me something unquestionable.

All I could think was, how much blood was Avery talking? He shouldn't be suffering serious side effects unless—

Tristan interrupted my thoughts with a playful swat at my chest. "Iron is a blood thing, though. Maybe it is a vampire!" He was messing with me, and on the verge of giggly, but I couldn't collect myself enough to play along. "Why're you so interested, Edwin? Huh? Like oh my god, imagine if *you* were a vampire. I'd so be freaking out right now."

Tristan devolved into full on giggles like he was having a great time. I was in shock, wrung out from an emotional whirlwind. He took advantage of my position, sitting up against the headboard and straddled me. Our naked bodies rubbed together. Tristan leaned in and kissed my neck.

"Are you like five hundred years old? Here to take advantage of little innocent me?" he crooned before licking my neck.

My pulse jumped to my throat. It was a joke. "I'm not five hundred," I managed to say.

"And I'm not innocent." Tristan had a wicked, sexy note to his voice. He nipped at my neck.

I was too off balance to be enticed. I needed to fix this so we could go back to the soft, almost loving mood of a few minutes ago. My hands slipped around Tristan's waist, pushing his back slightly. "You could stay here."

Tristan stopped his worshiping of my neck to look me in the eye. "I mean yeah, I was planning on staying over tonight."

"No. I mean, yes. How about on a longer-term basis?" I knew this wasn't the right thing to say but couldn't stop myself. Tristan couldn't move in with me, but he couldn't go back to that apartment until Avery was gone.

I had no idea why my mind jumped straight to sharing a home. What was happening to me?

"Wait—live with you? Because of a few bug bites?" Tristan looked sure it was a joke, but when I didn't speak, his expression soured. "Seriously? I said it wasn't a big deal, Edwin. My house is fine. Not everyone can be rich and perfect like you. That doesn't mean I'm some poor guy needing your sympathy. You don't need to rescue me. I'm doing great on my own."

My stomach dropped. "That's not—"

Tristan's face settled into something hard, like he was done messing around and putting up with me and all my shit. "Well, what did you mean? Why ask me that now? You won't even date me!"

He was right. *Fuck.* The hint of pain in his voice sent my anxiety to a new place. "I'm sorry, Tristan. Please. I'm just worried."

"Again, because I have a few red spots on my wrist?"

Tristan looked at me like he'd never seen me before, then removed himself from my lap. "Maybe I'll head home after all."

I reached out for him, only to pull back my hand in mute horror as he climbed out of bed. "No, I'm sorry. You don't have to go. I'm being ridiculous."

Tristan pulled on his underwear. "Yeah, you are. Why though?"

I had no idea how to answer. My actions were as much a mystery to me as they seemed to be to him. *I should be able to handle this better*. Sorting out this kind of magical misuse was my damn job. I'd been keeping magical secrets for over a century. But Tristan wasn't just anyone. He should know he was different.

I swallowed. "I care about you. I'm only trying to help."

He gave me an exasperated look full of confusion and hurt. "I'm not sleeping with you because I need you to look after me. Try caring about me without being condescending. Let me in. Talk to me. Don't try to fix my life when I didn't ask."

No. That wasn't what I meant.

I climbed out of bed, almost tripping. I hastily pulled on a robe. "I'm sorry, Tristan. Please stay. I'll make it up to you."

"How? In bed?" He pointed at the rumpled sheets in accusation.

"I—" That was what I had in mind, and all I apparently had to offer, but his tone was not inviting.

"I know that's all this is, but *fucking hell*." Tristan picked up my shirt and threw it at me. It fell to the floor. "I do have some self-respect, and I dunno, expect to be treated like an equal. You can't just take me to bed, then insult me, and expect another orgasm to fix it like nothing else matters. Like I won't notice what little you think of me."

I tried to run through our conversation to figure out what he was talking about but was too scattered. "No—that's not—I didn't insult you."

"Didn't you? Acting like I can't take care of myself? Like you know better? Expecting you can give me *nothing* and still ask me to alter my life for you? A drink out was a big fucking deal, but also I should live with you? You don't care about me or what I want, Edwin, only what you want from me." Tristan's eyes shone in the low light, his cheeks red with anger.

My chest was hollow and my stomach in shreds. "No. Please—I don't give you nothing. That's not—" Something deep inside me stole my voice.

How would Tristan know I shared so much tonight when even the things I gave I kept hidden? I looked at him, feeling stricken, and saw a new level of disappointed wash over his face at my failure to speak.

Tristan let out a heavy sigh and pulled on his shirt. "See, you can't even deny it. Whatever this thing is we're doing—I'm done."

"Please, darling—" I scrambled for what to say, feeling like I was falling, and still came up with nothing.

In the back of my mind, I envisioned myself shouting *I love you*. But I didn't, that wasn't what this was. I barely knew him, and he didn't know me at all. So why was losing him pulling me apart?

Tristan stared at me, waiting. He wasn't expecting love but he was expecting more than the nothing he thought I was giving him.

The assurances Tristan needed to hear weren't ones I was willing to say—due in part to magic but really, this was just who I was.

Tristan pulled at his hair in frustration, swiping it back from his face and looking around the room, likely for his pants. He turned back to me. "Please what? If it's not nothing, what is this? What do you want?"

*Everything*. But if this moment proved anything, it was that I couldn't actually have more than our casual affair without screwing it up.

"You know what I want, Tristan. This is just a misunderstanding."

Tristan's hardened manner didn't relent. He put a hand on his hip. "Explain it then. What am I missing?"

"I—I don't know—" I clutched at my robe, twisting it in a tight fist.

He turned away and finished dressing in a hurry, barely looking at me.

Helpless to stop him, I walked Tristan out. After the door shut the whole ridiculous conversation bounced around the empty walls of my too-large apartment, making my head ache.

The place felt haunted without him.

## 18

## EDWIN

The next morning, I set myself up on a cross street corner near Tristan's apartment to wait for Avery.

It was a quiet Saturday. I did nothing for hours but ruffle my newspaper as Mortals walked by, running through everything from last night's argument in my head, trying to see it as Tristan had. Some of the things he'd said had seemed to come out of nowhere, giving me the sense I'd been missing a whole lot more than siphon marks on my lover's wrist.

He easily believed I was the kind of person who'd tell him what to do, demand he change his life without consulting him, and that hurt on so many levels. I'd never try to control or manipulate anyone. And not only because that was what Wyatt had done to me; it was wrong, and the thought of people not being able to make their own choices maddened me. I knew how bad it could get, what it was like for someone to disregard you completely and see you as a thing that existed solely for them. Giving that impression to Tristan without realizing made me doubt everything about how I'd handled myself with him.

Tristan still thought I didn't care about him, and maybe he was right in a way. Not that I only cared what I could get from him, but that I cared more for myself than I did for him. My actions always put me first. Sometimes that was necessary, especially after living a life where I was no one's priority, not even my own. But I didn't like where that mentality had taken me.

I had no idea what to do about it all or if I could fix it. I wanted to show Tristan that wasn't who I was.

With no way to solve the problem of what, if anything, came next for Tristan and me, I tried to focus on the more immediate issue. The situation with Avery was tricky. There was no evidence of a crime other the residual magic on Tristan's skin. I couldn't go dragging him into Witch-court to get an arrest warrant, so I'd need a confession from the culprit, or some other physical evidence, to justify bringing her in.

Hopefully Avery's knowledge of who I was would be enough to get her to talk. She'd recognized my name when we'd met and been skittish whenever I was at the apartment. Perhaps she'd acted that way, not due to my reputation and legendary magical power, but because she was committing crimes right under my nose. I was a fool for not seeing the problem sooner.

Avery and Tristan's apartment was full of magic, but nothing sinister or illegal. I'd scrutinized the spells cast on the dwelling the first time I'd come over. They were mostly standard protections and enchantments to help the various plants grow. Avery wasn't casting blood-spells at home, so it was likely she was selling what she was stealing from Tristan.

At last Avery emerged from the apartment building. She didn't head in my direction, so I folded the newspaper I'd been pretending to read and strode after her.

I thew the paper in a trashcan right as I caught up to her. "Miss Heyde."

Avery jumped, looking around. "Oh. Hi, Mr. Bickel. Tristan's back at the apartment." She turned to go.

I kept pace with her. "I'm here to see you, actually."

She stopped. "W-why's that?"

I adopted the superior, bored tone I was known for. "Don't you think we should talk? There's quite a lot of magic in Tristan's life for an unsuspecting Mortal."

"I'm not going to Tell Tristan about magic," Avery said in a rush. "I know who you are."

"Do you?" I leveled an icy stare.

She took a half-step away from me. "Sure. Uh. Rumors, you know. I never thought I'd find *you* dating a Mortal." She laughed nervously.

Her causal assumption gave me a hot flash, almost like embarrassment. Was she laughing at me? What did she mean? There shouldn't be rumors circulating about me, other than the ones I'd cultivated. Avery shouldn't have heard anything about my personal life. All those stories were decades old and contained within the Authority.

"You think you know anything about me? You utter fool," I snapped, covering all my other emotions with anger.

"Hey!" Avery crossed her arms and glared. "No need to be a dick. Why are you sneaking up on me in the street, huh?"

"You've been caught." I projected smugness, reveling in how acting like this washed everything else away. My face was a hard mask. This persona didn't crack, the resulting man I became didn't take shit or care about anything, and I could almost ignore all the cold dread pooling inside me.

Avery gave another nervous laugh and took a step as if to walk away. I didn't make any move to stop her, not needing to do more than track her with an unblinking stare.

The color drained from her face and she stopped. "Caught doing what? Magic in my own home. Tristan's skeptical as hell. There's no risk he'll believe when I'm not trying to enlighten him."

I scoffed. "You thought I wouldn't notice?"

"Notice what? I'm not doing anything." She avoided my gaze, her voice wavering.

I casually flicked my wrist, stretching my arm so my suit jacket pulled back, exposing soft skin and faintly outlined veins. Then I let my eyes do the rest.

People assumed my stare was part of my magic, but it was a mundane talent, only giving the impression I could see more than you wanted to reveal.

Avery couldn't take her eyes off my wrist. "I-I'm not doing anything." Her words came out in a fearful whisper.

I tapped my exposed skin and her eyes flicked up and were caught by my cold ones. "A few little marks say otherwise."

Tears spilled onto the young Witch's cheeks.

I shook out my sleeves and folded my hands behind my back. "Did you think you were slyer than me? Doing this under my nose?"

"I had no choice." Avery swiped at her tear-filled eyes.

I shrugged, letting my frigid disapproval go and replacing it with boredom. "You'll face the court all the same."

Distantly, I wondered if this uncaring aspect of my persona had crept into my actual personality. Tristan might think so. But, I was supposed to act like a prick here, with Avery. No one liked Bickel and now was not the time to change that.

Avery shook her head. "Please, I'm sorry. I can explain."

"I'd expect you to. That's not an enticement. Cooperate and maybe—"

The Witch's cheeks bloomed in splotchy red as she raised her voice. "I had no choice! I—I wasn't hurting him."

"Yes, you were." My restraint snapped and I stepped into Avery's personal space, looking down my nose at her.

"Hey!" A familiar voice yelled from down the street. My heart sank as Tristan rushed up to us. "What the hell are you doing?" he shouted as he stepped in front of Avery, shielding her from me. "Why are you yelling at Avery?"

"I wasn't yelling." Sudden dizziness clouded my head. There was no way to explain. I'd screwed myself beyond hope of ever reconciling with him.

Tristan looked as though he despised me. "I fucking heard you. Why are you here, Edwin? This can't be about the bug bites!"

Avery grabbed his arm. "Tristan, it's okay. Just go home."

He turned to her. "What do you mean it's okay? Of course it's not. What's going on?"

"Tristan—" I reached out and he backed away.

"No, Edwin. Just stop. You make no fucking sense. I said we were done. Are you following me? Harassing my roommate? What are you playing at?" The rage pouring off Tristan was palpable and my chest became so tight I feared I was going to have a heart attack.

The urge to explain overwhelmed me. If he knew the whole truth, he wouldn't be mad. If he knew, he wouldn't leave me.

Not that I ever had him.

I felt myself cracking. If he knew we could be together. I could give him everything with nothing held back. The wild thought made me blind with hope. I wanted to be Tristan's so bad it had to be wrong. A red flag. Nothing should be as potent as my need for him. It went against everything I'd built to keep myself together and protected from hurt.

Except this hurt a hell of a lot in itself.

No. I couldn't Tell him about magic. Not like this. That was a bigger risk than letting him in and this wasn't the right way to go about it. Blurting out the truth wouldn't happen without consequence.

Tristan's anger only seemed to grow in response to my silence. He shook his head and turned to Avery. "Come on."

"I can't let her get away with what she's done to you. It's my job." I clenched my fists at my sides and took a step after them. *Am I really doing this?*

Avery looked at me in silent shock as if she'd had a similar thought.

"Done to me? Your job?" Tristan practically growled, voice still raised. "Just 'cause you're a PI doesn't mean you can stalk people!"

Avery tugged on Tristan's arm. "He isn't stalking me."

"Don't defend him." Tristan pulled Avery close so they were pressed side to side. "Let's go. We don't have to listen to this."

Avery gave me a helpless look. Tristan didn't miss it. I could practically feel his confusion, but nothing cut through his anger or urge to protect who he thought was his friend. He turned and walked away from me without another word.

It couldn't end this way, not when I still wanted so many things I hadn't had the time to come to terms with.

I rushed after them.

I didn't know what I was going to do, only that I couldn't let this happen. Tristan could leave me if he wanted—we'd never been together—but he couldn't leave me for reasons that weren't true. He deserved an informed choice. I deserved a real chance.

Damn everything to hell.

I grabbed Tristan's hand and spun him around. He looked like he might hit me.

"*Darling, please*." My voice was strangled, on the verge of tears.

He pulled his hand from mine. "Don't darling me. There's nothing you can say."

"We're Witches!" I didn't let myself think, only went with my deepest, most burning desire. "Magic is real and I'm a Witch. So is Avery. She's been siphoning your blood. The bites. The fatigue. That's why I freaked out!"

Avery gasped.

Tristan didn't seem to know where to look. His eyes roved over me, then flitted to Avery and back again. Confusion seemed to finally win out and he deflated. "Come on. Edwin, what's happening with you? Are—are you okay?"

Closing my eyes momentarily, I took a deep breath.

He probably thought I was having some sort of delusion. At least he'd stopped yelling.

I could still back out and be sensible. Tristan's moment of belief hadn't hit yet. However, it was now too late for me. The only way was forward. Perhaps this had been coming since I'd met Tristan in that hotel. All this time I'd been on the slow, slippery road to giving in despite knowing better.

My heart finally won out, and I resigned myself to letting the rest fall where it may.

I opened my eyes to find Tristan's concerned expression focused on me. "I'll explain everything. Here. I can show you magic. If you feel nauseous, don't worry. That's normal, all right Tristan?" I took his hand.

He didn't pull away. "Edwin, what?"

I held his hand tight. "Magic is real. I'll take you home and we'll talk about it. I'll explain everything."

"Oh-kay—" Tristan sounded out the word like he didn't know what else to do but agree.

I pulled us through negative space, teleporting us in an instant to the living room of his apartment.

Tristan swayed.

I caught him and held him firmly against me. "It's all right. Just nausea. It happens to everyone and will pass soon."

He groaned and dry-retched as his body reacted to the disorientation of unnatural space travel. I held him steady, his face pressed close to mine.

The moment Tristan realized magic was real was tangible.

As the disorientation subsided, he looked around the room and there was a subtle popping sensation in the air.

Tristan dug his fingers into my shoulders and held me painfully tight. He trembled, taking a shaky breath.

"You're all right," I said in my most tender voice.

He squeezed me harder, in a grip that would surely bruise. "How is this happening? How did we get here?"

"Magic. I'm a Witch who has the unique ability to manipulate space and time. I teleported us."

"No." Tristan shook his head, his eyes wide. "That's not possible. It's a trick."

Tristan looked at me with the most lost expression I'd ever seen. It was pure innocent confusion. No one wanted their world changed this drastically without warning. I knew that in theory, but hadn't been ready for the reality. I needed to ease Tristan's fear, and hoped desperately that he wouldn't regret that I'd done this.

I swallowed. "Magic makes it possible. Witches like me can do all sorts of things."

"What the *hell*?" Tristan gave my shoulders a little shake. He let his forehead drop to my chest and laughed. It was too manic to be relieving, but maybe we were heading in the right direction.

I stroked his hair in the way I knew he liked best. "I'm sorry. I didn't know how to show you in a way that wouldn't shock you. Are you okay, Tristan?"

He straightened up and gave me a gentle shove, putting space between us. "No. This is in no way okay. Or real. Are you fucking kidding me? I mean—I mean—Are you sure we aren't on drugs? Or—I dunno—something?"

"Most certainly not. Nor are we under a spell."

He frowned. "A spell—"

"I've never used magic on you, Tristan," I said in a hurry.

"How would I know?" He eyes went wide in alarm. "You said —Avery—" He looked wildly around, eyes landing on the couch, then shifting to his wrist. When his gaze found mine, it was pleading.

Oh god, this was going to get worse before it got better.

I ran a hand through my hair. "Avery is a Witch. She's been siphoning your blood. I'm sorry I didn't realize sooner. I'm sorry I handled this so badly. I should have done better last night, but I upset you and it made everything worse. I'm so sorry for the confusion and making you think I didn't care and all those things you said."

Tristan didn't appear to be listening. "Avery can't be a Witch."

"Look around." I spread my arms outward. "She's the most blatant Witch I've met in years."

"No. It's just. It's just—" He picked up a candle and turned, gesturing wildly around about the room. "She's just quirky!"

"No one's this quirky, Tristan. These symbols, the crystals. It's all part of magic."

Tristan glared at the magical items surrounding us, the look of panic in his eyes growing more pronounced. It settled on me. He put the candle down. "She's—what did you say she's doing to me?"

My gut twisted at having to explain this to him knowing it was only going to make him feel worse. "Avery is siphoning your blood. That's where the marks are coming from, not bug bites."

"No—she can't be. She—I thought she was my friend." Tristan choked on the last word and looked away from me.

I didn't know how to comfort Tristan, or cushion the reality of lost trust without denying or minimizing Avery's betrayal, so I fell back on facts. "What she's done is illegal. It won't happen again. You have my word."

"She's stealing my blood? But why?" Tristan wiped at his

eyes before any tears could fall. "I don't get it. You said vampires weren't real!"

"They aren't. Mortal blood is a powerful substance used for certain types of magic."

Tristan wrinkled his nose. "Fucking yuck."

"Indeed." I couldn't help smiling faintly.

Tristan echoed my grin, but it looked ghostly. He fidgeted uncomfortably. "This is too much, Edwin. The blood, *this* is why I'm unwell? Because of what Avery did to me?"

I nodded.

"But she kept trying to help. Giving me all the vitamins and tea and shit. Nothing makes sense." He sat down on the couch as if in defeat, cradling his head in his hands, sending his long curls falling in front of his face, his purple nails bright against his black hair. "Last night—why not tell me everything then?"

"I'm not supposed to Tell. Witches have to keep magic secret —to protect Mortals. There are rules." I took off my jacket, suddenly feeling too hot. I let it fall on the couch.

"Why not break the rule last night?" Tristan looked up at me, red-rimmed eyes wide and pleading.

I opened my mouth but nothing came out.

Why was this so hard? I'd gone for the big secret, but that didn't make anything easier between us. Revealing magic gave us an opportunity, it put us in the same room, but didn't fix my inability to trust or share things that mattered.

*So now what?* I tried not to panic when I still couldn't give Tristan what he wanted. I couldn't open up about all the reasons I personally never planned to Tell him about magic. They were too wrapped up in why I wouldn't date and what was going on between us. I couldn't go there, so I said nothing at all.

An echo of the expression he'd worn last night appeared on Tristan's face. "You let me walk away when I didn't have to."

"I—" My hands fluttered uselessly. "None of this was planned, Tristan."

He chewed on his lip frowning more severely that I'd have thought him capable of. "You'd rather have kept magic secret? And have me leave?"

"If I'd rather that, we wouldn't be here. It just took me a night of panicking to decide I should throw all my principles out the window and Tell you." I flopped on the couch next to him, dropping my head back to look at the ceiling. "I didn't want you to walk away. Not at all, but especially not like that. It hurt both of us—and you're right, it didn't have to."

Tristan sat up from his crouch and leaned against my side. "I don't know what to make of any of this."

I encircled him with my arm and he pressed his face into my shoulder. "It's okay to be unsure—afraid," I whispered, unable to escape the fact I was talking to myself as well as him.

Tristan put his arm around my waist and we held each other tight as my breathing shallowed and my throat burned. I wondered if I was going to cry.

No tears came. I caught my breath and tried to collect myself. "This will all be less shocking with time. Please know I won't ever use magic on you. You don't have to fear magic, despite what's happened with Avery. I've got you. Looking after your wellbeing is my responsibility now."

Tristan tensed in my arms. "Why? I'm an adult. Not anyone's responsibility."

"Yes, but I Told you about magic. Like I said, there are rules. I have to be responsible for the consequences of bringing you into the Witchy world. There's a lot to explain about Witches and our laws. I didn't go about revealing the secret the right way, so we'll have to go to court—"

Tristan jolted away from me. "*What!*"

I shifted to face him squarely. "Don't worry. They'll give us time before we're summoned. I'll handle everything. You can ask Owen, he and Aria had to go. I'll have to guide you through the system and ways of our world." I was rambling, but suddenly it was important he know I was fully committed to this, if nothing else. "It will be all right, Tristan. I won't let any of this negatively impact you, I promise. And if you're mad I Told, you can tell the court. They'll fix it, if you want."

"Wait. *Owen* knows about all this?" Tristan's last shred of composure vanished in disbelief. I didn't know if he'd heard anything else I'd said.

*Hell.* That wasn't something to spring on him. Finding out the person who meant more to him than anyone had kept a secret like this wasn't something Tristan should have to wrap his head around right now. I should have known better. But I wasn't thinking. This whole Telling had the makings of a disaster. I was handling everything poorly, creating more problems than I was solving.

"Is nothing normal? Is everyone in on it?" Tristan's voice was strained. "You probably aren't even a private investigator, are you? Everyone's what? Just lying to me?"

"No. Well—yes and no. Not everyone is lying. I'm an investigator for the magical Authority, kind of like Witchy law enforcement. I do freelance PI work with Juliet on occasion."

Tristan's expression was blank. "She's a Witch?"

"Yes. Juliet is a Witch. So is Aria. She Told Owen about magic a year and a half ago." *God, if only facts could rescue me.* But I suspected I was still saying all the wrong things.

"I need—I—I don't know—" Tristan looked pale. "I don't know what I need." Tears filled his eyes again. "I don't know what to think. Not about any of this. I don't know what's going on. I don't know anything. Except that everything's a lie."

I pulled him close. His body was vibrating with tension. "Not a lie, just not the whole truth. Understanding will come."

Tristan gave me a wild look full of exasperation and something I couldn't quite place. Maybe he was about to start shouting again. But instead he crushed me into a kiss. He was a force, pushing me back into the couch, fisting his hands in my hair.

"Edwin, I can never think straight around you." The way he was kissing me left no room for my reply. "All I know is I want you. You're a liar and I don't fucking get you, but I still want you more than anything."

Tristan's tears spilled onto my face as he kissed me. I held him back long enough to wipe his eyes. He blinked rapidly.

"Tristan—" I was silenced by his hand on my lips.

"Please," he whispered, squirming against me.

I pressed my lips to his forehead. "Last night you didn't want me to pretend to fix things with sex. I think we should follow that logic now too."

"I just want to feel good for a little while." He grabbed at the front of my waistcoat with a desperation I'd never seen in him.

I almost gave in.

Was sex the only way I could make Tristan feel good? I wanted to be more than a physical comfort for him.

My hands carefully covered his. "Let's find another way."

Tristan huffed, letting go of me. "Okay. Fine, let's talk. Go for it, Edwin. Tell me where this is all going. Tell me what you really want from us." He waved his hand in a flourish.

And I fucking froze.

# 19

# TRISTAN

Edwin didn't suddenly open up and tell all. He didn't say anything.

My disappointment wasn't surprising. He never said anything. Why would that suddenly change?

Maybe it was for the best, everything he'd said so far only left me more lost than before.

I got off the couch, turned in a circle and tried to pace the crowded room. Adrenalin was doing odd things to my emotions. I was oscillating between highs and lows at a sickening rate, my thoughts a jumbled mess.

Magic was too much to process. Its existence was beyond shocking but didn't explain or excuse everything. The only thing magic cleared up was Edwin's erratic behavior over the last twenty-four hours. It lent no clarity to *us,* or our dynamic. Edwin still confused the hell out of me, acting like he cared only to backpedal or not follow through if it meant opening up in any way, not matter how small.

"Tristan—" Edwin said my name like it was the start of a thought, a conversation, but nothing followed. As usual, his face gave nothing away and I had no clue what he was thinking.

God forbid he tell me.

I was sick of asking for more and being shut down. I was done being the only one taking risks. Done opening myself up time and again, only to be met with confused nothings.

Why Tell me about magic if he was going to stop there? Why couldn't he admit that not wanting me to walk away over a misunderstanding meant this thing between us wasn't disposable, or was I really just that wrong about everything?

The apartment door opened with an ominous creak.

Avery. I whirled around to face her as she entered the cluttered living room. Her eyes were puffy, her face drawn. As she came closer, I recoiled instinctively. You'd think magic would be fun and exciting, but finding out it existed and was used on you without your knowledge killed that pretty quick.

"I'm sorry, Tristan." Avery wrung her hands, looking distraught. Not that I could trust how she was acting. She'd only been lying to me this whole time.

"I thought we were friends." More tears streaked down my cheeks. "But you—you were sucking my blood!"

Avery reached out helplessly and I shifted further away, though my progress was hampered by the tree fern. "We are friends, Tristan. I'm so sorry!" Her posture drooped. "I didn't mean to hurt you. I swear."

"But you did." My throat burned. Everyone around me knew about magic, yet left me alone, falling head-first into it.

"It wasn't my choice!" Avery looked at me imploringly. "They forced me. I don't know why you were feeling so sick, Tristan. I was doing everything to help. All the teas, nutritious food, little health spells. I wasn't taking that much blood. I don't understand!"

"But you were stealing my blood. *Why?* Don't you get how fucked that is? You seemed so nice, Avery. I want to say this isn't like you." I laughed humorlessly.

Avery straightened like she was steeling herself. "Yes, I was taking your blood. I know it's fucking wrong. I'd put you into a trance when you were on the couch and I hated it, but—but—I only took small amounts."

"Why?" My voice came out near a shout.

Avery stumbled back and almost knocked over a chili plant. She steadied herself and readjusted the pot, not looking at me. "My mom died recently. I didn't know she had debt, and not to the bank. They came to collect, said I had to pay a lump sum, but that was impossible. They wouldn't take monthly payments, not in cash, only blood. Then you moved in. I had nowhere else to get the blood payment. I thought you wouldn't notice."

"Who are *they*?" Edwin asked from the couch, calm as ever.

Avery turned toward him. "There's a magical pawn shop not far from here. The owner gives out dodgy loans with ridiculous conditions. I can't believe my mom signed. I couldn't get out of the contract. The conditions shifted with her death, cursing me to repay them. Under life penalty."

"Hm. Are you talking about Mystic Pawn?" Edwin waited for Avery to nod. "I hadn't heard Al did loans. He kept that unusually quiet." Edwin sounded almost bored, like all this was routine.

He'd sent me through the wringer; *not* Telling me, then *Telling* me about magic, all because he'd been freaking out about what Avery was doing. Now it was like he didn't care about any of it.

"I'm so sorry, Tristan." Avery turned back to me pleadingly.

Both of them—fuck—I was tired and didn't want to be here.

I looked at Edwin, cool and collected on the couch, no visible trace of how devastated he'd been pleading with me out on the street, or how he'd held me and said not to be afraid like he'd needed to hear it even more than I did.

I had nothing more to say to him if I was the only one capable of being open.

I checked my pockets for my wallet and phone. “I’m going out.”

Edwin stood up. “Tristan, we need to discuss a few things. I have a responsibility here.”

Not, *Tristan, please don’t go. I want you to stay.*

“I don’t know what we have to talk about, Edwin. You said you worked for magic law enforcement.” I gestured to Avery. “Seems like there’s work to do. Or is it okay for Witches to hold Avery hostage like that, make her steal my literal blood?”

“No, the contract sounds highly illegal. Even if blood wasn’t stipulated in the wording, using a magical agreement to curse someone to obtain it isn’t—”

“Right.” I crossed the room to the hall. “You two work that out. You hurt me, Avery, like emotionally. I’m sorry you were in such an awful position, but I can’t do this right now.”

So I left.

# 20

# EDWIN

Entering the Authority building on Sunday to begin dealing with Avery's situation was stifling. The place wasn't as busy as it'd be tomorrow, but Witches were always here, weekend or no.

For a judicial enterprise, confidentiality within the organization was bafflingly non-existent in some instances. Like Telling. Everyone seemed to know that Edwin Bickel had Told a Mortal about magic without approval.

The enchantments monitoring Mortal knowledge had revealed Tristan's and my identities to the compliance department. That small pop had been like a beacon, naming me as the one to reveal Witchery to Tristan. I didn't see why anyone felt sharing the news around the rest of the Authority was appropriate, but I could tell people knew by the way they watched me from the moment I arrived.

I locked my emotions down as I moved through the building. Acting like a coldhearted bastard was my coping mechanism. Except, in this case, I feared my rigid persona was part of what made my recent actions so intriguing to my colleagues.

Nothing this surprising had happened since Judge Herrera's

downfall. That had been dire, this was more sensational, but it didn't help that I'd been involved in both instances.

Judge Raven was waiting in my office, staring out the window, when I arrived. I held back my surprise. The move was both rude and an annoying little power play on his part, so I ignored him and went to sit behind my desk.

"You're full of surprises, Edwin. I think it's safe to say no one saw this coming. Why'd you do it?" He gave me a look of mild curiosity, his dark gray hair slicked back, matching the color of his drab suit.

"That will be outlined in court." I turned on my computer and waited for my email to boot up.

Raven walked casually away from the window to stand before my desk. "I thought you might like to explain yourself sooner."

"Not really." I clicked the mouse to make it seem like I was busy even though the program was still loading.

The judge didn't appear impressed. "I'd never have thought you'd be caught out by love. Again."

"What? Who said anything about love?" I gaped at him, horrified, both at his causal mention of my past and that he had the gall to refer to what had been between Wyatt and me as love.

Raven gave me a twisted, smug smile. "Love of one sort or another always makes people Tell. I'd have thought *you'd* had quite enough of all that nonsense."

I leveled a cold stare at Raven, cursing myself for reacting to his baited comment. "Thank you for those irrelevant observations, but I have work to do. Or is there some reason I can't wait until the situation is examined in court, with the other party present to tell their side?"

"No, no. I'll let you get on with—whatever you're doing. But I hope this little incident isn't telling, no pun intended. You're good when you're following the rules Edwin, otherwise you're a liability." Raven raised a brow as if daring me to disagree.

I couldn't seem to keep quiet. "People in the Authority Tell as often as other Witches do. Sometimes it's the only way." Retroactive approval for unplanned Tellings happened, if not regularly, then as a matter of course as long as no one was being malicious or negligent when they revealed magic. I shouldn't be treated differently than any other employee, or any other Witch, but I'd been letting Raven and the other Judges do that to me from the start.

"Yes, sometimes these things happen." Raven flicked a pale dismissive hand. "But you should have Told in the correct manner, not recklessly. You hadn't even mentioned to anyone that you were thinking of Telling. You should have sought advice from the appropriate departments. I'd have expected better of someone in your position. This failure speaks volumes."

"I don't need advice," I muttered.

"No? How's the Mortal? Happy and well-adjusted already?" Raven was the picture of skepticism.

My insides went cold, but I wouldn't let myself react. "The Mortal is fine."

Judge Raven shrugged and turned to leave.

His departure gave me no relief. Everything was not fine. Tristan hadn't responded to any of my texts or calls. He was understandably upset. I had to show him things would be okay, that we would be okay.

I could accept that I wanted some form of *we*, even if I still had things to work out within myself. I'd come that far, but was it far enough?

I needed to regroup, find Tristan and try despite my fears.

I had to talk to him.

## 21

## TRISTAN

Jonah came through for me in a big way.

After fleeing my apartment, I met him for a drink. I was miserable company, but Jonah didn't press me for an explanation. He just invited me over for dinner, saying his roommate's lasagna wasn't to be missed.

I made up a story about my current predicament, telling Jonah I had generic housemate drama, and lasagna turned into two nights on his couch. I returned his kindness by subjecting him to a lengthy, one-sided bitch-fest about guys who wouldn't commit—cough, Edwin—but Jonah was all ears.

My mysterious Witchy not-boyfriend called and texted all weekend. Not excessively, but coming from him it was significant. Even though I was surprised I didn't respond to any of the messages.

It was so hard to get my head around Edwin being a Witch, and space to silently freak out was what the situation required. That and Jonah's favorite ice cream, which had pieces of pretzel in it, and was best eaten to the sound of his breakup playlist.

Everything about hanging out with Jonah was normal and predictable. It was exactly what I needed and honestly, if the housemate problems I'd outlined for him had been the full story, I'd have been well over it by the time he was through with me.

Too bad it wasn't that simple.

The fact that I hadn't called Owen burned inside me, but I needed time to be upset. I had to wait until I was thinking straight before I talked to him or Edwin.

I WOKE up on Monday feeling better. Not great, but I was going to take what I could get.

Jonah and I arrived at work to find Edwin waiting outside the entrance to our building. He seemed the same as ever, the idea he could do magic almost like a dream.

He nodded cordially to Jonah, who was sporting an impressive I-don't-like-you glare, which Edwin ignored. He turned to me. "Tristan, may I take you out for coffee?"

It was such a normal question that it comforted me. Sure, he couldn't start talking about magical blood stealing in front of Jonah, but the things I'd been most emotional about over the weekend were personal, normal problems that could have come up with any commitment-phobic guy. Magic was shocking and uncomfortable, and had to be addressed, but I needed to sort out all the questions about Edwin I'd been harboring for the last several months before I even considered the rest.

Upon closer inspection, Edwin looked tired and less composed than I'd seen him outside our intimate moments. As I hesitated, things running through my mind, he seemed to brace himself.

I turned to Jonah. "Go on, I'll be there in a bit."

Jonah looked from me to Edwin. "You sure?"

I nodded and he turned to enter the building with a promise

to tell our manager I'd be along soon. Not that they'd care, going by past experience.

Edwin stood silently, making no further move.

I shoved my hands in the pockets of my coat. "Why do you want to take me out for coffee?"

"Why?" he echoed, not hiding his confusion.

I waited.

Edwin looked away, seeming uncomfortable. It was hard not to jump in and reassure him. I wasn't pushing him to be mean and didn't want to see him squirm. However, I needed him to make an actual effort. I wasn't going to fill in the blanks with guesses, try to read him, or to steer us toward any particular next step.

I needed to know what he wanted.

"I thought it would be nice to get coffee together." Edwin reached up as if to run his hand through his hair but was foiled by his hat. He fumbled it, setting it slightly off center. "Coffee used to be our thing. Sort of. I mean, I thought you might like to get coffee and I needed to do something. You didn't call me back."

"I didn't want to talk this weekend."

"I understand." Edwin looked almost sad about it. He wasn't guarding his expressions anywhere near as closely as he usually did. "What about now? Can we talk?"

I desperately wanted to talk, or more specifically, him to talk. I wanted to believe he'd open up even if past experience told me that was wasn't likely. Edwin was here, seeking me out and taking a risk, and that was new. There was no way I was going to turn him down. If coffee was anything, it was just the start, but I had to give him a chance before we got any further.

"There's a place around the corner we can go." I gestured down the street and started heading that way.

Edwin tentatively followed. "Thank you for taking the time."

"Sure, Edwin."

*He's a Witch.* The unhelpful thought came out of nowhere. And okay, maybe I wasn't as able to push magic aside as I kept trying to tell myself I was. The unpleasant feelings I'd successfully ignored since waking up this morning were creeping back. Being unsure about Edwin and me and our not-relationship was manageable, even if it hurt, but Witches existing on top of that pushed my capacity to deal with things.

"A lot happened this weekend," Edwin began, as if reading my mind. When I didn't respond he went on, his voice turning soft. "Are you okay, Tristan?"

"I'm overwhelmed and confused, and not just about magic." I kept my eyes ahead, letting him hear my frustration.

Edwin moved closer to me, our shoulders brushing. "I'd like to try and help with that." He sounded earnest, almost desperately sincere.

I didn't move away, continuing to brush up against him as we walked. "You have to talk to me." It came out more like a plea than I'd wanted it to.

"I plan to. I know you needed it before." Edwin's fingers trailed across mine, in what I assumed was an invitation to hold hands. "My inability to be forthcoming had been a problem—but I'm here to talk to you now, Tristan."

"I really hope so." I brushed the back of his hand with mine before taking hold of it.

I was an optimist, I'd always give him a chance if it seemed like he was trying, even if doing so put me at risk of getting hurt. It would always be worth it if there was a possibility things would turn out for the better.

Edwin gave my hand a gentle squeeze. The feeling landed somewhere in my chest.

We arrived at the busy cafe, ordered our coffees and found a seat in the back corner. The place was nowhere near as welcoming as Coffee Cat, the furniture plain and tables a little too close together.

Edwin lifted his espresso cup only to set it down without taking a sip. He looked at me with his usual focused attention, but his expression seemed much more open and almost malleable. A furrow creased his brow. "I'm sorry I insulted you, Tristan."

"Oh, yeah, well—" I squirmed in my seat. "I get how I misunderstood the reasons behind you saying I couldn't go home and should stay with you. It was a reaction to what Avery was doing. But you get why you offended me, right?"

"Yes. I'd never try to tell you what to do. I'd never try to 'fix' or manipulate your life. Of course you shouldn't tolerate that sort of behavior. I'm sorry that I made unfair demands of you. Even if the situation arose from a misunderstanding, that's no excuse." Edwin had a hurt, almost pleading edge to his voice that I wasn't sure was completely to do with us. It gave the impression of being too deep somehow.

I almost asked who'd been the one to treat him like that. Instead I stayed focused. "As long as it doesn't happen again, then let's forget about it. Apology accepted. Okay?"

"All right." Edwin sounded relieved and looked down at the table.

We both sipped our coffees. My latte needed more sugar. Not that now was the time to get up and sort it out. Even if the silence was awkward, I wasn't trying to run away from it.

I could have helped the conversation along but opted not to, and waited. Edwin had wanted to talk to me, this was his show.

"There's a lot going on here," Edwin continued eventually, setting his cup down. "If you'd like to end our—um—time together, I understand. But now that I've revealed the true nature of things to you, we need to stay in touch, at least for a time. We need to address magic and the purpose of the court hearing. It's nothing you can't handle, but everything won't be done in a single conversation."

Yes, I could handle it—whatever it was he was talking about. It was important to me he knew that. Edwin seemed genuinely committed to working through magic's existence with me and given he was so averse to commitment, I found this reassuring.

"Is it bad that you told me about magic?" I found the idea of a court hearing confusing and didn't like thinking I was in trouble when I didn't even know why.

"No." Edwin sounded completely sure of himself. "Witches reveal the secret from time to time. It's not bad that you know. We need approval to Tell, but we can get that after the fact just fine. Any questions you have, I promise to answer."

My mind blanked. I almost didn't know where to start but it didn't take long for my worries to surface. "Are there Witches everywhere? Should I be concerned more people are doing magic on me like Avery?" The thought could be paralyzing if I let it.

Edwin shook his head. "The Witch population is much smaller than that of Mortals. I'm the only Witch in this coffee shop, and we didn't pass any others on the street. It may seem like we're everywhere, but you only know so many of us because Juliet and I know Aria. Meet one and you might come across their friends."

"It was bad luck with Avery, huh?" I tried for a joke, but it fell flat. What she'd done made me feel so helpless.

"Yes." Edwin was serious. "But most Witches never cast spells on Mortals without their consent. You don't have to worry that every person you come across is a Witch with a sinister agenda. But if you are worried, you can always call me. Any time. No concern is too small."

"Yeah, okay." Warmth flooded my body. I trusted Edwin. The way he was looking at me, I believed he would be there for me without question if I was ever in magical trouble, no matter what else happened between us.

Right now he seemed to care fiercely and that didn't come out of nowhere. Edwin caring for me had to be what gave our intimate moments so much intensity. Him hiding it the rest of the time had made me wonder if it was really there, but sitting here it was so plainly written on his face that I suspected he might have cared this deeply all along.

Why hide it? What about me made him want to hold back? I didn't understand caring for someone and not wanting to show it constantly.

Edwin continued on. "There's something I wanted to ask you. Um. If that's all right? I was wondering if I could tell you about my work? My actual work. I think it would be a good way to explain certain magical aspects to you, in a way that's relevant to both of us."

"Sure, I'd love to hear more about you, Edwin. I've always been interested, even before I realized you had a magic job. But first, can we go back to us for a minute?" I might trust him as far as Witches and magic went but it was clear that was a separate commitment from *us*. We still had a lot of personal unknowns that I wasn't okay with leaving unaddressed. Caring didn't add up with how he acted most of the time and I wasn't interested in more baffling inconsistencies.

Edwin looked at me nervously, giving the tiniest of nods.

My coffee cup and saucer clinked in my unsteady hands. "I don't want our time to end necessarily, but I don't want to go back to the arrangement we had before. It didn't feel casual to me. Did it feel that way to you?"

Edwin looked strained, new lines appearing on his face in a complex tangle of emotion. "No. It didn't, but I—I have a hard time opening up to people."

"I kinda suspected that." I smiled and after a moment Edwin did too.

"It was obvious, I'm sure—uh—I usually avoid personal connections completely. I don't have a lot of friends, to say the least. And romantic relationships are—um. Challenging for me. But this is me trying to be more forthcoming." He gestured to us and our coffees.

"By telling me about your work?"

"And asking for your help." Edwin seemed completely out of his comfort zone, his grip on his espresso looking a little too tight.

I had the somewhat embarrassing realization that the problems between us might not be all about me and what Edwin thought of me. I'd told him I'd suspected he had trouble opening up, but maybe I hadn't realized the extent of what that meant for him. Maybe not committing wasn't about me not being good enough, or anything lacking on my part. That was just the insecurity my mind always went to.

I'd never thought Edwin might be hiding his emotions from me because he found relationships and showing his feelings personally challenging.

I reached across the table and stroked his knuckles with my index finger. His grip on the cup loosened and I withdrew my hand. "I'd love to help, Edwin. What did you have in mind?"

He seemed to grow more confident, his posture taking on that poised quality I found so magnetic. "It's a case that I'm working on for the magical Authority. I was hoping you could help me with part of the investigation, but I'll need to explain it first."

"Really?" The level of surprise in my voice was almost comical.

Edwin quirked a brow. "Yes. Avery's situation is most likely connected to the increased black market blood trade we've been trying to get to the bottom of."

"What's going to happen to Avery?" I felt sorry for her, even if what she'd done was a violation. She'd seemed conflicted and like she'd hated having to do it. Now that I'd calmed down from the shock of everything, I felt bad for running out on her. If she was coerced into action, I hardly blamed her.

Edwin frowned. "Avery and I came to an agreement. She'll provide information on the individuals she was supplying, and anything she knows about their blood operation. The Authority will get her out of the illegal contract, and she'll pay her due for the crime against you in the form of a fine."

I grimaced at my coffee. "What about the dodgy loan people?"

Edwin gave me a conspiratorial look. "That's a bit more complicated. We don't actually want them knowing Avery's been caught, so we're arranging for her debt to be paid without drawing suspicion. The Witches she was supplying could help lead us to the larger problem—if it's all connected as I suspect. We won't arrest or prosecute the 'dodgy loan people' for anything yet. See, the amount of blood on the market couldn't come from one small group of people, like the ones who had a hold over Avery. It's a large scale, organized effort. And most likely not the work of fragmented groups, as evidenced by consistent pricing, lack of competition and steady distribution of product. We want to find the Witches running the whole thing."

I leaned forward, full of interest and a hint of renewed fear. "Wow, okay. So this is like a really big deal. But I thought you said sinister Witches weren't lurking everywhere. And yet I'm not the only one getting my blood stolen."

"This situation really isn't ideal for introducing you to the magic world." Edwin tapped his fingers on the table. "It's like anything. You can't judge any group based on the actions of individuals. Not all Witches are bad or use magic to take advantage of Mortals, but some do. The main point of the Authority is to protect Mortals from magic. Most of the structure of our society is built around that goal. Knowing about magic can be a positive thing, I promise. I can show you the more fun side, or the more day-to-day life-of-a-Witch side if you want. Maybe that would help?"

The urge to see Edwin do magic overcame me. It would be so cool—and maybe kind of hot? I didn't think I'd ever heard him describe anything as fun. Getting to know this side of Edwin would be amazing. I wanted to put aside my fear and embrace the kind of excitement you always expect to come with spells and mystical things.

"I'd really like for you show me more magic."

Edwin gave me a soft smile. "I'd like that too, Tristan."

We stared at each other for a long moment. It was a tender, more exposing version of the kind of staring we'd so often got caught up in in the past. Edwin wasn't unreadable beauty, he seemed almost hopeful.

He broke eye contact first, looking down at the table as color tinted his cheeks.

I cleared my throat. "I see what you mean about not making assumptions about Witches based on this horrible situation Avery got caught up in." I sipped my coffee. "But how are you hoping to solve it? What kind of evidence do Witches need? Can't you catch the dodgy ones with magic?"

Edwin picked up his coffee as if he were grateful for it as well as the shift in subject. "We can obtain evidence through magical means, to present in our Witch-run court, but we still need tangible evidence, like you'd expect in any Mortal case." He took a sip, seeming to relax fully back into his usual self, but not in a closed off way. "Avery can testify against the Witches forcing her to supply blood, but we need to think bigger than that. I've had word that more blood than Avery could have acquired passed through the pawn shop the loan came from. So who else is supplying it?"

"There's no spell to tell you who's behind it?" I couldn't help asking even though there mustn't be, or else he'd have done it. I just really wanted to engage in the conversation, keep it going, and see what else Edwin might tell me.

He seemed happy to oblige. "It's not so simple. Magic is just another force in the world with its own limitations and natural laws, it's not the perfect solution to all problems. And we're going after Witches, concealment spells are complex and very effective if done properly. But that brings me to the idea I was hoping you'd help me with."

I laughed in surprise. "What am I gonna do? I've only known about magic for like five minutes."

"True. But your blood is involved. This can be helpful if you're willing to go on a little investigatory mission with me?"

I was floored, and excited. Magical investigating seemed so beyond cool, especially if it was something Edwin and I could do together. "I'm in."

Edwin saluted me with his espresso cup. "Thank you, Tristan. I knew I could rely on you. And I'd also like it if things weren't over between us. I want to try again and be more like this together."

I suppressed a grin. "More like this as in, *not* pretending we're a no strings attached, sex only thing?"

"Right. I was thinking something more honest." He looked a little bit terrified of the prospect.

## 22

# EDWIN

Tristan and I arrived at Mystic Pawn that evening to find Mason at the counter bent over a laptop muttering to himself.

"Goddamn nonsense—oh. Mr. Bickel, apologies but I have this stupid fucking email to reply to."

"What seems to be the problem, Mason?" I leaned up against the counter. He didn't look at me, continuing to glare at the screen.

Tristan stood at my side, bouncing slightly on his toes as he took in the strangeness of the shop.

Mason jabbed at a button on the laptop. "Al had this screwy idea we need to promote Mystic Pawn. Now this Mortal marketing pleb is emailing me. What am I supposed to say? Our target market is Witches. Advertising via Mortal means is pointless."

"Couldn't you use a Witch advertising agency?" I suggested.

"No. Al's signed something with these Welsh people already." Mason gestured at the laptop with ferocity, putting the machine in danger of being knocked to the ground. "*Please tell us the aim of your campaign.* What utter bull—" The shopkeeper finally seemed to realize I wasn't alone. "Who's he?"

I placed a hand on my—oh god was he my boyfriend?—on the man-beside-me's shoulder. "This is Tristan Tomás, he's here to help us with the blood problem."

Tristan offered his hand to Mason and the two shook. "I'm a copywriter and marketing pleb myself, if you want a hand with your email."

Mason narrowed his eyes. "Hm. Y'all employing Mortals now?"

I removed my hand from Tristan's shoulder. "No. His blood may have been in some of the vials. I wanted to bring him here and see if we could find the trail."

Mason stroked his chin, looking at Tristan like he was sizing him up. "Going to do some residual magnetism—interesting."

"It's worth a shot, even if the trail is cold. Can you show us exactly where the box was?"

"Anything you need, Mr. B." Mason led us to the back room.

Tristan drank in everything around us with keen attention. "That is a pile of bones," he whispered, grabbing my arm.

"Don't worry. They're animal bones," I assured him. The items back here tended to be even odder than those out front.

Mason grabbed the small enchanted mirror off a shelf. "Might as well check this thing again. Though it's been pretty useless."

Tristan watched, his features arranged in an undeniably cute *huh* expression, as the shopkeeper sifted through the images by tapping on the glass.

"Wait, look at this." Mason turned the mirror toward me.

The glass showed Al was coming in and out of frame, placing wrapped parcels in a box.

"It could be more blood," I hedged.

"But you can't see shit, can you?" Mason gave the mirror a

dirty look. "This was two nights ago, and I haven't seen that box here, so there's no way to know what's in those bundles."

"Ah, well. Hopefully Tristan can help us find something. Are you ready?"

Tristan looked up from the mirror. "Yep. Enchant away." He spread his arms playfully like he was ready to take part in a performance. He may have been trying to cover any nerves he had about the upcoming spell but there was an underlying confidence to Tristan that made me think he really was okay with magic and how things had turned out.

The relief I'd felt all day turned into something wholly comforting that had me wanting to wrap him up and bury my face in his neck.

"So the box was here both times." Mason pointed to a corner.

Tristan and I went to stand in the spot indicated.

I handed him a small blue crystal on a necklace. "This will help focus your awareness during the spell." We'd gone over the details already, but to make sure Tristan was fully comfortable I went through it again. "I'm going to enchant you so that any blood you lost will be drawn back to you. If your blood was ever here, you'll be able to feel an echo of its pull. Something fundamentally part of you will always have a magnetism to you. If the connection is strong enough, you'll be able to follow the path your blood took from here."

Tristan put the necklace on. "And I won't be in a trance?"

"No. You'll be aware and in control the whole time. The spell shouldn't feel overwhelming, it's more like a suggestion. If it's uncomfortable we can always undo it and try something else."

Avery's method of incapacitating Tristan when taking his blood was bound to make him wary of magic that altered his state of being. I didn't discount Tristan's trust in me in agreeing to do this.

"Okay. Got it." Tristan shook out his arms and took a steady breath.

I took his hands, for comfort rather than out of spell casting need, and recited the incantation. He closed his eyes, an unnecessary but common reaction amongst Mortals. When I stopped speaking, he cracked one eye open.

"I—uh—don't feel anything." Tristan frowned and looked around the cramped storeroom.

"Give it a minute." I squeezed his hands before letting go. "It's only a subtle sensation. Breath, concentrate. Let the crystal guide you."

Tristan closed his eyes again and we waited.

"Oh, I feel tingly!" He beamed at me as excitement took hold of him, seeming to banish the last of his uncertainty. "Let's go over here."

Mason and I followed Tristan toward the back exit. He carefully opened the door and stepped outside.

Tristan paused in the small back alleyway. He wandered back and forth between the buildings, up to the cross street and back before stopping in front of me. "I think I'm getting the hang of it. Like I can tell when I'm going the wrong way because I start to lose the weird tingling in my head."

"Excellent. Shall we see where it goes?"

Tristan nodded.

"Have a nice walk. I'll be here if you need me." Mason waved us off and shut the door, grumbling about getting back to the computer.

Tristan led me to the entrance of the alley, rolling the blue crystal between his thumb and forefinger. "I feel like we should go right." He gestured into the gathering dark of the quiet street, a familiar lopsided smile brightening his face.

I felt his grin catching hold of me. "Are you enjoying this?"

"Kinda, yeah. I mean, it's magic." He grabbed my hand. "And

—you know—us. Even if the context of Witches selling blood is creepy as fuck, I'm glad we're doing this together."

"You're amazing." I let the sentiment out in a rush. Not holding back at coffee this morning had been uncomfortable, but right now it felt like breathing fresh air.

Tristan blushed, only noticeable in the night because I was so attuned to his subtleties. "Says the guy casting actual spells. Come on."

He led me quite a ways. The initial thrill had worn off by the time we stopped on a street corner in Queens.

"We're almost at the end. I don't know how I know, but I'd say the blood came from in there." Tristan pointed to a bar two doors down.

"Came from?"

"Yeah. I have this feeling that the trail ended at the pawn shop and started here. Not the other way around. Could that be right?"

"Avery told me she never brought her payments directly to the pawn shop." I pulled out my phone to check my notes. "She mentioned this place as a drop off, so you're right. It could have come from here.

"So my blood went from Avery, to"—Tristan squinted at the half lit up sign—"the Fizz Bar, and then ended up at Mystic Pawn in a box?"

"Looks like it." I tucked my phone back in my pocket. "I'd hoped to find out where the blood went after Al collected it, but never mind."

Tristan looked disappointed. "I'm kind of surprised the whole following-the-tingling-feeling worked. Like I know magic is real, but still."

We walked slowly down the street passing the bar. It looked relatively empty inside with only a few people standing around a pool table.

"I know what you mean." I moved us past the window before anyone inside the bar could catch us looking. "Magic probably still feels unreal."

"Yeah." Tristan frowned at a closed deli as we continued down the street. "And the fact that I went the wrong way and followed the path backward instead of forward was a bit of a fail."

"Not at all." I stopped as an idea struck and motioned for Tristan to follow me back to the Fizz Bar. We stood at the edge of the building, out of sight of the window. "Do you think you could keep following the trail from here all the way back to your house?"

Tristan concentrated. "No. It feels like it stops here. And I'm not just saying that because I don't want to walk all that way."

I chuckled and led him away again, crossing the street. "I'd say that means your blood was stored at the bar for a significant time, or else the trail wouldn't come to an end. This is excellent Tristan."

"Really?" He looked at me skeptically.

"Knowing that your blood was stored here points to the bar's direct involvement. If Avery's keepers had picked a random, unassociated spot to meet her, they wouldn't have kept anything here for more than a few hours, and the trail wouldn't have seemed to end. I can probably justify an official look into the bar owners if they're Witches."

Tristan followed me toward the subway. "Hm. If you say so. But maybe we should go back to the pawn shop and I can try again."

"I was thinking the same thing."

With some difficulty we were able to pick up another trail. To save us walking around all night, Mason offered to drive us in his van, but this made it harder for Tristan to concentrate on the residual pull of his blood and he became less sure the farther we got from Mystic Pawn.

When Mason pulled over at last, we were outside Tristan's office building all the way in Manhattan.

"Sorry." Tristan looked confused as he and I exited the van. "I must've lost it somewhere. I thought I was feeling something, but I've just taken us back to work. That can't be right. Must have been my subconscious taking me somewhere I knew."

"That's okay." I was starting to feel tired from a long day, not to mention a weekend of emotional stress. I could only imagine how Tristan was feeling. "You've done really well considering how new to interpreting magical sensations you are."

"I could try again," Tristan offered, looking back at Mason where he was waiting, van idling.

"There is another way that leaves less room for doubt." I hesitated. "It would mean donating blood, Tristan. And I understand if you don't want to, so please don't feel obligated. But we could have Avery give her keepers one last blood payment infused with a concealed magical tracking spell."

Not surprisingly, Tristan seemed wary. "Do you think Avery would be up for that?"

"I'd say so. The more she can help us, the more the Authority will be willing to forgive her own rule breaking."

Concern flashed across Tristan's face. "But I don't want her to feel like she has to. Could it be dangerous? The dodgy Witches wouldn't be able to detect the spell, right? I wouldn't want them to know Avery was working against them."

"No, that wouldn't be good for her. I'm confident they won't be able to detect anything different about this last payment. I wouldn't suggest it otherwise."

"Yeah, if Mr. Bickel does the spell work, you're all aces," Mason called from inside the van.

"Anyway. If you're comfortable giving up some blood, I'm sure Avery will agree." I hurried on, not wanting to explain what Mason had meant.

I hadn't lied to Tristan in the coffee shop about wanting to open up, but I had to do it slowly. I wasn't ready to explain exactly who I was in Witch society. It felt too caught up in my past and all the things about me I wasn't ready to share.

Getting to the point where I'd stopped lying to myself about what I wanted with Tristan had been hard enough. I still had to figure out how far I wanted this relationship to go. All the way was a daunting prospect, and even if I wanted to get there, it wasn't happening all at once.

I had to make sure I was ready for each next step when it came. And if that wasn't possible I had to face it, be honest with myself about what I wanted but also what I could and couldn't handle.

Tristan cringed and for a moment I forgot what we'd been talking about, worried I'd somehow communicated my self-doubt with my expression. Then he said, "Okay, I'm in. Take my blood. Might as well use it for something good."

Right. Blood. The case.

Allowing myself to be more honest was going to be minefield of new worries if I stopped controlling my every small expression. It made so much of interacting with Tristan feel exposing. Except, I wanted to be comfortable with it.

I hoped I could be.

# 23

## TRISTAN

That Friday evening Edwin took me to see Owen.

We appeared in front of the door to Owen and Aria's apartment, inside their building at the top of the stairs, where no one was at risk of seeing us. I was instantly overcome with nausea and went completely light-headed, my balance left somewhere back in New York.

"Teleporting takes some getting used to," Edwin said as he helped me stay upright.

"Why does it feel so awful?" I groaned into his suit jacket before making half an effort to compose myself.

"Your body isn't used to occupying the space between." Edwin brushed my hair back, giving me one of his tender looks, letting his fingers find their way to my scalp in a soothing hold.

"If you say so." I remained queasy and burrowed my face into him once more.

We'd had a chat about magic and Witch stuff after our run around the city chasing my blood. I was now less lost-in-a-sea-of-secrets and tentatively confident about the new place Edwin and I were in. We hadn't talked more about our relationship, but

I didn't know if we needed to yet. We were feeling things out and that was okay.

"Thanks for taking me to see Owen." I glanced at the apartment door but didn't knock. I hadn't told Owen much other than I was able to be in SoCal for the weekend.

Edwin removed his hand from my hair. "You're welcome, Tristan. I'm happy to take you to see him anytime."

I resisted telling Edwin he didn't have to do that. It was a caring gesture on his part. Wasn't that what I kept telling myself I wanted from him? To know he actually cared, for it to be out in the open and acknowledged by both of us? I didn't know why it was simultaneously hard to accept.

I shifted away from Edwin and rapped my knuckles on the door.

After a few moments it flew open. "Oh my god, Tristan!" Owen pulled me into a crushing hug.

"Ow. Hi." I hugged him back.

He released me, only to pull me inside for a hug from Aria.

"I can't believe you waited 'til this week to say you were coming out," she admonished.

"Oh, well—" I squirmed and it was about then my friends noticed Edwin standing in the doorway.

"Hello." He gave them an incredibly awkward wave, then took off his hat and fiddled with it.

My friends stared mutely for a second too long.

"Hey, Mr. Bickel. Come on in." Owen recovered with a sincere seeming smile.

"Oh no, I won't stay." Edwin put his hat back on. "I'll talk to you later, Tristan." He disappeared.

Owen's mouth fell open. He turned to me in mute panic.

Aria gasped. "What the hell?"

Piña, Owen's cat, poked her head out from behind an armchair to hiss at the spot where Edwin had been.

"Yeah, so I found out about magic." I attempted a casual shrug.

The two of them became—I'd have thought impossibly—more shocked than before. Owen was doing a pretty good impression of a fish and Aria laughed in a way that was clearly not meant to indicate humor.

She slammed the door shut.

I probably should have told them in advance, but I hadn't wanted this conversation to happen over the phone. Partly because I didn't know where to start.

Owen wore the guiltiest look on his face. "Tristan—when?"

"Um, last weekend." I squirmed some more. "Look, Edwin told me you had no choice about keeping all this from me. So I'm not mad or anything."

"You sure? Because this was one hell of a way to bring it up."

Aria put her hand on Owen's shoulder and he visibly relaxed. "I think we all need a drink."

Owen and I nodded and she disappeared into the kitchen.

"Okay, I was maybe mad at first, before I really figured out how all this works." I gestured more frantically than I meant to, betraying my heightened feelings about the situation. "But I don't think Edwin meant to let slip that you Knew. It was just all very intense, and I didn't know what to say to you. I had to take a serious beat by myself. Then I just wanted to see you. And now I've made it weird, haven't I?"

"No, it's fine." Owen ran a nervous hand through his short hair, making it hard to tell if his assurance was true. He seemed nervous. "I wish Aria and I'd been able to tell you firsthand, rather than Bickel saying god knows what about us, but—" His words fizzled out and we just looked at each other.

Aria returned with a bottle of wine and three glasses. I slunk over to the couch and Owen followed, sitting on the end opposite me. Aria curled up in an armchair and we all drank in silence.

The cat, possibly sensing Owen's discomfort, jumped onto his lap and allowed herself to be patted. We were quiet for a few more sips. Suddenly, Aria snorted, almost choking on her wine, startling Owen and me.

My wine sloshed.

"Sorry." She put her hand over her mouth. "But come on. *He Told you?* I can—not—fucking—believe it." She grinned like a devil.

"Aria." Owen gave her a *be cool* look that I felt Piña did a good job of echoing. The cat had never seemed to like Aria, if I was honest.

"No. This is just—after the way Bickel acted when I accidentally revealed magic to you, Owen—I'm *never* letting him hear the end of this."

Owen paused his cat patting. "We don't even know what happened."

"Why, what happened with you guys? Are you mad Edwin Told me? Was this supposed to be a secret forever or something?" I had a weird sinking feeling in my stomach and abandoned my wine on the coffee table, then brought my legs up to my chest so I could rest my chin on my knees.

"It's not like that at all, Tristan." Owen also abandoned his wine. "I wanted to Tell you so bad, but I literally couldn't due to the magical restrictions on Mortal knowledge. And Aria would have been in serious trouble with court if she Told you after what happened with me."

"I have a complicated past." Aria knocked back her drink and poured herself another.

"But we were going to tell you," Owen insisted, deep brown eyes imploring. "It's just a whole process."

I wrapped my arms around my legs and looked at my green

polished fingers. "Yeah, Edwin told me about the pre-approval thing. Witches seem to have a lot of rules."

"You can say that again." Aria rolled her eyes. "But really. Tristan, this wasn't something we wanted to keep from you. And we weren't going to, not forever. I just never would have guessed Bickel would let it slip."

"Is that why you pretended not to like him? You didn't want me to date a Witch who'd lie to me about magic?" I glanced from Owen to Aria, searching.

She made a face. "No, he's just a total prick."

"*Aria*," Owen hissed.

The cat mewed.

Aria didn't look concerned. "We did worry about you trying to date a Witch who'd never be honest with you about anything. It seemed like a recipe for disaster. It was hard to imagine the two of you working out when we knew you wanted a partner, Tristan. You needed someone who cared just as much as you did."

"But he isn't a prick. And he is honest with me about things." *Sometimes.* At least he was starting to be. But for some reason my voice was coming out at a strange pitch. "I think it's just really complicated. We only agreed to like, be together for real and see where things go after the whole magic mess. I don't think Edwin would have Told me he was a Witch if he didn't care."

Edwin did care. He'd been slowly showing me all week, even if a handful of days out of the past couple months of sleeping together wasn't a lot, it was a start. And all the moments I'd tried to tell myself I'd read into nothing were probably something. I was more confident in that belief now that I was beginning to understand Edwin.

"You're right." Aria lost her usual grumpy edge. "Bickel wouldn't have Told you if you didn't mean everything to him. It's just, he doesn't act like a person who cares around the rest of us.

And I know he puts on an act that has something to do with how he wants Witches to see him, but Owen and I always worried how that would mean he'd treat you."

I looked between them. "What sort of act do you mean?"

Aria began ticking things off on her fingers. "He gives the impression everything in life is boring and not worth his time. He's overly pretentious and purposely intimidating. He doesn't let anyone of inferior power or place in Witch society call him by his given name. And some of his above-it-all-ness isn't show. Bickel has a lot of power as far as Witches go. He's like legendary. The most powerful Witch in modern times."

"Oh." I hugged my knees tighter. "So what, do Witches have some sort of powerfulness-ranking system?"

Aria blinked in confusion. "I mean—no."

"Then how do you know he's actually more powerful than everyone?"

"Well he might not be *literally*, when you consider world population, but coupled with his unique gifts that allow him to stop time and move through negative space—or teleport—which no one else can do, he's way out of everyone else's league."

I grunted acknowledgment, begrudging her point. "I'm just saying, most powerful Witch of modern times is a bit of an over dramatic way to put it."

"I feel like you're focusing on the wrong thing here." Owen's lips twitched with the ghost of a smile.

"Am I?" I gave him a haughty look that he'd know not to take too seriously. "You're the ones making a big deal out of Edwin's reputation."

"Maybe—but you'd never fall for someone like the Bickel Aria first met, or even the one she and I know now." Owen picked up his wine and had a sip. "He goes out of his way to be unlikeable."

"But why would he want people to think he's awful when he's actually really sweet?"

Owen quirked a brow like he was intrigued. "He's sweet to you?"

"I mean, yeah. He holds a lot back and isn't exactly easy to understand or particularly open, but I think that might be changing. He said he wants to be together and try and open up."

"That sounds like a pretty big deal, coming from Bickel." Aria didn't hold back her look of surprise.

Yes, it was a huge deal.

I'd already known that our meeting in the coffee shop had been a major step, even without this extra context. Now, I was even more sure that Edwin hadn't been holding himself back because he didn't see me as partner-material. He kept everyone at a distance, to an even more extreme degree than he'd ever done with me.

I couldn't help prying for more details even though I knew I should talk to Edwin firsthand. "So you don't know him personally, at all?"

Owen shook his head. "No, but I don't see him much. Not like Aria does at work."

She sipped her wine slowly before commenting. "I wouldn't say I know him personally either. All I know is that Bickel isn't as awful as he likes to make people think he is. But at the same time, whenever he does or says something nice to me, he always ruins it with something cutting. I guess I still judge him for acting that way, even if I know it's fake. Choosing to be like that still means something."

"Juliet knows him well. They're friends," Owen added, possibly in an effort to be more encouraging about the whole situation.

"We really just didn't want to get involved," Aria insisted. "It was too hard without being able to explain most of this stuff to you, Tristan."

"That's fair, I guess." Everything swirled around in my head. I let go of my knees and flopped back onto the couch. "I wonder if magic had anything do with why Edwin pushed me away after that first night."

Owen considered. "Maybe. You could ask him about it."

I could, but the idea made me nervous.

What if there was something else holding Edwin back beyond his discomfort with letting people in? Maybe it was just Witchy stuff. If so, he might not have wanted to leave us at one night, which could explain why Edwin had been so affectionate when we'd reunited. But I wasn't sure. Were Witchy differences *that* much of a big deal, or was I still missing something significant? Like the key to why Edwin had two vastly different personalities.

Bypassing all that as something I could stew on later, I told my friends about Avery, the blood siphoning and last weekend's roller-coaster. They were mildly horrified about the whole thing, but something in the story perked Owen up.

He was making mushy eyes at me. "He's totally in love with you, Tristan."

"I don't know about all that." I'd completely uncurled from my knees-up ball-position but wished I was still tucked in and hiding.

"I might have to agree with Owen on this." Aria looked more serious than lovey-dovey, but that was just her style. "Telling wasn't about the blood at all. He could have sorted that out covertly—"

"Actually, he kind of went off the rails from the moment I mentioned the bites, so—"

Aria cut me off with an *oh please* look. "Bickel wasn't thrown off by the crime. He was thrown off by you. The only thing pushing him to reveal magic was you leaving him, Tristan. Plus, there's the whole Coffee Cat thing."

"Wait, what Coffee Cat thing?" I looked between my two friends.

"Tristan, he lives in New York, yet kept coming *here* to get coffee." Aria pointed down through the floor to where the cafe lay beneath us.

"Yeah, but you and Juliet must see Edwin all the time. He travels for work," I insisted, even as the pieces fell into place.

"Does he?" Owen cocked his head with a very knowing grin. "Or is he a teleporting Witch who only had *one* Tristan-shaped reason to frequent my coffee shop?"

# 24

# TRISTAN

The rest of the night passed like I was floating in a glass of champagne.

With no more forced secrets between us, Owen and Aria were overflowing with stories. They told me all about how they'd thought the cafe was haunted back when Aria first moved in, and I found out her psychic ability was real, just not in the way I'd expected.

Even the idea of having to go to Witch-court with Edwin next week seemed less daunting. Owen said it would be a breeze, that Edwin and I would have no trouble based on our story. Aria agreed, saying Edwin's big-deal Witchy persona would probably work in our favor. Plus, her brother was a lawyer if I wanted to ask anyone for actual advice.

After months of regret about moving and general life dissatisfaction, everything felt like it was falling back into place.

THE NEXT DAY I helped Owen in the cafe and had a blast. Tess was so happy to see me she didn't even try to coerce me into getting a tattoo. Which was her loss because I might have gone for it.

I made lattes like a pro and ate—what some might consider —too many sweets.

After we closed up Coffee Cat Aria insisted we go to the beach. As she was off in the spare room looking for a frisbee, Owen and I finished one last cup of coffee at the kitchen table, Piña rolling around on the floor between our feet.

I hadn't heard from Edwin, but didn't feel like I'd needed to. I was committed to taking this new stage of our relationship slowly. Things felt like they'd shifted, and as long as it was real progress that didn't disappear the next time I asked him a question, I was supper happy with it.

Of course, finding out Edwin had *totally* been coming to Coffee Cat to see me helped boost my confidence. Him not making a move or talking to me much even made sense, knowing how averse he was to letting anyone get to know him.

I drained the last of my coffee, checking my phone notifications and personal email. I groaned at the sight of the first unread message.

Owen put his coffee cup down. "What's up?"

I slouched warily in my seat. "Just my mom. Come see."

Owen came around the table and leaned over my shoulder. We stared at the subject line: *Please Tristan, I want to see you.*

"She's outsmarted your not-reading-her-messages tactic." There was a hard edge to Owen's voice.

"Yeah." I grimaced at the phone. "I mean, I assumed she wanted to see me. That's what she always says eventually."

"What do you want to do?"

My thumb hovered. I'd told my mom not to contact me about a 'visit' until she was actually in town, but I'd never told her I'd moved. I had the sudden worry that the boundaries I'd set were unreasonable, or that I was being immature in how I was handling her.

Maybe neither of those things were true, but a mess of guilt, self-doubt—and the inescapable truth that even after all this time I wanted to see her too—made me click on the message anyway.

*I REALLY MEAN it this time kiddo. Miss you! Message me back!*

"NOT THE LONGEST message she's ever sent." It left me feeling a bit dumbfounded.

"Not the first time she's said she really means it either," Owen reminded me gently.

I swiped the email app away and turned my phone face down on the table.

I didn't want my mom to miss me. I'd wanted her to care so badly when I was younger. She should have missed me when it counted. And all right, she probably had, I didn't think she was a monster, but she should have *showed* me. The more my mom told me she missed me, the more I'd thought about how she'd never had to leave me behind and miss me in the first place.

Now *I miss you* felt like a guilt trip. *I miss you so how can you ignore me?* That sort of thing. I didn't believe her sentiment anymore. She never acted like it was true.

Fuck it. I was spending today with Owen, someone who cared about me unconditionally. I had Aria too now. And Edwin. I didn't need more than that.

I STOOD in the atrium of the WMS building on Monday morning full of jittery energy.

As I waited for the elevator I rocked back and forth from my toes to heels. Music blasted from my earbuds. My email app was open on my phone and I slowly tapped out a message.

*HI MOM, we've talked about this. I know you want to see me but it hurts when it never happens.*

I PRESSED SEND BEFORE I could think about it.

A man standing beside me said something. I popped out an earbud and looked at him. Great. It was Emerson Walsh.

"Hey, it's Tristan right?" He pointed at me and I nodded. "I bet you anything that elevator you're standing in front of isn't going to arrive." The man beamed at me, teeth too white, graying hair too perfect.

"Are they broken?"

"I'm not saying *an* elevator won't come. *That* one you're standing in front of isn't going to—" He was interrupted by the arrival of an elevator behind us and to the left. "See."

Man, he was a strange one. Who cared about the elevators and who noticed what pattern they arrived in?

I had no choice but to follow Emerson into the elevator. Luckily a few lawyers from the firm on the floors above WMS piled in after and I was saved having to chit-chat with the man.

He gave me an odd smile from across the crowded lift, his eyes lingering too long. Emerson needed to attend a workshop on social skills. Maybe I'd suggest one at our next corporate brainstorm.

There was all kinds of nonsense going on at the office when I got to my floor. A fancy-pants espresso machine had appeared in the writers' breakroom and people were enthusiastically getting their part-time barista on.

I avoided the crowd and went to my desk but by the afternoon I'd stopped pretending not to be as thrilled about the new coffee set up as the rest of my colleagues.

Jonah was inspecting the variety of coffee beans that had been supplied as I waited for a turn with the machine. He picked up a dark roast and sniffed the bag. "I say it's all a passive aggressive way to tell us to stop dozing off in meetings."

"There's less expensive ways to do that." Rochelle glanced over her shoulder at us as she steamed milk for her third mocha of the day. "Why does it keep splattering?" She frowned at the silver jug in her hand.

"You're letting too much air in, here." I turned off the steam and took over for her. "Am I the only one who's ever worked in a coffee shop?"

"Doubt it. You should have seen the thing Graham made earlier. Serious Starbucks vibes." Jonah poked into the fridge, eyeing all the syrups that had appeared along with the rest of the stuff.

"Seriously though, do you remember what that last meeting was about?" Rochelle asked us.

We'd come out of the conference room and beelined for the coffee. Most of the team was back at their desks by now, but we were committed to quality hot drinks done right.

"I feel like it had to do with team building." I finished off Rochelle's coffee and started making myself an almond milk latte.

"I think I was snoring," Jonah said without shame. "Was I?"

"No idea. I was so dazed I must've fallen asleep too." Rochelle sipped her mocha and sighed. "Tristan, I love you."

"No, you don't, you love chocolate. How is it that we all fell asleep?"

"You too?" Jonah frowned and itched his neck. "Our manager can't be that clueless. She must have noticed. There were only a dozen of us in the room."

Rochelle took another loving sip of her coffee. "In my own defense, I've been feeling really tired the past few months. Especially on weekdays."

I'd been doing better since Avery had stopped siphoning my blood, but I couldn't say I felt back to normal. I'd assumed it was a recovery time thing, however this conversation had me feeling paranoid.

Why were we all so tired?

"I don't see how all three of us missed everything from that meeting, and yet no one's calling us out." Jonah took a coke out of the fridge and popped the tab. "Also, what was last week's all-staffer about?"

Neither Rochelle nor I could come up with anything concrete, though we'd both attended.

I set down my almond latte and surreptitiously checked my wrists. No marks. I was being silly. No one at Walsh Marketing Solutions was stealing our blood. It had to be something else.

"I hear fluorescent lighting is terrible for you." Rochelle shielded her eyes from the admittedly excessive lighting in the break area. "Maybe that's what's making us tired."

"The light gives me headaches for sure," Jonah agreed.

"Wellness week is coming up. We can suggest reconfiguring the lighting," Rochelle began making her way back to the desks and Jonah and I followed. "It's not just us getting headaches. Viv's been getting migraines since working here."

"Brutal," Jonah sympathized. "My dad gets those. It's no joke."

Back at my desk I couldn't shake the unease settling over me. It was suspicious as hell that none of us could remember what today's meeting had been about, and combined with so many people feeling constantly tired and unwell, it was hard not to think something was wrong.

The thought of being entranced and siphoned at work scared me. Magic induced sleep was no different than being drugged, and call it what you want, stealing blood was assault. How the hell could something like that be going on in an office? Or maybe I was overly sensitive after what had happened to me.

I had to talk to Edwin.

I picked up my phoned aiming to text him but was distracted by a new email.

It wasn't surprising that my mom had responded so promptly, that was typical. We were in the attentive phase, so I told myself not to read into it as I opened the message.

*I KNOW we've talked about it, Tristan. I just want to see you. Please. I'm so happy to hear from you! I've looked online, your LinkedIn says you're in New York City. Is that true? That's so exciting! I'll be up there this weekend. That's why I messaged, just like you said to do. Please say you'll meet me kiddo?? xx love mom*

WAIT, what? She'd been looking me up online. What did that mean?

I turned to Jonah in shock. "My mom is like stalking my online shit. She found my LinkedIn."

Then the rest of it hit.

She was coming to New York.

Had she really done what I'd asked? But I couldn't help feeling hurt she'd looked me up rather than try and ask me how my life was going. Unless—

I found the two previous emails from her that I'd ignored. The first was just a short hello, no questions about me or anything. The second was her saying she was going to be in New York, back in September.

When had she looked me up? Was it something she did often? The thought almost made me worried I'd pushed her away, made her resort to leaning about my life through a damn business profile, but that wasn't true. I'd tried with her for so long.

And she was finally making an effort to see me on my terms.

Nerves fluttered inside me.

Jonah swiveled in his chair. "I think it's a mom requirement to creep on their kids online. Don't worry. Back in college, my mom found a picture of me doing a mostly nude keg-stand on a weekend I told her I was too busy studying to go home for a visit. Finding your professional profile is pretty tame."

"Right. That's— Sorry, gotta go—" I scrambled away from my desk and slipped into the stairwell.

I called Owen, who answered promptly as usual, and the whole thing came spilling out of me in a run-on sentence.

"What do you want to do?" Owen asked when I stopped to catch my breath.

"I mean, I should see her right? She did what I asked. Said when she's going to be here. Twice now." I trailed my nails along the wall feeling a mix of guilt and regret for not looking at her messages sooner.

But she'd tried again, even after I'd ignored her, and that made me think she was serious.

"It's great that she finally listened to you, but—are you ready to actually meet up?" Owen sounded equal parts skeptical and cautious.

I didn't have much room for cation with the rest of the emotions taking hold of me. "Am I ever going to be ready? I can't say no now."

Owen snorted. “Yes, you can. But I get what you mean. It’s not that you can’t say no, it’s that you don’t want to.”

“*Ugh*. My stomach hurts already.” My head replaced my hand on the wall. “We have so much to talk about. So much I need to understand about what’s been going on the last half of my life. But—I dunno—am I a chump for giving her a chance? After everything?”

“Not at all. Just be careful. Stay realistic. Be prepared to be let down. Even if the meet-up doesn’t fall through and you actually see her, it might not be everything you’re hoping for.” Owen paused. “If you’re really thinking of doing this—I could come out. Go with you.”

“Owen—” I protested.

He didn’t wait for me to elaborate. “Or Edwin could go with you. I’m sure he’d support you if you asked. Have you told him—”

“No. We haven’t talked about stuff like this. I can handle things myself, you know.”

Owen was silent in a way that felt heavy. “That doesn’t mean you have to.”

# 25

## TRISTAN

That night Edwin met me at the door to his apartment with a drink in hand. He was tense, his features carefully reserved in that closed-off way I was all too familiar with.

I had no idea what had him looking like that. We'd agree to meet up tonight after Edwin had picked me up from Owen's on the weekend. I hadn't had a chance to tell him about my WMS suspicions yet.

"Darling, am I glad to see you." With an apparent effort, Edwin let his guard down. His expression didn't land in the realm of happy.

I slid off my coat and he hung it up for me. "Are you all right?"

"I'm better now." Edwin pulled me close and kissed me with careful, whiskey flavored lips.

"Better is good," I murmured as we broke apart, trying not to worry about his comment or the kiss being deflections.

"Let's get you a drink." Edwin gestured down the hall and I followed him to the living room bar.

He mixed me a whiskey sour, complete with a cherry because Edwin never did anything halfway. He had a real talent for cocktails and once he'd realized the straight stuff wasn't really my thing, he'd always made me something that fit my tastes.

I settled on the couch and took a sip, watching Edwin replenished his glass. He adjusted his champagne-colored bow tie, poised and beautiful as ever, but still looking tense.

After checking everything was put away on the bar, Edwin joined me, sitting tucked close to my side. I put my arm around him as I suspected he wanted.

He rested his head on my shoulder. "I've had a day of sorts."

No matter how vague the statement was, relief he'd said something rather than pretend nothing was up washed over me, banishing my growing worry. "Is it work?"

Edwin turned his glass around in his hands where they lay in his lap. "In a way. It's complicated. Work doesn't usually bother me."

Questions flooded my mind. The desire to know exactly what was going on so I could help him feel better was almost overpowering, but I took a moment to rub my hand up and down Edwin's arm and reminded myself comforting him had to come on his terms.

The tension in Edwin's body lessened the longer my hand moved back and forth.

"If you want to talk about it, I'll leave the invitation open."

"I—" Edwin pulled away from me just enough so we could look at each other. He let a ripple of conflicted emotion show.

"It's okay if you don't. Just. Anytime okay, Edwin?"

He gave me the tiniest nod.

I kissed Edwin in an act I hoped he could tell was pure comfort, trying to make it clear I wasn't pushing him to talk. He accepted my lips with a soft sigh and we kissed sweetly, not escalating to anything lusty, just connecting.

After a long tender moment we broke apart. The sense of intimacy slowly lapsed and Edwin raised his glass to his lips.

I ate my cocktail cherry and placed the stem on a coaster. "I had an odd day at work, actually. Would you be able to tell if I was still being siphoned?"

"What?" Edwin went rigid with alarm, looking immediately to my wrists, but I didn't miss his flash of relief at the shift in subject.

That was fine. I'd taken us back onto familiar, working-together-on-a-thing-that-isn't-us ground on purpose.

I conveyed my suspicions that something strange was happening at Walsh Marketing Solutions. My mom's email could have been part of my recount of the unusual day, but I didn't want to go there. It was hardly as pressing as potential blood stealing.

Edwin abandoned his drink on the coffee table as he examined my wrists thoroughly. "I can't detect any trace of magic."

I sagged in the beginnings of relief. "That's good."

"Potentially." He rubbed his thumbs over the veins showing faintly through this lighter part of my skin. "It's possible for a skilled Witch to cover their tracks. Avery wasn't experienced in siphoning, and didn't try to hide the evidence."

"Oh. Then what if when we followed the blood trail, and I led us back to my office building, it wasn't me messing things up?"

Edwin wore a devastating frown, brow crinkling as it often did when he was deep in thought. "It's a possibility. But if you're potentially being siphoned at work, why would your blood go from Mystic Pawn *to* your office?"

"Maybe it was another backward trail?"

"Hm." Edwin looked out the expansive window as the furrow in his brow deepened. "I suppose it doesn't matter if, or how the two are connected, at least not yet. We first need to know if you're right about why you and your colleagues keep coming out of meetings like someone's entranced you. Avery was adamant she wasn't taking enough blood to cause the side effects you were experiencing. Being siphoned from two different places would explain it. And an office would be a good captive source."

"Oh *god*. It would, wouldn't it?" I swallowed the rest of my drink, ready for another. Somehow the reality of what I'd suspected was hitting me in a new unsettling way. "I thought this job was my break, not some creepy-ass sham. No wonder they wouldn't let anyone work remotely."

All of my low-key regrets about moving came bubbling back up. I'd traded everything I enjoyed for this job and it might just be a bunch of bullshit.

"We don't know that it's a sham." Edwin examined my wrists again. "Even if you're being siphoned, it doesn't mean the job is illegitimate. Who knows if the Mortals at the company even know what's happening. *If* anything is happening."

"But it all feels like a big mistake." I'd prioritized all the wrong things. I'd been happy with my life before, why had I felt I needed a better career?

Edwin looked at me with concern. "What feels like a mistake?"

"None of this would have happened if I didn't move. I thought I'd always wanted a flashy job like this, but maybe I didn't. Maybe it was what I thought I was supposed to want."

"Do you not enjoy copywriting?"

"No, I do. But part of me took this job and moved because I wanted to be a certain kind of successful, and it might all be for nothing. The job is just a blood farm. It makes me think I've ruined everything for nothing."

Edwin gave me a look of confusion, lines appearing around

his eyes. "We don't know the job is all about blood, or even if it's partly about blood. Why is everything ruined?"

Because I'd let other people's judgments push me to take a job that was better on paper even though I knew in my gut that I'd wanted to stay in California. Who was I even trying to impress? Old exes I'd never see again, faceless people who treated me like I wasn't as good as them? Was I that afraid I wasn't good enough on my own that I had to satisfy arbitrary expectations to reassure myself?

Part of me knew I was good enough, without any job or anything. I had Owen, he'd stuck around though all my ups and downs and wouldn't be going anywhere. But no one else had even come close.

I wanted to be worthy of someone sticking around, even though I knew a certain job wasn't the magic way to achieve that. If someone didn't think I was good enough that was their problem, I knew that intellectually, but ever since my mom left I'd been looking for ways to trick people into seeing me as worthy. If there was a reason they'd leave that I could fix or counteract, how could I not try?

Except I'd been doing all this without really thinking about the root of my actions, and been doing things for hypothetically judgmental people. Even when I knew people with those kinds of views, they weren't who I wanted in my life. It was embarrassing to realize I'd moved across the country just to quell one of my insecurities. Filling my need to be unquestionably good enough, and validated by something concrete I could point to—like see, look at my job, I'm not nothing—and it had come at the price of everything I actually valued.

Edwin was waiting for me to respond as I squirmed under the weight of my own thoughts, but I didn't know how to talk to him. I was spiralling and we didn't even know if WMS was stealing blood for sure.

"Hey—" Edwin took my hand.

"Sorry." I tried not to look around at his fancy penthouse apartment. I knew me being so far from Edwin's position in life wasn't why he'd held back, I knew me thinking that was about my insecurities, but what if it became a thing for us? What if it was a little bit of the reason there was so much distance in our relationship?

"There's no need to apologize, Tristan." Edwin sounded serious yet tender, and looked oh-so-perfect in his vintage suit, surrounded by his artful home.

"Right. You're right. And not everything is ruined." I squeezed his hand. He was the only good thing to come out of me moving. I wouldn't let myself worry he'd leave when I didn't live up to the rest of his life. "We need to find out what's going on at WMS. If they're hurting everyone working there, that's so fucked up."

Edwin hesitated like he might want to bring us back to my unvoiced messed up worries, but he let it go. "We'll do everything we can, without delay. Luckily you're perfectly placed to help me poke around undetected."

*Yes*. Being able to do something about the problem was what I needed. Even if blood siphoning was only the surface issue. "Do you mean I'd be like, undercover, on the lookout for Witches at work?"

Edwin nodded. "If you're all right with that. There are other ways if you don't want to go back to your company given what you suspect."

"No, I have to go back. I need to look out for my colleagues. But how will I figure anything out if I keep being put to sleep?"

Edwin gave me an admiring look, like I'd said something impressive. "I can cast a protection spell on you that would make you resistant to most enchantments. But it could still be dangerous if you discover something, or if the Witches involved suspect you're immune to whatever they're doing."

"You'll have my back though." I was confident in this, if nothing else. I trusted Edwin. "We're a good team, when we try. Don't you think?"

Edwin smiled. "That we are."

EDWIN PERFORMED his protective spell on me, and the rest of the week crawled by. I was unsettled at work, expecting to see blood sucking Witches around every corner, and shaking off the realizations I'd had about my motives for taking this job proved harder than I'd have liked.

At least I'd managed to patch things up with Avery. There was still some tension between us, but I wasn't moving out and we said we wanted to try and give our friendship a second chance. I didn't blame her for her situation, but it was still hard to get over what had happened. It was a constant reminder that magic was unfair and dangerous, and that even with Edwin, Owen and Aria I was still in this weird new world that had somehow always been there, and there wasn't much I could do if a Witch had it out for me.

*But I'm not alone*, I reminded myself constantly.

Edwin kept me updated on the investigation. He'd tracked the last vial of blood Avery handed over, just as we'd planned, but it was currently sitting around at the Fizz Bar doing nothing and leading us nowhere. It turned out the bar was owned by Witches even if they were otherwise unnoteworthy and unsuspicious.

At work, I missed the only meeting scheduled for Tuesday. Not due to falling asleep but because Emerson Walsh called me to his office. Apparently, he'd picked a few people from each division to participate in a focus group to do with the new website and I was the lucky junior writer.

It was all a bit random. I didn't have strong opinions on the new layout or design, but didn't mind a change in routine. However, this meant a disruption to my normal meeting heavy schedule while I was stuck in a conference room with the focus group. It took up the majority of the week.

On Friday Emerson took us out to lunch as a thank you. I'd have liked to skip it but couldn't think of a way to without being rude.

"You seem distracted, Tristan." Emerson was sitting next to me at the restaurant and leaned in to practically whisper in my ear.

I scooched back, away from him. "Sorry. I have a few things on my mind." This awkward lunch wasn't doing much to distract me from the fact that I'd committed to seeing my mom tomorrow. She was even beginning to eclipse my worries about blood siphoning and the fact that Edwin and I were due in Witchcourt on Sunday.

Would she show up? If she did, then what?

Emerson was still very close to me. "Anything I can help with?"

"It's not work related—uh—thanks." I picked up my water glass and had a long sip.

"I'm good for advice in other areas. Something to keep in mind." He winked at me before turning away to ask a woman from finance about her daughter's science project.

The weird vibes coming off Emerson just didn't let up. He was too friendly, never to the extent it felt inappropriate, just oddly attentive. He'd chatted with me—or attempted to—more than anyone else at the table. I couldn't exactly fault that, but my intuition didn't like it.

I was a low-level employee, Emerson shouldn't care about

me. And he probably didn't. Making friends with everyone was very much part of his corporate-execs-are-just-like-you attitude. But it felt like I'd caught his attention.

Was he in on the alleged blood sucking? I wished I could tell if he was a Witch, but surely he wouldn't be. What Witch would opt for an office job and voluntarily sit through meetings on web traffic and click rates if they were also running some big blood scam?

## 26

# EDWIN

Tristan strode into my apartment and slipped off his coat, revealing a rumpled button up work shirt. His hair looked windblown and tangled, his soft brown cheeks flushed from the cold of the evening.

He was lovely, as striking as ever.

"You might want to hang on to that." I gestured to the coat as Tristan went to hang it in the closet. "I was thinking we could go out."

"Yeah?" The crooked grin that lit his face pulled on something deep inside me.

"For dinner. If that sounds good to you?" I grabbed my own jacket.

"I'd love to." Tristan slipped his coat back on, hair catching under the collar. He pulled it free, the curls noticeably longer than they'd been on our first night together. The new length suited him. "Looks like you're in a dreamy mood."

"Huh?" I'd been staring and even though it was far from the first time, getting caught left me flustered.

"Seems like going out for dinner has you all—" He waived a glittery hand at me, smiling in an affectionately amused way.

"Maybe so. Um. I thought we could use a nice night out. After everything." I busied myself exiting the apartment and locking up behind us.

"I guess so." Tristan buttoned himself up and pulled an impossibly scrunched scarf out of a large pocket. He seemed to get lost in thought, his bright mood dipping somewhat.

Had I said the wrong thing?

I eyed his hands where they were restless on the scarf. "How was work?"

"Hm?" Tristan looked up. "Fine. The same as the rest of the week. No opportunity to see if anything was going on. And next week's short. I wish I'd been able to make better progress." He pressed the elevator button.

That was right, I'd forgotten the holiday coming up. Meaning I hadn't asked Tristan what his plans were. Would he want me to? I usually teleported over to Juliet's on Thanksgiving, but realized I hadn't talked to her about it either. What if she was busy with Mea? The blue-haired Witch actually had relatives she might like to visit.

We rode down in the elevator. Tristan's mood remained dampened, whether by mention of work, lack of holiday plans, or my implication dinner was about needing a pick-me-up after stress, I wasn't sure.

I should have just told him the real reason I was taking him out, but now didn't feel like the right time. I went with what was easier. "We'll figure out what's going on. It might be a short week, but at least no one will be in danger of siphoning over the holiday. And there's still a chance you found nothing because there's nothing to find."

"Maybe." He shrugged.

"This case had been frustrating since the start. The fact that you've uncovered nothing in a week isn't surprising. It's been slow all around. No one at the Authority is pleased with the progress."

"Is that why work was bothering you the other day? The blood case isn't going well?" Tristan glanced at me and then away, as if he were worried about calling too much attention to his question.

"Maybe in part." I tried to distract us from my vague answer by exiting the elevator. Evading Tristan's concern gave me a pang of—not guilt—something more like uncertainty.

The truth was, my low mood on Monday had been about the upcoming court hearing and how Telling Tristan about magic continued to influence people's interactions with me. I could tell Witches at the Authority were whispering. It seemed this latest intrigue had renewed gossip about what happened with Judge Herrera at the start of the year, and from there, my past.

The judge had tried to frame me by planting evidence at a property I owned, one that had been deeply entangled in Wyatt's criminal business. I'd sold the place now but that didn't prevent it from being the detail that jogged everyone's memory. It reminded them I'd always been suspect and peripheral to those breaking the law.

None of my superiors were even pretending to assign me work anymore. Judge Geer said this was a courtesy, a break before the Telling hearing, and maybe he believed that, but I didn't trust that something else wasn't going on.

Confiding any of this in Tristan was too complicated. I didn't want to explain why old rumors still hurt me, or how convoluted my position at the Authority really was.

My carefully constructed career was unraveling. Judge Herrera was the first thread, and I might have been able to patch that up, but I'd gone and broken an actual law. There was nothing in Telling Tristan about magic that the judges shouldn't be able to excuse, but I suspected that being held to different standards than others was about to bite me.

"Like you said"—Tristan grabbed my hand—"we'll figure it out. And your work will be pleased if you make progress on the case."

"They will," I all but lied. "Let's try and forget about it for now. Enjoy the evening."

I led Tristan outside to where my town car was waiting. As I opened the door for him, Tristan treated to me an odd smile, almost like the interaction baffled him.

Should I have let him open his own door? I tried to brush my nerves away as I slid into the seat and buckled my seatbelt.

The car pulled away from the cub.

Tristan eyed the driver with suspicion, or was it more like discomfort? I couldn't tell, but he seemed to be avoiding catching my eye too. Maybe Tristan didn't like to talk with someone able to listen in and was disappointed we weren't alone. Whatever it was, the pure joy he'd displayed upstairs seemed to have disappeared.

I almost asked if everything was all right, however the feeling I was over thinking and creating problems in my own mind held me back.

There was nothing wrong with the car. I couldn't teleport everywhere. This was normal.

As we made our way through the city Tristan looked quietly out the window, his mind seeming far away. Which was understandable given the circumstances. His uncharacteristically subdued manner didn't necessarily have anything to do with me, or the fact that we were finally on a date together.

The quiet had me feeling awkward, if only breaking it now didn't feel so forced. It would be good once we got to the restaurant. The atmosphere would bring the evening back to where it was supposed to be. There was nothing to worry about.

Tristan didn't exactly perk up as we exited the car. He looked up and down the street before inspecting the restaurant as if we'd gotten out on the wrong block.

"This is one of my favorite places to dine." I'd taken us to what was, in my opinion, one of New York's finest steakhouses. A place that had been open for decades and had never served me a disappointing meal.

"Good thing I'm not in a T-shirt." Tristan opened the restaurant door.

It was on the formal side, but I'd never really thought about it. "Should I have let you go home to change?"

"No. I just never guessed I'd be someplace like this tonight."

I wasn't sure what to make of the comment. Perhaps he didn't appreciate not knowing our plans in advance, though I'd have guessed Tristan was someone who liked surprises. Maybe I was wrong.

I gave my name and someone took our coats before we were whisked off in a familiar direction. I had a particular table toward the back where I always sat. Being here with Tristan and sharing one of my routines with him felt oddly intimate for such a public setting.

As we settled in a small, single sided booth that curled around a table for two, a waiter delivered a whiskey and a whiskey sour.

"We didn't order." Tristan looked at the man in confusion.

"I always start with a drink." I waved the waiter off, trying to ignore a renewed flutter of nerves. "They bring it out as I arrive, so I called ahead to say I had company. If you'd like a different drink—sorry I assumed. That was rude of me."

Tristan watched the retreating waiter. "No, it's fine. You come here often?"

"About once a month." Admitting I had a standing reservation didn't feel like the right move. "I don't cook, and so eat out a lot. Though I'm a fan of food delivery apps."

"You don't cook at all?" Tristan smiled at me like he wasn't surprised.

I relaxed a fraction. "I've kept my culinary skills to cocktails."

"Well, you're very good at those." He scooched closer to me so we were almost touching. "I can't believe we're on a date. There's a candle on the table and everything."

I blushed and had to look away from him. "These last couple weeks together have been really good, Tristan. I've—opening up to you more has made me feel so—um—happy, I guess."

When I had the courage to look, Tristan was giving me the sweetest most lopsided smile, drinking in all my clumsy words and nervous tells like they were things he liked. "It's made me happy too, Edwin."

I was relieved he didn't ask why it'd taken me so long to get here, but of course he would never focus on the negative. Tristan wouldn't try to cast me in a bad light. He'd done nothing but give me a chance and allow me to be what I could for him.

"I thought—well, we haven't really defined what's going on." I gestured between us. "But I'd like to be able to call you my boyfriend. And I'd love to be your boyfriend. If that's all right with you?"

"Sounds awesome to me." Everything from Tristan's words to his eyes were filled with all his beautiful sincerity.

"Awesome," I agreed with a lighthearted laugh.

He raised his glass, glittery nails sparking in the candlelight. "To us being official."

We cheersed and he leaned in to kiss me. A soft peck on the lips. I was so wildly happy it hurt.

"This is very fancy for a first date," Tristan said as he looked down at the menu.

"It's nothing, really." Which wasn't true, but I was a bit embarrassed.

I always made such a production of things. Champagne on that first night, all this just to say I wanted to be his boyfriend. But to me each step was worth celebrating. I was in a place I'd never thought possible, where I could trust this man and trust myself to let him in without so much fear.

I sipped my whiskey and tried to explain. "My life is quiet and full of small constants, like coming here. I wanted to share a favorite with you. Besides, I don't know if this classes the same as a typical first date. Not with you, Tristan."

The meal was beautiful. Delicious food, fine wine, smiles and stolen kisses. Tristan talked and laughed like a man enjoying himself even if I found him almost flustered at times.

He insisted dessert was too much, so I asked him to join me again next month. Tristan loved sweets and shouldn't miss the crème brûlée. On a whim I suggested we come here just for drinks and dessert next time. I'd never done that, but it felt like an ideal way of blending two small bits of our lives together and creating something new.

Tristan agreed with obvious pleasure.

On the ride back to my place Tristan lapsed into silence once more, staring out the window. It was almost like he'd left his laughter and light mood back in the restaurant.

"Is there anything on your mind?"

"Nothing major." Tristan turned his attention to me. "I've got a busy day tomorrow, that's all."

"You must have a full-on weekend then. Are you worried about court on Sunday?" I pulled his hand into my lap.

He ran his thumb over my knuckles. "Not so much. I feel like I'm ready for it, between you and Aria's lawyer brother. And tomorrow's nothing you can't keep me distracted from."

He was right about that.

THE NEXT MORNING Tristan was up early. I rolled over to find him getting out of bed almost two hours before his usual time on a Saturday. I murmured an incoherent plea he come back to bed.

"Damn, I woke you." He grimaced in apology.

I rubbed a hand over my stubble-lined face. "It's been a while since I had a boyfriend, but is it customary for you to try and sneak off in the morning?"

Tristan didn't react to my teasing tone. "I have somewhere to be and need to get home to change."

"I can summon anything you need from your wardrobe, if getting dressed here is easier."

He hesitated, then climbed back into bed. "Thanks. Actually that will be good. Saves me backtracking."

I pulled Tristan close and we fell back asleep for a while.

Later, he proved indecisive on what to wear and in the end I teleported us back to his place rather than risk bringing all of his shirts through negative space, one by one, only to pile up on my bed.

Direct access to clothes didn't improve Tristan's selection process. He hadn't yet managed to get past the socks and underwear stage of dressing.

"Do you mind waiting? Giving me a magical lift?" Tristan asked as he held up two wildly different shirts, one a worn T-shirt and the other a patterned button down I'd seen him wear to work. "I've dawdled too much and I'm going to be late."

"That's my fault for keeping you in bed. I'll take you to—wherever you need to go."

"Thanks." He threw both shirts aside and grabbed a pair of

chinos and a pair of jeans to contemplate as he told me the name of the diner he was apparently going to.

Tristan finally settled on a simple casual outfit, jeans, a tidy T-shirt, and a bomber jacket. His visible nerves had worsened now he'd finished dressing. With no purposeful motion left to him, he fidgeted and fussed with his long hair.

I wanted to ask, but couldn't bring myself to pry. He could have mentioned his plans if he'd wanted. Really, it wasn't my business. Tristan allowed me to open up at the glacial pace I required, the least I could do was respect his need for privacy in return.

Tristan checked his phone for the third time in about two minutes. "I can't believe I'm running this late."

"It's all right. I've found a good place to teleport to. There's a foreclosed cafe down the block. It'll be empty." I stowed my phone in my pocket and held out my hand.

We were there in a flash.

"Thanks, Edwin." Tristan sounded guilty as we stepped out of the closed down cafe. "I won't make a habit of this sort of thing."

I used a quick spell to relock the back door. "It's no trouble. I can take you anywhere, anytime. Teleporting isn't making you so dizzy now. I don't think you so much as lost your balance."

We were in NoHo, not an area I often visited. Tristan and I made our way down a small alley to the street. He caught my hand before I turned to leave and pulled me in for soft kiss.

I was overcome with a giddy sort of smile. "I'll see you soon, darling. Have a good—"

"*Tristan!*" a voice called from up the street.

He went rigid. A woman whose facial features and curling black hair suggested she was a relative approached in an excited hurry. Tristan didn't move or call back. He looked stunned.

Before long the woman was upon us. "Kiddo. *Oh*, look at you." She pulled Tristan into a hug which he didn't return.

"Hi."

She released him, touching his shoulders and fussing over the collar of his jacket. "You're so handsome. And if you tidied up your hair. *My god*—I can't believe how much taller you are."

"Yep, like a full-grown man or something," Tristan muttered.

She stopped touching him and pursed her lips. Her too-familiar brown eyes focused on me. "Who's this?"

Tristan looked blankly between me and the woman, words failing him. It didn't seem like he wanted the situation to unfold this way and gave the impression of someone who was woefully trapped.

The woman frowned.

"I'm Edwin Bickel." I offered my hand and she shook it. "Lovely to meet you."

She turned back to Tristan expectantly. "I didn't know you were bringing someone."

"Edwin is—he's my—boyfriend," Tristan said as if he wasn't sure. "Sorry. Edwin can't stay. That's why I didn't mention it. He was just dropping me off."

"It doesn't look like he's dropping you off." The woman looked toward the street as if searching for a car.

Tristan squirmed. "Uh—"

"Never mind. He should stay. I want to get to know him." She turned back to me with an assessing stare. "Unless you aren't the type of man a mother would approve of?"

I faltered. "N-no, not at all. But Tristan wanted to spend time just the two of you. I don't mean to intrude."

"You're not. It's only coffee. Come on, boys. I'm freezing, don't make me stand out in the cold." Tristan's mother turned and walked down the street.

"Sorry," I muttered, trying to gauge what Tristan wanted me

to do but he still looked blank. “I can go. I’ll tell her I have an appointment if you’d rather I wasn’t here.”

Tristan remained silent as he stared after his mother, expression unreadable. After a long moment he slipped his hand into mine and pulled me along, his grip near crushing.

# 27

# TRISTAN

This was a disaster already. I should have sent Edwin away but couldn't let go of his hand.

I couldn't do this alone.

Why had I tried to? Owen was right, he should have been here. Edwin had no clue what was going on, and I still didn't want him to. It was too exposing. But fuck if I didn't need him.

Mom entered the diner, not waiting for us. The door swung closed.

I couldn't believe she'd come. That had to be why I was screwing this up; I'd never expected her to show. Getting stood up was something I could do on my own, and something I didn't want others to see, but this, this could be good, and that was so much scarier.

Someone exited the diner and held the door for us expectantly. I led Edwin inside. He said something I didn't register. It was like I couldn't concentrate, everything sounded like it was under water.

We sat in a booth. Mom on one side, Edwin and I on the other. I forced myself to let go of his hand.

Mom looked so much like I remembered. We had the same

light brown skin, same black curls. Her hair was up as always, long ponytail draped over one shoulder, wrists decorated with more bracelets than you could count, sporty clothes, unpainted nails. The glasses were new. There was no mistaking how much time had passed. She looked older but somehow less tired. Like being away from me suited her.

I didn't try to sit still. The plastic-covered booth made those annoying squelchy sounds so I settled for jiggling my foot and trying to figure out where to put my hands.

My mom picked up her menu. "So how'd you two meet?"

"What?" My voice came out hoarse.

She smiled at me. "How'd you and Edwin meet?"

"At a coffee shop." I swallowed. "I used to work there, and—back in California—my friend owns it." It was like I'd lost the ability to organize my thoughts even though I'd gone over things in my head, trying and prepare for this moment. There was so much I wanted to say it left me paralyzed now that my mom and I were actually together.

My mom's eyes roved over Edwin. I had no idea what she'd make of his vintage suit and teal bow tie. He looked pleasantly impassive, like he wanted to make a good impression while also attempting to fade into the background.

"Have you been together long?" The question was directed at the man beside me.

"Not terribly." Edwin took off his hat and set it beside him on the seat. He ran a hand through his gray-flecked hair. "Though we've known each other a while."

Mom turned back to me. "I thought you were doing something with writing?"

"I am." I blinked, baffled by everything she said. Were these the most pressing topics, really, after fifteen years? Boyfriends and work?

"Did you help Tristan get his job here?" Mom asked Edwin.

"Um—no." Edwin frowned. "I don't work in marketing."

"Oh. I just thought—going from working in a coffee shop to something so different?" Mom raised a brow at me.

I explained how I'd been doing copywriting part-time for years. Which she could have seen from my LinkedIn, but I guess she hadn't looked into all my past stuff.

It was hard to gauge my mom's interest as I rambled. She kept looking back and forth between me and Edwin like she was trying to piece things together. She'd known I was gay, so I didn't get what the hang-up was. Maybe she was just as flustered about seeing me as I was her.

There was a lull when I stopped talking.

"Well, I'm glad I was able to track you down, Tristan. I've missed you."

"I missed you too." My voice was too quiet and I had to blink a bunch to fend off tears.

But mom was looking at her menu again and didn't seem to notice. She flagged down a waiter to order coffee and pie. Edwin ordered a coffee each for me and him. I was too busy looking at the table to say anything, so mom ordered me a piece of pie as well.

"It's hard to know where to begin, kiddo," she said after the coffee was poured.

"Yeah." I squirmed.

"I guess I never thought you'd be so much like me." She gave me a sad look, like she was trying to smile but it didn't quite take.

"I don't know what you mean."

Mom gave Edwin a pointed glance over her coffee mug. I followed her gaze to the man next to me, lines of worry forming around his eyes.

"God, Tristan." Mom sighed. "He's got to be about my age."

"He's sitting right here," Edwin said in a tight, surprisingly cold tone.

"Wait—*what?*" I stared at my mom in shock.

She'd had me when she was twenty, and so yeah, she was only six years older than Edwin but—

"It's just, you've seen how this goes, Tristan." She clicked her tongue.

"Excuse me?" Edwin's voice remained cold, but I couldn't bring myself to look at him.

"Mom—" She gave me more of that sad, knowing look. I shook my head. "No. You can't just come in here and— That's so — I mean, you don't know Edwin. Hell, you don't even know me. It's been fifteen years."

She flinched. "Thank you, Tristan. There's no need to shout about it to the whole room."

"I didn't shout." I'd been at half-volume at best.

"I'm sorry if I've hit a nerve, but you know what that means." Her expression said you-can't-deny-I'm-right. "It doesn't matter how long it's been since we've seen each other."

"It matters to me." I looked at my lap and Edwin's arm slipped around my shoulders. It wasn't until his touch calmed me that I realized I'd been trembling.

I wanted to go back in time and start over. Out of all the things I thought my mom and I would say today, judging my romantic life hadn't factored in.

Edwin held me steady. "Whatever you think you know about me, I can guarantee it's way off the mark."

"Okay, but I won't apologize for looking out for my boy. It's worth it if it keeps you honest." Mom picked up her coffee.

I couldn't believe she'd gone there. Saying she was looking out for me cut into my already raw emotions, recalling all the times she hadn't been there.

"So where—what about all the other years?" I tried to ask.

Mom waited briefly for me to say more. "Sorry, kiddo. I don't know what you mean?"

"I haven't seen you since I was in high school. Why? What about when I had my first boyfriend? What about—" But I wasn't even sure I knew what.

My mom looked surprised. "Tristan. That time is hard for me to talk about. Discussing your high school years isn't why I'm here."

"It's hard for me to talk about too." I ran a hand through my hair. "But I need to know why you kept saying you'd see me and never did. You were supposed to come back. I need to know what happened with us."

"Nothing happened. It wasn't deliberate. Sometimes you just miss each other's paths."

But that wasn't how I remembered it. Maybe some of the times, but every attempt we made to reconnect, all the unreturned calls? How was me saving up for flights to visit her and reaching out to confirm dates, only to not hear back for months, *missing each other's paths*? It had felt like avoidance.

I wanted her to apologize for it. Or explain how I'd got it so wrong.

The pie arrived, which was just as well. I was too incoherent to talk.

"Look." Mom eyed me, fork poised above her plate. "I want to start over. I can't change the past. All I can do is spend time with you now."

"Yeah, okay." I gulped down some coffee.

I wanted to know my mom and have her in my life. I wasn't going to insist we argue about our past if it was going to push her away. I wanted to repair our relationship not dwell on all the bad stuff. But I did need to acknowledge our history in some form or another. If we didn't, how could we build anything real going forward?

Maybe today just wasn't the day. Over a decade of hurt feelings weren't going to heal in one morning at a crowded diner. Maybe after we were used to each other again, comfortable like we used to be, then we'd have that talk.

I had to be patient, as long as she was making an effort. "So what's—um—new with you?" I had another sip of coffee.

"I'm actually in town with my husband." Mom ate a bite of pie and smiled. "His son—your step-brother—is a freshman at NYU."

"I—oh. When did you get married?" I pushed my own pie away.

"Come on. I told you." She reached across the table and patted my hand, bracelets clinking. "Almost four years ago now."

She hadn't told me. There was no way. "But I would have come to your wedding."

"We didn't do a wedding." She waved me away so casually. "Just signing the papers with Steve's sister and son, Levi. Close family only."

"But—" I sputtered and my throat burned. Edwin tightened his arm around me and I had to resist tucking my face into his chest.

My mom seemed to realize what she'd said. At least she had the decency to look horrified. "Fuck, Tristan. Kiddo. Sorry. I—I just didn't want to ask you to fly all that way for a trip to the courthouse. You had your own life, there was no need to disrupt it. And Levi took some time to warm up to me, we didn't want to overwhelm him. I tried to come visit you that year. But look—" She brightened deliberately. "That's why I'm here. I know we wanted to see each other sooner, that you'd have been there for me, but now is perfect. It's time for new memories. You should come to dinner tonight. Meet the rest of the family. Your brother."

"I—I don't think tonight is good."

"Aww, please. Why not? Bring your boyfriend. I'm sorry about what I said earlier. Really, Edwin." She glanced at him demurely. "You know me, Tristan"—a self-deprecating laugh—"I always say the wrong thing. How often did that get me in trouble? It was just like déjà vu, seeing you and old memories coming up. I worried. Still, I'm sorry. Of course not all older men are the same. Though kiddo, I ended up with a younger one. Just saying." She winked at me. "Oh! God, what if you and Steve are the same age?"

Edwin was at his most unreadable. "I'm sure that we aren't."

I felt dizzy. "Can we just leave the age thing? Regardless, I can't do dinner tonight." I was due to talk to Luca Belmonte before court tomorrow. Hell, after this Witchy judgment day was going to be a breeze.

Mom pressed cheerfully on. "Well, what about next week?"

"Next week?"

"Thanksgiving, kiddo. Steve and I are driving back down to Jacksonville with Levi, come with us. We can even bring you back to the city."

"I have work this Monday and I'm flying to California on Wednesday."

"Why?" My mom looked bewildered, like me having a reason to go back never crossed her mind.

I couldn't keep up with this conversation. She'd ripped my heart out and then proceeded to offer me a family road-trip I'd have killed for fifteen, ten or even five years ago. It all hurt just as bad as her obliviousness to anything about me. "Owen's in California."

"Well, who's that?" She gave me a bright, over-interested smile.

"He's my family."

She blinked and looked at Edwin. "Am I missing something?"

"I mean, other than my whole adult life?"

"Tristan—" She looked genuinely hurt. "There's no need to be like that. You can just say you don't want to spend the holiday with me."

"That's not what I meant, sorry. I appreciate the offer, really mom. But I booked this trip months ago. Why don't we plan something else?"

"Yes, of course." She picked up her fork and poked at her pie. "I can't expect you to always have time. I mean, we've both had our own things going on for years. But now that Levi goes to school here, and you aren't so far, I'm sure we'll see each other more."

I nodded and finished off my coffee. I'd been too distracted to put cream or sugar in it. The taste was horribly bitter.

Mom nudged my pie plate back toward me. I picked up a fork. She'd ordered us cherry, my favorite. I tried to hold on to that as she told me all about Steve and Levi.

The pie tasted like nothing.

The more she talked the more I was confronted with how sickeningly jealous I was of Levi. Some eighteen-year-old kid I'd never met. It was impossible to be happy for my mom and her not-so-new life when all I could see was me being replaced. And in part, that wasn't fair. My mom should be able to be happy. She sounded like she was doing really well, and had decent people around her for once. That was good. She deserved it. But I didn't know why I couldn't have been there too.

## 28

## TRISTAN

My mom hugged me goodbye outside the diner. "See you soon, kiddo."

I hugged her back this time. "I'm sorry I'm busy next week." I sniffed, too aware of the fear I might not see her again now there was no concrete plan.

"That's all right." She pulled back and patted my hand where it was still on her shoulder.

I nodded.

As long as we didn't leave it like this and never see each other again. This meeting had been too mixed. I still had so much to say.

"I'll look forward to seeing you *both* next time I'm here." Mom waggled a finger at Edwin. "I'm going to keep you on your toes."

"I'll get my point shoes ready." Edwin didn't sound or look remotely amused.

"Ha." My mom ruffled my hair. "Bye now." And she walked away.

Edwin and I looked at each other in silence as people moved around us on the busy sidewalk.

"That was—" His unreadable face slipped into concern.

"I'm so sorry." I choked a little and cleared my throat. My vision blurred. "Fuck."

Edwin stepped forward and his arms encircled me. "You don't have anything to apologize for."

"Yes—" I choked again, the sound slightly muffled by Edwin's shoulder.

He held me and whispered assurances in my ear. I tried to let everything fade away and focus on Edwin, but the street was too loud, the air too cold. Someone on the street wolf-whistled.

"I need to get out of here," I said into Edwin's suit.

He led me back to the foreclosed cafe and soon we appeared in my bedroom. Clothes were everywhere and even though I was the one who'd tossed them about, the sight startled me. The room felt cramped and unwelcoming.

"I should clean up."

Edwin grabbed my hand as I reached for a shirt. "Tristan—"

I faced him, our hands clasped in the space between us. "I'm sorry. I can't believe I dragged you into that."

"You can drag me anywhere you need."

"I did need you. But I didn't want to tell you. I—I don't know what I'd have done alone."

I sat on the end of my bed and let the whole story out. My self-consciousness about sharing with Edwin hadn't been cured. It was eclipsed by a desperate need for him to understand. Maybe talking to Edwin would help me understand.

I'd never felt more different from Edwin than I did spilling my guts in my messy room. He was poised and flawless even while he expressed his concern for me. I felt raggedy and insecure, like I had nothing to offer other than problems and failures. I couldn't remember what I'd ever thought Edwin might value in me.

I was cute. I was good in bed. That seemed to be the sum of it.

Why was he here? Why did he care?

"I can't even tell if the meeting was bad or not, or if I messed it up." I was barely processing my own tumbling words. "She really does seem like she wants to try. She's listened to me. But seeing her felt so—and she's kind of right. It feels like everything has come to a point. My whole life is just— My job. The blood. Moving for the stupid job to begin with—"

"Tristan, take a breath." Edwin sat next to me, perched on a pair of discarded pants, his hand tight on my shoulder.

But I couldn't stop. "She was right, we don't make any sense together. She didn't even have to say it on so many words."

He took has hand away like he'd been burned. "What—no—"

"Yes. Why else would her comment hit me like that? Yeah, it was rude and insulting to both of us. But we don't match up. I'm just not good enough and I have to stop trying. Like with this job, who was I aiming to impress? And it's not even that impressive. Edwin—I know you held back from me for your own reasons, but don't you think part of it was because I'm not right for you?"

"What?" It came out in a breathless puff. I couldn't make myself look directly at him.

I rubbed my eyes. "You're older than me, richer than me, more put together than me. You were happy to just get off with me. Leave it at that and send me on my way. If Avery never siphoned me, if there was no blood scheme, would I still just be a convenient fuck you kept at arm's length like I wasn't good enough for the rest of your perfectly constructed life?"

"No. None of that is true." Edwin got off the bed and knelt before me, compelling me to look at him. His eyes shone. "Our differences in age and wealth had nothing to do with why I resisted a real relationship with you."

I averted my gaze. "How can it not be why? Why didn't you want me? Why did I have to push so hard?"

He grabbed my hands and when I didn't resist, held them tight. "Tristan, you are good enough, just as you are. I've always wanted you. I—I had no idea you felt this way. I used the boundary of a casual relationship to hide from my own fears. I want to be able to live up to you, your kindness, your acceptance, your joy and the way you live your life. That's what I see in you. Not your job or the price of your clothes. My—my hesitance was about my own insecurity. My own inability to be vulnerable and show you who I was."

"Oh god, Edwin." I pulled out of his grasp and put my head in my hands. "I'm sorry. You told me you had a hard time opening up, and I thought I was past this. It's not that I don't believe you, I just can't let go of my doubts. I'm never good enough. It has to be part of the problem here too. We're so glaringly different." I make a choked sound. "And even if we weren't. I've never been good enough for anyone. How is that ever going to change?" My breaths were coming short and strangled. "I just wish I was someone she'd found worth keeping."

Edwin wrapped me up and accepted my tears. He sat back on the bed and pulled me into his lap. It was awkward and I felt unbearably lanky, but he seemed to be holding me with everything he had. "You are worth keeping, darling. I'm not letting you go. I'm sorry I couldn't show you how much you meant to me."

"It's okay." I tucked tighter into him.

"I think it's really not. I'm selfish and flawed. I've been hurting you in order to sooth my own—I don't even know anymore."

I sniffed. "I'm not trying to make you feel guilty. I know a lot of this is actually about my mom. But I've spent a lot of time wondering if that's how you felt about me, and I guess it kept coming back up, popping into my mind whenever I wasn't sure about us. I couldn't keep holding it in."

"You don't have to hold it in. I shouldn't be reinforcing the doubts your mother's given you." Edwin buried his face in my hair. "I wish you'd told me how you felt. I wish I'd seen it, or stopped and thought about how my behavior came across rather than obsessing about myself."

I took a very shaky breath. "Guess we both aren't great at saying how we feel."

"No." Edwin handed me a handkerchief and I shifted off him to mop my face. "Do our differences bother you? My age or financial position, magic even?"

"I want to say no; if it's not why you pushed me away then it doesn't matter. But it could matter. Like if you think you have to take care of me just because you're wealthy and I'm not. I want to be able to take care of each other. I don't want you to expect to solve my problems just because you can. I don't want things I can't reciprocate. I don't want fancy stuff, and I don't want you to think I need it."

Edwin thought for a moment. "Last night's date, was that the kind of thing you don't want?"

"I want to date you, as in be a couple. It's not about the going out specifically. I don't expect to be taken to fancy restaurants. Not that I didn't enjoy it. I get that you were sharing a special place with me and I really liked that. I just don't want everything we do to be me trying to fit into your lifestyle while you pay for it. If we can have just as good of a time eating pizza by the slice as we can at a restaurant with Michelin stars, and you don't see one as inherently better than the other, then I think we'll be fine. We can do both, not default to one or the other, just be equal."

"That sounds good. I never meant to push you to fit into my

life. That isn't what I want. I have a hard time expressing myself" —we shared a smile—"and I used the restaurant as an, I don't know, a representation. And I admit, I turn to luxury when celebrating, even if I know it doesn't add any more meaning than if I'd asked you to be my boyfriend on a street corner."

"I just want to talk about it." I twisted the handkerchief in my lap. "Ask me if an extravagant night is the way to go. Tell me why you want to go that way so I know you aren't just treating your life as a default over mine."

"So communicate." Edwin gave me a self-deprecating grin.

"Yeah, and I will too. Promise." A large part of the worry I'd been carrying around for months lifted.

I had to resist the urge to lie down and pulled the covers over me. I was exhausted.

"On that note, there is something I have to tell you." Edwin's expression shut down just a little. "My age—I—what if I lied?"

That brought me up short. The word *lie* felt like a cold stone in my gut. "What do you mean?"

Edwin closed his eyes briefly. "It's a Witch thing. When you first asked how old I was, I wasn't able to tell you the truth, and I wasn't sure when to return to the topic after Telling you about magic. Now it feels overdue. If there's a chance our age difference bothers you—" Edwin's posture hunched like he was feeling ill and didn't go on.

"Look, I'm sorry my mom kept bringing that up. But it's the same as the money. If you don't act like we're on different footing because your older, and don't plan to dump me just for getting wrinkly so you can replace me with someone younger, then the difference doesn't concern me. But lying about it might." I wasn't sure how this could be a Witch thing.

Edwin didn't un-hunch. "That's understandable. I wouldn't have lied about it if there'd been a way to explain from the start, but Witches live for centuries. Um. We don't age like Mortals.

That's why you're Mortals. We don't live forever," he added in a rush, responding to my apparent shock.

I breathed a sigh of relief.

Edwin looked at his hands, straightening the cuffs of his jacket in his lap. "I'm one-hundred-and-thirteen and may live another two centuries, or so."

"Oh." As the words sank in my eyes roamed, from Edwin's flecks of gray, to his youthful yet lined face, to his exquisite vintage clothes. It made a strange sort of sense when considered all together. "Well, you're definitely not the same age as Steve."

Edwin snorted and looked up. Relief shone in those sharp blue eyes. "Yes, I did say— But Tristan, seriously."

"Sorry, just soaking it in." I was as surprised as he seemed to be with my non-reaction, but I'd always sensed there was something impossible to pin down about Edwin's age, his mannerisms, the hint of formality in his interactions.

"It's okay if this bothers you," Edwin said heavily, as if he thought my lacking comment had a negative context. "I'm sorry for deceiving you, but I don't feel a hundred years old, honestly." Edwin crossed his arms tight over his chest, like he was trying to hold himself together, his expression imploring.

"I don't know if it can bother me. Being that old doesn't seem real in any way I can grasp. But I'm also not totally surprised. Maybe seeing you walking around like you're off to a fancy speakeasy helped the truth go down." I tweaked his bow tie and he grinned, leaving it off kilter rather than fixing it. "I guess—what does your age mean to you? How do you think it impacts us? What's it like?"

Edwin flopped back on the bed, his head coming to rest on one of my stray T-shirts. I stretched out beside him and we faced each other, both propped up on our elbows. Right now he looked youthful, freckled and bright eyed, relieved and a bit silly with the crooked teal bow tie.

My very-much-older Witch-boyfriend ran his delicate fingers over the rumpled bedspread and the button-down shirt trapped beneath us, looking thoughtful. "I don't think my age affects us in the immediate future. It's one of the strange things about being a Witch, where you live multiple lifetimes but also don't feel as though you've aged. It gives the sense of things passing you by, the world changes and you do too, but at a different rate. Like I feel able to keep up with the times and progressing views but also very similar, in some respects, to the man I was thirty years ago. Mea thinks it's just our excuse for remaining immature." He smiled. "But I don't know. I've never been in a relationship with a Mortal. I don't know how this aspect of who I am will affect us."

"So does this mean you won't get old?" I felt the first squirm of uncertainty, because of course I wanted to think we'd work long term.

"Not at the same time you do." Edwin tucked a stray curl behind my ear. "But there are different ways to deal with that. Some Witches might stay with their Mortals lovers for a lifetime, then grieve at their passing and move on. Some find that too hard to accept and sacrifice a portion of their Magic to grant their lover a matching lifespan. I don't know if either scenario is a commitment level we're ready to navigate. I'm certainly not ready." Edwin looked away.

"I'm not ready for that either." He looked back at me with some relief. "I mean, I was just freaking out about not being good enough for you. We have a long way to go, but that's okay. Working on big stuff is what relationships are about. I actually feel all right about this, and magic and everything. It seems like you're open to different options for us, and like you've considered some sort of future, and I think that's a good sign."

"Thinking about a future with you used to scare the hell out of me," Edwin mumbled, his attention directed to the bedspread.

I poked his leg with my toe. "And now?"

He looked up. "Now, I'm more manageably worried about my ability to do this."

"Progress. Can't argue with that."

Edwin moved closer, putting an arm over me. "See, Tristan. This is what matters. You—your ability to accept and care. This is what I've always seen in you. Not your job or other markers of status. And I won't say those things don't matter, because they clearly do to you, and affect both of us, but this matters so much more."

I kissed him and felt his lips turn up in a smile. "Careful, Edwin. You're sounding pretty wise. Age might actually come into play after all."

Edwin laughed. "I'm not wise. It's just the gray hair."

I ran my fingers through it. "So can I ask, why do you hold back from connecting with people?"

Edwin's eyes went round with panic and it seemed like I'd ruined the moment. "I know I've been good at sharing today, Tristan, but I still need time. I could blame my slow progress on being a Witch, but I'm pretty sure that's an excuse. There are things I'm just not ready to share."

"That's okay." I appreciated he could say he wasn't ready instead of hiding the whole thing. "I wasn't ready to share my mom with you."

"True, but I'm glad you did share that part of your life with me. Now I have a better understanding of where you're coming from." Edwin frowned. "So, ah—maybe I should try to give you some context too."

I let him think about that and tried not to sway him with a *yes, please, I just want to know you* face.

"Before you," Edwin said tentatively, running his fingers

through my hair. "I hadn't had a boyfriend since the late eighties."

"Oh," I breathed.

Edwin didn't shy away as he continued, keeping his intent blue eyes focused on mine. "I never planned to have another relationship. I didn't want one. And I'm not ready to talk about why, or what that last relationship was like. I was content with my isolated life and my one friend, Juliet, who isn't dissimilar to what Owen is to you. But a lot has changed this past year, and it hadn't been easy. That's why I held back. I was afraid to change and didn't want to take risks. I didn't want to open up again. Not doing so had worked for so long. But lying here, I wonder if it ever worked the way I thought. I'm glad I've tried, even if it might not seem like I've made much progress."

"I can tell you've opened up," I said as gently as I could. "And I can be patient about the things you're not ready for. I don't mean to push. You can tell me if I'm asking something of you that's out of your comfort zone, but hopefully I have a better handle on that now."

"I will. And you too? Tell me if something is bothering you?" Edwin brought his face close to mine.

"Yes." I rested my forehead against his and we stayed like that, feeling the tentative new understanding we shared. It was nerve wracking and sweet, and full of all the potential I'd hoped for.

"Tristan, there's something else I'd like to share," Edwin whispered, rubbing his nose over mine. "That first night with you, I hadn't had sex in a very long time. Not as long as it'd been since I'd been in a relationship, but close."

I wanted to pull away and scrutinize his expression, but our closeness felt important. I put my arm around him and gently stroked the back of his neck. "Oh, Edwin. I hope it was what you needed. I hope I was—"

"You were everything. I walked away because I'm terrible at dealing with my feelings. And that night, Tristan, I had a whole lot of them. You were very special to me. I just wasn't ready to be special to you."

My heart just about burst. "And now?"

He kissed me, laying me flat on my back. "I'm yours."

# 29

# EDWIN

Tristan and I spent the rest of the weekend apart.

He had an appointment with Luca Belmonte regarding the court appearance the following evening, and it wasn't for me to sit in on. Strictly speaking, he didn't need a lawyer, but he'd talked to Luca on Aria and Owen's suggestion, and the man had offered to come to the hearing. Apparently he was due to be in town with family.

I hadn't understood Tristan's motivations for engaging the lawyer until now. I suspected it was his way of confronting magic as independently as possible. He wanted to be on an even footing with me in court, not reliant on me to take care of things. It wasn't about trust in me, or any lack, it was about him feeling secure in himself. He'd told me he hoped the court would take it as a show of initiative, a sign he was happy to know about magic and deal with all it entailed.

It was a good idea. Tristan's committed attitude gave me confidence. My initial fears that revealing magic had gone horribly wrong seemed almost laughable now. We'd come a long way.

I arrived at the Authority building on Sunday evening to find Luca waiting outside.

The court always scheduled Telling hearings outside the Mortal's working hours out of courtesy, and in this case it helped me too. There would be less people around, watching and talking.

As I approached Luca, a man exited the building. I recognized Mr. Belmonte, Luca and Aria's father, whom I'd met along with the young lawyer when I'd endure an awkward visit to their home a year and a half ago.

"Good evening, Mr. Bickel," the older Belmonte said.

I tipped my hat. "Evening."

Luca looked up from his phone. "Tristan's messaged to say he's on the way. There was a delay on the subway."

The lawyer was smartly dressed in an—I'd say—tailor-made suit. He had brown hair down to his shoulders, a stubble-lined jaw and skin slightly darker than Tristan's. Luca projected the same serious demeanor I'd found in his sister, but without her air of indignance.

"Too bad you and Luca didn't get to know each other better last year." The older Witch considered his son and me thoughtfully. "He could have saved you all this trouble."

"I'm sorry?" I blinked at the man, keeping my face carefully neutral.

"I just think my boy would suit you better. That's all. And I know I'm not exactly impartial, but what can you do?" He made a show of chuckling.

Was he really commenting on my personal life? Suggesting I date his son just because he was a Witch? "I don't know why you'd think that." I leveled a cold stare, then turned to Luca "No offense."

He was a deep shade of scarlet. "No worries. Dad, why don't you leave me to it. I'm working."

"And always networking. If you'd remembered that when Mr. Bickel was our guest, perhaps we'd be standing in an entirely different place right now." He patted his son's shoulder and left.

"I'm so sorry." Luca couldn't quite look at me.

I should have said it was fine, his father's presumptuous behavior was hardly his fault, but I was already lost in my thoughts.

Why did people always feel they could comment on my private life?

How had Mr. Belmonte even heard my Telling had to do with a boyfriend? As if this hearing really was so much trouble that I'd consider another partner more preferable. Telling wasn't the problem. The issue was my work situation, my colleagues and superiors' reactions.

Comments like that were the problem.

Mr. Belmonte must have been unaware of my history. He'd never consider me good for his son if he weren't, or maybe he put that much value on power. My standing outside the Authority was enviably high, but no one had yet taken that as an invitation to rope me into furthering their ambitions. Maybe I was becoming too likable. Too approachable.

What an uncomfortable thought.

I stewed on all this as Luca tried to occupy himself with his phone. Mercifully, Tristan arrived.

"Shall we go in?" I opened the door for the other two to proceed before following them across the quiet foyer to the elevators.

I was ready to get this over with, and reminded myself that Luca being here was a good thing from any angle. An audience would make it harder for the judges to find fault in my Telling just because they didn't like me.

I just had to get this ticked off and deal with the issues it had created at work. Then everything would go back to normal and I could relax, focus on my relationship, sort out how to get through my remaining hold-ups.

If I wanted something lasting with Tristan I couldn't hide parts of me forever. I had to get comfortable with the reality of where this was headed and trust I could handle whatever came of it.

To do that I needed to focus, not be distracted by work drama and the damned history I was trying to get over. I wanted to leave the whole business with Wyatt far behind me and never look back.

We entered the elevator and I selected the button for the top floor.

"This place isn't very Witchy," Tristan observed as the door slid shut. He was carefully dressed, wearing a tie—which I'd never seen him do—and I could have sworn he'd polished his shoes. He'd even redone his nails in a shimmering blue.

"I told you no one was as Witchy as Avery." I nudged his shoulder and he smiled. "Mostly we're as stiff and boring as anyone else."

"More so, some might say," Luca muttered, his face impassive.

"I bet Aria thinks that." Tristan laughed.

The same thought had occurred to me.

Luca snorted, allowing a brief smile through. "Any last questions, Tristan?"

"Nope, I think I'm all good." He grinned at me and took my hand as the elevator opened. "How about you, Edwin?"

I relished the comfort of his touch. "Looking forward to after. Maybe we can have dinner together."

"Yeah, perfect—there's this taco place near my house you need to try."

"That sounds lovely."

We walked down the empty hall to the court room. The door stood cracked, the faint mummer of voices coming from within. Luca checked his watch and pushed the door open.

The courtroom was large and unadorned. The gallery seats were empty, however the bench at the front was lined with all seven of the judges who sat on the local Judicial Committee.

"Owen said it would be like, one person and a notetaker," Tristan whispered.

I squeezed his hand. "I thought so too, that's standard. I don't see why they all came just because it's me." And in all the passing comments about my hearing, no one had thought to mention it ahead of time.

"I'm sure it will fine. The procedure has to follow the appropriate format." Luca sounded stern and authoritative. It was almost comforting.

We progressed to the front of the room. I went to stand to the right as Tristan and Luca took the space to the left.

"Right on time, excellent." Judge Geer sat in the middle of the panel, hair wild and a pleasant look on his face.

Judge Pérez sat beside him, peering over her glasses. "We'd expect nothing less than timeliness."

I hadn't had a meeting with all seven Judges since the beginning of my employment. Even during the investigation into Judge Herrera I'd only seen a few of them at a time, though that had been taken over by another district due to obvious conflict of interest.

It didn't bode well that they were all here.

"Shall we begin?" Judge Raven sat at the far end of the bench. He was in all black and looked like he was attending a funeral, or perhaps a memorial for his hair, which always looked like the slickened gray pelt of some unfortunate animal.

"Yes, yes. Let's get on." Geer clapped his hands, rubbing

them together like he was looking forward to it. The others remained neutral.

Pérez adjusted her glasses. "The New York Judicial Committee is now in session." She picked up a stack of papers, a gesture whose sole purpose appeared to be allowing her to look intimidatingly over it in Tristan's direction. "I, Judge Pérez, will preside over this hearing. Be reminded that lying to the court is an offence that may be prosecuted. Our newest member, Judge Lee, possesses the psychic talent and will be validating the truths spoken today, as we go. Objections?"

There was a heavy pause.

A glance at Luca suggested he was surprised, but he hid it well. His only reaction to this less than standard imposition was a clenching and flexing of his magically tattooed hand. "No objection. However, I note the extra precaution is a deviation from procedure."

The lawyer practically had no other choice. He might have objected based on overreach but establishing grounds would be unlikely, and there was the risk the court would take protest as an indication we had something to hide. It was a sneaky move on their part and I didn't like it.

"Very well." Pérez turned her attention to me. "Mr. Edwin Bickel, you have been called here for Telling Mortal Mr. Tristan Taylor Tomás about the existence of magic without prior approval. Before we ask you to explain what led you to reveal magic, we turn to the Mortal. Mr. Tomás, in your own words please describe your relationship with Mr. Bickel."

"Romantic?" Tristan's voice came out steady but quiet enough that I suspected his nerves had mounted since we'd walked in the room.

"Is that a question?" Pérez arched a brow.

Tristan cleared his throat. "No. We're dating."

"And this began when? How did you become acquainted?"

She was belaboring the point. The judges only needed to establish the dynamic between Witch and Mortal, making sure I hadn't carelessly Told a random person. There was no reason to request details. I tried not to let this make me anxious.

Tristan paused. "Um—since September? We met over coffee."

Judge Lee leaned forward in her chair. "Why are you unsure?"

Tristan's fidget caught at the corner of my vision. "These things are hard to define, um subjective and all that. We met a year and a half ago."

"I'd say we have all we need to know." Geer looked around at the others for agreement.

No one gave it, giving the impression that the line of questioning might have gone on, but no one contradicted Geer's point either.

From here I was asked to outline what happened. I kept my account focused on discovering Avery's crime against Tristan and his confusion upon finding me trying to deal with Avery. "I had to explain what was really going on. He had a right to know he was being assaulted by someone he trusted."

"And it was the only way to get back in Mr. Tomás' good books. Stop him leaving you," Raven added.

The rest of the judges peered at me keenly.

"No. Not to stop him, but to give him a fully informed choice about staying with me or leaving." I folded my hands behind my back and clenched them together, hard.

There was nothing wrong with admitting I'd Told for personal reasons. I wasn't ashamed to acknowledge the significance of my feelings for Tristan, but I resented having to give those details to this group of people in particular. I didn't trust that they wouldn't pry out of idle curiosity or even maliciously in pursuit of gossip.

They'd made me divulge more than I'd felt was strictly necessary in my trial regarding Wyatt's criminal network, forcing me to detail the abusive nature of the relationship while casting judgment and doubt on everything I said. Then someone had shared my story around the Authority for no justifiable reason.

I feared them prying now. Doing so because they could, and because they loved to dislike me, or considered me guilty despite my verdict and still wanted to punish me, make a powerful Witch like me feel less than.

Judge Herrera had always hated me, even before I'd befriended her daughter, and she'd always asserted that I shouldn't be here. I hadn't hoped that her removal would prompt the rest of them to reevaluate their attitude toward me—I wasn't that naïve—but I didn't take any pleasure in being right about nothing changing.

Pérez shifted her attention back to Tristan, moving on. "Do you have anything to add?"

It was a relief they weren't lingering over me breaking Witch-law because my lover had left me, but I resented the feeling. I shouldn't have had to worry in the first place. At least Pérez didn't seem so bad. If they'd let Raven preside, I had no doubt I'd have been in for a humiliating experience. It was too bad Geer wasn't in the top seat today.

Tristan had no comments, other than to state his agreement that he had a right to know about magic after what happened to him with his housemate.

"And how are you feeling about magic, Mr. Tomás?" Pérez ticked something off on her papers.

"It will take time to get used to, but I'm not worried." Tristan came across more confident now, his voice free of hesitation.

"You're not worried?" Pérez sounded skeptical. "Even after being blood-siphoned unknowingly in your own home?"

"But it wasn't Avery's fault." Tristan was adamant.

"Regardless of fault it seems surprising you'd be unconcerned about magic. Aren't you worried about being placed under spells you're unaware of again?"

"Isn't it illegal?" Tristan gestured at the judges. "I shouldn't have to worry about it any more than anyone else would. And I'm fine with magic in general. I had no concerns about letting Edwin do the spell on me to follow that trail at the pawn shop."

"Was that the first spell you cast on the Mortal, Mr. Bickel?" Raven cut in.

Everyone looked at me.

"Yes, of course it was." Anger simmered below the surface, but I managed to keep it out of my voice.

"Really, Judge Raven. That seems unnecessary to clarify." Geer sounded disapproving. "We've no reason to think Edwin used magic on Mr. Tomás without his knowledge."

Raven leaned forward to peer around Judge Davis, whom he was sitting next to, and regarded Geer with distaste. "We are duty bound to check the Mortal is all right."

"He seems fine to me." Pérez didn't look at Raven. "Unless you have a justification, I suggest we get back on track."

"I believe I do." Raven looked smug, his smile twisting. "I wonder, Mr. Bickel, were you with Mr. Tomás on the sixteenth of September?"

"I couldn't say precisely. Why?" This wasn't good, even if I wasn't quite sure what he was getting at. Anxiety took hold of my chest and I prayed my outward appearance remained calm. Of course, the psychic Judge Lee couldn't be fooled.

"I have a report bearing that date." Judge Raven brandished a piece of paper. "Was Mr. Tomás the Mortal mentioned here?"

"If that's the report I'm thinking," Geer cut in before I could answer. "Then the Mortal detection was a mistake."

"But compliance never found a fault with the monitoring enchantments." Raven passed the report to Davis for the other judge to examine and hand down the line. "Mr. Tomás, were you with Mr. Bickel on this date?"

"Um—" Tristan glanced at Luca, but of course the lawyer had no idea what anyone was talking about. "I can't remember. That was more than two months ago. I mean, maybe I was, but if so there was no magic."

Raven gave me a look of great significance. "Mr. Bickel, surely *you* remember. You wrote the report, after all."

*Curse everything*. I was trapped. I couldn't lie with Lee watching. That would be a crime they'd love to get me for. "The report is inaccurate," I began slowly, keeping myself as calm as possible. "Tristan was with me at the day and time indicated, but I resent having to explain. I agreed to be monitored in good faith. It shouldn't be used to force me to give out personal details, or justify my magic use outside of work."

"What was personal about stopping time?" Davis asked mildly. "In the last twenty-odd years you've only ever done it in pursuit of some case or another."

My heart thudded uncomfortably. "It was accidental. I was distracted, and Tristan didn't notice the brief pause in our surroundings. I lied on the report because it was no one's business why it happened. I shouldn't have to make reports for things that aren't work related, but I'd failed to consider that back when we set up my employment. I don't use my time altering magic much, I never have. And there's no law saying I have to tell you what I do with my magic, or what I do in my personal life."

"But how was it accidental?" Raven looked as if the idea alarmed him. I wondered if the wide-eyed look was for show.

"It seems no harm was done, Judge Raven." Pérez passed the damning report on to the next judge with hardly a glance. "Magic wasn't revealed on the sixteenth of September and Mr. Bickel says stopping time was an accident." Everyone looked at

Lee for confirmation, which she gave with a nod. "How the accident happened hardly seems important. We can't claim Bickel was trying to manipulate Mr. Tomás if he wasn't acting intentionally, but I suppose it was good to check."

"But he lied." Raven pointed at me. "Following the blood trail wasn't the first time Bickel enchanted the Mortal."

"It wasn't an intended lie." Lee peered down the line at Raven. "Misremembering or getting caught out on technicalities isn't a punishable offence if no deceit was meant. Since the first magical incident was unintentional, it's fair for it not to count in Bickel's eyes, or ours."

Raven scowled. "Lying in the report is a violation of Bickel's employment agreement. It doesn't matter if he thinks he shouldn't have to explain *personal* circumstance"—Raven made air quotes as he said the word personal—"he agreed to be monitored and failing to uphold his end of the deal is grounds for dismissal."

Luca cleared his throat. "I'm sorry but I'm going to have to object. This is no longer relevant to Telling. I ask that we return to the procedure and conclude the session."

"Agreed." Geer nodded approvingly.

"I argue it is relevant." Raven looked me dead in the eye. "Mr. Tomás should know what he's dealing with. Mr. Bickel is being deceitful and the court has a duty to the Mortal."

My pulse thudded in my ears. This was so unfair. Raven didn't care about Tristan. I wanted to shout at them for being such pedantic, hateful little shits. I wasn't bad and they couldn't keep treating me like I was just because I once knew a bad person.

Geer's naturally good-natured demeanor had vanished. "Our Telling-related duty doesn't involve passing judgment on Edwin for his work conduct."

Raven grinned. "But it does involve judging the Witch's character, and determining if there's a risk they will abuse their power over the Mortal. After all, that's the whole point of the secret. It would be irresponsible of us not to look closely at Mr. Bickel due to his past."

My hands trembled behind my back. They couldn't do this. But some of the judges were murmuring agreement.

"I don't see it that way at all." Geer twisted around to look at Raven. "Holding onto Bickel's past is prejudiced." Pérez seemed to agree with that, nodding as Geer went on. "Nothing wrong has been done here. The Mortal seems perfectly fine. He even has his own lawyer and other supportive Witches in his life."

"You don't wish to un-do this Telling, do you Mr. Tomás?" Lee asked. "If you would like to return to your ignorance of magic, the court can erase your memory. This will include everything from the moment of Telling up until now. The process is irreversible and requires your fully informed consent. We can have a Witch discuss the procedure with you further, if you're considering it."

Tristan adamantly declined and didn't hold back in telling the judges he trusted me.

Pérez seemed satisfied, leaving Raven's concerns behind, and took Tristan through the rest of the formalities.

I couldn't concentrate. Even as they outlined my responsibility for assisting Tristan in the magical world for the remainder of his life. I hoped Tristan wasn't put off by the wording. He didn't seem to be. We'd talked about this, but that was before learning how he felt yesterday. I was making a legal commitment to him—it was my job to keep him informed about the Witch world and help him if magic ever become a problem, with legal consequences for me if I failed in my duties—I hoped it wouldn't affect our relationship, but I could deal with that. Once I got out of this room, I could deal with anything.

The last of the official business was completed. I was

detached, going through the motions without faltering only because I was so familiar with the processes and used to acting coldhearted in the company of Witches.

As we were dismissed, Raven raised a hand in protest. "Thank you, Judge Pérez. Now that's done I'd like to address the matter of Bickel's breached employment terms, since we're all together. The Mortal and his lawyer may leave."

I looked over at Tristan, feeling helpless. I didn't want to be left alone in here. "They can stay."

My boyfriend's sharp features displayed a deep concern. I kept my eyes on him as the judges argued in front of me. Raven pushed for my dismissal as Geer raged against technicalities. I tried to block it all out.

None of them wanted me here. Those that professed to only liked it better than having me loose in the world, with the exception of Geer. This wasn't a new revelation, but it still felt like rejection.

In the end they suspended me. Six months with a review upon my return and a requirement all my work be directly supervised. It was ridiculous. The false report had only hidden private information. It didn't interfere with anything. It should have resulted in a warning, but I wasn't trustworthy to them and at this rate it seemed like I never would be.

# 30

## EDWIN

Tristan, Luca and I exited the courtroom.

The lawyer ran a hand through his hair. “I’m not entirely sure what happened back there.”

I rounded on him. “There’s no reason for you to know, and if you repeat any of that—”

Luca put up his hands in surrender, but his expression was hard. “I’ve actually heard of confidentiality, thanks. It’s my job.”

“Well then how did your father know I’d Told a boyfriend?”

“Edwin—” Tristan put a hand on my arm.

“I didn’t tell my dad anything.” Luca looked offended that I’d even considered it. But if he hadn’t, that was almost worse.

Who did Mr. Belmonte know? And what, were people not content to keep gossip within the organization anymore?

I gave the lawyer my coldest stare. “Well, someone told him. So you can see why I’m concerned. You’ll regret it if you go around spreading things.” Maybe implied threats weren’t reasonable, but I had lost my ability to feign calm.

“Edwin—” This time Tristan sounded surprised.

I kept my gaze fixed on the lawyer.

He didn’t react. “I think I’ll leave you two for now.” Luca

pressed the elevator button. "If you need anything further, let me know, Tristan. And Mr. Bickel, if you want someone to look over your employment contract, I can. It sounds highly irregular."

*Hell.* He was being kind. I deflated in what felt distinctly like shame. "I—I'm sorry—" *for snapping at you when I really want to yell at someone else.*

Luca nodded and got in the elevator. The doors closed.

I teleported Tristan back to my apartment. We appeared right next to the bar and I was already grabbing glasses.

Tristan passed me the whiskey. "Edwin, what just happened?"

"I've been having trouble at work." I set the glasses down, my stomach so unsettled I didn't even want a drink.

"Do they always treat you like that?" Tristan sounded tentative and a glance proved he was full of concern, brown eyes wide.

"What? No. I don't know—" His comment felt somehow exposing. I wasn't sure why.

We looked at each other for a long moment. I felt frozen, like I was clamming up completely, from my brain to my muscles. My hopeful confidence from yesterday was nowhere to be found. Opening up then had felt almost freeing; now it was as impossible as it'd ever been.

Tristan poured us each a whiskey. "Were they saying that you stopped time once, with me?" It was as if he knew the way to get me to unclench was to direct me toward us, the present, a recount of events, not an explication of my muddled past so wrapped up in bad feelings.

Even if he couldn't possibly know all that, I breathed more easily. The judges had used the incident against me, but I could explain it to Tristan without feeling violated. It was a memory of him and me, and could still be something good between us. Our private moment.

"That day we ran into each other in the street—" I took a sip of the drink Tristan handed me. "We came back here, and well, you know. I got so lost in you I didn't mean to use magic at all. Didn't even realize."

"You didn't want it to end," he whispered, giving me a tender, comprehending look.

I blushed in a reaction that started out pleasurable only to turn sour. "They had no right to know about that. I shouldn't have had to explain."

"Hey—" Tristan put an arm around me. "They don't know what that night meant to us, or what we were doing. They wouldn't try to ask you about your sex life."

I felt cold. *Wouldn't they?* It was a relief I hadn't had to spell it out, or imply. But I was upset by the idea they'd deduce my magic had come out in an intimate moment anyway.

Tristan's arm tightened on me. "What's wrong?"

I couldn't answer. I hadn't accepted having to share the worst parts of myself with him. I couldn't explain why court had gone so badly without delving into my past, and was nowhere near ready to face Wyatt's lasting impact on my life so openly. After everything he'd done, he was still reaching through time to influence my current employment and ability to Tell my boyfriend about magic. I couldn't seem to get over the unfairness of it all. That old relationship shouldn't be something I had to deal with any longer. Wasn't it enough that I'd gotten away from him? Couldn't I just be rid of him?

"It's too hard to explain," I said at last.

Tristan ran a hand up and down my arm. "You don't have to tell me everything. But what about like yesterday? A bit of context. Is there any way you can help me understand?"

"That was different." I hadn't been confronting my past

directly, or risking Tristan seeing things I didn't like to think about.

It had felt like so much progress to accept the risks of being vulnerable with him. My newfound trust had been like a gift. Now all that felt small. I was still hurt and the more it came up, the more it felt like it would never go away. I didn't want to give my past so much space in my present, and I wasn't ready to share just because someone else had brought it up and made Tristan wonder.

"Hey." Tristan took my glass from my too-tight grip. "I'm not going to push you if you're not ready to talk. I'm just worried about you, Edwin. They suspended you from your job for something that doesn't seem like it should matter. Some of those judges were outright hostile. It seemed like they pounced on you, like it had been planned."

"It probably was."

"The fact you're not surprised seems like a red flag. I— Have you talked to anyone about what's been going on at work?"

I looked at my hands. "No. I was handling it."

Tristan brushed back his hair. "Okay, but it feels like something is seriously wrong, and I don't even know the details. What about your friend Juliet?"

The question jolted me unexpectedly. "What about her?"

Tristan gave me an almost exasperated smile. "Can you talk to her? If she's your Owen, like you said. I just don't like how all that went down. Even Luca seemed sus. You don't have to talk to me, but I think you should talk to someone."

I was thrown. The proceeding had been awful, and caught me off guard since I'd thought the report forgotten, but it wasn't that bad. That was just how the judges were. How things were when I first started work. How they'd been leaning all year, ever since the damned thing with Judge Herrera.

I turned away to look out the window. "Talking to Juliet is a good idea. I just didn't want to bother her. She's had a lot to deal with this last year."

"I don't think she'll feel bothered. She'll want to help you."

*Do I need help?* I could deal with this. True, today had been the opposite of ticking a box and getting back to my usual life, but that didn't mean I couldn't sort it out.

If anything, court proved I still needed to be here, at the Authority. Again, the judges had handled things in a less than fair manner. I'd let them put extra restrictions on my employment, but I should have still been treated like anyone else. Geer was right that recalling my past was prejudiced.

The whole reason I'd come to work here was to try and stop these sorts of things from happening. I'd been slowly building up their trust, so that they would listen and hopefully improve their conduct. So far only Geer had warmed up to me, but that was progress. It wasn't time to give up. I still had a lot to do, and now I was suspended, set back.

I needed to prove them wrong. Show I was trustworthy and someone who did his job well. I couldn't let this derail me from my original purpose.

I watched the sky outside darken into full night. The city lights twinkled.

"Why don't we order some dinner in?" Tristan's soft voice pulled me out of my thoughts.

I had no idea how long I'd stood in silence. "All right."

I WOKE SUDDENLY in the middle of the night drenched in sweat.

My past loomed, pushing itself to the forefront of my mind like a bad dream.

Tristan slept peacefully beside me, a presence that seemed almost unreal in the quiet dark. His understanding, the fact he'd stayed even after I'd declined to talk, was a reality I wasn't accustomed to. It shouldn't have surprised me. He was a very caring person. But his acceptance made me acutely aware of how ingrained my expectation of dismissal was.

I slipped out of bed and went to shower. As I scrubbed the sweat from my body, my thoughts failed to stay away from Wyatt. Even though I tried not to, I imagined his reaction to today's events, if he'd been in Tristan's place. Living out that scenario in my mind served no purpose. Still, I felt his judgment as if it were real.

I braced a hand against the tiled wall and took a deep breath.

I needed to shake the damn man off. I deserved good things and should be able to enjoy my life without Wyatt lurking. My current situation was nothing like that. Tristan would never use guilt to punish or manipulate me. He would never sneer at my emotions.

I knew that, and also knew what Tristan did or didn't do wasn't the problem. It was more than just shaking Wyatt off. Acting like it was unreasonable that Wyatt's abuse had a lasting impact wasn't fair to myself. Of course something like that would affect me, I just didn't want it to anymore.

As I crept back into bed, Tristan stirred.

He half opened his eyes, gentle fingers reaching out to touch my head. "Is your hair wet?"

"I had a shower. Trouble sleeping."

Tristan moved closer until our bodies touched. He was soothingly warm as he wrapped his arms around me. I tucked my face into his neck. My legs found their way between his, tangling together.

"Today was hard," I murmured, wondering what it would be like to say more. To voice what I'd felt just now in the shower, tell Tristan about that relationship and all the ways it still dogged my steps.

But I didn't. I just breathed in the scent of his skin.

After a pause Tristan whispered, "I'm here for you."

"Thank you." I kissed him as gratitude welled up inside me. "I've never had a partner who was."

The admission was terrifying. I didn't know if I could do much more than this. I didn't know if I could ever share everything.

Tristan ran his hand through my damp hair, then traced my face with a soft touch. "You'll always have it with me."

Something relaxed in my chest, like a vise I hadn't realized was there.

I might have floated away if Tristan hadn't held me.

# 31

## TRISTAN

The next morning Edwin and I stood waiting for coffees at a cafe around the corner from his apartment.

"We're still looking into WMS, right?" I didn't want to bring up his suspension, but I was under the impression no one at the Authority knew about the WMS lead. Edwin had been waiting to present something solid and we couldn't just forget about it now.

He didn't seem bothered by the reminder. Edwin had been determined and confident this morning. Not hiding his emotions or trying to pretend like nothing had happened. Instead it seemed like he was actively trying to focus on things that didn't upset him.

"I'm still a licensed investigator. My infraction was against my employment contract, so I don't feel there's any problem helping you look into WMS privately. That is, unless you'd like to report your suspicions to the Authority, or ask another PI to handle it." A flicker of doubt crossed his face.

I huffed. He couldn't actually think I'd go to someone else.

"Can't say I'm keen to ask Authority Witches for help with much of anything after yesterday."

Edwin grimaced. "Fair. Keeping the Authority on its toes has always been my main objective, but I want to prove them wrong about me. If anything is going on at WMS—I won't say it's fortunate—but it could help me out of this suspension hole."

I frowned. "You don't have anything to prove. They treated you really unkindly, Edwin. Why do you want to keep working for them?"

He looked away and was conveniently distracted by the appearance of our coffees on the counter. When he turned back, he had a defiant set to his jaw. "It's my life. They don't get to do this to me, Tristan. They aren't even punishing me for lying in a report. The damn thing was irrelevant. I won't let them do this."

"Okay. I hear you." I took my almond latte from him. "It's unfair, and you're right; they shouldn't be treating you this way. We'll look into my company because it's still the right thing to do, and if that helps you, even better."

I held back from telling him he shouldn't go back to the Authority. It wasn't for me to decide, but I found it hard to believe it would be good for Edwin to keep working there.

We exited the cafe in silence.

I hesitated before turning toward work. "I hope we figure something out soon, for both our sakes."

"So do I. Let me know how your day goes." Edwin adjusted his hat infinitesimally. "I'm off to see Juliet. I might ask her to help our investigation."

"That's great, Edwin." I hoped he talked to her about more than the blood.

He'd seemed to accept yesterday's events, and the judges hinting at some past issue in a clearly biased way, with little resistance or surprise. It made me really concerned remembering Edwin's passing comments about having a hard time at work. What the hell had been going on?

Of course I wanted Edwin to tell me, but he'd shut down so hardcore after court. Whatever this was impacted him in a big way. I wondered how long he'd worked at the Authority and if the working environment could have contributed to his closed off nature. I'd have guessed his trust issues were mostly due to the long-ago relationship he'd mentioned, but maybe it was more than that.

His desire to prove himself to people who seemed to have little interest in treating him respectfully was concerning. I just didn't know how to help the situation when I had no idea where it was all coming from, or what Edwin was comfortable having me do for him.

If Juliet could help that would be good.

My morning went slowly. I couldn't concentrate and honestly didn't try very hard. Working here had lost all its appeal. I'd rather be back in California, and not just because of the potential blood thing.

Jonah rolled his chair into my desk space after lunch, interrupting my procrastination. "Hey—did you get Graham's email? He needs a hand. I don't have space to take on any more projects, but I told him you might."

"Sure. I'll take a look. A few of my smaller pieces finished up last week." I scanned my inbox.

"FYI, Graham said the client has been difficult."

I waved him off. "That's fine."

"Oh, also." Jonah wheeled his chair even closer and we leaned together conspiratorially. "Emerson came looking for you earlier."

I sat back abruptly. "Emerson Walsh?"

"Yep. Said it had to do with the website focus group."

"Couldn't he have emailed?" I glanced at my messages again, there was nothing from him.

"Dunno. He was disappointed not to catch you, but didn't say more. Gave me another company mug." Jonah rolled back to his desk and picked up a mug full of pens, next to his identical mug full of coffee.

I frowned at the twin company logos staring back at me. "He's weird, right?"

"Emerson? Oh, totally." Jonah put the mug down, his agreement more of a relief than I'd thought it would be. "It's like he learned how to run a company off internet fluff pieces and memes."

I laughed. "You know, I've had that exact same thought."

"Anyway—" Jonah turned serious. "I'm organizing drinks for tomorrow in preparation for the holiday weekend. You in?"

A FEW HOURS later I followed the rest of my team into a meeting room. I was on edge, both wanting something to happen so we'd know, and not wanting to be right about getting our blood stolen.

As our manager flicked through a presentation, two men entered the room. No one acknowledged them or even looked in their direction.

They were wearing some heavy-duty necklaces of crystals and dried herbs. Distinctly Witchy. And it was super unnatural the way they were moving around obtrusively yet catching no one's attention.

Except mine.

It took all my effort to gaze placidly at the projector screen and not gawk at the intruders. They did a quick incantation and everyone around me went slack. I almost gasped.

The manager was still standing, mouth open, eyes glazed like she was in a trance.

My heart pounded in the silent room. I had to act like I'd been entranced too, and willed myself to go limp. I picked a spot on the wall and stared at it, trying not to breathe like I was running a marathon.

The Witches went for the neck, not our wrists. Across the conference table, two little holes appeared by magic in Jonah's skin. Blood leaked out in dark red lines. The floating droplets were collected by a hovering glass vial. It was creepy as hell.

"Something's wrong with this one." One of the men was right behind me.

The other looked up. In my peripheral vision I could tell he was staring at me. "Did he just twitch? Can he hear us?"

"I don't see how. But his heart rate is off. It's way too fast."

"Better skip him. He's the unwell looking one from before, maybe he's got a condition." The Witch moved out of my line of sight.

"Yeah, fine. We're hitting the HR and admin teams tomorrow morning. We'll get plenty." The other also moved away.

They gradually made their way around the room. My neck hurt and my face itched. I just hoped I wouldn't sneeze.

The two circled back to me when they were done. One of the Witches leaned in close, hovering over me from behind. "His pulse is still going a-mile-a-minute, wonder if he's on drugs."

"Better not be. Too many of them start being off limits and we're going to have to put influencing spells on the coffee, keep them free of substances."

Before leaving, the Witches skipped to the end of the presentation and undid their enchantment on the group. Once everyone started stirring, the manager reminding us blankly to keep the client forefront in our minds, I bolted to the bathroom and threw up.

I called Edwin from the toilet stall and told him everything.

"I'm sorry, Tristan. Are you all right?" I could picture the concerned crease in his brow as clearly as if we were video chatting.

"Kinda freaked out, to be honest."

"Are you alone?"

I ran a hand through my hair. "Yeah, hiding in the bathroom."

Edwin appeared in the stall with me.

"Hey!" I scrambled, blocked by the wall. "Wait—I don't want you to see me when I'm all pukey." I'd wiped my face but a rank taste lingered in my mouth. The space was tight, we were chest to chest.

"Sorry. Here—" Edwin flicked his fingers and my mouth tingled, tasting suddenly minty.

"Oh my *god*. Did you just brush my teeth? Magically?" I laughed as a warm feeling flooded me despite everything.

Edwin brushed back my hair. "Was that too presumptuous?"

"No. It's just—I don't even know. Sweet, I think, but weird."

Edwin grinned. "Would you rather be pukey?"

"Definitely not. We aren't ready for that stage of the relationship. Let's get out of here."

Edwin teleported us away before I could remind him I needed to get my coat, or mention I still had half an hour left of work, but I couldn't bring myself to care about either.

We appeared in his living room, next to the bar.

Behind it stood a woman with blue hair. She was arranging a line of martini glasses. "Oh good, you brought him with you."

"Um, hi?" I glanced from her to Juliet, who was sitting in an armchair.

"This is Mea." Edwin extended a delicate hand toward the

woman as she began vigorously putting the cocktail shaker to use. “And you’ve met Juliet.”

I waved as she got up and made her way over to us. It was true I’d met her before, at Coffee Cat, since she was Aria’s boss, but I’d never really talked to her.

Edwin filled the others in as Mea doled out the martinis. I stared skeptically at the olive in mine, before taking a sip. I tried not to make a face.

“No good?” Mea’s eyes flashed at my failed attempt to hide my reaction to the strong drink.

“It’s—I’ve just brushed my teeth so—” I shrugged apologetically.

Edwin snorted, trying not to laugh. He looked happy and surprisingly relaxed given the news I’d just delivered about serious blood-crimes at WMS, but then again, he was with people he cared about and obviously trusted.

My boyfriend swirled his martini like it was second nature, or like he’d been making the gesture for a hundred years and it didn’t require any more coordination than breathing. “Juliet and Mea have graciously agreed to help us look into your company.”

“As if we would have declined.” Juliet gave Edwin and admonishing look, her deep brown eyes full of loving exasperation.

“You could have been busy,” he protested.

“I don’t know what you imagine we’re busy doing all the time, Edwin.” Mea shook her head as if she found him hopeless.

“Well—lots of things I’m sure. And there’s the holiday—”

“Please.” Juliet set her drink down and crossed her arms. “I expected you to pop on over for that like always.”

“Oh.” Edwin smiled sheepishly, trying to hide it behind his martini.

Juliet squeezed his arm and I felt all gooey inside. It was so nice to see Edwin with other people. Not quickly teleporting away like he had at Owen and Aria's, or being formal to the point of strained as he'd been with Avery, even before the blood thing. He was at ease, and including me in this moment with his friends felt like a big deal.

"Never mind about Thanksgiving. We need to make a plan." Edwin focused on me. "I checked up on that tracked blood sample of yours. You'll never guess where it was moved to over the weekend."

"No—"

"Yes. After a lengthy stay at the Fizz Bar it's found its way to the same building as Walsh Marketing Solutions."

I WAS DISTRACTED WAITING to go up to the office the next morning, worried that anyone around me could be in on the blood-stealing scheme. I wasn't cut out for this kind of high stress day-to-day.

Knowing Edwin and Juliet would be in the building with me was somewhat calming, but my regret for taking this job had begun to consume me. Why had they been hiring so many writers at once when I'd applied? Had something bad happened to the last batch of employees? Had the company grown recently to fill a need for more bodies to harvest blood from, or had Witches latched on to a completely unsuspecting Mortal business?

I picked some upbeat music to blast my ears with, reminding myself I hadn't necessarily been hired just to fill blood bags. The interview and reference checks had been real. But even if it wasn't all bullshit, the value I'd once seen in WMS didn't feel like it was ever coming back.

Emerson came up next to me and waved to get my attention. I popped an earbud out.

He gave me a good-natured smile. "You're waiting in front of the wrong elevator again."

"Is this the same one as last time? I didn't notice." I couldn't make myself smile back and flicked my eyes away rather than look up at him.

An elevator to the left dinged. Emerson walked in and put his hand out to stop the door closing, waiting for me. Just my luck no one else was currently going up. We had the small space to ourselves.

The CEO leaned casually against the elevator's side wall, looking directly at me instead of facing forward "Excited for the days off, Tristan?"

"Oh yeah, sure. You know." I busied myself putting my earbuds away and shoved my hands in my pockets.

Did Emerson know what was going on at his company? Something in his demeanor freaked me out this morning, but I didn't know if that was just paranoia.

Emerson's concentrated gaze seemed to drill into me like I was a puzzle to solve. "There's something just so—I don't know—familiar about you, Tristan."

"It'd be weird if I wasn't familiar, given we work together." That was maybe a bit rude, but silence didn't feel like my friend.

Emerson's eyes flashed with annoyance. It was the most real expression I'd ever seen on him but it vanished as the elevator opened onto my floor.

"Wait—" He grabbed my arm. "I might, uh, be in touch about my next cross divisional project. You were good to have on the team."

I stared at his pale fingers.

Emerson let go. "So keep an eye out, and have a good day." The smile he gave me felt oily, like he was trying too hard to hide something.

I muttered a goodbye and rushed off.

# 32

# EDWIN

Juliet and I were off to WMS this morning to see what more we could uncover about the siphoning Witches. Tristan had given us the details of where to find the meetings the two had mentioned yesterday, so we'd start there.

Mea was staying behind to do some research on the company and hadn't emerged from the guest bedroom. Juliet found me waiting in the living room, ready to go.

She tweaked my bow tie with affection, setting it off center. "You're looking really well."

I set the tie right. "I had a nice time last night. The four of us together was almost dreamlike, even in the circumstances."

Juliet slipped on a jacket to complete her pencil skirt suit set. "And would you like to talk about those circumstances?"

My pulse jumped. I'd only mentioned in passing that I'd been suspended. "I don't know what else there is to say."

"Given you've said almost nothing, I'd think quite a lot." Juliet arched a brow and waited.

I didn't know why I was resisting, other than it was what I always did. Being there for Juliet was so much easier than accepting her returned support. But I needed it. When I let myself think about Sunday, I felt terrible.

I outlined things as quickly and painlessly as possible, which wasn't very.

Juliet's concerned frown turned to outrage when I admitted things started going downhill after her mother's attempt to frame us. "This whole time? Edwin, I wish I'd known."

"There was nothing you could do. It's not like you could corral the judges and tell them off."

She gave me a look that said, *oh yeah?* "What I would have done, or not done, doesn't matter now. Are you sure you want to go back? It's getting hard to see the point."

"No." A pain jabbed at my chest. "I mean, yes, I'm sure. No, it's not hard to see the point. You know this district needs watching. Someone to push them in the right direction."

"I don't disagree, but what about you?"

"What about me?" My words came out harsher than I'd intended.

She made a frustrated gesture. "You need to look after your own wellbeing."

I turned away, not understanding why hearing that bothered me. "Come on." I made my way down the hall.

Juliet followed. "I just think it's worth discussing options. You should talk to Mea about her new position. Joining her team would be perfect for you. Take an official position keeping the Authority accountable for its actions, and since it's a pilot program you could help form the new way of doing things."

I turned back to Juliet. "And what? Just let everyone here get away with this—this shit? Let them chase me away? This city is my home."

Juliet grabbed my arms and held me still, her sharp brown eyes cutting into me. "You know that's not what I'm saying. You need to do what's best for you. You'll always have your home here, that's not in question. Geographical space doesn't even matter to you. I used to see you constantly when you needed coffee as an excuse to visit Tristan. You could easily work with Mea and base yourself here. And you might find you can do more outside of New York. Don't be stubborn."

"I'm not." I looked at the ceiling.

"Edwin," Juliet scolded.

"Fine. I'll think about it, but any progress made out in California isn't going to affect this district. Not unless Mea's program is expanded." I smoothed the arms of my suit jacket as Juliet released me from her grasp. "I just don't know if I'm ready to admit I've failed."

Her determination dissolved into something sadder. "You haven't failed."

I'm sure Juliet believed that but almost thirty years later it felt like nothing had changed at the New York Authority. What else could you call that but failure?

"We should get going." I pulled out my phone to check the time.

"If you insist." She seemed displeased, but we really did have a schedule to keep. "Get on with casting your spells."

The Witches Tristan had seen yesterday sounded like they'd used diffusion spells to render themselves, if not invisible, then compulsively forgettable. Tristan was only immune, and able to remember them, because the protection I'd cast on him was stronger than anything the other Witches could produce.

I set about placing diffusion spells on myself and Juliet, without the need of bulky necklaces due to my superior power, and teleported us into the stairwell leading to Tristan's floor of WMS. From there, Juliet and I followed his instructions, making it to the boardroom on the floor above without incident.

As we approached, I could feel the magic thrumming from within the room.

We entered to find a few dozen people slumped in their chairs. Three Witches walked around, conducting floating vials and suspended streams of blood with twitching, crystal-clad fingers and muttered words. Their movements displaying practiced efficiency as if they went through the process often.

Juliet took photos with a camera I'd altered to be immune to the spells the Witches were using to mask themselves—outmatching everyone in power really had its advantages—and I placed tracking spells on the illegally collected blood.

We didn't need an official warrant for any of this. Juliet and I were licensed investigators, so all Tristan had to do was hire us to look into illegal magic. As a Mortal aware of magic, he could give us permission to poke around and look for anything Witch-related. Anything Tristan could access by walking around his company, we could access on his behalf. If we delved into anything that Tristan had no right to, like restricted company information or locked storage, we'd have to get a warrant.

The Witches steadily filled a box with vials of blood, creeping around as Juliet and I crept behind them. Once they were done and the Mortals awoken, we all slipped back into the hall. To my surprise the Witches discarded their spelled necklaces and pushed the cart laden with boxes along in full view.

It was true diffusions worked less well on objects than people, but hiding in plain sight spoke to a level of confidence I wouldn't expect unless they'd already gotten away with this routine countless times. That, or certain members of the company were in on it, and the Witches had no fear their presence would be challenged.

Our strange group of five made our way to the main elevator bank. A Mortal waved and wished one of the siphoners good morning. Juliet snapped his picture.

When we got to the elevators, one Witch walked right up to a closed set of doors on the end, looked around for bystanders, and pressed a small crystal to the metal. A subtle popping sensation accompanied the opening doors.

Juliet and I followed them carefully into the elevator. The same Witch who'd opened the door ignored the buttons in favor of pressing the crystal to the back wall. The doors closed and we made our descent.

The space was crowded, and even pressed up against the wall as we were, the Witch with the cart kept pushing it confusedly into Juliet's foot. She glared at him.

The doors slid open onto a dimly lit space unlike anything found in a modern office building. I guessed we were underground, and from the off feeling of the place, this space was constructed with the assistance of magic.

It was chill, not quite like a freezer but close, and housed hundreds of boxes just like the ones on the cart. The Witches offloaded their take, labeling everything with dates and the source, then returned to the elevator.

"Oh my," Juliet said once they were gone.

"This has to be the heart of the whole operation." I walked up and down the rows of boxes. "There's blood going back weeks, according to the labels. They must house it here until it can be distributed. This alone is enough to keep the black market ticking along for months."

Juliet followed, photographing everything. "How many people work at WMS?"

"Tristan said a few hundred. Enough to be the source of most—if not all—of this, assuming they're siphoning each employee a couple times a week." I paused, pointing at a box to my right. "Look, this box is labeled from Mystic Pawn. I don't know why they'd bother with suppliers like Al when this company is a fountain of blood."

"Unless it was more like absorbing the competition than

bothering with small suppliers." Juliet snapped a photo of the box. "We should track all of this."

I agreed and set about wandering up and down the narrow aisles, placing a spell on each box.

"The chill down here is unnatural." I flexed numb fingers. "Guess it's to preserve the blood, but it feels strange, don't you think?"

"Hm." Juliet slung the camera strap around her neck, and muttered a quick incantation, the crystals on her rings flashing. "My warming spell isn't working."

I tried and found the same problem. "The magic maintaining the room must be drawing on a powerful source if I can't get past it."

Juliet knelt down. The floor was bare dirt and rock, the walls too. She dug her manicured fingers into the soil, head bowed as she assessed the magic humming through the place. "There's a complicated containment spell at work. I'd almost say it's been bound to the earth for power. It's blood magic for sure."

One way a typically powerful Witch could outmatch me was turning to blood, but using the earth to enhance the magic, rather than say a single crystal, added a whole other level of complexity. No wonder I couldn't get through it with my basic warming spell.

I offered a hand to help Juliet up. "We've done what we can for now. Let's go."

We returned to the elevator. There was no way to call it, though that wasn't a surprise after seeing how it had worked coming down here. It was a good trap for any other Witch.

I took Juliet's hand and made to teleport us back to my apartment. Nothing happened. I tried again and a wave of nausea swept over me, a sensation like I hadn't experienced since I'd mastered this power.

Beside me, Juliet swayed. "Edwin, what's happening?"

We helped steady each other as the unbalancing effect passed.

"I can't separate us from this space." I closed my eyes, calling upon my magic to feel everything around me, picking through the room's magical construction. "It's like the spell has incorporated us into the room itself. I can't feel the distinction between us and our surroundings the way I normally can."

"If we can't warm up, we won't be able to wait for the Witches to come back." Juliet's voice pitched with nerves.

"I know. I'm thinking."

The blood Witches probably didn't come down here every day, and even if they did, it was a damned holiday weekend tomorrow. Tristan had said all of WMS had been given Wednesday and Friday off in addition to Thanksgiving. Unless they were back with more blood today or coming to take boxes away, no one would be here for days. We'd freeze just as any Mortal would.

It'd been a long time since my magic wasn't enough and I didn't care for the thrill of uncertainty coursing through me.

Juliet knelt and ran her palms over the dirt floor again. "The spell is well done. If you're right and it's linking us here, I don't think anyone would be able to get out without the elevator. That crystal must break the containment somehow."

I grimaced. "There's always one sure way to break a spell."

Juliet stood, shivering, and brushed the dirt from her hands onto her skirt. She didn't look any more pleased than I felt. "Go on then."

We grasped each other's icy hands. She closed her eyes, likely thinking about the last time we did this almost thirty years ago. I bit back the urge to apologize for reminding her.

It was possible for me to break any spell, no matter how strong, by disconnecting the subject from time, space and all other worldly influences. It was the most extreme manifestation of my power and much more abstract than teleporting. It ripped us from the physical world irreversibly. I'd put us back, but no matter how short a moment we were in this altered state, we'd be different and disconnected from who we'd been before.

The difference itself was abstract, other than the removal of any magical influences. At least I'd considered it so after last time. It wasn't like we were about to forget ourselves or come back with different personalities. Yet knowing we wouldn't be the same, that our bodies essentially stopped existing in the form we knew, only to be remade, made this a trick I avoided at all costs.

I released my magic with a loud crack that sent a shudder through the floor. A weightless sensation descended upon me, creating an almost dreamlike state. The cold disappeared. I felt nothing but Juliet's presence beside me as everything else became distant, like a slowly fading memory. Even she didn't feel physical, it was more like I was aware of her thoughts buzzing next to mine. A haze of otherworldly sensations shrouded my mind.

Our surroundings blurred, like we were no longer in the room, or the reality it existed in, but able to access it. As we drifted in this in-between, I teleported us to my living room, only peripherally aware of the change in location. We were like fish in a bowl looking out at a thick fog.

"I wondered last time—" Juliet's voice came to me as a faint echo. "If this is what dying might feel like."

I'd had that impression too. It was the only other time you left your body.

Accessing beyond the physical world was only ever done through seance. This plane wasn't a shadow world, despite the haziness, and it wasn't an afterlife even if being here felt like a glimpse into a deathly state of being. It was something else.

You shouldn't be able to come here, it was too fundamentally different. We were in my apartment and also so far out of reach that reality might become a distant memory. Even the notion of a solid form, earthly needs and concerns, were slipping into the abstract.

I let out another surge of power, forcing us back into our rightful place. I didn't like spending time on that other plane, like I might get stuck or forget to come back.

The world began to move around us, the feeling of unnatural calm gone so suddenly it hurt. My legs wobbled and I collapsed onto the couch, letting my hands trail over the fabric, soaking in the rightness of knowing I was within my own body.

Juliet remained standing, rubbing her arms with her hands in an absent warming gesture.

A sadness overwhelmed me. It made no sense, and was completely out of place, but it was familiar. I focused on Juliet. "Are you all right?"

She met my gaze, brown eyes filled with emotion. "It reminds me of before. The feeling—" Her voice faded to nothing. Juliet's memories of our last trip to unreality weren't fond ones and I didn't expect her to elaborate.

The last time I'd used this trick to break a spell was to free Juliet from unspeakable magic. Reminding her of that time wasn't something I was happy to have done. Yes, our friendship had grown from that low moment, but it'd started in an undeniably dark place for both of us.

The sensation of altered reality brought the aftermath of Wyatt and my ruined life to my present in an onslaught of memory. It was a trigger like nothing I'd experienced before. Like I'd been transported back in time. I hadn't forgotten how hopeless I'd felt back then, but the resurgence of that exact emotional cocktail made my throat burn.

A few deep breaths had me more level-headed. The old emotions slipped away, and the more I thought about current events, focused on a sweater Tristan had left on one of the armchairs, the more I felt like me.

My life was more of a mess now than I was happy with, but it was nothing like it'd been in the late eighties, early nineties. That man wouldn't recognize me and I was proud of that.

I pulled out my phone to message Tristan. I longed for him, wanted to convey that this odd moment held significance and that he was very much a part of that.

Not knowing what to say, I sent a single emoji heart. He sent back a string of five hearts less than a minute later.

I smiled. How was it possible to feel this loved, just like that?

MEA AND TRISTAN joined us that evening to debrief on the day's events. We were in my living room, Juliet standing at the window looking down at the fall-colored park, Mea sitting cross legged on the carpet, and Tristan curled into the corner of the couch with his shoes off and sock-clad feet tucked beneath him.

I paced absently as Juliet and I recounted our trip to WMS.

Tristan's attention perked up as we mentioned the magically influenced elevator. "Our CEO's been babbling to me about the elevators. A particular one on the end, right side."

Juliet turned away from the window. "Really?"

"He kept saying it didn't work, or wouldn't come. Man, I knew he had to be in on it." Tristan frowned off into space, wrinkling his nose like the thought of the executive repulsed him.

"This would be Emerson Walsh we're talking about, right?" Mea had a laptop open on the ground beside her. She clicked a few times like she was bringing something up on the screen. "I cross-referenced everyone on the company roster you gave me, Tristan, with the Authority's database on Mortals who've been Told. Emerson Knows about magic."

"*Ugh*. Figures out of everyone he'd Know." Tristan sounded annoyed.

"We don't know he's involved. At least not yet," I reminded him gently. "It's possible Mr. Walsh noticed the elevator irregularity naturally, though I'll admit that seems unlikely." I stopped my pacing to hover over Mea. "Who Told him about magic?"

She pulled up the database to check and read the information out to us. "Emerson Walsh was married to a Witch who Told him seven years ago. They've since divorced and he's applied to the court for a new magical guide on the grounds that she's no longer suitable, and might not bear his best interest in mind. The application is pending. Hm. It looks like Walsh keeps postponing the court date." Mea closed the tab. "I didn't find anyone else at WMS who'd been Told."

Tristan uncurled, sitting up straight. "Emerson makes me uncomfortable. I know that's not damning evidence, but it adds up if he's in on this. He could be taking advantage of everyone working for him. That's despicable, I mean—wait—he couldn't know *I know* about magic, right?" Tristan looked from Mea to me in alarm.

"No," I assured him. "Only Authority members can access the Telling database. Unless you have common magical acquaintances, there's no way he could find out."

"Good. It's just, he's noticed me." Tristan fidgeted. "Emerson picked me to be part of an inter-departmental project, and came looking for me at my desk after it was over. Then, today he said I was somehow familiar. It's all weird. Everyone thinks he's weird, not just me."

I joined Tristan on the couch. "Familiar how?"

He shifted so our shoulders were touching. "That's it. I don't know. Like duh, I work there. It was such an awkward comment."

"Oddities aren't exactly a crime." Juliet turned back to the window.

"I know." The man next to me remained determined. "But Emerson's strange behavior makes sense if he's hiding something. Like his niceness is fake and over the top *because* he's fucking everyone over. And he has the means to be one of the orchestrators of the blood scheme. It's not like finding out Bill from accounts knows about magic." He gave me a pointed look.

I smiled. "True. If Walsh is selling out his employees, there has to be a financial benefit. Money, or magical influence to improve his Mortal business dealings—which is illegal in itself. That's what we need to start looking for, as well as any connection between Walsh and the Witches we already know are involved in the scheme."

"I've already found a connection between WMS and dodgy Witches." Tristan adopted a smug expression.

"What? How?" Juliet abandoned the window entirely and joined us, perching on an armchair.

Mea snapped her laptop shut.

"Mystic Pawn hired WMS to do their marketing. A guy in my team asked me to take over the account today. He's sick of trying to deal with it. Mason must have never replied to that email."

"Not surprising, knowing Mason." I resisted laughing. "That's excellent, Tristan."

He beamed at my praise. "Yeah, there's no way Mystic Pawn would benefit from Mortals at WMS—who're ignorant of magic—running an advertising campaign when it's a Witch business. So it's hard to believe the pawn shop hired us genuinely wanting our services. But why would there be a connection like this? What's the point?"

I let myself think out loud. "If Al is one of the blood suppliers, complimentary advertising might be part of his payment, even if it seems odd. But that would mean the company is definitely involved at the heart of things, not just being leeched from outside."

"And if no one else knows about magic but me and Emerson, he *has* to be in on it." Tristan gave us all a triumphant look.

"Now we just have to prove it." Mea's reminder got a begrudging nod from Tristan.

"With any luck we're on the right track and might be able to get to the Witches running everything through Emerson. He has to know who they are if he's helped set this all up." I felt a satisfying thrill at potentially being able to hand the judges the culprits in this dragged-out investigation after everything.

"We should start by getting a warrant to search the company records." Mea stretched and got off the ground. "See if we can find anything in the paper trail between the pawn shop and WMS—assuming there's even a contract for the services. Looking for financial information to prove Emerson, or the company, is being paid for the blood would also be a good bet. Really, an auditing team should look for any magical influence in the business, but we might need to find proof there's something odd in the pawn shop deal first, to justify that."

"I wonder if we could try and see someone tonight." Juliet put an arm around Mea as the other woman sat on the arm of Juliet's chair. "Thanksgiving would be a good day to search the company, since we'll need the Mortals out of the way."

I frowned. "Who would we go to for the warrant?"

"Why not Geer?" Mea suggested.

I agreed, trying to ignore my feelings of reluctance. "I'm sure he'd be happy to sign it off for you, Mea. Even if you bother him at home the night before a long weekend."

Things had gone well for Mea after she'd helped expose Judge Herrera's crimes. Mea had come out of everything with a new—rather groundbreaking—position overseeing Authority activity in Southern California aiming to correct the organization's mistakes and improve areas where gaps in its service existed.

For the first time the unfairness of this struck me. True, Mea had never been implicated in the framing plot, but the difference in reaction between her involvement in exposing the judge and mine was uncomfortably vast.

Mea hopped back off the arm of the chair. "Let's go then."

Bitterness settled over me. They didn't need me, I could just let Mea take it from here. "You think I should come with you?"

"Why not?" Juliet looked at me sternly. "Geer will know you and Tristan have put us onto the case. Mea and I are the only people you work with, so you might as well come. It's not like he'll refuse us because of your suspension. Not with this kind of evidence, and because *he likes you*. Might even be glad to see you, Edwin."

"Why would he be glad?" I gave her baffled look, then glanced at Tristan as if he could somehow explain it to me.

Juliet sighed. "Honestly, it's still as if you've never heard of the concept of friends. Hasn't the man been trying to become one of yours for ages?"

I blinked at her. "But Geer and I aren't friends."

Juliet got up and patted my arm. "I know, never mind. Let's go, before it gets too late. There's no need to inconvenience the Witch more than we need to."

# 33

# TRISTAN

We took Edwin's town car to Judge Geer's home. As we sat in traffic my phone buzzed in my pocket.

It was an email from my mom. I had a flash of mixed emotions. There was the anxiety that always accompanied hearing from her, feeling like an almost Pavlovian response, but I was also relieved.

It was good to hear from her less than a week after seeing each other. She wasn't dropping off the face of the earth.

Her message was short, just saying hi and 'hope you have a good holiday.' She told me the road trip was going well and included a picture of her, a middle-aged man and a teen, who I assumed were Steve and Levi.

An initial pang of longing hit me. They all seemed so happy. But after a minute of staring at the screen, I smiled. This was good, the message felt like the first step in building something, even if it was complicated.

I sent a quick reply and attached a photo of Edwin, Juliet, Mea and me from last night. We'd gone out for pizza and it'd been really fun.

Eventually we got to Geer's place, a beautiful brownstone

rather than an apartment building. Lights blazed in every window.

He'd been the least shitty judge by far, but that was a low bar and I wasn't exactly pleased to be seeing him again so soon despite what Juliet said about him wanting to be Edwin's friend.

A gray-haired white woman opened the front door. "Hello, Mr. Bickel." She had the tone of a seasoned hostess. "Charles didn't tell me you were coming but it's so nice to see you again."

"Uh." Edwin took off his hat. "I only sent him a text an hour ago. This isn't a planned visit."

"You're not here for the party?" The woman cocked her head.

"Party?" Edwin sounded pained.

"Everyone's here to kick off the holiday season. Come in, all of you." She gestured us inside. "Your best bet is finding Charles in the library. Feel free to stay for dinner after you see him."

"I don't think this is a good idea," Edwin muttered as the woman, who I assumed was Geer's wife, walked away.

"We're already here." Juliet directed Mea to the front of the group. She wasn't looking particularly pleased about word of a party either. "We'll find Geer and be on our way."

Music and voices drifted forth from the back of the house. It wasn't an open-plan living set up so we were able to navigate the hall and the stairs without running into anyone.

In the library we found Judges Geer, Pérez and Davis along with a few people I didn't recognize. A hush settled over the room as we walked in.

"Hello!" Geer bounced out of an armchair in obvious delight.

No one else echoed the greeting. They all just stared.

Judge Davis followed Geer forward. "Ms. Herrera, I'm surprised to see *you* in New York." He might as well have asked Juliet what the hell she thought she was doing here from the nasty look on his face.

"I'm on a case." Juliet seemed completely unperturbed. "Tristan requested Mea and I look into suspicious behavior at his workplace."

Davis frowned at me, eyes turning amused like I was some sort of joke. "How do you know Juliet Herrera?"

"My friend Aria works for her." I did my best not to let any unease show. I didn't want to be intimidated by the judges.

"It's great you all stopped by." Geer greeted us each enthusiastically before more could be said. "Get drinks. Dinner is in an hour so plenty of time to mingle beforehand. I'm pleased to see you, Edwin." He clapped him on the shoulder. "And you, Juliet."

Edwin seemed stiffer than usual, his features neutral, eyes unreadable. "Thank you, Charles. I didn't mean to crash your party. We'd hoped to find you less occupied."

"I have a favor to ask of you," Mea added, tone apologetic.

The older Witch gave Mea and Edwin a good-natured smile. "I'm at your service."

"I appreciate it." Mea seemed much more relaxed than our other two companions. "Like Juliet said, we're looking into problems Tristan noticed at his office. He's uncovered blood siphoning—"

"Why are you still working on that case?" Davis directed the question to Edwin. He'd inched closer to our group while the rest of the room's occupants watched in silence.

Edwin looked blank, completely unreactive to the man's words.

I crossed my arms. "I asked him to help me. That's Edwin's job or whatever, now he's responsible for me in the magic world, right? You outlined it all in court."

Davis narrowed his eyes at me. "True."

"I'm here about a warrant to search the company," Mea cut in, addressing Geer. "Maybe we can go discuss it—"

"The time altering magic detected today was you *investi-*

*gating*, was it, Bickel?" Davis interrupted. He hadn't been kind in court, but he hadn't been this hostile either. The guy was shaping up to be as bad as Raven. "I don't like you going around altering reality and not having to account for it."

Edwin glared. "Perhaps you shouldn't have suspended me, then I'd have checked in."

"To give us more lies?" Davis shook his head. "I was talking to Judge Raven about the legality of your power just today. Wondered what we might be able to do about it."

Geer blustered. "Hey, now. We don't change laws to single out things we don't like. Edwin has always been cooperative."

"*Always?*" Davis sneered.

Everyone but me reacted, the room feeling collectively on high alert. Edwin's nostrils flared and Juliet looked murderous.

"Yes, always." Geer set his drink down on a side table. "Why don't you four join me in my office?"

"This isn't the appropriate time to seek a warrant." Davis turned his disapproval on his colleague.

"Oh, I don't mind." Geer waved the other judge away like the nuisance he was. "Not when it's important. Delaying action for a dinner party isn't right. We have a responsibility. I mean, siphoning in an office, right here in the city—my goodness. I'm happy to go over warrant papers now. Really Davis, you can't argue things aren't in good hands with Mea here."

"We can when Bickel's lurking behind her." Raven had snuck in without me noticing and stepped up to Davis's side, mirroring the other man's look of distaste.

"So we shouldn't look into the crimes they've discovered?" Geer flapped his arms wildly as his frustration seemed to grow. "Do we need to call in some of our investigators after hours, just to have Mea explain everything to them so they can get the warrant? Which one of us will still need to sign."

Raven didn't come up with an immediate retort and Geer led the way out of the room, the four of us hastily following.

"You're an unlucky man, Mr. Tomás," Raven called after me.

"Huh?" I stopped, tunning to look at him without really thinking. Edwin stopped with me as the other's disappeared down the hall.

Raven waved his drink lazily. "Siphoned by not one, but two perpetrators. It's almost unbelievable."

I was itching to get out of here but felt trapped by courtesy and the awkwardness of walking away from someone directly addressing me. "What do you mean unbelievable? It's not like I'm lying."

"It's strange," Raven continued, turning to Davis. "A young Mortal caught at the center of our biggest crime in decades. A case of strange connections to Edwin Bickel all around."

Davis chuckled and the hair on the back of my neck stood up.

We needed to get away from these devious people. Everyone else was still watching like we were putting on a play, fascinated by the drama. It was unnerving.

"I wonder," Raven mused, eyes on Edwin. "You kept your boyfriend's presence out of your reporting. What other personal links did you leave out of your other files?"

Edwin narrowed his eyes. "None."

"No? Then why did I find an undisclosed connection to you just this morning?" Raven sipped his drink, grinning like he was enjoying whatever this was.

Edwin faltered. "I don't know what you mean. There was nothing like that in any of my work."

"You're a good liar, Bickel." Raven's amusement turned to naked hate. "One needs to check facts when you're involved, so I looked over everything to do with your recent cases and lines of investigation. The Fizz Bar, for example, illuminated an interesting connection."

I glanced at Edwin. A flicker of confusion passed over his face.

"Or do you really not know?" The judge sounded almost gleeful.

"Know what?" Edwin snapped.

"The owner of the bar is a Witch named Bethanie Boyle."

"I've never heard of her." Edwin grabbed my hand. "Let's go. I'm sick of this."

We turned away but only made it one step before Raven's voice washed over us. "Cousin to Wyatt Boyle. We all know you've heard of *him*."

Edwin stopped dead, his face so blank the sight made my stomach drop.

He swallowed, not turning to face the judges. "Everyone has cousins." The statement came out as nastily as any of Raven's had. I'd never heard anything like it, not even when Edwin had given Luca that death glare outside court and practically shouted at him.

A nervous sweat broke out on my palms. Something major was going on and I had no idea what.

"You really didn't know?" Raven came around to stand in front of us, cutting off the exit. "*Tsk-tsk*. You should've made the connection. Yes, everyone has cousins, but I can't say everyone has criminal associations quite like Wyatt Boyle, or you for that matter."

"There's no evidence Wyatt is involved in this. There's no evidence he's in the state of New York," Edwin said as if every word were laced with poison.

"I wouldn't be so dismissive." Raven didn't react to Edwin's frightening tone, he was way too happy about something. "Or have you been keeping close tabs, watching Wyatt's movements? Have you been in contact with him?"

"The Authority would know if Wyatt returned to New York," Edwin insisted, ignoring everything else.

I wanted to ask who the hell Wyatt was, but from the look in Edwin's eyes, maybe I didn't want to know. We really needed to get out of here. I tugged on his hand, but he didn't move.

"All the more reason to look into this connection," Raven pressed. "True, Wyatt went West after his release, but his name coming up for the first time in ten years should have been a red flag, Bickel. Unless you chose to ignore it."

"His name didn't come up, his *cousin's* did. A cousin I was unaware of. Now if you'll excuse me." Edwin's grip tightened on my hand. "We need to find Geer."

Edwin pushed past Raven and out of the library.

"What—?"

"Not now, Tristan." His hand shook slightly.

Juliet, Mea and Geer came out of a door to our left, making the hall overcrowded.

Juliet took one look at Edwin's face and went from quietly pleased to worried. "What is it?"

Edwin ignored her, turning to Mea. "Do we have what we need?"

"Uh—yeah." Mea looked quickly around as if trying to piece together what she'd missed.

"Thank you, Charles." Edwin sounded clipped, like he was trying to cover up his distress. "We'll leave you to your party."

"Oh, you can't go yet." Geer looked genuinely disappointed. "I'm sorry about the others back there. Talking about the legality of your power like that. I can't say I'll be inviting everyone from work next time I have a party. After the way this year has been I should have known better. Please stay for dinner. All of you. I'd like to get to know Mr. Tomás better." He smiled at me. "May I call you Tristan?"

"I'm afraid we can't stay." Edwin let go of my hand and turned away, heading for the stairs.

Raven popped out of another door—not the library one we'd exited—maybe there was a second door in the large, book-filled room I hadn't noticed. He was perfectly positioned, blocking our path out.

There were officially too many people in the cramped hallway.

"I don't think running away will help." Raven radiated the same satisfied glee as before.

Edwin stopped in front of the judge.

"Who's running?" Geer tried to peer around everyone else to see his colleague. "Why not make yourself useful, Raven, get my guests drinks? Then you can leave us alone to enjoy ourselves."

"Enjoy yourselves?" Raven called down the hall. "Haven't you heard? Wyatt Boyle is back."

"There is no evidence of that," Edwin half shouted. Juliet pushed past me and squeezed his arm. He ignored her

"Really, Raven—" Geer looked nervously around at everyone, finally picking up on the tension. "Where's this coming from? I haven't heard a peep of this."

"Not surprising, Charles. Bickel didn't want us to know the blood problem could be related to his ex-lover. Not when he's already covering things up because of his current one."

Raven looked at me like I was the scum on his shoe. Like what the fuck was this guy's problem—also—*ex-lover?* Possibly the infamous haven't-had-a-boyfriend-since-before-you-were-born ex-lover. No way this all went back to Edwin's personal life. That just felt wrong.

Juliet drew closer to Edwin, putting her arm around him.

She looked livid and fiercely protective of her friend. "Excuse us." She tried to push past Raven.

He didn't move, making it impossible for Juliet and Edwin to get by without knocking into the man or shoving him out of the way. "No. I'm not happy with any of your involvement in this case. We can pick this up on Monday. Until then, leave it be."

"Edwin's past has been dealt with and has no bearing." Geer's tone was a clear warning. "And Mea Dubois is perfectly capable of overseeing this warrant. If Wyatt is involved, I'm surprised I didn't hear about it. No one but you seems to think he's done anything of note in decades. He's monitored by the Authority. How could he get back in the state without us knowing? There must be a mistake."

"It's the modern age, like one needs to be physically present to be involved." Raven looked at his colleague like he didn't find the man worth his time.

"His cousin's involvement means nothing." Edwin had gotten quieter, which I found more worrying than him shouting.

"Why do you sound so desperate for that to be true?" Raven glanced from Edwin to me again and my blood boiled. "Maybe you've stopped dating criminals, gone for someone soft. A Mortal you can be in charge of more easily, but you're very touchy about the possibility Wyatt is back. How do we know you're not tempted to throw in your goodie-goodie act and join him again? I'm sure he could tempt you. It was too easy for him to do it before."

"Shut up," Juliet snapped, more vicious than anything else said tonight. "You have no right. You hateful, power-abusing excuse for a judge."

Edwin pulled his arm out of Juliet's grip. He looked around jerkily, eyes finding mine. Then he disappeared.

# 34

## EDWIN

I shouldn't have run away.

But I did, reappearing in Juliet's twilit yard. I was unnaturally cold in the comparatively mild Southern California air.

I shivered.

A sob escaped my throat and I clapped a hand over my mouth. There was no point holding it in. The twinkling trees and magically glowing underbrush blurred around me as hot tears wet my cheeks.

Raven was a bastard, cruel and unjust, but I didn't think he was lying. His claim Wyatt was tangled up in the current problem was farfetched, but not impossible. It made me sick with dread. He was supposed to be in my past. Wasn't it bad enough he invaded my thoughts?

I didn't know what to do, how to fix this. The investigation didn't matter, other people could see to that. It was my life. How was I supposed to go forward? Ignoring everything and shutting out all my problems no longer felt possible, but addressing them was as challenging as it'd always been.

I was backed into a corner, being forced to confront things I didn't want to look at.

I cried in the enchanted woods behind Juliet's house until George the purple-maned pony found me and nosed me into patting him. I stayed out there most of the night feeling guilty for turning my back on Tristan—not to mention Juliet and Mea—and unworthy of the concern they were probably feeling for me.

But Tristan wouldn't see it that way. None of them would resent me for acting like this. They were kind and I wished I could accept that more easily.

I wanted Tristan here with me and wasn't sure why I couldn't bring myself to go back to him. He wouldn't push me to explain anything I didn't want to, so what was I hiding from? I didn't know why I was so afraid to accept his support, still, after everything he'd shown me.

Unless I did know why, and I was avoiding that too.

I was clinging to my isolation even though I knew it wasn't the answer. It might never have been. That seemed so apparent standing here, alone in the darkened yard. Solitude certainly wasn't what I wanted for my future. It was a coping mechanism I'd held onto for so long I didn't know how to let go, even though it was hurting me.

I should have gone back if being alone wasn't what I wanted, but I didn't.

By the next afternoon I was still avoiding everything. Maybe my grand plan to get through life via isolation had been hindering me this whole time, but that didn't mean I was ready to change everything the second I admitted the flaw to myself.

I'd stayed at Juliet's, with my phone switched off for good measure. I needed to regroup, be upset at Raven and his ghoulish theatrics, be mad at myself for pushing good people away along with the bad, feel regretful and wallow.

I'd closed off because I'd needed to. It had been the only way to cope with being at the Authority. I didn't regret my decision to work there, or the things I'd been trying to achieve; the situation was more complicated than that. But it hadn't been a healthy environment for me and I'd acted like ignoring that would solve the problem. Maybe I should have left before now, taken another approach to my goals, but I hadn't seen the situation with that kind of perspective.

Avoidance had already been ingrained in my life by the time I'd gone to work for the judges. Protecting myself by shutting everyone out had been a response to Wyatt first. It was the only way I could try and take back control, to not be hurt again, so when I took that approach at work it felt natural.

The two had always been too tangled together. Wyatt, my trial, what that experience prompted me to do with my life after.

I wasn't going as far as to say closing off had been wrong from the start, but somewhere along the way avoiding people, my past, my own emotions had become a problem.

My life had slowly snowballed out from a single reactive decision. Then one day I'd looked up and realized everything had become an unmanageable disaster, waiting to crumble out from beneath my calm unaffected façade.

I didn't want things to go back to normal as I'd wished only days ago, and didn't want to maintain my intimidating, heartless reputation any longer. I wanted to open up to Tristan without limits and didn't want him to be the only one who saw a more real me. I wanted a life that felt different, one where I chose things out of joy rather than fear.

So I started by summoning George an apple out of nowhere and feeding it to him. The pony tossed his head in appreciation. I smiled.

"New friend?"

I spun around. On the path between the trees stood Tristan.

"I— How did you get here?" My hands went to my rumpled waistcoat, the buttons undone at my neck. My bow tie was in a crumpled lavender ball in my pocket.

Tristan walked forward holding two coffee cups. He looked radiant in the long afternoon light, casually dressed and as stubble ridden as I was. His hair was messily tousled as if he'd been running his hands through it. Fall leaves crunched under his mauve Converse-clad feet.

"Here." He handed me a small espresso cup. "The cafe isn't open today, but I popped in to make it for you. Hope it's not cold."

"But—?" I took the coffee.

Tristan smiled. "I had my flight out here for Thanksgiving, remember? Juliet thought you'd have come here. Aria came by to check last night. Apparently she can use her psychic sense to detect human presences."

"Aria?" I was almost disappointed she hadn't traipsed back here to pester me.

"You could have left your phone on if you didn't want us resorting to such in-person means," Tristan admonished, but in a way that was clearly meant to be friendly.

I hugged him and he returned it with force.

"I'm sorry," I said in his ear.

Tristan shook his head, his hair tickling me. "No need to be." We pulled back in unison as if each of us needed to see the other's face. "I don't mind coming to find you. Why don't you show me around?"

"Oh." I blinked. "It's not as nice now the enchanted lights are out. You should see this place at night. And—um—I suppose I should introduce you to George."

The pony hadn't gone far.

Tristan and I walked around the large wooded yard, coming across the ducks on the grass. A leisurely stroll was not what I'd expected, but it felt right. Even though we weren't talking about what had happened last night it didn't feel like avoidance. We needed a moment together, or I needed it at least. A normal, sweet moment, one that wasn't about all my problems but about good things.

We ended up sitting under a large oak tree, our empty cups nestled in the roots beside us. We sat shoulder to shoulder. Quiet, but not in that expectant way that made silence feel like the empty space proceeding someone's next words.

It was companionable.

I enjoyed it for a very long time, and Tristan seemed to as well.

"I'm not going back to my job at the Authority," I said after a while.

Tristan leaned his head on my shoulder. "Are you happy with that, or do you feel like you can't go back?"

"It's the right choice for me, but I'm not exactly happy. I'm disappointed that I put so many years into working there and trying to prove myself to people who were so determined to see bad in me. But I'm not leaving because I don't want to face the judges and their endless vendetta. I don't have anything to prove to people like them. Changing their minds doesn't somehow validate me as a good person. Their beliefs are up to them and I don't have to put up with it."

"They were awful to you, Edwin." Tristan grabbed my hand. "You really don't have anything to prove. You're a good man."

My chest ached and I cleared my throat. "I want to work with people who think that too."

Tristan made a pained sound. "I'm sorry you ever had to deal with anything less."

"It felt like the right thing at one time." I squirmed my shoulder so that Tristan stopped leaning on it, then shifted around so we were sitting facing each other. "I used to be very different from who I am now. I used to be more average, as far as my lifestyle. I had friends and lovers and didn't pretend to hate everyone. I didn't push people away."

"When was this?" Tristan asked tentatively.

"Oh—for the first sixty years of my life or so. My power was known, but not as widely as now. Things were generally less sensational. Witches saw me more or less like anyone else. Then I met a man and fell in love with him. He was charming, full of life and fun. Everyone loved him, and he was so taken with me. I held nothing back with him. We were together for about fifteen years."

Nervousness made me pause. Juliet was the last person I'd told this story to and that was so damn long ago. I remembered how telling her had felt, gut-wrenching in the moment, but after it had been a relief.

Tristan watched me carefully. I wondered if he was nervous too. He reached out a hand and I took it.

"It wasn't a good relationship," I went on, trying not to avert my eyes from his too much. "Not after the beginning. He was manipulative, emotionally abusive and controlling. A devious, self-centered man driven by his ambitions. He built himself a gang of Witches, slowing taking control of illegal magical dealings in the city. And I had no idea. When we met, I honestly don't think he'd started it yet. The growth of his network had to have been gradual to go unnoticed, but he hid his crimes from me well, for a long time.

"Wyatt and I lived together but I didn't know what he did all the time and he discouraged my prying. Afterward I found out he'd used our relationship to his advantage. People assumed I was in on everything he did, or maybe he told them I was directly. Either way, anyone who knew about his enterprise thought I was at his side, supporting all of it.

"As his operation grew, he began claiming I was not only in on it, but secretly in charge. The irony of that still makes me mad. Wyatt controlled my whole life and had the gall to paint me as the one telling him what to do. He spread stories about my unique power and used it to scare people. The things I could do while time was frozen, with no one able to stop me. Witches gave in to his demands more easily when they feared I might be the one to visit them next time. And I was oblivious as this thing grew around me, too consumed by our toxic relationship, trying to earn his love. I'd been isolated, conditioned not to question him or look to closely. I saw what he wanted me to see.

"I wanted to leave him, but he was an expert at manipulating me to stay. I was powerless. And later no one believed that I—the legendarily powerful Witch—could have been trapped by anyone."

Tristan's jaw clenched. "That's bullshit though. It's not about physical or magical strength."

"I know. But not everyone saw it that way, there were too many unlikely truths for the likes of Raven and Judge Herrera to swallow. It made more sense to them that I was behind the criminal enterprise, as rumor suggested.

"Near the end I think I was almost willfully ignorant of what Wyatt was up to, afraid to find out. I knew he was hiding something big. He started pushing me to do favors for him, trying to make me use my power for him outright, but I never did—I've always been very careful what I do with my extra gifts. My refusal made him worse. He had me buy a property for him instead, as a concession, and I never asked what he used it for. No one found that believable either.

"But one day I went to the place. I was preparing to leave, getting my things in order and planning to sell the property out from under him and disappear. At the warehouse I found blatant evidence of his operation. I'd been shocked and also not surprised at all, feeling like a fool.

"I turned him in and it became a nightmare. The court picked apart my life. Wyatt tried to blame the whole thing on me and the only way to disprove that was to tell people what actually happened, including the abusive nature of our relationship."

Tristan squeezed my hand. "Edwin."

My vision blurred. I leaned into Tristan and he put his arms around me. It was awkward, sitting on the ground, but it felt so damn good. The past was very far away.

Tristan spoke soft words in my ear. I murmured back thickly through my tears, and didn't think I'd ever been comforted like this, by someone who cared for me like Tristan did.

Eventually, I wiped my nose and settled between Tristan's legs, my back to his chest.

"I can't imagine telling those Witches such a personal story. Or going to work for them after." Tristan was soft with understanding, his voice quiet and close to my ear.

I picked at a leaf on the ground. "I didn't become an investigator right away, that was almost a decade later. I'd wanted to help people. And I wanted to work with those judges in particular because they'd messed up in my case, blamed the victim and then gone and shared personal details of my story around when they shouldn't have. I wanted to make sure they didn't keep acting that way."

"I don't know what to say, Edwin. I feel like sorry doesn't mean anything, but I wish none of this had ever happened to you, or that there was something I could have done, even though it was too long ago for that to be possible."

I smiled, turning to look at him over my shoulder. "This is perfect, Tristan. Talking."

"Yeah?" He raised his brows.

I nodded before turning around to lean back into him. "You're the one person I should have been able to confide in. I resisted because it felt like you were the only one who didn't know. I just wanted to control my own story. I shouldn't have had to resist telling you because others treated the information carelessly. I knew you wouldn't judge me, but I just wanted my past to stop defining me, and keeping it from you felt like the only way I could assert that."

"I can see that. But I'm glad we're doing this now." He hesitated. "What changed, do you think?"

I shrugged in Tristan's arms, feeling them move with me. "Nothing really, it's more that I want things to change. I want to be comfortable letting people in again. I want a job that doesn't revolve around Witches that make me miserable. I don't want all my energy to go into trying to mold others' opinions of me at the expense of being who I want."

"That all sounds really good, Edwin. And I'll be here for any of those things or whatever else you want in life. I wonder though—" Tristan shifted his position so he could hold me better. "Have you ever talked to anyone about all this, over the years?"

"You mean like in therapy?" I ran my fingers over his jean-clad knee as I stared forward into the yard. "No. But I probably should have a long time ago."

"I wouldn't worry too much about what you should have done. Just do what's right for you now."

"You're very wise." I squeezed his leg.

"Not really. I just know it can be helpful, done a bit of it myself."

"Well, now that I'm so willing to change my ways, I might as well go for it." I let out a breathy sound almost like a laugh, surprised at my own lightness.

"Sounds good, Edwin." Tristan nuzzled my ear.

George was off eating the grass, purple mane shimmering in the setting sun. The first of Mea's enchanted lights started popping up around us. It was beautiful.

We both seemed content to sit here and watch the night unfold around us.

"What do you think you'll do now that you aren't going back to your job?" Tristan asked when it was almost fully dark.

"I'm not sure. So I guess nothing for now. I inadvertently broke all the monitoring spells the Authority had on me when escaping the blood-room yesterday, so I'm truly free of those Witches if I want to be. Mea has a new role along the lines of what I was trying to achieve by myself. Officially checking on her local Authority's actions. If something like my trial happened now, the person would have somewhere to turn for assistance. At least in the Southern California district. Maybe I'll look into joining her. I could probably make more of a difference if I worked away from New York and all the Witches who dislike me. Leave that mess for Mea to look into if she's so inclined."

I was sure she would be, but bringing accountability to the Authority in any region was a complicated task. I knew firsthand you couldn't do it alone and there was no way to know how the new program would be expanded throughout the country. What Mea was doing now was just the start. It was a good thing she had a team of determined Witches at her disposal.

"I don't really know what I want to do next either." Tristan seemed hesitant. He hadn't mentioned he was considering a change himself before now. "I might want to move back here, and—actually, that's not true. I do know what I want. I am coming back." His voice became more confident. "I miss the cafe and being close to Owen. The things I've gained by leaving all the good parts of my life behind aren't worth it. Other than getting the opportunity to know you, Edwin. And I feel like we can make it work even if we don't live in the same city."

"If my Coffee Cat days proved anything, it's that you won't even notice the difference."

"Ha. Sounds like things will work out perfectly then." Tristan kissed me behind my ear and down my neck. "I'm fully on board with as much magic in our relationship as you want, by the way. Teleport me anywhere."

I chuckled. "I've a few far-flung date locations in mind already. And I can always take you back across the country to see your mother. If that's something you want."

Tristan squeezed me. "I love that you knew I'd be worried, being so far from her again. It shouldn't matter, she should be able to keep in touch with me anyway, but I want to see her, not email her. Figure out if we can have some sort of relationship again."

"Any way I can help, let me know." I twisted around to look at him. "Would you like to spend the rest of the holiday with Owen and Aria? I'd like to get to know them better."

Tristan stretched and stood, putting his hand out for me and pulling me up. "Hearing that makes me so happy, Edwin. They're going to love you, I promise. And I think you'll like them too. But I actually told Owen I was going back to New York with you."

"Very presumptuous of you," I teased, not bothering to brush the dirt from my clothes.

He picked up our coffee cups and we made our way toward the house. "But I was right, wasn't I? We need a little alone time."

"We do."

Tristan linked his arm through mine. "You can come for Christmas. Owen and I do a whole thing."

"I'd love that more than anything."

Tristan grinned and I kissed the lopsided curve of his lips as the enchanted trees glittered around us.

# 35

## EDWIN

After a quiet night to ourselves and a long lazy morning in bed, Tristan and I joined Mea and Juliet for the holiday.

It was shamelessly the best time I'd ever had.

Tristan and Juliet cooked, bringing my kitchen to life, while Mea kept up a running commentary and made everyone laugh. I was in charge of cocktails and setting the table, and I did what I could about decoration. On a whim, I place a bow tie at each table setting and insisted we all wear them during the meal.

It was silly and seemed to please Tristan to no end.

By the early evening we were all happily slumped on the couch, but the night was far from over.

MEA WANTED to make use of her warrant while WMS and the other businesses in the building were closed for the holiday. Tristan was game to go with her and Juliet to guide them around and help with anything he could.

I was joining them even though I didn't need to see this line of investigation through for professional reasons, since I didn't technically have professional reasons after deciding to quit my job. Tristan would be in good hands with the other two, but given Juliet and I had nearly been trapped once already, it would be foolish to assume that something similar couldn't happen again.

The cocktails we'd drunk earlier had worn off and we'd all had naps before Tristan roused us with coffee, not that I was feeling at my sharpest as we got ready to go.

At midnight I teleported the four of us into the building's lobby.

"This feels a lot like trespassing even though I work here." Tristan's voice echoed across the empty space as we made our way to the elevators. "I know the security cameras can't see us after that spell you did, Edwin, but that almost makes it worse."

Mea pressed the up button. "Magical warrants don't work like Mortal ones. It's a complicated system, having laws apply to non-magical folks without them knowing. They can't be aware we're searching, there's no way to explain without Telling, so we have to conduct our search in secret."

"And we just have to trust you're doing it right?" Tristan gave her a skeptical look.

The elevator arrived and Mea led the way in, waiting for Tristan to select the correct floor. "It's the same as trusting we aren't putting spells on unsuspecting Mortals. Which maybe isn't a great example, given everything. Trying to mediate the power imbalance of magic by restricting Witches with its secret leads to all kinds of subsequent problems. That one restriction creates a society based around rules and enforcement. It's all supposed to be in Mortals best interests, but you're right, when things go wrong there's no one to catch it."

"But Mea's seeing to that, aren't you?" Juliet looked at her girlfriend with pride, and maybe a hint of teasing.

"I really don't know." Mea seemed momentarily doubtful, running a hand through her hair and looking around at us.

"I think it's a good start," I assured her as the elevator doors opened.

She smiled at me gratefully.

We stepped out onto the executive floor of WMS.

"Being here in the middle of the night is eerie," Tristan whispered, even though keeping quiet was unnecessary due to the diffusion spells hiding us.

Not that we expected to see anyone in the middle of the night after a holiday, but he was right, there was the distinct sense that we shouldn't be here.

"Better be as quick as we can then. Let's start in record keeping." Juliet, forever keeping us on task, looked to Tristan to lead the way.

He took us to a windowless room filled with filing cabinets and two desks arranged facing the door. Mea and Juliet took up a chair each and switched the computers on.

Tristan looked over Mea's shoulder. "I don't know these passwords."

Mea inserted an Authority branded flash drive. "I've got a way around that. Mixing magic and technology really is fascinating." Tristan didn't look sold on the idea. Mea gained access to the computer anyway. "We should search for the documentation relating to Mystic Pawn first, then move on to financials."

The pawn shop was listed as a client, but neither Mea nor Juliet could find any sort of contract or agreement in the electronic files. Tristan and I browsed the cabinets until we came to the M's.

"It's not here." Tristan flicked through manila folders in frustration.

He stepped back and I had a fruitless look of my own. We checked under P for pawn and T for treasure, as well as under A and S, to correspond to the owner's initials. There was officially nothing.

"Should we just try to look for evidence that Emerson is being paid for the blood?" Tristan asked.

Juliet swiveled around in her chair. "That's not an easy thing to look into. And finding nothing here isn't meaningless. If Mystic Pawn's deal was solely related to the blood, the record is probably missing on purpose. Hiding the connection."

"We could look for more missing files." I walked over to the computers. "Since the pawn shop was listed under the clients, there'll be a way to cross reference. If more are missing, that might mean all those deals are dodgy as well."

"Do you mean go through every client and every file?" Tristan looked aghast.

Mea grinned. "Paranormal Investigating is so glamorous, isn't it?"

Soon we were all looking bleak. It was tedious work, and nothing seemed out of place for a good hour. Then we slowly started finding missing records. Nothing on the computer and nothing in the cabinets, just a name on the client list.

"But I don't get it," Tristan said at about quarter to two in the morning. "I've worked on this firm's most recent campaign. It's not a Witchy business like the pawn shop. They're a huge account and probably pay WMS loads, so it's not like their deal would be off book for any Mortal reason, but I can't see how it'd be related to the blood."

"It probably isn't directly related, as far as the Mortal business goes." I looked down at the list of clients for whom WMS had no records. "I wonder if Emerson isn't being paid for the blood directly with cash. Maybe he's being paid in magical favors. Witch-for-hire is a good job, and very attractive as a service for aware Mortals. If these contracts are missing, and some are for large accounts as you say, then I wonder if the contracts for service between WMS and the clients were magically influenced."

Juliet was rubbing her eyes, but paused to nod her agreement. "A spell on the contractual papers could trick the client into signing a bad deal, buying services for inflated prices unknowingly, or force them to pick WMS over competitors. It would be as illegal as the blood stealing itself."

"And exactly the kind of evidence we need." Mea narrowed her eyes at the client list she was examining. "Magic like that has to be done on paper, so we need to find what was signed to see if it's been tampered with."

Tristan had his eyes narrowed. "Witches would really use magic to help someone get corporate advantages?"

"Yes, Witches do it themselves, well, not all the time, but often enough." I closed the cabinet Tristan and I had been looking through. "I've had more than a few cases where a Witch tried to use magic to say, buy out all their biggest competitors with magically tampered mergers. We don't all work in Witchy businesses like Mason, lots of Witches work in Mortal industries, but using magic to disadvantage others, or put yourself on top, is illegal."

"That has to be the most boring thing to use magic for." Tristan tried to stifle a yawn.

I laughed.

Mea's lips twitched briefly as she turned away from her computer. "So where do we think these potentially spelled papers might be?"

"I really hope they aren't in the blood-room." Juliet looked at me in dismay. "I didn't see anything that looked like a place to store files, but we weren't exactly looking."

"No." I shoved my hands in my pockets. "They could have been in any one of those boxes. I read their labels as I went but not all of them were visible. I could have easily missed a tampered contracts box."

Juliet tapped her nails on the desk. "If there's anywhere else they might be, we should check there first."

"Agreed. I'm not keen to have to break us out again."

"You don't have to tell me twice," Juliet muttered, turning back to the computer.

Tristan was yawning again. "Uh—sorry. Why don't you summon the missing contracts?"

"I have to have a general idea of where an object is. Down to the room at the very least. And if anything is in the blood-room, it wouldn't come anyway."

"Damn. Okay." Tristan considered. "If it were me, and I was running a blood scam from my company in exchange for magically guaranteed deals, I'd keep the incriminating stuff where I could keep an eye on it. That, or I'd hide it away so no one ever found it. *Aww man*, what if the papers are locked in a safe deposit box or buried in someone's yard? If so, we're fucked."

"I'm not so sure they would be." I had to resist laughing at his dramatic dismay. "Company records will likely all be here in the building. Their complete absence would be suspicious, during a Mortal audit, for example."

"Right." Tristan stretched and made for the door. "Let's go look in Emerson's office then."

Juliet and Mea opted to continue the inventory of the records room so we would have a full list of the missing information and potentially influenced deals. I took the list of clients we'd already identified and followed Tristan to Walsh's office.

The CEO occupied a corner room with large windows and a bunch of wasted space. A few leather couches and a coffee table were set up in the far corner and a glass top desk sat closer to the door. The two walls that weren't windows were lined with mostly bare bookshelves.

"How minimalist." I made directly for the desk, but there was no point checking it closer. There was nothing on it but a laptop, keyboard and mouse.

"It's weird. Doesn't look like a space used to actually work." Tristan assessed the room with narrowed eyes. "Why are there no books, pictures, or rich-guy knick-knacks? Just nothing, with so much shelving. Oh, but there's six rows of company mugs. That's no surprise."

The bottom quarter of each bookshelf housed a closed cabinet. It had to be where anything might be kept in the bare room. We each went to open one, but they were locked. I flicked my fingers in a silent spell and Tristan tried his cabinet again. It still wouldn't budge.

"Hm." I knelt down and placed my palm on the wood door, over the latch. "An unusually strong spell was used to keep these shut. I'd say it was infused with blood from the feel of it."

"Gross." Tristan made a face. "But at least there's a good chance something worth hiding is inside. Can you open it?"

"Blood magic could potentially be strong enough that I can't break it, without the extreme measures I used to get Juliet and me out of that room, but I think a little more power should do the trick here." Magic fizzled in the air around me as I did the spell again.

With a faint pop, all the cabinet doors opened.

We peered into the nearest ones, Tristan joining me in kneeling on the ground.

"There's more here than I'd expect from the bare room." Tristan pulled out several packed manila folders, leaving twice as many behind, and plopped into a sitting position.

I examined a stack of my own, feeling for magic before reading. "All of these documents are untampered with." We looked through them anyway. Discovering the missing files without traces of magical influence would mean we'd been wrong and have to go back to financials or something else.

We kept the lights off as we searched, the twinkling city out the windows and full moon casting enough light to see by. I fought off exhaustion, Tristan's constant yawns proving horribly contagious. Just as I was about to suggest we pass this tedium on to a team of Witches still employed by the Authority, I found something.

One of the missing contracts was at the bottom of a bunch of repetitive phone lists. It practically reeked of magic. In the same cabinet, Tristan and I found several more missing records interspersed among drafts of WMS's mission statement and other random things. The next cabinet proved similar.

I vanished the papers, sending them to Geer's office at the Authority for safekeeping. Mea and whoever took over this case could parse out the exact nature of the spells later.

Tristan was reading yet another magically influenced document, two more sitting beside him. "You know that thing you said about mergers?" I indicated I did and he frowned. "Yeah, well. I think Emerson did exactly that. These"—he picked up the other papers—"were some of the companies bought out before I started. It looks like absorbing these businesses' clientele and employees made WMS go from just another average marketing firm to the behemoth it is now."

I looked at the date on the documents. "That's not long before all the blood started showing up for sale. Looks like he created WMS with the explicate purpose of harvesting blood, rather than Witches approaching him for access to what he already had. He'll probably know exactly who else is running this. Ha. The Authority is going to be stunned when Mea wraps this whole thing up after so long without any good leads." I chuckled, wondering if the tiredness was getting to me, but really I was just pleased everyone in New York branch was going to look lacking. "Her bosses are going to love her. I bet she'll want to bring Walsh in for questioning right away—"

"He might have an objection to that," said a deep voice from the doorway.

Tristan and I looked up in unison. A man stood on the threshold of the room, cast in shadow. No one should've been able to see or hear us through my diffusion spell.

"Hello there, Tristan," the man said without moving. "I think I've finally figured out why you seem so familiar."

Tristan stood up, thrusting the rest of the magic papers at me as I got off the floor as well. I vanished the documents behind my back so the intruder wouldn't notice.

"I really don't know what you mean, Emerson." Tristan's words came out steady and tinged with anger.

Walsh laughed.

I felt a flash of panic but I wasn't sure why. Everything was off: his voice; his ability to see us when he was a Mortal, not a powerful blood-Witch.

There was something else I couldn't place.

"I can't believe you, this isn't funny." Tristan clenched a fist at his side. "We know what you're up to."

"I see that." Walsh sounded almost delighted. "I'd never have thought you knew about magic, Tristan. If I'd realized, we could have been much better friends."

*Wrong.* Everything about the man was wrong.

"We aren't friends at all," Tristan snapped, near a shout. "You're using people."

Emerson let out a dramatic sigh that set my pulse thumping. He was still cloaked in shadow and for an odd second I was almost grateful. "People are here to be used. Not you, Tristan. I'd like a man like you at my side. Aren't you curious why you're so familiar?"

"No." Tristan moved a fraction closer to me so that our shoulders brushed.

My mind raced, a realization sitting out of reach, hidden like Emerson's features. Why was I cold and clammy? This Mortal put fear in me, almost like nothing I'd ever felt, yet it was chillingly familiar.

My heart was already in my throat when Emerson stepped forward into the faint light streaming through the windows.

It wasn't Emerson Walsh at all.

36

# EDWIN

"You've been letting Edwin cast spells on you, Tristan." The man's manner was chiding, his greedy eyes deliberately avoiding mine. "His magical signature caught my attention when we were alone in the elevator. I used to know it so well—the way his spells felt—though I'd forgotten him enough to be confused by the sensation. Edwin is a forgettable kind of man, but you know that, I'm sure. Funny, I'd thought his *magic* would always be clear in my memory, regardless of him."

"You're not Emerson Walsh." I meant to shout, or sneer, but my words were almost inaudible.

He looked at me then, very briefly, familiar gray eyes as cold as I remembered. "Am I not? Tristan, what do you think?"

Every time he said Tristan's name my stomach cramped. My mind seemed to be moving sluggishly. This wasn't possible. But even so, I should be doing something. I must have been in shock because I just stared on as Tristan refused to answer the man in front of us, his shoulder pressing tighter against mine, his steady hand brushing my trembling one.

The man calling himself Emerson pulled a small vial out of

his pocket. "This contains your blood, Tristan. I couldn't ignore the puzzle of you, and so I tracked it down to figure out what was so familiar. Now that's been cleared up, I can use this for other things."

He uncorked the vial of blood and brought it to his nose, swirling the dark liquid as he sniffed, then he poured a large drop into his palm before corking the vial and stowing it back in his pocket. Emerson dragged his index finger through the blood.

Tristan shuddered beside me and made a gagging noise, but he seemed to rally quickly. "So what if it's my blood? You're not a Witch, just a fucking creep."

"Not a Witch? Hm. But Edwin said I'm not Emerson Walsh. So which is it?" He paused, looking at us with exaggerated expectation. He scowled when we didn't play along. "Well, you're both wrong." Emerson clapped his hands together with a squelch. He muttered an incantation and the blood turned to a dark red powder, coating his palms and spilling on the carpet.

"Uh—" Tristan looked at me in confusion that was quickly turning to panic.

I had to focus. This wasn't the time to freeze up. If only I could collect myself by sheer power of will as I'd done so often before.

At last I found my voice. "You're Wyatt Boyle. Like I wouldn't know."

"I'm not so sure you would," Wyatt said casually, all trace of his previous disapproval gone. "I *am* Emerson Walsh now. You won't find anyone in the company to say otherwise. No Mortal would disagree. Most Witches wouldn't even be able to tell, not even Emerson's ex-wife."

Tristan grabbed my hand and gripped me hard. I tried to squeeze back but found my muscles weak.

"How sweet." Wyatt leered at us. "Edwin and the pretty Mortal. Seems you've heard of me, Tristan. Don't believe a word of it. He made me take the fall for all his bad behavior. Edwin is an excellent liar. But you must know that. He pretended I was so big and bad when he's the one with all the power."

"That's not true." My words were waspy even to my own ears. "You can't deny—don't deny what you did to me."

"Me? Did to you?" His offense quickly turned to anger. "I went to prison, Edwin. You sent me there unfairly. I wanted to leave you, get out from under *your* control, and look what you did to me?" He grabbed the front of his shirt and pulled on the fabric in a desperate gesture, like he was about to fall to his knees and sob. The red powder smeared everywhere. He looked wounded and pitiful, except for his cold, calculating eyes.

A hot flash of panic hit me, making me close to faint. His words were all wrong and everyone knew it, but I couldn't resist defending myself. "I did nothing to you. None of it was my fault. Everything—you—you did. It was all you."

"Fine, we can pretend lies are true if you want. As *fun* a reunion as it's been, Edwin, I've got more pressing things going on. You're old news. I have a new life." Wyatt looked down at his messy shirt. With a swipe of his hand and a muttered word, all the powder was neatly piled in his palm again. He looked up. "I see we both found Tristan mildly interesting."

Tristan made a sound almost like a growl. "What did you do to the real Emerson Walsh, you piece of shit?" He squeezed my hand twice in quick succession like he was trying to tell me something.

Wyatt rolled his eyes. "I stole his identity—we Witches do it thoroughly. A mildly complex blood magic ritual really does the trick. To do it I'd needed Emerson's blood, but it wasn't hard to get him to pop over to Denver, where I'd been holed up. The idea that his silly marketing empire could go out of state, that he could open offices all over the country, seduced him perfectly."

"So where is he now?" Tristan sounded apprehensive of the answer.

"Who cares? You never met him." Wyatt stared at the powder in his hand. "The ritual created an illusion of identity so strong that no one who knew the original Emerson would be able to see the difference. Even when I'm much more handsome. Aren't I good looking, Edwin?" Wyatt gave me a taunting glance. "You know you can't deny it."

Anger jolted me out of my haze.

We had him. And if I could shake off my shock I could use his arrogance to our advantage. I squeezed Tristan's hand back, feeling calmer. I might as well try to get as much information from Wyatt as I could.

"You wanted to run a marketing company?" I asked.

Wyatt's actions didn't make much sense when I considered everything Tristan had told me about Emerson around the office. Having a day job wasn't Wyatt's style, but by all accounts he was at the office five days a week calling meetings and handing out mugs to Mortals, being *visible*. Hardly the behavior of the powerful Witch in charge he yearned to be. I knew him well enough to be confident his ambition hadn't changed so drastically, not even in thirty-some years.

"Running a company wasn't my first choice, no. We had a much better setup than this, you and I." He sounded bitter. "You're the whole reason I'm here, Edwin. I had to get a new identity because of the slander you cursed me with. Even being out of state was no good. No matter where I went, a watchful cloud followed me. It was horrible living like that."

Wyatt turned away from us to glance out the window, playing with the powdered blood in his hand, absently sending it swirling with a magical flick of his finger. "I was in Denver when I met this Witch from Brooklyn. He knew my name from the old days, I think he once dated my cousin. Anyway. He and his brother were starting a new venture back home. See, *their* cousin married a Mortal, only to get divorced."

Wyatt threw a what-can-you-do look over his shoulder. "Emerson was bitter about the break up. He'd grown accustomed to having magic in his life and wanted to use it to set himself up. Boost his income. So he went to his ex-cousins-in-law with a proposal and the three of them hatched this whole scheme. Magic to build a marketing empire and make Emerson rich and successful in his field, in exchange for a permanent captive blood supply. Fucking genius."

Wyatt turned around, leaning against the glass. His excitement even seemed to reach his eyes. "They asked if I wanted in on the magic side of things, but that wasn't what I was after. It would be impossible to get away with, given my criminal history. So I sent them away and made my own plan. Emerson had it great, money and security guaranteed by magic. A place here in the city I missed so dearly. Stealing his life would be perfect. Masquerading my own magic in Mortal's blood was the only way I could get around the Authority's tracking and incessant monitoring. The end of Emerson was my new beginning. It came off flawlessly. None of the Witches involved in the siphoning even know I'm a Witch. No one knows I'm not Emerson. It's perfect to be hidden in plain sight, and I have all the blood I could ever need—it's the only way to do magic—I wish I'd tried it sooner." He made a fist around the powder in his hand, red sparks flying, lighting the cruel glint in his eye.

"You killed Emerson?" Tristan sounded hollow with disgust.

"What a crude way to put it. I don't see it like that at all. I needed all of his blood, a minor detail. He lives on with me. You see?" Wyatt left the window and came right up to us. He was taller; any closer and he would be towering.

Wyatt looked me up and down. "Edwin, you look so the same. Except I'm not sure what's going on with your outfit." He made a snorting sound. "What are we going to do now? I hear you've been a very good boy. Are you bored yet? Fooling everyone must be tiring. You miss me, don't deny it. I was mad at you for a long time, but I could forgive you. I'll take you back if you make it worth my while."

He thought that would work after everything? After all this time? He thought he could admit to killing a man and I'd come back to him? Wyatt didn't understand me at all if he thought he had the upper hand. I'd been vulnerable when I'd wanted his love, but that desire was long dead. He might have triggered fear and a mess of traumatic emotion in me tonight, but I didn't want or need anything from Wyatt other than to never see him again.

With my grip firm on Tristan's hand, I stopped time.

When everything went still, I felt myself relax. It took Tristan a moment longer to realize things were frozen. As soon as he did, he spun me around to face him.

"Holy shit. Are you okay?" He cupped my face in his hands, scrutinizing me.

I made a weird half-laugh, half-choking sound. "I'll survive."

Tristan wrapped me up tight in his arms.

"Really." I let my weight rest against him. "I could have done without that little confrontation, but it's all right. He's not part of my life. I'm going to deal with all the lingering effects he left me with and move forward. This doesn't change anything. I'm ready for something new."

## 37

# EDWIN

Tristan waved from down the street.

I returned it, smiling as he hurried up to me.

"Sorry, I'm late." He kissed me on the cheek.

"Not at all." I checked my phone. "You're right on time."

We entered the Authority building and made for the elevators. The place was busy but I didn't bother glancing around.

"How did it go?"

Tristan gave me a hesitant smile. "Good, I think. She wants you to come next time, but I think we were both glad it was just the two of us."

I ignored a group of Witches getting into an elevator, opting to wait for the next one. "I'll gladly join you two when she's in town next. What did you guys talk about?"

Tristan had met his mother for lunch this afternoon. She was back in the city to drop Levi at school and had seemed keen to see her older son.

"Actually she asked if we'd meet her and Steve for dinner tomorrow. Before they leave." Tristan led the way into an empty elevator.

I followed and selected the correct floor, not holding the

door for anyone behind us. I may be newly committed to not pushing people away, but I didn't find I had any desire to drop my unlikable act while in this particular building.

I focused on my boyfriend. "Would you like to have dinner with them?"

Tristan shrugged, a small smile twitching on his lips. "Yeah. Mom and I still haven't talked about the all things we need to, but I think it will be nice to catch up first. Get to know each other again. And if that part goes well we can move on the heavier stuff. Seeing her today was so much better than last time. We just chatted about little things. It wasn't a perfect visit but it feels like we could actually get somewhere. Eventually."

Warm affection filled me. "That's great, darling. I'm glad you're feeling optimistic. Of course I'll come to dinner with you." I adjusted my bow tie. "I hope they like me."

Tristan squeezed my arm. "They'll love you. And if there's any weirdness I'm going to address it head on. But I really don't think it will be like that."

I trusted him.

The idea of dinner with people who wanted to get to know me was still nerve wracking. It was the kind of social situation I felt lost in. But all I had to do was support Tristan. I knew I could do that. "I'm sure it will all go well."

"Yeah." Tristan's attention seemed to shift as he looked at me more closely. "But how about you? How are you doing?"

I took a moment to consider and found I was confident about being here, my feelings surprisingly uncomplicated. "I'm good. Really, I promise."

We exited the elevator and made our way to Geer's office.

I'd officially resigned the same night we'd caught Wyatt. Mea had brought the man in and taken care of all the official business while I'd gone to my desk one last time to email the judges.

Tristan and I had been asked to make witness statements

about our conversation with Wyatt and detail how we'd found all the documents, but other than anything that might still need to be ticked off in regards to that, I was done with the case and working at the Authority. The only reason I was here today was because Geer had asked to see me, saying it was personal.

I knocked on his door. It swung open immediately.

"What a week." The judge beckoned us in. "Drinks?"

We settled in the armchairs by the fire with glasses of whiskey.

I had a sip and set mine aside. "You seem frazzled, Charles."

"Do I?" He ran a ring-clad hand through his white hair. "Well, it's been busy to say the least. I'm sad you're leaving us, Edwin."

"Oh." I crossed and uncrossed my legs, feeling vaguely uncomfortable. I wasn't going to hide my emotions from Charles or stonewall his personal questions as I usually did. I'd resolved to come talk to him honestly.

I only regretted the decision a little bit.

But Tristan was here. I caught his eye and he gave me an encouraging look.

"I can't say I'm sad about it." I didn't quite meet Charles' eye.

"So there's nothing I can do to change your mind?" He sounded regretful. "This could change everything, you know. You've turned Wyatt in twice. There's no room for doubt on this current case. He's as good as convicted. You and Mea solved a major problem for us. We want to reward you, not see you go."

It had been almost a week since Emerson had revealed himself to be Wyatt in disguise. Once Wyatt had been caught, it was possible for Authority Witches to examine the identity spell he'd cast on himself using Emerson's blood. The results proved Wyatt had killed Emerson. Even without Tristan's or my attesting to Wyatt's confession, there was enough evidence to put him away for murder.

Once this became apparent, Wyatt gave up the other Witches involved in the blood-siphoning scheme to try and broker some sort of deal, but he was kidding himself. There was no escaping the consequences and no one else he could try and blame in his place.

The Authority cast restrictions on Wyatt in addition to detaining him to await trial, preventing him from ever being able to practice blood magic in the future. He wouldn't be finding any magical loopholes again.

From my perspective, the matter was dealt with. The man was back in my past where he belonged and I was committed to dealing with the lingering issues our relationship had left me with in a healthy manner.

I was ready to move on from this whole stage of my life. Remaining a part of the Authority wasn't something I was even going to consider. If I stayed here I'd never be able to move past things the way I needed to.

I cleared my throat, sitting up straighter. "While it's good there's no room for doubt that Wyatt was behind his own crimes this time, I'm still not happy about how long people here blamed me for what he did last time. I don't want to work with Witches who treated me with suspicion for decades. I don't care if they've finally realized I'm not the bad all-powerful Witch they assumed I was. I don't care if catching Wyatt again changes everything or vindicates me. Honestly, I wouldn't be surprised if people still blamed me for what happened in the eighties. The whole problem was their biased opinions. New facts might do nothing to sway them. Either way, I'm done with all of it."

Charles set his drink aside. "Then I won't try and talk you out of it. I'm sorry, Edwin."

I nodded, not feeling any need to tell him it was okay when it wasn't.

The judge folded his hands in his lap, deep frown lines

creasing his face. "I knew you weren't popular with everyone here, but I hadn't realized quite how much some of the other judges held on to the past. No one had brought it up so bluntly in front of me until the Telling hearing this month. Until then I'd assumed we'd all moved on long ago." He paused, dithering. "You never told me."

"I didn't want your help." My words sounded tight.

"No." He grimaced. "And you shouldn't have needed to ask. The way things were for you here wasn't your fault and I understand you leaving. I didn't fully when you sent your email, but think I'm beginning to now."

There was an awkward silence.

I still hated this sort of emotionally honest chat when it was with anyone other than Tristan but was glad to be having it. It felt like closing off a chapter of my life rather than running from it.

"Would you have any interest in keeping in touch?" Charles' gaze dropped to his glass. He picked it up. "I'd be sad to never see you again, Edwin."

I took a sip of my drink. "I'm not completely opposed to something social."

Charles brightened, his face falling back into its familiar good-natured happiness. "Excellent. And I'd love to get to know you too." He turned to Tristan.

"Uh, yeah sure." My boyfriend seemed a bit taken aback by the judge's interest.

"Why not start now?" Charles got up to retrieve the whiskey bottle from the cart in the corner. "We really should have done this years ago, Edwin."

I smiled. "Me quit the Authority? Or agree to socialise outside work?"

The answer didn't really matter. I was doing both now and I felt good about all of it.

# 38

## TRISTAN

Six months later.

About a year after our one night stand, I woke up in an equally lush bed with Edwin snoring softly beside me. We were in Tahoe on our first couple's vacation.

I rolled over and tucked up against him, laying my head on his chest.

He stirred, shifting to get his arm around me. "Good morning, darling."

I kissed where I could reach without moving, along his jaw and neck. "G'morning."

I was taking a week between leaving WMS and returning to Southern California, and Edwin had been adorably excited to plan a trip for us. We were in a cabin by the lake, surrounded by trees. It was refreshing after everything, our days filled with walks and simple joys.

It had been a long, stressful six months, so this vacation felt well earned. I'd been getting back into freelancing and had started working with old clients in my free time before I'd resigned from WMS. I'd needed to make some extra money before leaving, to cover the cost of moving and make sure I could keep up with my expenses once I quit my steady job. But lying here, all the work seemed worth it.

I was happy and knew I was doing the right thing for me.

Edwin had let me sort out my own affairs as if it was the most natural thing for him to do. Instead of offering to fund my move just because he could, he helped me in ways that mattered more from a couple's perspective.

He supported me as I worked through the complicated feelings that came along with abandoning my job and the old goals that had led me to take it in the first place. With Edwin's help I was able to do what I needed to without falling into feeling like the choice was some sort of failure. He let me know I was who he wanted, that I was enough, and I was starting to move past some of my old insecurities.

I never felt like he judged my life and was getting to a place where I could stop doing that so much myself.

And I was ecstatic about going back to the Coffee Cat Cafe. Owen and I had been bouncing new ideas off one another and were thinking of starting a community art night where local artists could host workshops.

From now on I wanted to treat my role at the cafe the same way I'd always treated my writing work. It wasn't a secondary job. Running Coffee Cat with Owen was what I wanted to do. I could even see myself phasing out my other work in favor of officially partnering with Owen like he'd always wanted me to. I couldn't wait to get into it and see how we could make the business grow.

Not to mention my favorite customer would be back, brightening my mornings with his bow ties and smiles.

Edwin hadn't yet landed on what he wanted to do next. He'd

been popping over to see Juliet more regularly again and sometimes helped her out with small cases, but he didn't seem interested in doing much more than that for now.

The man needed a break, and one a lot longer than a week.

He was still interested in Mea's team of accountability Witches—that's what I called them anyway—who were trying to find a way to sort out the Authority's missteps. It sounded really messy to be honest, so I wasn't surprised Edwin was taking a beat before diving back into that. He was working on himself and watching him flourish made my heart all mushy and full of pride.

Walsh Marketing Solutions had gone through a bumpy transition before I'd left. The company was under the impression Emerson Walsh had passed away after a heart attack. Attending the work memorial service had been surreal. On one hand, the real Emerson was dead and should be mourned, but most of the people at the service had only known the imposter.

The rest of it was a legal mess, magically and otherwise. Witch-lawyers had been present in droves trying to untangle the contracts where Mortals had been unfairly influenced, but the day-to-day operations of the company had slid back into normality with the Mortal employees unaware of what was going on.

The magically influenced buyouts and mergers couldn't be undone, only compensated for, so WMS lived on with a new CEO and, most importantly, no one getting their blood drained.

Edwin stretched, seeming to wake up fully. "Do we have any pastries left?"

"I'm pretty sure you ate the last pastry yesterday."

He ran a hand down my back. "Hm. Looks like you'll have to cook."

"So you're ready for your next lesson then?" I propped myself up and looked down at him.

He gave me a boyish smile full of freckles and bright blue eyes. "As I'll ever be."

We got up and dressed.

Edwin joined me in the cabin's kitchen, rolling up his sleeves to the elbow.

"No waistcoat or jacket." I looked him up and down in mock horror. "Are you sure you're dressed?"

He huffed and readjusted his coral bow tie. "Watch out, I might wear that other new T-shirt on our walk later today. After the one I wore yesterday, I'm surprised you're complaining about my lack of formal wear."

"Yeah well, you look pretty hot in hiking boots."

Edwin laughed.

I had the ingredients for making quiche out on the counter. I beckoned him closer. "You're going to learn how to make pastry."

"Am I?" Edwin sounded skeptical, as if these cooking lessons hadn't been his idea.

I handed him an apron. "Fine. You can watch this time. But once it's in the fridge *you're* making us coffees. And the filling is all you, whisking the eggs and all."

"I look forward to the eggs, but—" Edwin eyed the drip coffee machine unenthusiastically. "Are you sure you don't want me to pop out and get you a latte?"

"You just love that Owen now lets you teleport directly into the stairs behind Coffee Cat, don't you?" I got out a bowl and the measuring cups.

"It's so convenient." Edwin peered at the recipe on my laptop screen as he knotted the apron behind his back. "And smart on Owen's part. He's pretty much secured my coffee and pan dulce buying loyalty for life."

"Like it wasn't already."

Edwin pulled me close for a kiss. "You're right. I'd love to always be at your side, Tristan. Having coffee, seeing you at work, cooking eggs, walking around in boots. Anything. I love you."

"I love you too, Edwin." I hugged him tight and he squeezed me back. "I think we're going to be good together."

"We already are. I think we're going to be something wonderful. I'm so excited for the rest of my life, I can't even tell you."

I sniffled, smiling so hard my face felt funny. "You've got plans for us, do you?"

His blue eyes flashed. "A few."

"Then I can't wait to be there with you."

Edwin kissed me as best he could while smiling and we dissolved into happy laugher.

## THANK YOU FOR READING ONE WICKED NIGHT

Please consider leaving a review on your favorite site to help others find magical books they love. 🖤

More from the *Love & Magic* world

WITCH BOYFRIEND WANTED

COMING 6 FEB 2024

*Luca Belmonte & Theo Landon*

Would you like a free **bonus scene**? Head over to my website coletterivera.com and subscribe to my author newsletter. I'll send you Tristan and Edwin's very first meet cute - the look that started it all!

## ACKNOWLEDGMENTS

I would like to thank my editor May Peterson for her work on this book and for her enthusiasm for this series. It has been great working with you on these stories.

As always, I would like to thank TK for his support of me and for his continued love of my Witchy worlds.

Thank you to Sam Palencia for her beautiful cover art and bringing these characters to life.

And thank you to my readers, your love of Edwin throughout this series has been truly wonderful!

## WITCH BOYFRIEND WANTED

**When you need a Witchy boyfriend but not a *real* one.**

Luca Belmonte is sick of being set up. All his father wants is for Luca to marry well, to progress his career and standing in Witch society. Luca wants to be left alone. He's overwhelmed with work and needs a plan to get his father off his back.

Finding his own boyfriend seems like the best solution, except Luca won't risk the rejection that comes with real dating no matter how much he wants to be in love. A fake relationship sounds better, if he can find someone to play along.

Yet somehow his friend Marci convinces him to go on one last date...

Theo Landon is in a dating rut, that's the only reason he agrees to a blind date. He takes a chance and his date is hot. Charming. A man from his past he never wants to see again. The night is an epic disaster. But Theo has a secret. He's been lying to almost everyone about being in a steady relationship and when he gets spotted with Luca assumptions get out of hand.

So the two agree to fake it, just for a while.

Only Luca isn't the bad guy Theo thought. He's just the Witch Theo needs, especially when things start to go wrong at his apothecary shop. So what happens when there's nothing fake about the feelings growing between them?

## ABOUT THE AUTHOR

Colette is an award winning author of lgbtq+ paranormal romance. She lives on an island made of books where she creates HEAs fueled by coffee and baked goods.

Colette can be found on Instagram and Twitter @colette_rivera or at her website coletterivera.com.

## LOVE & MAGIC

GIVE A WITCH A CHANCE

KEEP YOUR WITCHES CLOSE

ONE WICKED NIGHT

Made in the USA
Middletown, DE
08 October 2023